WARRIORS OF ULTRAMAR

'PASANIUS, GET UP here. I need your flamer!' shouted
Uriel as a ripple of motion shuddered through the
membrane. He raised his bolt pistol and fired a succession of shots into the object, drawing an alien screech
of pain from within.

As he watched, a long claw ripped through the membrane and a grotesque creature bounded from the
object. Its hide glistened wetly, dripping fluids from its
bony exoskeleton, its mucus-wreathed head filled with
needle-like fangs. Two pairs of arms, each ending in
vicious barbed claws, clicked together as it landed
lightly on the mesh deck. It hissed at Uriel, its black
eyes nictating as it adjusted to its new surroundings.

A trio of identical creatures followed it from the
steaming chrysalis. Uriel could see many more behind
them and unloaded his pistol into the mass of creatures
as Pasanius finally arrived at his side.

A WARHAMMER 40,000 NOVEL

An Ultramarines Novel

WARRIORS OF ULTRAMAR

Graham McNeill

To Stephen, Susan and Arran
for your continued friendship.

A BLACK LIBRARY PUBLICATION

First published in Great Britain in 2003 by
BL Publishing
Willow Road, Lenton,
Nottingham, NG7 2WS, UK

10 9 8 7 6 5 4 3 2 1

Cover illustration by Alex Boyd

A CIP record for this book
is available from the British Library

ISBN 1 84416 000 9

Set in ITC Giovanni

Printed and bound in Great Britain by
Cox & Wyman Ltd, Cardiff Rd, Reading, Berkshire RG1 8EX, UK

See the Black Library on the Internet at
www.blacklibrary.com

Find out more about Games Workshop
and the world of Warhammer 40.000 at
www.games-workshop.com

IT IS THE 41st millennium. For more than a hundred centuries the Emperor has sat immobile on the Golden Throne of Earth. He is the master of mankind by the will of the gods, and master of a million worlds by the might of his inexhaustible armies. He is a rotting carcass writhing invisibly with power from the Dark Age of Technology. He is the Carrion Lord of the Imperium for whom a thousand souls are sacrificed every day, so that he may never truly die.

YET EVEN IN his deathless state, the Emperor continues his eternal vigilance. Mighty battlefleets cross the daemon-infested miasma of the warp, the only route between distant stars, their way lit by the Astronomican, the psychic manifestation of the Emperor's will. Vast armies give battle in his name on uncounted worlds. Greatest amongst his soldiers are the Adeptus Astartes, the Space Marines, bio-engineered super-warriors. Their comrades in arms are legion: the Imperial Guard and countless planetary defence forces, the ever-vigilant Inquisition and the tech-priests of the Adeptus Mechanicus to name only a few. But for all their multitudes, they are barely enough to hold off the ever-present threat from aliens, heretics, mutants – and worse.

TO BE A man in such times is to be one amongst untold billions. It is to live in the cruellest and most bloody regime imaginable. These are the tales of those times. Forget the power of technology and science, for so much has been forgotten, never to be re-learned. Forget the promise of progress and understanding, for in the grim dark future there is only war. There is no peace amongst the stars, only an eternity of carnage and slaughter, and the laughter of thirsting gods.

PHASE I – DETECTION

PROLOGUE

Low clouds scudded across the clear blue sky of Tarsis Ultra, drifting in the light breeze that bent the fat stalks of corn stretching in all directions as far as the eye could see. The air was warm, scented with the pungent aroma of crops ready for harvest.

A tall, high-sided vehicle lumbered through the gently waving fields on a road of hard-packed earth, flashing blades on extended tilt arms efficiently scything the crops on either side into a huge hopper on its back. The sun had yet to reach its zenith, but the hopper was almost full, the harvester having set off from the farming collective of Prandium before dawn's first light had broken.

Smoke from the harvester's engine vented through a series of filters and was released in a toxin-free cloud above the small cab mounted on its frontal section.

The harvester lurched as it veered to one side before one of the cab's two occupants pulled the control levers away from its more reckless driver.

'Corin, I swear you drive this thing like a blind man,' snapped Joachim.

'Well I'm never going to get any better if you keep taking the controls from me,' said Corin, throwing his hands up in disgust. He ran a gloved hand through his unruly mop of hair and stared in annoyance at his companion.

Joachim felt his friend's glare and said, 'You almost had us in the irrigation ditch.'

'Maybe,' admitted Corin. 'But I didn't, did I?'

'Only because I took over.'

Corin shrugged, unwilling to concede the point, and allowed Joachim to continue driving the harvester in relative peace. He removed his thin gloves and flexed his fingers, attempting to work out the stiffness in his joints. Holding onto the juddering control columns of a harvester and trying to guide it around the huge fields was punishing work.

'These gloves are useless,' he complained. 'They don't help at all.'

Joachim grinned and said, 'So you haven't padded them out yet?'

'No,' replied Corin. 'I was hoping your Elleiza would do it for me.'

'I wouldn't hold your breath, she already runs after you like she was your wife.'

'Aye!' chucked Corin, 'She's a good lass. She looks after me well, so she does.'

'Too well,' pointed out Joachim. 'It's time you got your own woman to look after you. What about Bronagh, the medicae in Espandor? I heard that she was sweet on you.'

'Bronagh. Ah, yes, she's a girl of rare taste,' laughed Corin.

Joachim arched an eyebrow and was on the point of replying when the world exploded around them. A thunderous impact struck the side of the harvester and both men were hurled against the cab's interior as the giant vehicle lurched sideways. Joachim felt blood on his scalp and reached for the controls as the harvester began to tip.

He pulled back on the column, but it was too late, the left track slid from the road into the ditch and the entire vehicle rolled over.

'Hold on!' yelled Joachim as the harvester toppled onto its side with a crash of twisted metal. Broken glass showered them and Joachim felt a jagged edge slice open his temple. The harvester slammed down into the field, hurling giant clouds of corn and dust into the air as it toppled onto the dry earth. Its enormous tracks ground onwards, churning air as the engine continued to turn over.

Almost a minute passed before the side door of the cab swung open and a pair of booted feet emerged. Gingerly, Joachim lowered himself out of the cab and splashed down into the knee-high water of the irrigation ditch that ran between the road and the field. He landed awkwardly and cursed, clutching his bruised and gashed head. Corin groggily followed him into the ditch, cradling his arm close to his chest.

Wordlessly, the two men surveyed the damage done to the harvester.

The hopper was a twisted mass of buckled metal, smoking fragments and the stinking residue of burned corn all that remained of its centre section, where it appeared that something immensely powerful had struck.

'Guilliman's oath, what happened?' asked Corin, breathlessly. 'Did someone shoot at us?'

'I don't think so,' replied Joachim, pointing to a pillar of white smoke billowing skyward some hundred metres further into the field. 'But whatever it was, I bet it's got something to do with that.'

Corin followed Joachim's pointing hand and said, 'What the hell is it?'

'I don't know, but if it's a fire, we've got to get it out before the whole crop goes up.'

Corin nodded and clambered painfully back into the harvester's cab, unclipping a pair of fire extinguishers from its rear wall and dropping them down to Joachim. With some difficulty they climbed the sloping rockcrete wall of the ditch, Joachim turning to pull Corin up as he reached the top.

Hurriedly, they made their way through the field, their passage made easier by virtue of the long, dark scar gouged in the earth that led towards the column of smoke.

'By Maccrage, I've never seen anything like this,' wheezed Corin. 'Is it a meteor?'

Joachim nodded, then wished he hadn't as hot stabs of pain thundered in his head. 'I think so.'

They reached the lip of the crater and pulled up in astonishment at what lay within.

If it was a meteor, then it didn't look anything like either man imagined it might. Roughly spherical and composed of a leprous brown material, it resembled a giant gemstone rippling in a heat haze. Its surface was smooth and glassy looking, presumably from its journey through the atmosphere. Now that they could see it clearly, the two men saw that it wasn't smoke that billowed from the object in stinking waves, but steam. Geysers of the foul smelling vapour vented from cracks in its surface like leaks in a compressor pipe. Even from the edge of the crater they could feel the intense heat radiating from the object.

'Well it's not on fire, but it's still damned hot,' said Joachim. 'We need to cool it down or it could still set light to the crop.'

Corin shook his head and made the sign of the aquila over his heart. 'No way. I ain't going down there.'

'What? Why not?'

'I don't like the look of that thing, Joachim. It's bad news, I can feel it.'

'Don't be simple all your life, Corin. It's just a big rock, now come on.'

Corin shook his head vehemently and thrust the fire extinguisher he carried towards Joachim. 'Here. You want to go down there, then go, but I'm going back to the harvester. I'm going to vox Prandium and get someone to come out and pick us up.'

Joachim could see there was no arguing with Corin, and nodded.

'I'm going to take a closer look,' said Joachim. 'I'll be right back.'

Slinging an extinguisher over each shoulder, he picked his way carefully down into the crater.

Corin watched him until he reached its base and turned back the way they had come. He touched his wounded arm, wincing as pain flared just above his elbow: it felt broken. He glanced over his shoulder, hearing a loud hissing, like water being poured on a hot skillet, but continued walking.

The hissing continued, followed by an almighty crack.

Then the screaming started.

Corin jumped, spinning around as he heard Joachim shriek in agony. His friend's scream was abruptly silenced, and a keening screech cut the air, utterly alien and utterly terrifying.

Corin turned and sprinted back towards the harvester, fear lending his limbs extra speed.

There was an autogun in the cab, and he desperately wished he'd brought it with him.

He stumbled along the gouge torn in the earth, tripping on a buried root and falling to his knees. The thump of heavy footfalls sounded behind him. Something large and inhumanly quick was speeding through the corn. He could hear snapping stalks as it came nearer and nearer; Corin was in no doubt that it was hunting him.

He moaned in fear, stumbling to his feet and running onwards. He risked a glance over his shoulder, seeing a blurred form ghost from sight into the swaying corn.

The tread of something large seemed to come from all around him.

'What are you?' he screamed as he ran.

He ran blindly, bursting from the corn and yelling as he fell headlong into the irrigation ditch. He landed hard, cracking his elbow against the rockcrete, swallowing a mouthful of brackish water as he screamed in pain. He scrambled backwards, spitting water and shaking his head clear.

He looked up as a dark shape blotted out the sky above him.

Corin blinked away the water in his eyes and saw his pursuer clearly.

He drew breath to scream.

But it was on him in a flurry of scything blows that tore him apart before he could give voice to it.

A lake of blood spread from the dismembered corpse. Corin's killer paused for the briefest second, as though scenting the air.

It scrambled easily up the slope of the ditch and set off in the direction of Prandium.

PHASE II – APPROACH

ONE

THE BASILICA MORTIS was home to the Mortifactors.

The ancestral home of the Mortifactors Chapter of Space Marines rotated slowly in the wan light of Posul and her faraway sun, its surfaces craggy and mountainous.

For nearly ten thousand years, since the Chapter's founder, Sasebo Tezuka, had been led here by the Emperor's tarot, the Mortifactors had stood sentinel over the night world of Posul, and since that time, these holy knights of the Imperium had trained members of their warrior order within the walls of their orbiting fortress monastery.

In appearance, it resembled some vast mountain range cast adrift in the void of space. The Imperium's finest tech-priests and adepts had come together to create this orbiting fortress; the Basilica was a marvel of arcane technical engineering that had long since been forgotten.

For millennia, the Mortifactors had sent warriors from the Basilica Mortis to fight alongside the armies of the Imperium in the service of the divine Emperor of Man. Companies, squads, crusaders and – three times – the entire Chapter had been called to war, most recently to fight the orks on the blasted wastes of Armageddon. The honours the Chapter had won rivalled even those of such legendary Chapters as the Space Wolves, Imperial Fists or Blood Angels.

At full occupation, the monastery was home to the thousand battle-brothers of the Chapter and their officers, with a supporting staff of servitors, scribes, technomats and functionaries that numbered seven and a half thousand souls.

Vast docks jutted from the prow of the adamantium mountain, spearing into space with slender silver docking rings rising from the jib. Two heavily armed Space Marine strike cruisers were berthed in the docks, with smaller, Gladius frigates and Hunter destroyers either returning or departing on patrol throughout the Mortifactors' domain. Battle barges, devastating warships of phenomenal power, were housed in armoured bays deep in the bowels of the monastery, terrible weapons of planetary destruction held in their silent hulls.

A beacon, flaring in the darkness upon the furthest jib of the docks, reflected the light from the hull of an approaching strike cruiser. The ship slipped gracefully towards the darkened fortress monastery, escorted by six rapid strike vessels of the Mortifactors. Ancient codes and tortuous greetings in High Gothic had been exchanged between the ship's captain and the monastery's Master of the Marches, but still the Mortifactors were taking no chances with security. The ship, the *Vae Victus*, drifted slowly, powered only by attitude thrusters that controlled her approach to the docks.

The *Vae Victus* was a strike cruiser of the Ultramarines, the pride and joy of the Chapter's Commander of the Fleet, and normally travelled with a full panoply of escort craft in her wake. But the ships of the Arx Praetora squadron lay at anchor near the system's jump point, forbidden to approach the ancient sepulchre of the Mortifactors.

The ship's structure was long, scarred by thousands of years of war against the foes of humanity. A cathedral-like spire, braced by ornamented flying buttresses, towered over her rear quarter and, in deference to the Mortifactors, her guns and launch bays were shuttered behind their protective blast shields. The portside of the vessel's prow gleamed where the shipwrights of Calth had repaired the horrendous damage done to her by an eldar ship, and the insignia of the Ultramarines shone with renewed pride from her frontal armour.

As the *Vae Victus* drew near the Basilica, her prow swung slowly around until her starboard was broadside to the mountainous fortress monastery. Here, she hung silently in space until a flurry of small pilot ships emerged from the Basilica Mortis and swiftly took up position on her far side.

Other ships, bearing vast mooring cables, each thicker than an orbital torpedo, flew out to meet the *Vae Victus* and attached them to secure anchor points as the pilot ships gently approached the portside hull of the Ultramarines vessel. Little more than powerful engines with a tiny servitor compartment bolted to its topside, the pilot ships were used to manoeuvre larger vessels into a position where they could dock. A dozen of them gently nuzzled the *Vae Victus*, like tiny, parasitic fish feeding on a vast sea creature, and flared their engines in controlled bursts. At last, their combined force overcame the inertia of the larger ship and, slowly, the *Vae Victus* eased towards the Basilica Mortis, the thick cables reeling her in and guiding her towards the enormous, claw-like docking clamps that would moor her safely to the fortress monastery.

Deep within the starship, armoured footsteps and the distant sound of the pilot ships on the hull were the only things to break the calm, meditative silence of her corridors. Well lit by numerous electro-candles, the marble-white walls seemed to swallow sounds before they had a chance to echo.

The gently arched walls were smooth and spartanly ornamented. Here and there along their length, tiny niches, lit by a delicate, diffuse light, held stasis-sealed vessels containing some of the Chapter's holy relics: the thigh bone of Ancient Galatan, an alien skull taken on the fields of Ichar IV, a fragment of stained glass from a long ago destroyed shrine or an alabaster statue of the Emperor himself.

Four Space Marines marched towards the starboard docking bays where they would at last be able to set foot on the Basilica Mortis. Leading the delegation was a bald giant, his skin dark and tough as leather, with a network of scars criss crossing the left side of his face. His features were drawn in a scowl of displeasure, his eyes darting to the corridor's roof at every groan of metal that came from the hull, imagining the damage the pilot ships were inflicting upon his vessel.

Lord Admiral Lazlo Tiberius wore his ceremonial cloak of office. The stiff foxbat fur ruff surrounding his shoulders chafed his neck and the silver cluster securing it to his blue armour scratched his throat. He wore a wreath of laurels around his forehead and the many battle honours he had won glittered on his breast, the golden sunburst of a Hero of Macragge shining like a miniature sun.

'Damned pilot ships,' muttered Tiberius. 'She's only just out of the yards at Calth and now they'll be buckling Emperor knows how many panels and arches.'

'I'm sure it won't be as bad as you think, lord admiral. And she will see worse before we are done with Tarsis Ultra,' said the warrior immediately behind Tiberius, the captain of the Fourth company, Uriel Ventris, his emerald-green dress cloak billowing behind him.

Tiberius grunted. 'As soon as we get back to Tarsis Ultra I want to put into dock at Chordelis and check. I'll not take her into battle without making sure she is at her best.'

As captain of the Fourth company, one of Uriel's titles was Master of the Fleet, but in recognition of Tiberius's greater knowledge of space combat, he had deferred the position to the lord admiral, who had taken on the role with gusto. There was no dishonour in this, as the warriors of the Ultramarines followed the teachings of their primarch's holy tome, the Codex Astartes, which stressed the importance of every position being held by those most suited to it, regardless of station. Tiberius and the *Vae Victus* had fought together for nearly three centuries and Uriel knew that the venerable lord admiral would make a better Master of the Fleet than he.

In the month since the destruction of the space hulk, *Death of Virtue*, the ship's artificers had done their best to repair the damage Uriel's armour had suffered, replacing his shoulder guard and filling and repainting the deep grooves cut by alien claws. But without the forges of Macragge, it was impossible to completely heal the damage.

Pinned to his green cloak was a small brooch with an embossed white rose, marking Uriel as a Hero of Pavonis, and below this a number of bronze stars were affixed to his breast-plate.

His face was angular, the features classically sculpted, but serious and drawn. His storm-cloud eyes were narrow and heavy-lidded, the two gold long-service studs on his left temple shining brightly below the darkness of his cropped scalp.

Uriel's senior sergeants marched in step behind him, Pasanius to his left and Learchus on his right. Pasanius easily dwarfed the others; his armour barely able to contain his bulk, despite the fact that much of it had come from an ancient suit of irreparably damaged Terminator armour. Both he and Learchus wore the green cloak of the Fourth company, and like their captain, sported brooches bearing the white rose of Pavonis.

Pasanius wore his blond hair tight into his skull and though his face was serious, it was also capable of great warmth and humour. His right arm gleamed silver below the elbow where the tech-priests of Pavonis had replaced it following the confrontation with the ancient star god known as the Nightbringer in the depths of that world. Its monstrous scythe had sliced through his armour and bone, and despite the attentions of Apothecary Selenus, the tissue touched by its glacial chill was beyond saving.

Learchus was a true Ultramarine. His heritage was flawless and of the finest stock, his every stride that of a warrior born. During their training, he and Uriel had been bitter rivals, but their shared service to the Chapter and the Emperor had long since overcome any such rancour.

Lord Admiral Tiberius tugged at the fur ruff around his neck and adjusted the laurel wreath at his temples as they rounded a bend in the corridor and approached the docking bay. A ringing clang that sounded throughout the ship told Tiberius that the docking clamps of the Basilica had them secured.

He shook his head, saying, 'I'll be glad when this is over.'

Uriel could not bring himself to agree with Tiberius. He was eager to meet these brothers of his blood, and the threat they were soon to face on Tarsis Ultra made him doubly glad the *Vae Victus* had come here.

Split from the Ultramarines during the Second Founding, nearly ten thousand years ago, the Mortifactors were descended from the same lineage of heroes as Uriel himself.

Ancient tales told of how Roboute Guilliman, primarch of the Ultramarines, had held the Emperor's realm together after its near destruction at the hands of the treacherous Warmaster Horus, and how his tome, the Codex Astartes, had laid the foundations of the fledgling Imperium. Central to those foundations was the decree that the tens of thousands strong Space

Marine Legions be broken up into smaller fighting units known to this day as Chapters, so that never again would any one man be able to wield the fearsome power of an entire Space Marine Legion. Each of the original Legions kept their colours and title, while the newly formed Chapters took another name and set out to fight the enemies of the Emperor throughout the galaxy.

An Ultramarines captain named Sasebo Tezuka had been given command of the newly created Mortifactors and led them to the world of Posul, where he established his fortress monastery and earned many honours in the name of the Emperor before his death.

Despite their shared descent from the blood of Guilliman, there had been no contact between the Ultramarines and the Mortifactors for thousands of years, and Uriel was looking forward to meeting these warriors and seeing what had become of them, what battles they had fought and hearing their tales of valour.

An honour guard of Ultramarines lined the columned approach to the starboard docking hatches and the four warriors passed between them. A thick, golden door with a locking wheel and Imperial eagle motif beneath an elaborately carved pediment lay at the end of the honour guard. A brass-rimmed light above the door flashed green to indicate that the passage ahead was safe and as the Ultramarines approached, a cybernetically altered servitor on tracks rolled forward to turn the wheel. It turned smoothly, steam hissing from the vacuum-sealed edges.

The door lifted from the hatch with a decompressive hiss, and slid aside on oiled runners, revealing a long, dark tunnel of black iron that led towards a dripping portal ringed with black skulls.

Icicle fangs hung from the jaws of the skulls and moisture gathered on the stone flagged floor of the docking umbilical. Tiberius shared an uneasy look with Uriel, who moved to stand alongside the lord admiral.

'Doesn't look particularly inviting, does it?' observed Tiberius.

'Not especially,' agreed Uriel.

'Well, let's get this over with. The sooner we are on our way back to Tarsis Ultra the happier I will be.'

Uriel nodded and led the way along the docking tunnel. He reached the door at its end, which was formed from the same dark iron as the rest of the tunnel. Behind them, the pressure door slammed shut, sealing with a booming clang. A rain of melting ice pattered from Uriel's shoulder guards, running in rivulets along the scores in his breastplate and soaking the top of his cloak. He raised his fist and hammered twice on the door, deep echoes ringing hollowly from the walls. There was no answer and he raised his fist to strike the door again when it swung inwards with a tortured squeal of metal.

Dry, dead air, like the last breath of a corpse, soughed from inside the Basilica Mortis, and Uriel caught the musty scent of bone and cerements. Inside was darkness, lit only by flickering candles, and the chill of the internal air matched that of the docking tunnel.

Uriel stepped through the skull-wreathed portal and set foot in the sanctum of the Mortifactors. Tiberius, Learchus and Pasanius followed him, casting wary glances around them as they took in their surroundings.

They stood in a long chamber, seated statues running along its length and its ceiling shrouded in darkness. Faded, mouldy banners hung from the walls. Water pooled behind them as it splashed in from the docking tunnel. Ahead, a softly lit doorway set in a leaf-shaped archway provided the chamber's only other visible exit.

'Where are the Mortifactors?' hissed Pasanius.

'I don't know,' said Uriel, gripping the hilt of his sword and staring at the statues either side of him. He approached the nearest and leaned in close, sweeping its face clear of dust and cobwebs.

'Guilliman's oath!' he swore, recoiling in disgust as he realised that these were not statues, but preserved human corpses.

'Battle Brother Olfric, may his name and strength be remembered,' said a deep voice behind Uriel. 'He fell in combat with the hrud at the Battle of Ortecha IX. This was seven hundred and thirty years ago. But he was avenged and his battle brothers ate the hearts of his killer. Thus was his soul able to go on to the feast table of the Ultimate Warrior.'

Uriel spun to see a robed and hooded figure standing in the doorway, his hands hidden within the sleeves of his robes.

From his bulk, it was plain that the speaker was a fellow Space Marine. A pair of brass-plated servo-skulls hovered above the man, a thin copper wire running between them and dangling metallic callipers twitching as they floated into the chamber. One carried a long, vellum scroll, a feathered quill darting across its surface, while the other drifted towards the Ultramarines, a red light glowing from a cylindrical device slung beneath its perpetually grinning jaw.

It hovered before Uriel, the red light sweeping across and over his head, and he had to fight the superstitious urge to smash the skull from the air. The skull moved on from Uriel to Pasanius and then to Learchus, bathing each of their heads in the same eerie red light. As it reached Tiberius, the lord admiral reached up angrily and swatted it away.

'Damn thing!' snapped Tiberius. 'What is the meaning of this?'

The skull squealed and darted back, rising into the air and hovering just out of reach. Its twin followed it, pulled up by the copper cable that connected them.

'Do not be alarmed, lord admiral' said the figure in the doorway. 'The devices are merely mapping and recording a three-dimensional image of your skull.'

Seeing Tiberius's confusion, the robed Space Marine said, 'So that upon your death, it may be placed in the position that most suits its dimensions.'

Tiberius stared open-mouthed at the figure, who pulled back his hood and stepped forward into the light.

His skin was the colour of ebony, his dark hair pulled back in long braids and woven with coloured crystals. Four golden studs glittered on his brow, his full features and dark eyes sombre as he addressed the startled Ultramarines.

'I am Brother-Chaplain Astador of the Mortifactors, and I bid thee welcome, brothers.'

THIS WAS NOT what Uriel had expected of the Mortifactors. After announcing himself, Astador had turned and marched from the chamber of corpses without another word, leaving the astonished Ultramarines to follow. The two servo-skulls floated alongside their master, bobbing just above his head and Uriel wondered what other technological artefacts the Mortifactors utilised. The Ultramarines shunned the use of

servo-skulls, preferring that the mortal remains of fallen
Imperial servants be interred whole that they might sit at the
right hand of the Emperor complete.

The halls of the Mortifactors were gloomy and silent as a
tomb. Every portal and chamber they passed through bore
more skulls and only now, as he looked closer, did Uriel
realise that none were carved or fashioned by human hand.
All were real, bleached and dusty with age. Though they saw
no inhabitants of the fortress monastery in their long journey,
the silence was broken by occasional snatches of hymnal
dirges and sombre chants of remembrance.

Uriel's sense of bewilderment rose the further they penetrated this dismal sepulchre. How could warriors of the same
blood as his dwell in such a morbid place? How could these
sons of Guilliman have deviated so far from the teachings of
the primarch? He increased his pace until he was level with
Astador.

'Brother Astador,' began Uriel. 'I do not wish to cause
offence, but has your Chapter suffered a great loss in its recent
history?'

Astador shook his head in puzzlement. 'No. We have
returned from the world of Armageddon with much honour
and the bones of our fallen. Why do you ask?'

Uriel searched for the right expression. They needed the
help of the Mortifactors and the wrong words could dash any
hopes of aid. 'The halls of your monastery suggest your Chapter is in mourning.'

'It is not like this on Macragge?'

'No, the Fortress of Hera is a place of celebration, of joy in
the service of the Emperor. It echoes with tales of courage and
honour.'

Astador was silent for a moment before replying. 'You are a
native of Macragge?'

'No, I was born on Calth, though I trained at the Agiselus
Barracks on Macragge since I was six years old.'

'And would you say that you were shaped by your homeworld?'

Uriel considered Astador's question. 'Yes, I would. I worked
on an underground farm from the day I was able to walk.
They breed them tough on Calth, and you either buckled
down and worked hard or you felt the birch across your back.'

'Did you enjoy your life there?' asked Astador.

'I suppose so, though I barely remember it now. It was hard work, but I came from a family who loved me and cared for me. I remember being happy there.'

'And yet you gave it all up to become an Ultramarine.'

'Yes, in Ultramar everyone trains to be a soldier. I discovered I had a natural talent for war, and I swore that I would be the best warrior Macragge had ever seen.'

Astador nodded. 'You are who you are because of where you come from, Captain Ventris, so do not presume to judge me by your own standards. The world below us was my home, and until I was chosen to become one of the Emperor's warriors, I knew neither sunlight nor joy. These things do not exist on Posul, only a brutal life of darkness and bloodshed. I took three hundred skulls in battle before I was chosen to become a Space Marine and since that day I have killed the enemies of the Emperor. I have since seen the sun, yet still I know no joy.'

'A Space Marine needs not joy, nor glory,' said Learchus. 'Service to the Emperor shall be his wine and sustenance, and his soul shall be content.'

Astador stopped and turned to face the veteran sergeant.

'You quote from the Codex Astartes, sergeant. We have grown beyond the need for such dogma and forge our own path from the wisdom of our Chaplains. To be bound by words set down an age ago is not our way.'

The Ultramarines halted in their tracks, horrified by Astador's casual blasphemy. To have the holy writings of Roboute Guilliman dismissed so lightly was something they never expected to hear from the mouth of a fellow Space Marine.

Tiberius was the first to recover his wits and said, 'Forgive us, Brother Chaplain. But it is surprising for us to hear one whose lineage can be traced back to the blessed primarch speaking in such a manner of the Codex Astartes.'

Astador bowed in respect to Tiberius.

'I apologise if my words caused offence, lord admiral. We venerate the primarch, just as you do. He is our Chapter's father and all our oaths of allegiance are sworn to him and the Emperor.'

'Yet you scorn his greatest work?' snapped Learchus, clenching his fists.

'No, my brother, far from it,' said Astador, moving to stand before Learchus. 'We look upon its words as the foundation of our way of life, but to follow its teachings without consideration for what we have learned and that we see around us is not wisdom, it is merely repetition. Repetition leads to stagnation. And stagnation dooms us.'

Uriel placed a hand on Astador's shoulder and said, 'Brother Astador, perhaps we should continue? We have come to speak with your Chapter Master and do not have time for theological debate. The world of Tarsis Ultra is under threat from the most deadly enemy and we would petition your master for his aid in the coming conflict.'

Astador nodded without turning, then spun on his heel and marched off into the darkness once more. Uriel released the breath he had been holding and unclenched his jaw.

'Damn it, Learchus,' he whispered. 'We are here for their help, not to antagonise them.'

'But you heard what he said about the codex!' protested Learchus.

'Uriel is correct, Learchus,' said Tiberius. 'We are all warriors of the Emperor and that is the most important factor. You know there are other Chapters that do not follow the words of the primarch as closely as we do. The sons of Russ follow their own path, and we count them as allies do we not?'

Learchus nodded, though Uriel could see he was not convinced.

Uriel's gaze followed Astador as he continued onwards through the darkness of his fortress monastery. The skulls of fallen Mortifactors stared back at him from the walls. Uriel sighed. Certainly time and distance could change a Chapter a great deal, no matter how similar their ancestry was.

Astador turned and beckoned them onwards.

'Come, Lord Magyar awaits.'

THE GALLERY OF Bone was aptly named, thought Uriel as he stood awaiting the audience with Lord Magyar, Chapter Master of the Mortifactors. A carven cloister of bone surrounded a stone flagged floor paved with hundreds of tombstones. Niches set within the columns of the cloister contained skeletal warriors clutching swords and the entire, domed ceiling was formed from interlocked skulls, their eyeless sockets glaring down at those who stood within their domain. The four Ultramarines stood in the centre of the wide space enclosed by the cloister, Uriel and Tiberius to the fore, Learchus and Pasanius standing at parade rest behind them.

Mortuary statues of angels flanked a vast throne composed of the bones of long-dead Space Marines. Uriel could pick out individual femurs, spines and many other bones as well as grinning skulls leering from the armrests and above the tapered top of the throne.

A bone-legged table stood beside the throne with a flattened bowl of dark enamel atop it. Everywhere Uriel looked, death was venerated and exalted above all things.

Astador stood close to the throne, the hood of his black robe cowling his face once more.

A deep gong sounded, and hidden doors behind the throne swung silently open. The first of a long procession entered the Gallery of Bone. Dozens of hooded figures shuffled into the chamber, some swinging smoking censers, others chanting a sombre lament, but all with their heads cast down. One by one they took up positions around the chamber until each skeleton-filled niche had a living twin standing before it. Two Terminators in dark armour decorated with bone trim marched into the chamber, each carrying a long, wide-bladed scythe. Their helmets were carved to resemble screaming skulls and Uriel could well imagine the terror that these warriors must evoke in their enemies. The Terminators took up position either side of the throne as a winged skeleton, no larger than a child, flapped into the gallery on fragile-looking wings with thin, membranous remnants of tattered vestments fluttering between each of its wing bones. It settled upon the top of the throne and squatted there, silently regarding the shocked Ultramarines. Brass wire glittered at its joints and Uriel could see a tiny suspensor generator attached to the spine between its wings.

Uriel's lip curled in distaste at the sight of the winged familiar as a tall figure, clad in armour of bone entered the gallery. His movements were slow and unhurried, every step considered and solemn. His breastplate was formed from long ribs, bent and fashioned into shape, the Imperial eagle at its centre as skeletal as the winged familiar that watched the proceedings below. Every piece of this warrior's armour, from the greaves to the vambrace, cuissart and gorget was formed from bone. He carried a gigantic scythe, its blade silvered and sharp, the haft gleaming ebony.

Lord Magyar, for it could surely be none other, stood before his throne and bowed to the Ultramarines. His long, silver hair was tied in numerous crystal-wrapped braids reaching to the small of his back and his coal-dark skin resembled a lunar landscape, cratered and ridged with numberless wrinkles. A long, forked white beard fell to his waist, waxed into sharp points.

His eyes were dark pinholes and though it was impossible to guess the age of the Chapter Master, Uriel was certain he must have been at least seven hundred years old.

Lord Magyar sat upon his throne and said, 'You are welcome, brothers of the blood.'

Uriel was shocked at the strength and powerful authority in the ancient warrior's voice, but hid his surprise as he stepped forward and bowed.

'Lord Magyar, we thank you for your welcome and bring greetings from your brothers of Ultramar. Lord Calgar himself bade me convey his regards to you.'

Lord Magyar nodded slowly, accepting Uriel's greeting.

'You come with dark tidings, Captain Ventris. Our Chaplains have seen grave portents and they have seen you.'

'Seen me?' asked Uriel.

'Seen you drenched in blood. Seen you triumphant. Seen you dead,' proclaimed Magyar.

'I do not understand, my lord.'

'Long have we known of your coming to us, Uriel Ventris,' nodded Magyar, 'but not why. Tell me why you have come to my monastery, brother of the blood?'

Pleased to be on a topic he could understand, Uriel bowed again to Lord Magyar.

'We come before you in hopes that you will honour the Warrior's Debt and join us in battle against a terrible enemy.'

'You speak of the oath Guilliman swore on Tarsis Ultra during the Great Crusade.'

'I do, Lord Magyar.'

'Such an oath binds your Chapter still?' asked Magyar.

'Yes, my lord. As has been our way since the blessed primarch swore his oath of brotherhood with the soldier who saved his life, we are sworn to defend the people of Tarsis Ultra should their world ever be threatened,' said Uriel.

'Is it so threatened?' asked Magyar formally.

'It is, my lord.'

'You are sure?'

'Yes, my lord. A tendril of the Great Devourer is moving towards it and will attack soon. My warriors and I recently boarded and destroyed a hulk codified as the *Death of Virtue* that was bound for Tarsis Ultra. The accursed vessel was filled with genestealers and we fought them with courage. Upon returning to our ship, our astropaths detected the psychic disturbance known as the Shadow in the Warp moving towards us. The tyranids are coming, my lord. Of this I am sure.'

'And what do you wish of me?'

'My Chapter is honour bound to defend these realms and I call upon the blood that flows between us for your aid. The tyranids are a monstrous foe and we will be sorely pressed to defeat them. With your valiant warriors by our side, we would stand a much greater chance of victory.'

Lord Magyar grinned, exposing brilliant white teeth. 'Do not think to appeal to my warrior's vanity, Captain Ventris. I know of this debt and the bond that exists between us full well.'

'Then your warriors will fight beside us?'

'That remains to be seen,' said Magyar, beckoning to Astador.

Astador stood beside his lord and master, awaiting his command.

'You will perform a vision-quest, Brother Chaplain Astador?'

'Yes, my lord. As you command,' said Astador opening his robe and allowing it to fall to the tombstone floor. His armour was the colour of spilt blood, dark and threatening, the trims formed in gold. Obsidian skulls adorned each shoulder guard. He carried a golden-winged crozius arcanum, his weapon and a Chaplain's symbol of authority.

He leaned down and removed one of Lord Magyar's gauntlets, placing it next to the bowl on the table. Next, he raised the razor edge of his crozius and slashed it across his master's palm, allowing the blood to spatter into the bowl. Lord Magyar clenched and unclenched his fist repeatedly to prevent the blood from clotting until the bowl was full.

Astador lifted the bowl and offered it to Lord Magyar who
accepted it with a respectful nod. The Chapter Master supped
his blood and handed the bowl back to Astador.

The Chaplain lifted it to his lips and poured the blood over
his face in a red rain. He drank deeply of his master's blood
and Uriel grimaced in distaste. What manner of barbaric ritual was this that required the blood of fellow Space Marines
to enact? Had the Mortifactors become so debased that they
had fallen into rituals more commonly associated with the
Ruinous Powers? He glanced over at Tiberius.

The lord admiral's face was unreadable, but Uriel could see
the muscles bunched at his jaw and took his cue from him.
Astador groaned and reached out a hand to steady himself.
The bony familiar perched atop Magyar's throne took to the
air and flapped noisily towards the swaying Chaplain, catching the bowl as it fell from his slack fingers.

Uriel could contain himself no longer and shouted, 'What
is he doing? This reeks of impure sorceries!'

'Be silent!' roared Magyar. 'He seeks guidance from our
revered ancestors. Their wisdom comes from beyond the veil
of death, unfettered by the concerns of the living. He seeks
their counsel on whether we should join you in this fight.'

Uriel was about to answer when he felt an iron grip on his
arm. Lord Admiral Tiberius shook his head slowly.

'The Devourer comes from beyond the galaxy, and even by
naming it, men betray their ignorance,' groaned Astador. 'The
immortal hive mind controls its every thought. So many
beings... A billion times a billion monsters form the overmind and there is none here who can comprehend its scale. It
comes this way and seeks only to feed. It cannot be negotiated
with, it cannot be reasoned with, it can only be fought. It *must*
be fought.'

Astador dropped to his knees and vomited a gout of glistening blood, but the winged familiar was there and caught
the vital fluid in the bowl. It flapped towards Magyar and
handed him the blood-filled bowl before resuming its perch
above the Chapter Master.

Lord Magyar locked eyes with Uriel and smiled, before
drinking a measure of his returned blood.

Uriel heard Learchus retch behind him, but forced himself
to conceal his revulsion.

The Chapter Master of the Mortifactors wiped a rivulet of blood from his beard and said, 'The omens are not good, Uriel Ventris of the Ultramarines.'

Uriel's heart sank, but Lord Magyar was not yet done. He rose from his throne and crossed the floor of the dead to stand before Uriel. The Chapter Master of the Mortifactors leaned over Uriel and offered him the bowl. Saliva-frothed blood swirled in its bottom.

'Will you seal the pact of our brotherhood, Captain Ventris?'

Uriel stared into the bowl. The blood was bright scarlet.

He felt his gorge rise, but took the proffered bowl from Lord Magyar.

He raised it to his lips. Blood-stink filled his nostrils.

Amusement glittered in Lord Magyar's eyes and Uriel felt anger flare.

He tipped the bowl, feeling the hot blood fill his mouth, and swallowed.

It slipped down his throat, and Uriel could taste a measure of Lord Magyar's vitality and strength fill him. The blood carried the weight of ages in its hot, metallic flavour and Uriel gagged as a powerful vision of slaughter suddenly filled his senses, redolent with an eternity of death. He saw a pair of alien, yellow eyes and once again he felt the touch of the Nightbringer stab into his mind.

Lord Magyar took the bowl from Uriel's nerveless fingers and turned to face Astador, who nodded.

'We will honour the Warrior's Debt, Captain Ventris. I shall give you a company of my warriors and Chaplain Astador to lead them. You shall fight beside one another as equals. The blood has spoken and you have renewed our bond of brotherhood.'

Uriel barely heard him, but nodded anyway, sick to the pit of his stomach.

But whether it was the blood or the memory of the Nightbringer, he could not say.

TWO

THE VAST CITY of Erebus shone like a bright jewel in the flanks of the Cullin Mountains. It was built in a great wound in the rock, as though a giant had taken a shovel and cut a gigantic oval scoop into the south-western flank of the tallest peak. Set within a steep sided, rocky valley, fully nine kilometres wide at its opening, the city cut deep into the mountains for nearly forty kilometres. Bisected by the River Nevas, and home to some ten million people, Erebus was a crawling anthill and the most populous city of Tarsis Ultra.

Hab-units, factories, hydroponics domes, pleasure boulevards and other structures vied for space on the steep sides of the valley. Huge, teetering metal structures of glass and steel rose like metal flowers from the valley's side, and almost every square metre of rock was built upon or bolted to. From the valley floor to the soaring majesty of the luxury habs and exotic spices of the flesh bars, every available sliver of rock was festooned with girders, beams, angles and unfeasibly slender columns, supporting an architecturally eclectic mix of styles that clashed jarringly with the simple, marble elegance of the ancient structures built by the Ultramarines ten millennia ago.

When Erebus City, as it had been known then, was constructed, it was a model of the perfect city, but a lot had changed since those heady days. Where once the city had served as an example of all that was good about human society, ten thousand years of continued expansion had taken its toll on its utopian ideal, bringing it closer to the grim reality of hives on worlds such as Armageddon or Necromunda.

Zooming sculptures of steel rose steeply above the sides of the mountains, each wrapped in hab-units. As each structure climbed higher and higher, accidents became more and more common. Lattices of steel would give out under the horrendous loads imposed upon them, tearing free of the valley's side, to slide majestically down the rock face, pulling walkways, bridges and people with it until they crashed spectacularly to the valley floor in a jagged jumble of twisted metal, rockcrete and bodies.

Yet even here at the bottom, amidst this constant turmoil of debris, people thrived.

The brooding underbelly of the city – the Stank – held twisting baroque corridors and chambers of anarchic splendour that gave sanctuary to the skum gangs – the outcasts and the lawless. The Adeptus Arbites, known locally as the Bronzes, had declared some of the wilder zones of the Stank as no-go areas and even the toughest members of the Arbites Execution squads took care to travel in groups, combat shotguns locked and loaded. Feral gangs roamed the depths of the Stank, scavenging what they could from the ruins of collapsed habs, production towers and each other.

Violent skirmishes would often break out as rival gangs battled for control of newly collapsed structures, eager to plunder their resources.

Or sometimes they fought simply for the hell of it.

SNOWDOG VAULTED OVER the counter of the Flesh Bar. Bullets ripped towards him, blasting the wooden front to splinters as he rolled across it. He racked the slide of his shotgun and dropped behind the bar as bottles shattered and the mirror behind him exploded into reflective daggers. The barman screamed and collapsed next to him, clutching a bloody wound on his shoulder. Glass had cut his face open and red lines streaked his features.

Snowdog winked at the weeping man. 'I guess this really isn't your lucky day.'

The pounding music almost drowned the roar of gunfire. Six Wylderns carrying some heavy-duty weaponry had just walked in and hosed the bar, killing its patrons indiscriminately with bursts from automatic weapons. Who'd have seen that coming? Snowdog took a deep breath and crawled to the end of the bar. He shouldered his combat shotgun. Its blue-steel surface glinted like new, and now more than ever was he glad he'd killed the Bronze who'd carried it.

Screams and panicked yells filled the bar as people sought to make themselves scarce, desperate to avoid getting caught up in another of the gang wars that were becoming an all too common occurrence in Erebus hive.

Heavy blasts of gunfire echoed through the bar and more screams sounded. The music died as the speakers blew out in an explosion of sparks. People dropped, craters blasted in chests and bodies torn in two by heavy calibre shells.

Snowdog risked a glance around the side of the bar. Tigerlily was pinned down behind an overturned table, a throwing knife in each hand, and Silver had found shelter behind a thick steel column. He couldn't see Jonny Stomp or Lex, but figured that one was too smart and the other too lucky to have been caught in the initial salvo of autogun fire.

Damned Wylderns! Life for a fledgling gang leader was hard enough without these crazies making it even more precarious. It was bad enough that the Bronzes came down like an iron hammer on anyone who broke the law – which meant just about everyone in this part of the hive – from their grim and imposing fortress precinct on the edge of the Stank, the worst of the city's badzones. Not even the Bronzes would come in here without some serious hardware. But the Wylderns…

He couldn't figure them out. He robbed and killed for money, and to be the top dog of the Stank, but these psychos just killed. There was no telling where or when they'd strike, bursting in with powerful weapons and blazing away until everyone was dead. Killing for profit he could understand, but he could see no reason for these massacres and that bugged the hell out of Snowdog.

'Come out, come out wherever you are,' shouted a Wyldern in a singsong voice.

Snowdog heard the snap of more ammunition being loaded and nodded to Tigerlily. Like a coiled spring, the young redhead rose and hurled a throwing knife with unerring accuracy. The thin blade plunged into the eye of the nearest Wyldern and he crumpled wordlessly.

Tigerlily ducked back as gunfire blasted sparking chunks from the metal table she sheltered behind. Her black catsuit had been torn by a spinning shard of the table and Snowdog could see she was really mad now. As soon as the Wylderns were distracted, Snowdog rose from behind the bar and yelled, 'You picked the wrong bar to patronise, boys!'

He put another Wyldern down with his first shot and winged a second before they reacted and sprayed the bar with fire. Snowdog leapt aside, hundreds of bullets turning the bar to matchwood as he rolled.

Silver burst from hiding, a pistol in each hand. Her long, white hair was pulled in a severe ponytail and her ice-blue eyes were cold and unforgiving. She calmly double tapped another two Wylderns before spinning back behind the pillar, her long black coat billowing around her.

'And then there were two,' he muttered, seeing the sudden fear and confusion of the remaining two Wylderns. He stood and walked from behind the bar, sauntering into the middle of the blood-soaked killing ground. Bodies littered the place and it reeked of gunsmoke.

'Didn't expect this kinda welcome, did you?' asked Snowdog. 'We're the Nightcrawlers, and you interrupted our business here.'

'We'll kill you all!' shrieked one of the Wylderns, but there was no conviction in his voice.

'I don't think so, man,' said Snowdog, catching sight of Jonny Stomp and Lex on the upper balcony of the Flesh Bar, circling behind the Wylderns. He shook his head. Where else would Jonny and Lex be but with the girls and sex drugs, sampling the wares before doing the job?

'What do you say to you guys putting your guns away and letting us get on with this, huh?' said Snowdog.

He could see their hesitation and knew he had to appeal to their sense of self-preservation before their stupidity or bravado could resurface. He said, 'Look, no one else has to die here, okay?'

His voice was soothing and he slowly lowered his shotgun, taking in their high-priced clothing and coloured hair. Their faces were pierced with metal spikes and their full features spoke of healthy eating. Expensive looking electoos writhed up their arms and around their necks, throbbing in time with their racing heartbeats. These were rich kids on some narcotic high; he could see it in their eyes.

And suddenly it all made sense. They were thrill killers. Rich kids who killed because they were bored and because they could. But now that the tables had turned, the killing frenzy had gone out of them.

He continued to slowly walk towards the Wylderns and set his shotgun down on the bar. 'You just want out of here in one piece.'

The Wylderns nodded and Snowdog spread his arms.

'I can understand that,' he said, 'but it ain't going to happen.'

His eyes darted up towards the balcony.

'Now, Jonny,' said Snowdog mildly.

The Wylderns registered puzzlement for the briefest second before all one hundred kilogrammes of Jonny Stomp landed on them, smashing them to the ground. Jonny swiftly rose to his feet and dragged the first Wyldern to his feet, snapping his neck with a dry crack and rounding on the other as he tried to scramble away.

'No, please!' he begged. 'My family's rich, they'll give you any—'

'Not interested,' said Jonny and thundered his fist into the young Wyldern's face.

Blood and teeth flew as Jonny beat the young man to death with his bare hands.

Snowdog turned and lifted his shotgun from the bar, resting its barrel on his shoulder. He took a deep breath now that the fight was over, running a hand through his bleached and spiked hair as he leaned on the splintered bar. Flickering neon bathed his rugged features in an unhealthy glow and glass tinkled as it fell from shattered frames.

He rapped his knuckles on the bar. The dazed barman rose to his feet, hands clasped on top of his bloody head.

'Okay, man. Now where were we before all this unpleasantness?' said Snowdog.

He grinned ferally. 'Oh yeah, now I remember. This is a raid, hand over all your money.'

'GOOD TAKINGS?' ASKED Lex, eyeing the pile of cash on the upturned crate.

Snowdog eyed Lex suspiciously. 'Good enough, Lex.'

He pushed the money back into his small backpack and rose to his feet, flipping open a carton of bac-sticks and dragging one out. He pulled a brass lighter from his pocket and lit the aromatic stick, drawing in a lungful of smoke. He lifted the backpack by the straps and dumped it on his iron bed-frame.

Snowdog sat on the bed and watched as Lex shrugged and sloped off to join Jonny Stomp in the front room of their current hideout. Night had well and truly fallen and the glittering lights of the valley sides shone in through the holed roof and windowless frames. There was a sharp chill and Snowdog could feel a harsh winter coming on the air.

Lex was a problem. Snowdog knew it would only be a matter of time before Lex got himself killed. Normally, Snowdog would have cut him loose and moved on, but no one knew explosives like Lex. The things he could cook up with everyday items were beyond belief and many of the Bronzes had cause to regret an over-eager pursuit of the Nightcrawlers when they'd run into one of Lex's booby traps.

Lex didn't say much about where he came from, but Snowdog had seen a cog-toothed tattoo on his upper arm and guessed he'd once been apprenticed to the tech-guilds that worked the factory hangars and forge temples further down the valley. He'd come to them nearly six months ago and it didn't take a genius to figure out why he'd been kicked out of the guild. Lex was an addict, probably had been for years, permanently strung out on kalma or spur and was too dumb to realise that routine chem-screens would pick them up.

He banished Lex from his thoughts and rested a hand on the score from the bar. There was enough here to pay for some real big guns, then they could really carve themselves some turf. And he knew just the guy to get those weapons from.

Yeah, it had been a good heist, but the Wylderns had stolen the show and that bugged him. How was he supposed to build the Nightcrawlers into the most feared and respected gang in the Stank with practically no one left alive to spread the word? Perhaps they should have let the last Wyldern live, but Snowdog quickly dismissed that thought. Trying to stop Jonny Stomp from killing someone when his blood was up wasn't a healthy option if you wanted to stay alive yourself. The big man was a stone-cold killer, pure and simple, but he was useful and trusted Snowdog utterly.

Which just went to show that Jonny wasn't the sharpest tool in the box, but Snowdog would take what muscle he could get. He took a last draw on the bac-stick then dropped it on the floor, crushing it out beneath his boot. He stretched and lay down on the bed.

Snowdog was of average height, but was blessed with a wiry musculature that belied his whipcord-thin body. He wore tiger-striped combat fatigues, tucked into a heavy pair of boots he'd pulled from a dead Bronze and a white t-shirt with a faded holo patch of a mushroom cloud that expanded and contracted as he moved.

The score at the Flesh Bar would keep the wolves from the door, but he'd need to think of another pretty soon if he was to keep his crew together. They would follow him for as long as they thought he was good news. But he needed a regular gig that would keep the cash flowing with the minimum amount of effort.

He looked up as he heard a tap on the doorframe and smiled as Silver strolled up to the edge of his bed and sat beside him.

'Some day, huh?' she said.

'Some day,' agreed Snowdog. 'Where's Tigerlily?'

'She went off to a pound club with Trask,' answered Silver sleepily. 'Kominsky's, I think.'

'Maybe I'm getting old, but this pound music is something I just don't understand. Loud music I get, but it's like a sonic assault on the senses.'

'A lot of people like it,' pointed out Silver. 'Hell, even I don't mind it.'

'So why didn't you go with her?'

'I couldn't be bothered with Trask. You know what he's like with stimms.'

'Tigerlily obviously doesn't mind.'

'That's cause she's too young and dumb to realise what a loser he is.'

'You're cynical tonight.'

Silver smiled and Snowdog felt himself loosen up as she bent down to kiss him.

'I'm tired,' she said. 'And besides, what can Trask do for me that I can't get better from you?'

Snowdog chuckled, remembering the last time Trask had gotten overly amorous towards Silver after a heavy night on the stimms. The poor bastard hadn't walked straight for a week afterwards. He decided to change the subject. 'How're the rest of the troops?'

Silver shrugged, 'Okay, I guess. Lex is getting antsy and Jonny wants to head out to bust some heads. He keeps talking about taking on the High Hive gangs.'

Snowdog chuckled. 'They're gonna find Jonny face down in the sump if he thinks he can take on the High Hive gangs. Tell him he'd better stick to busting up Jackboy parties if he knows what's good for him. We ain't ready for that kind of action yet.'

Silver yawned and slid off her long coat, pulling her albino-white hair free of its ponytail and allowing it to spill around her shoulders. She climbed over Snowdog to lie with her back to the wall, laying her arm across his waist and resting her head on his chest. Snowdog kissed her forehead and put his arm around her shoulders.

'Did you notice that there weren't any citizens' militia units around the Flesh Bar?' asked Silver, pushing her hand beneath his t-shirt and running her fingers through the hair on his stomach.

'Yeah, I did. That was kinda weird, wasn't it?'

'I wonder where they were? Normally you can't move in the upper valley without seeing at least a few of them.'

Snowdog nodded slowly. 'I don't know, but now you mention it, the whole city has been pretty wired recently, on edge. I seen a lot of Bronzes, but it's been pretty quiet in the way of soldiers. I wonder why? And those Wylderns. Normally they'd never dare hit a bar that close to the High Hive.'

'What do you think is going on?'

'Damned if I know, hon, but if it keeps the militia and the Bronzes off our backs, then I'm all for it.'

Snowdog could not have been more wrong.

THREE

URIEL WATCHED THE landscape speed past the Thunderhawk, circling round white-capped mountains of soaring majesty. A hard winter was coming to this part of the world and the beauty below was breathtaking. Frozen mountaintop lakes glittered in the thin light and the rugged splendour reminded him wistfully of the landscape surrounding the Fortress of Hera.

The Thunderhawk banked, following the line of the mountains, and Uriel caught a glimpse of the black gunships of the Mortifactors as they turned in formation with those of the Ultramarines. His expression turned sour as the memory and taste of Lord Magyar's blood surged strong and vivid through his senses.

The Chapter Master of the Mortifactors had laughed, calling him brother, and slapped his palms on Uriel's shoulder guards, leaving bloody handprints. How any Chapter descended from the blessed Roboute Guilliman could have fallen so far from his vision of a sacred band of warriors was utterly beyond him. He also had the feeling that it had been his drinking of Magyar's blood that had convinced the

38

Chapter Master to send his warriors rather than any bond of shared brotherhood. How could such a Chapter operate, let alone thrive, without recourse to the Codex Astartes?

Upon returning to the *Vae Victus*, Uriel had immersed himself in prayer and rituals of cleansing, but the lingering vision that ripped through his mind could not be purged. He could not deny the feeling of power he had experienced drinking the blood and he knew that part of him, Emperor forgive him, longed for that power again.

In the month it had taken them to return to the Tarsis Ultra system, there had been precious little contact with the Mortifactors, a situation the Ultramarines were more than happy with. It had been a shock to everyone to know that a Chapter founded from their honourable legacy had changed so much.

They would fight alongside the Mortifactors, but Uriel knew there would be no renewal of brotherhood and no pledges of loyalty sworn anew between the Chapters.

They would face the common threat and that would be the end of it.

He realised he was clenching his fists and slowly released a deep breath.

The Thunderhawk began descending as they cleared the mountains and Uriel tried to shake his angry thoughts, returning his gaze to the world below.

They flew over ordered farming collectives, their sprawling fields a striking green amid the patchy white frosts of oncoming winter. Gleaming train tracks and hydroways snaked across the landscape, efficiently connecting the scattered communities and, every now and then, Uriel caught a glimpse of a silvered land train speeding between them.

The view was eerily reminiscent of the surface of Iax, sometimes called the Garden of Ultramar, one of the most productive worlds of the Imperium. Uriel briefly wondered if the inhabitants had also built their own version of Iax's fortress city of First Landing.

So far as he could tell from the air, Tarsis Ultra looked to be a model world that would not have been out of place in Ultramar itself. But Uriel knew it had not always been this way.

Ten thousand years ago, it had been enslaved by the lies of heretics for decades, before its liberation by Roboute Guilliman and the Ultramarines during the Great Crusade. Its grateful populace had incorporated their liberators into their world's name, that they might always remember and honour them. When the Ultramarines Legion moved on to fresh campaigns, Roboute Guilliman left the foundations of an ordered world, established on ideals of justice, honour and discipline, instead of the blasted wastelands many of his brother primarchs' victories left. Guilliman left teachers, artisans and people skilled in the ways of engineering and architecture to help with the rebuilding of Tarsis Ultra.

Its civilization was remade in the image of Ultramar, its society ordered and just, its people content and productive. Once more, Tarsis Ultra became a functioning world of the Emperor. Its output was prodigious, but unlike many other industrial worlds, whose unthinking plundering of their natural resources led to them becoming polluted, toxic deserts, sustainability and a careful husbanding of resources assured that Tarsis Ultra remained a verdant and pleasant world.

After the grim revelations regarding the Mortifactors, Uriel was looking forward to setting foot on a world touched by the primarch. What he had seen on the Basilica Mortis had shaken him to the core, and it would do him good to see a physical reminder of Roboute Guilliman's legacy.

And what he had seen thus far of Tarsis Ultra and its defences had impressed him greatly. Hulking star forts hung in geo-stationary orbit above the primary continental mass and already a sizeable fleet had been assembled in the months since their warning of the approaching tyranids had been given.

The *Argus*, a Victory class battlecruiser, and veteran of the First Tyrannic War, headed a detachment of fearsome vessels of war, including the *Sword of Retribution*, an Overlord battleship, three Dauntless cruisers and a host of escort ships. Flotillas of planetary skiffs, laden with the men and women of the Imperial Guard, were constantly shuttling back and forth from the planet's surface and four vast transport ships hanging in orbit. Within days, the entirety of two vast regiments, the 10th Logres and the 933rd Death Korp of Kreig, would be deployed to Tarsis Ultra.

More ships were being diverted to the system by segmentum command at Bakka and fresh regiments raised from nearby systems and sub-sectors, but they would not arrive for several months. For now they were on their own.

Lord Admiral Tiberius was even now planning the strategy for the combined naval forces with Captain Gaiseric of the Mortifactors strike cruiser *Mortis Probati*, and the commander of the fleet, Admiral de Corte, a student of Lord Admiral Zaccarius Rath himself.

'Two minutes,' came the pilot's voice over the speakers.

Uriel shook himself from his reverie and watched as Learchus paced the length of the Thunderhawk, his normally stoic features alive with anticipation. It seemed as though Learchus was more anxious than anyone to set foot on Tarsis Ultra.

Pasanius sat opposite Uriel, looking relaxed and unconcerned that they were about to see a world touched by their primarch. His heavy flamer was stowed above him and he nodded to Uriel as the Thunderhawk came about for its final approach. 'This should be interesting,' he said.

'Interesting?' laughed Learchus. 'It will be wonderful. To see the handiwork of the blessed Guilliman halfway across the galaxy is proof that our way of life is the way forward for humanity.'

'It is?' asked Pasanius.

'Of course,' said Learchus, surprised that Pasanius had even queried his statement. 'If the way of life we have followed for millennia thrives here, it can thrive elsewhere.'

'Is it thriving here?'

'Obviously.'

'How do you know? You haven't seen it yet.'

'I don't need to see it, I have faith in the primarch.'

Uriel let his sergeants argue the finer points of Guilliman's vision as he caught his first glimpse of Erebus city, a dark scar on the snow-covered flank of a vast mountain filled with silver towers. A huge reservoir glittered on the adjacent plateau, high above the kilometres-wide valley mouth, its rocky slopes crowned with white marble buildings and elegant, columned structures. A wide, statue-lined road rose through the centre of the valley, towards the first of the city's defensive walls, throngs of buildings crowding in on all sides. The interior of the city was a glittering spiderweb of silver and white.

Save for the buildings at the very edge of the valley, Uriel could see no discernable pattern to the city's construction. Here and there he recognised flourishes of Macraggian architecture, but where there should have been space and light, he saw newer, brasher constructions, towering carbuncles overshadowing the elegance of the oldest buildings.

The Thunderhawk gained altitude and altered course so that it was flying parallel to the valley. Uriel could see that the valley floor rose the further into the mountain it penetrated until it reached a long, defensive wall, a foaming waterfall at its centre, that in turn rose towards another, shorter wall as the valley narrowed. The stepped structure of the city's defences continued towards the valley's end and now that he could look down into the city, he saw ruined areas, collapsed structures that looked as though they had been shelled. Hundreds of jumbled structures squatted here in the frigid shadows of the high towers of the deep valley, thin plumes of white smoke rising from a multitude of cooking fires.

The sense of disappointment in what had become of Guilliman's legacy was a physical pain in Uriel's chest. He sat back in his captain's chair and felt his fists clenching again.

He looked over as he heard a shocked intake of breath from Learchus.

'What is this?' he breathed. 'Are we too late, has the war begun?'

'No,' said Uriel sadly. 'It has not.'

THE GUNSHIPS OF the Space Marines touched down on the upper landing platforms of Erebus city, the screaming of their engines drowning out the pomp and ceremony of the hundred-strong band that played rousing tunes of welcome. Uriel marched down the ramp of the gunship, feeling the sharp bite of the cold air as he moved away from the heat of the engines.

'Now this is a welcome,' said Pasanius, raising his voice to be heard.

Uriel nodded in agreement. The platforms were awash with men, thousands upon thousands of soldiers drawn up in ordered ranks before the Space Marine gunships. Vast banners flapped from standard poles thirty metres high, supported by a dozen men with suspensors and guy ropes.

Gold braid fluttered and the blue and white of the Ultramarines Chapter symbol rippled hugely on their fabric. The company banners of all ten of the Ultramarine companies were present as well as those of individual heroes from Chapter legend. At the forefront of the banners, Uriel could see the heraldry of Captain Invictus, and next to that, the banner of the Fourth company. He did a double take as he saw that a battle honour in the shape of the white rose of Pavonis had been added to the design.

Chaplain Astador joined him from the ramp of his own Thunderhawk.

'It seems your fame precedes you, Captain Ventris,' he said.

Uriel nodded, staring at this full ceremonial reception. He had expected to be met, but this was insane. How much time and effort had been put into this welcome that could have been better spent strengthening the city's defences or training? Did these people not realise that they would soon be at war?

An honour guard of perhaps two hundred armoured troopers formed up in ordered ranks either side of the Thunderhawks, dressed in ridiculously impractical blue armour. Fashioned to resemble power armour, the soldiers looked absurd next to the bulk of the Ultramarines.

A cold wind whipped across the landing platforms as another column of men strode towards them between the honour guards. The soldiers marched in perfect step, their drill flawless and uniforms spotless. In front of them came another group, headed by three men who, judging by the elaboration of the leader's dress, commanded this gathering.

The lead officer wore the same ceremonial blue armour as the honour guard, with a silver trim and gold braid looping around his shoulders and trousers. He wore a dazzling silver helmet with a long, horsehair plume that reached down to his waist, and he carried a golden, basket-hilted sword before his face. His chest was awash with gold and silver insignia and his boots were an immaculately polished black leather. His companions obviously eschewed such frivolous adornment, preferring the simple dress uniforms of their Imperial Guard regiments.

Uriel recognised the heavy greatcoat and fur colback of the Krieg regiment and, from the silver laurel and pips on his collar, deduced that this was that regiment's colonel. The final member of the group was a thickly-waisted older man, with a neatly trimmed beard, wearing simple, well-pressed fatigues and a thickly padded jacket with a fur collar. Like the colonel of the Krieg regiment, he wore a fur-lined colback and, also like his fellow colonel, seemed deeply uncomfortable at this ostentatious welcome.

'Captain,' said Pasanius, pointing towards the edges of the landing fields.

Further down the valley, huge crowds gathered beyond the high fencing that surrounded the platforms. Expressions of worship and awe stared back at the Ultramarines and Uriel could see people praying and weeping tears of joy.

The delegation of officers came to a halt before them, their over-dressed leader slashing his sword through the air in an elaborate gesture of salute. He sheathed the sword and stepped forward, bowing his head and dropping to one knee before Uriel.

'Honoured lords, I am thine humble servant, Sebastien Montante, Fabricator Marshal of the world of Tarsis Ultra, and in the name of the Divine Master of Mankind I bid thee welcome,' said the man in tortured High Gothic. 'May your beneficence shine over our world at the glory of your return. A thousand times a thousand prayers of thanks shall be offered up in praise of your names. Many are the salute–'

'I thank you for your welcome, sir,' interrupted Uriel brusquely. 'I am Uriel Ventris, captain of the Fourth company.'

Montante looked up, startled and more than a little crestfallen to have had his speech halted in its tracks. Uriel saw he was about to continue, and hurriedly said, 'These are my senior sergeants, Pasanius and Learchus. And this is Chaplain Astador of the Mortifactors.'

Realising that he wouldn't be able to finish his speech, Montante rose to his feet and brushed his trousers flat. He bowed nervously to Astador and said, 'Chaplain Astador, we have heard of your illustrious Chapter and bid you welcome also.'

Astador nodded and returned the bow. 'Your display of welcome is overwhelming, Fabricator Montante and we thank you for it.'

Montante smiled crookedly and nodded, turning to face the two colonels who had accompanied him.

'Allow me to introduce the senior officers of our brave defenders,' said Montante, recovering well.

The leader of the Krieg regiment stepped forward and snapped a curt salute to the Space Marines, saying, 'Colonel Trymon Stagler, regimental commander of the 933rd Death Korp of Krieg and overall theatre commander. I apologise for this waste of time, but Fabricator Montante kept it from us until an hour ago.'

Stagler ignored Montante's frown of indignation as the second man stepped forwards and offered his hand to Uriel. 'Colonel Octavius Rabelaq, commander in chief of the 10th Logres regiment. Pleasure to meet you, Uriel. Heard a lot about you from Sebastien. Looking forward to fighting with you. Well, not fighting with you, but you understand, eh?'

Uriel took the proffered hand and Rabelaq enthusiastically pumped his hand up and down, gripping Uriel's elbow with his other hand as he did so. Eventually, he released Uriel and stepped back with a brisk salute as Montante nodded briskly in the direction of the honour guard.

'Yes, yes, well, now that we all know each other, we should get on with the formal inspection, yes? Then onto the feast of welcome, eh? Don't want to let all that delicious food and amasec go to waste,' smiled Montante, again indicating that the Space Marines should follow him towards the honour guard.

'Fabricator Montante,' said Uriel. 'We do not have time to tarry here and should begin preparations for the coming battles. The tyranid fleet is probably less than a month from your system at best and you would have us indulge in frivolity?'

Montante's mouth flapped as he considered this breach of formal welcoming etiquette and looked towards the Guard colonels for support.

'Captain Ventris is correct' said Colonel Stagler. 'We must begin planning. The enemy is at the gates.'

Uriel thought he could detect just a hint of anticipation in the colonel's voice.

'Indeed it is,' said a figure emerging from the honour guard behind Montante.

Uriel saw a hooded adept with a retinue of scribes, lexmechanics and green robed astropaths limp painfully towards them using a claw-topped silver cane.

'The enemy is indeed at the gates,' repeated the hooded adept. 'My astropaths tell me that the first vanguard drone-ships are even now entering the outer reaches of the system. The rest of the hive fleet cannot be far behind.'

'And who are you, sir?' asked Uriel.

The man pulled back his hood, revealing an ancient, weathered face, with a tonsured crown of silver hair. His features had the pallid, waxy texture of frequent juvenat treatments, but his eyes had lost none of the fire that Uriel remembered from the numerous images of him in the Chapel of Heroes on Macragge.

'I am Lord Inquisitor Kryptman of the Ordo Xenos, and we do not have much time.'

SIXTY THOUSAND POUNDS of thrust roared from the twin engines of each Fury attack craft as they howled along the internal flight deck of the *Kharloss Vincennes*, a Dictator class cruiser, and shot from the launch bays of their cruiser's flank like bullets from a gun.

Two squadrons, each of three fighters, lifted off and circled back around, ready to begin their intercept. An anomalous contact had registered on the powerful surveyor systems of Listening Station Trajen, a lightly manned orbital anchored at the edge of the Tarsis Ultra system. Their job would be to investigate the contact and, if circumstances were favourable, engage and destroy it. Should that not be possible, they would provide exact positional data and allow the heavier guns of the *Kharloss Vincennes* to obliterate it.

The Furies were aerodynamic fighters with swept-forwards wings and twin tails with a rack of high-explosive missiles slung under each wing. Designed to shoot down incoming torpedoes, intercept attacking bombers and destroy other fighters, Furies were the workhorses of the Imperial Navy.

Each Fury carried extra fuel in a centreline tank, which would enable them to remain on patrol for longer periods of time without having to return to their carrier.

The Fury could carry up to four crew, but for scouting missions, a pilot and a gunnery officer were all that was required.

'Angel squadrons, sound off,' came the voice of the ordnance officer from the *Kharloss Vincennes*.

'Angel squadron nine-zero-one, clear,' acknowledged Captain Owen Morten, commander of the *Kharloss Vincennes'* fighter squadrons, thumbing the vox-toggle on his control column as he checked left and right for his two wingmen. He waited for Lieutenant Erin Harlen, lead pilot of the second squadron of Furies to call in as Kiell Pelaur, his gunnery officer, fired up the surveyor link to the *Kharloss Vincennes*.

'Ditto. Angel squadron nine-zero-two. We are clear, and that's official,' came the drawling voice of Erin Harlen over the vox-net.

'Cut the chatter nine-zero-two. Combat readiness is in force. Do you understand that at all, Lieutenant Harlen?' replied the ordnance officer in a voice that suggested he had been through this routine many times.

'Yes, sir! That order has been understood, sir!' shouted Harlen.

'Harlen, keep it down for a second will you?' said Pelaur over the internal vox-net. 'Let's find out where we're supposed to patrol before you start driving us all mad, huh?'

'Understood, Lieutenant. We were beginning to wonder that ourselves,' replied Harlen's gunnery officer, Caleb Martoq.

The Furies circled the *Kharloss Vincennes* as they awaited navigational data to be transferred into their own attack logisters.

The voice of the ordnance officer came again. 'Angel squadrons, confirm patrol circuit.'

Kiell Pelaur checked the pict-slate before him as the tactical plot of their squadron appeared and thumbed the vox. 'Confirmed. Circuit is acquired.'

'Confirmed. Angel squadrons one and two are weapons-free and cleared to engage. Good hunting.'

'You bet we'll have good hunting. We don't take prisoners,' said Harlen. He glanced through the toughened canopy to where his squadron commander and the rest of his squadron were flying on station with him.

'Ready, Captain Morten?' he said, the anticipation in his voice unmistakable even over the vox-net. Morten smiled beneath his helmet and said, 'Angel squadron nine-zero-one has the lead. Harlen, take our lower quadrant and stay close.'

'Understood, Captain. Nine-zero-one has the lead.'

Captain Morten turned his control column to the required heading, took a deep breath and opened up the Fury's throttle.

It felt as though he had suddenly been kicked in the back as the giant engines thundered and hurled the craft forwards. The suspensor wired pressure suit expanded to prevent his blood from pooling, counteracting the horrendous forces exerted on his body by such rapid acceleration.

Super-oxygenated blood pumped directly into his body via spinal connections and the contoured helmets both he and his gunnery officer wore exerted outward pressure on the surrounding air to prevent them from blacking out.

This was what it was all about, he thought to himself with a wide, boyish grin. The long years of training, the unbelievable physical demands and the risks were more than made up for by moments like this. Powering through space at the command of one of the most sacred pieces of military hardware ever forged, with the power to bring righteous death to the enemies of the Emperor, was as close to perfection as life ever got.

His two wingmen were keeping station with him in a standard 'V' formation. Satisfied, he rolled his fighter slightly to make sure that Harlen was in position below him. Morten knew that despite his often cavalier attitude, Erin Harlen was one of the best pilots in the squadron, if not Battlefleet Tempestus itself. For that reason and that reason alone he was cut a little more slack than would normally be allowed in such a regimented place as an Imperial Navy starship.

As Harlen's squadron commander he was entrusted with the often troublesome job of keeping him in line and not allowing him to stray beyond his already widened boundaries of discipline.

Sure enough, Harlen's squadron of Furies were right where they were supposed to be, slightly below and behind him on his starboard wing. He rolled level again and continued on course. This intercept should take less than an hour and until then there was very little to do except sit back and keep an eye on the gauges to make sure they were flying within the tolerances of the craft. There wasn't much of anything to look at through the canopy, and, without a fixed point of reference, it was impossible to perceive their motion.

Thirty minutes of their patrol circuit had passed before the surveyor screen before Lieutenant Pelaur picked up their target.

'Target acquired, captain. Bio readings consistent with tyranid life forms. Bearing, zero-three-six right, range one thousand kilometres,' said Pelaur from his slightly elevated position in the cockpit behind Morten, 'Recommend approach vector mark four-six.'

'Affirmative, lieutenant,' said Morten, adjusting his course so as to come in from the optimum attack position in space combat – behind and above the target. Pelaur's course would also put the light of the sun behind them, such as it was, and hopefully mask their presence a fraction longer.

In space combat, where death could travel the distance between combatants in seconds, the difference between life and death could often rest on those fractions.

'Lieutenant Harlen, come in.'

'Captain Morten! My gunnery officer has a contact.'

'As does mine, Lieutenant Harlen. Approach vector mark four-six.'

'I concur,' said Caleb Martoq.

'Thirty seconds to attack run,' said Pelaur.

They were fast approaching the point where they would make their final turn before beginning their attack. From here onwards they were on a war footing.

'Confirmed,' said Morten, starting the countdown to their turn and cutting the throttle back, decelerating towards combat speed.

'Twenty seconds,' counted down Pelaur.

The pilots rapidly bled off speed from their engines, slowing so that they would be able to attack without shooting past their target.

'Lieutenant Harlen. Ten seconds, be ready.' said Morten, flexing his fingers on the control stick.

'Aye, captain. In ten.'

'Turn on my mark,' said Pelaur, his face fixed on the pict-slate before him. 'Mark!'

Morten banked the Fury sharply right and downwards, following the plot on his attack logister. The other Furies swung in smoothly behind his fighter like a flock of hunting birds.

'What do you have, lieutenant?' he asked.

The icon displayed on Pelaur's screen flashed and held a steady red.

'I have a hostile contact, captain.'

'Affirmative,' said Martoq.

'Attack pattern delta four,' ordered Morten. 'I want a volley from your squadron, Lieutenant Harlen.'

'Attack pattern delta four confirmed,' said Harlen. 'Breaking right.'

The three Furies in Harlen's squadron peeled away to the right and increased speed as they closed with the target.

'Missiles ready,' said Martoq.

'Fire at will,' returned Morten.

Morten watched the Furies of Harlen's squadron shudder as a missile detached from each of their wings and his cockpit was suddenly brilliantly illuminated as the rocket motors ignited and the six missiles flashed into the darkness.

'Missiles away!' shouted Harlen.

'Angel flight nine-zero-one, with me. Let's go,' ordered Morten.

He pushed the throttle open again and sped off after the missiles, arming his own and powering up the lascannon. If anything flew out from the target to try and intercept the missiles, he and his Furies would be waiting for them. He mouthed a quick prayer to the Emperor and checked his display. The pict-slate showed the flashing red icon of the target with two green arrowheads rapidly converging on its position.

His own flight were following the missiles in, leapfrogging Lieutenant Harlen's and leaving his flight to cover them. Any element of surprise had been lost the instant they had fired, but it had been maintained long enough.

'Impact in two seconds,' said his gunnery officer.

Morten focused his eyes beyond the canopy and saw a blossom of white fire in the distance.

'Missiles have impacted. I say again, missiles have impacted,' called Martoq over the vox-net. 'We got him!'

'Good shooting, Angel nine-zero-two!' said Morten, even though he knew that Martoq's assessment of the target's destruction was premature. They couldn't know that for certain yet.

'Did they get it, Kiell?' asked Morten.

'Looks like it, sir. I'm not getting any bio-readings any more. I think we got it.'

'You bet we got it! We blew it back to the warp!' cawed Harlen.

'Alright, we're going in for a closer look. Cut speed and we'll go in and see what we can see. Harlen, you're covering.'

'No problem, captain,' acknowledged Harlen. 'Lascannons are armed and ready. Anything that so much as twitches is going to be sucking vacuum.'

'Okay, let's take this nice and easy,' cautioned Morten. 'Kiell, keep your eyes and ears open. If we need to get out of here in a hurry I want to know about it right away.'

'Affirmative,' replied Pelaur, concentrating on the threat boards.

Morten pushed the control stick over and headed straight for the location of the explosion he had seen through the canopy. As his craft drew nearer, he saw a large, tubular object spinning in space, huge craters blasted in its side. He pulled the speed way back and moved in for a closer look. Perhaps forty or fifty metres long, the object's surface was a mottled green and pierced with undulating sphincter orifices. A tattered, fleshy frill ran the length of the creature and long, cable-like tentacles drifted behind it. Its front resembled a giant, serrated beak and ichor foamed in an expanding purple cloud from the wounds in its side, spilling into space like blood. If this thing had once been alive, it now looked very dead.

'Are you getting any bio readings?' he asked.

'No, sir. All surveyors say it's dead.'

'Good.' said Morten. 'Well, log it in the cont–'

'Look out!' screamed Lieutenant Harlen suddenly. 'Three o' clock high!'

Morten instinctively slammed the control column right and pushed out the throttles to full power. He caught a glimpse of a fleshy, toothed torpedo-like object that had spurted from the side of the supposedly lifeless organism through one of the rippling orifices.

He rolled hard left, slamming them around the cockpit as it flashed over their heads.

As though in slow motion he saw the organism sail past his cockpit.

He continued his roll left, levelling off and easing up only when he had done a full circle. By the Emperor that had been close! They had almost–

'It's still on you, captain!' shouted Harlen, 'It's right on your tail!'

'Emperor's blood, this thing is persistent!'

He rolled right and dived, twisting his Fury in a looping spiral.

'Range, one hundred and fifty metres!' yelled Pelaur, 'Too close! Get us out of here!'

'What do you think I'm doing?' snapped Morten, climbing hard and pushing the throttle all the way out. If the damned thing was still with him now then it was only a matter of time before it caught them.

'Range, one hundred metres and closing!'

It was too close for any of his wingmen to shoot at and Morten could only hope that the thing, whatever it was, had to impact to detonate, or whatever it did.

'Captain!' shouted Harlen, 'Break right, Mark nine-three. Now!'

Without question Morten obeyed, hauling right and diving at full speed. He was just quick enough to see the shape of Harlen's Fury flash past his canopy, lasfire blasting from its underside.

Though he couldn't hear it, he felt the enormous pressure wave of the tyranid weapon's explosive death throes as the flurry of lasfire blew it away.

But it had been too close for them to avoid its vengeance completely. The rear quarter of the Fury lurched drunkenly sideways as hundreds of chitinous fragments scythed into the fighter's body.

Morten fought for control of the shuddering craft as it spun crazily. His helmet smashed into the side of the cockpit and his vision swam as warning lights winked into life all over the control panels. His suit expanded and despite the pressure helmet he could feel himself on the verge of blacking out. If that happened it was all over. The centrifugal forces would tear his ship apart, leaving their bodies to freeze in space.

Sparks and smoke obscured his vision and he could only just make out the shape of the throttle. Morten strained to reach it over the rising forces in the cockpit.

He could hear the squeal of tearing metal and knew that his Fury was beginning to disintegrate.

With one last effort he lunged forwards and hauled the throttle back to idle.

Almost immediately, the violent shuddering of his wounded craft ceased, to be replaced by the soft creak of twisted metal, Pelaur's rapid breathing and the protesting whine of the engines as they powered down.

The Fury drifted and spun sideways for a while, before Morten repressurised the cockpit, cleared it of fumes and gently restored power to the engines.

'You okay in the back?' he asked, craning to see how his gunnery officer was doing.

'I've been better, captain. But I'm still here. Nice work,' gasped Pelaur, obviously shaken by their close call.

'Yes, real nice work. I should have known there could be active bio-weapons.'

'We're still alive,' pointed out Pelaur.

'Yes, I suppose we should be thankful.' said Morten, making the sign of the aquila and pressing his glove to the small shrine beside him. He could see Harlen's squadron paralleling his course. From the lumps of flesh drifting past his canopy, he could see that as well as shooting down the bio-weapon, Harlen's squadron had also vaporised the original target.

He thumbed the vox and said, 'Nine-zero-two, we're allright here. A little shaken up, but other than that we're fine. By the way, thanks. That was nice shooting.'

'Don't mention it, sir' said Harlen lightly. 'Hold still now. I'm going to give you a once over, see how bad you're hurt.'

'Right. Holding steady,' replied Morten, which was easier said than done as the Fury fought his every attempt to hold her in a straight line.

Harlen's craft slid below and round the stricken fighter and came to rest off Morten's port wing.

'How bad is it?' he asked, almost afraid of the answer.

'It's not good, that's for sure. You've taken a lot of hits on the engine vectors so she's going to be hell to steer. And it looks like you're losing fuel. Not much, but we better get you home to the *Vincennes* before you run dry.'

Morten suddenly realised how close they had come to dying. If even one piece of the bio-weapon's chitin shrapnel had hit the centreline fuel tank, they'd have been incinerated in a raging fireball.

'Thanks. Get your squadron home to the *Vincennes* and we'll be back as soon as we can. If we need help we'll let you know,' said Morten. 'And let the tactical officers know about these things. I have the feeling we'll be seeing more of them.'

'Yes, sir. You sure you'll be allright?'

'We'll be late, but we'll get there. Now get out of here before I have to order you.'

'Yes, sir,' acknowledged Harlen as his three Furies accelerated to combat speed and were soon lost in the darkness.

'You ready to go home, Kiell?' asked Captain Morten.

'More than ever.'

Captain Owen Morten gingerly rolled the limping Fury towards home and slowly fed power to the engines, grimacing as the vibrations on the twisted airframe increased.

It was going to be a long ride home.

FOUR

THE UNKNOWN ARTIST had used the entire chamber as his canvas. A mosaic of enormous proportions covered the walls, the ceiling and even the floor. The workmanship was exquisite: none of the shards of coloured glass that made up the mosaic bigger than a thumbnail. Larger than the Chapel of Heroes on Macragge, the scale of such a work was breathtaking: the chamber stretched over two hundred metres long and its barrel-vaulted ceiling rose thirty metres or more above them.

Uriel and the Ultramarines walked in rapture around the perimeter of the long room, speechless in wonder at the magnificent sight, any faded expectations of Tarsis Ultra swept aside by the spectacular mosaic. Pastoral images of a rugged land of primal beauty stretched before them, the colours wondrously bright and vivid, the skill of the artist perfectly capturing the wild majesty of his subject. Glass mountains soared above glass seas of glittering azure, vibrant emerald fields teemed with proud animals.

Uriel reached out and touched the wall, half expecting to reach within the mosaic and feel the sea breeze scudding across the foaming waves that broke on cliffs of dazzling white. Atop the mountains, he recognised a majestic marble fortress with columns and golden domes that made his heart ache with longing. The Fortress of Hera, rendered in such loving detail that he could almost taste the salt of Macragge's seas and smell the sweet sap of its highland firs in his memory.

He could see the mosaic was having the same effect on Pasanius and Learchus, their faces alight with joy. Uriel craned his neck upwards, seeing a host of glass warriors at the hunt, mounted on horseback and wearing blue chitons, the loose, knee-length woollen tunics worn by men and women of Macragge in ancient times.

Leading the hunt was a giant of a man with golden curls and alabaster skin, his face alive with love and strength, carrying a long spear and oval shield. Uriel froze before this image, overcome by emotion, as he recognised Roboute Guilliman. Many times had he gazed upon the pallid, dead face of his primarch in the Temple of Correction on Macragge , where his lifeless body was held immobile in a sepulchral stasis tomb, but seeing him portrayed like this, with so much life and animation, filled Uriel with a terrible ache of sorrow for his passing. Until this moment, Uriel had never given any credence to the tales that the primarch's wounds were slowly healing, and that he would one day arise from his deathly slumber, but seeing this sight, he could now understand why people needed to believe that such a mighty warrior could return from the void.

Further along were scenes of battle, images of war from a bygone age when heroes stood as tall as mountains and could topple the earth with their strength. Here, magnificent and noble, Roboute Guilliman fought the armies of evil. Behind him, slinking from the shadows, an unseen champion of evil poised to deliver a treacherous deathblow. As Uriel's eye travelled further along the fresco he saw a warrior save Guilliman's life, masterfully rendered in chips of sapphire and glass as he thrust his bayoneted rifle deep into the enemy's belly. Sprays of rubies and garnet glittered from the wound.

Another portion of this section of the ceiling showed Roboute Guilliman on bended knee, swearing his bond of brotherhood with the warrior people of Tarsis Ultra. To see such a display of humility from one so mighty as their primarch was a sharp reminder to Uriel of everything the Ultramarines fought to protect.

Everywhere around the chamber there were new wonders and fresh visions of incredible beauty, but Uriel forced himself to tear his gaze away from the fantastical mosaic. Pasanius and Learchus stood by his side, similarly overwhelmed by this work of genius.

'It's…' began Learchus, searching for words to do this masterpiece justice.

Uriel nodded. 'I know. I have read of the Tarsis fresco, but had never believed it could be as magnificent as this.'

Footsteps echoed through the chamber and the spell was broken. The mosaic was just a wall and the images upon it nothing more than glass shards. Uriel turned as Fabricator Montante, changed into more practical plain grey robes, led the council of war into the room. The senior officers of the regiments, each with an entourage of scribes, flunkies and adjutants trailing a respectful distance behind them, followed Montante towards the centre of the chamber.

This portion of the room was sunken into the floor, where a number of marble benches and a long, low table were set, bearing clay jugs of mulled wine and wooden bowls of fresh fruit. Uriel stepped down into this sunken area and took a seat, examining his fellow commanders as they arrived.

Montante was thin and seemed pathetically eager to please. His features were delicate and ascetic, though intense. He did not look like a warrior and Uriel wondered how he had achieved his position of authority here. Was the rule of Tarsis Ultra hereditary, democratic or did it still follow the primarch's meritocratic ideals? Was Montante capable of leading his people in time of war or would he need to be replaced? Was that decision even his to make? Montante busied himself pouring wine for everyone and Uriel politely shook his head when offered a goblet.

Stagler had the look of a warrior. Uriel had heard tales of the Krieg Death Korp and how their colonels requested the most dangerous warzones for their regiments to fight in, the most lethal enemies to face. If Stagler conformed to type, then he had chosen a prime assignment for his soldiers. He sat ramrod straight and appeared deeply irritated with Montante, also declining the wine.

Rabelaq had the look of a man to whom soldiering was a way of life, though his ample gut told Uriel that the rigours of the battlefield were but a distant memory to the colonel of the Logres regiment. He enthusiastically accepted a goblet of sweet wine and sipped appreciatively.

Chaplain Astador accepted some wine and raised it in a toast.

'May this brotherhood be united in its cause,' he said.

'Hear, hear,' agreed Rabelaq draining his goblet and pouring himself another, but Astador was not finished with his salutation. 'And should any of you fall, I shall ensure that your skulls are granted a place of honour in our Gallery of Bone.'

An awkward silence fell, until Montante said, 'Thank you, Chaplain Astador. That is most gratifying to know.'

Uriel shared a glance with his sergeants as the last members of their group entered the chamber. Lord Inquisitor Kryptman limped towards their gathering, followed by a white robed acolyte wearing a cog-toothed medallion of bronze around his neck. Unusually for a member of the Adeptus Mechanicus, his hairless features were largely organic, save for the bionic attachment that covered his right eye. A number of hinged lenses of varying size protruded from the side of his skull, each capable of sliding forward to drop before his glowing red bionic eye.

Kryptman stepped down to the benches with some difficulty and as his Adeptus Mechanicus companion joined him, Uriel was shocked to see that he moved on metallic caliper-like legs that protruded from the bottom of his robes. As the acolyte descended the steps to take his place behind Kryptman, his robe parted and instead of legs and torso, Uriel caught a glimpse of a thick, flexing brass tube connecting his chest to his artificial legs.

The lord inquisitor eased himself down onto a bench, irritably shaking his head as Montante offered him some wine. He cast his gimlet gaze around the assembled company and grunted to himself, though Uriel could not tell whether it was in satisfaction or resignation.

'This is a grand adventure,' said Montante, finally sitting down. 'Most of my time involves accounts, ledgers and all manner of boring logistical work for the factories. I don't think I've ever entertained such an esteemed group in the palace.'

Kryptman gave Montante a withering stare. 'Fabricator Marshal, this is no adventure we are upon. It is a matter of the gravest urgency and most fearful nature. A tendril of hive fleet Leviathan approaches your world and you think it will be an adventure?'

'Well, no, not an adventure in the traditional sense, you understand,' said Montante hurriedly, 'but it's certainly exciting, isn't it? I mean, it's not every day we get to fight a war, and I for one am looking forward immensely to giving these beasts a bloody nose.'

'Then you are a fool, sir, and would do well to leave the defence of your world to those who understand the grave danger of a tyranid hive fleet.'

'I object to your tone of voice, sir,' protested Montante. 'I am the planetary governor, after all.'

'For the time being,' threatened Kryptman. 'Now, if we may continue? Let us be clear on one thing: I have seen, first hand, what it means to fight these aliens and it will not be an adventure, there will be no glory and little honour in their destruction.

'I declared their species Xenos Horrificus two hundred and fifty years ago and since that day I have studied, hunted and killed them, yet still know but the tiniest fraction of their xenology.'

The inquisitor indicated the Mechanicus adept behind him.

'To fight the tyranid you must first know it,' he said. 'This is Genetor Vianco Locard of the Magos Biologis, and he knows more about these xeno abominations than any man alive. He will be of great help to us. Magos, if you please?'

Locard moved to stand before them and a brass rimmed monocle whirred into place over his red eye. As he laced his hands before him, in the manner of an academic, Uriel saw they were a smooth black metal.

Without preamble, he launched into his discourse. 'The tyranids are a bio-eugenic race of xenomorphs from beyond the Emperor's light, first discovered in the 745th year of this current millennium by Magos Varnak of the Adeptus Mechanicus outpost of Tyran Primus in Ultima Segmentum, some 60,000 light years from holy Mars.'

'Bio-eugenic? What does that mean?' interrupted Colonel Stagler.

'It means that the tyranids are able to assimilate entire worlds and races, break them down into their constituent genetic building blocks and incorporate said constituents into their own physiology,' explained Locard.

Seeing Stagler's, and everyone else's confusion, Kryptman said, 'Thank you, Magos Locard, but perhaps I should explain and keep things at a level everyone here can understand.'

Uriel bristled at such a casual insult to his intelligence, and could see others frowning too, but Inquisitor Kryptman's notoriety preceded him and there were no objections as he continued: 'The tyranids are a monstrous nomadic race of predators from beyond our galaxy who ply the depths of space in vast hive fleets. Like locusts, they consume everything in their path, and as each foe is defeated it is assimilated, each future generation of tyranids becoming better adapted to hunt their prey. When they attack, they attack in their millions, swarming across a world like a plague and just as destructively. Everything, every blade of grass, every indigenous creature is engulfed by the teeming hordes. Millions of years of evolution is destroyed and uncounted millennia of hard-won development and growth are annihilated by the tyranids' insatiable hunger. The world's oceans are drunk dry, its skies boiled away and digested until nothing remains, save a barren rock, stripped bare of every living thing.'

'But can they be defeated?' asked Stagler simply.

Kryptman laughed humourlessly. 'Oh yes, Colonel Stagler, they can be defeated, but only at terrible cost.'

'The cost is irrelevant,' said Stagler brusquely. 'All that matters is that we can defeat them, yes?'

Inquisitor Kryptman arched an eyebrow before inclining his head towards Uriel saying, 'Colonel Stagler has a point. Perhaps Captain Ventris would favour us by recounting the tale of Hive Fleet Behemoth and the Battle of Macragge?'

'It would be my pleasure, lord inquisitor,' said Uriel proudly, standing and clasping his hands behind his back.

'Hive fleet Behemoth came from beyond the halo stars of the eastern fringe, its numbers too vast to count. Their alien ships descended upon Macragge, but the noble Lord Calgar, forewarned by Lord Kryptman here, had assembled a powerful fleet to defend the holy soil of our homeworld. Fearsome battle raged in space until Lord Calgar pulled back, drawing the hive fleet onto the guns of Macragge. Whilst the aliens were spread out and vulnerable, he turned and struck, his vessels crippling one of their accursed hive ships and fatally disrupting their fleet.'

'I don't understand, Captain Ventris,' said Colonel Rabelaq. 'How could the loss of one ship cause so much damage to their fleet?'

'I will answer that,' put in Magos Locard. 'To understand the motivational imperatives of the tyranids, one must first understand the nature of their consciousness. A hive fleet is made up of billions upon billions of living organisms produced in the hive's reproductive chambers by the Norn Queen. Essentially, each ship is a living creature, every organism that makes up that ship existing only to serve the ship, and each ship functioning only as part of the fleet. A gestalt consciousness links every creature in the fleet, from the mightiest warrior beast to the tiniest, microscopic bacteria of the digestion pools, creating a vast psychic consciousness we call the overmind, that is capable of exerting a monstrous will and alien intelligence. Of course these creatures have no individuality of their own and exist simply to serve the hive mind. If one can disrupt the psychic link between them, the lower organisms become confused, often reverting to their basic, animalistic natures. It is the key to defeating them.'

'Yes,' continued Uriel, 'when Lord Calgar's fleet destroyed the largest hive ship, they were able to reap a great tally in bio-ships as the aliens' attacks became increasingly uncoordinated and random. Their fleet was driven from Macragge, and though thousands of spores, each bearing a tyranid organism, had been released above the polar defence fortresses, Lord Calgar gave chase to the fleeing enemy.'

'He left his world undefended?' asked Stagler, disapprovingly.

'No, colonel, far from it,' said Uriel. 'The polar defence fortresses were held by Terminators of the First company as well as brave warriors from the defence auxilia and Titans of the Legio Praetor. Lord Calgar was confident they could hold, and pursued the tyranid fleet to the ringed planet of Circe. Together with recently arrived ships from Battlefleet Tempestus, he destroyed the tyranid fleet in a great battle. We had defeated the tyranids, but at a grievous cost. Hundreds of thousands died, the flagship of the Tempestus fleet, the *Dominus Astra*, was lost and our entire First company was killed, including my own ancestor, Lucian Ventris. Only now does it regain its full strength.'

Uriel sat back on the bench as Kryptman picked up the tale.

'Hive fleet Behemoth was no more, but the tyranids had learned from their defeat and when they returned at the head of a new hive fleet – which we named Kraken – less than a decade ago, it was on a much greater scale. Entire sectors in the eastern fringes have been swallowed by the psychic interference of the tyranid warp shadow, and yet there is worse to come. I have detected a pattern amongst a seemingly random series of attacks across Segmentum Tempestus, Ultima Segmentum and even Segmentum Solar that leads me to believe yet another hive fleet is attacking, this time from below the galactic plane. I have named it Leviathan and it appears that a splinter fleet from Leviathan threatens this world. We must stop the tyranids, gentlemen. Here and now. For if the Shadow in the Warp is allowed to smother the divine light of the Astronomican, then Humanity will surely perish. Ships will be unable to navigate the warp, communication across the galaxy will cease and the Imperium will collapse. Make no mistake, we are fighting for the future of our very race and I am willing to make any sacrifice to ensure its survival.'

The assembled commanders were silent as they took in the scale of the coming conflict, the stakes and their part to play in it. Even Montante now seemed to appreciate the seriousness of the situation and nervously chewed his bottom lip.

'What measures have been taken to prepare this system for the tyranids' attack?' asked Astador.

'Lord Admiral Tiberius is working with Admiral de Corte to devise a strategy to delay the tyranid fleet before it reaches this world,' answered Uriel, 'but, it is apparent that the defences of this city have fallen into disrepair in many places, and we will need time to ready them for the coming assault.'

'Captain Ventris is correct,' nodded Kryptman. 'I have requested the deployment of warriors from the Deathwatch, the Chamber Militant of my ordo, and we will be able to count them amongst our forces before long. However, we must delay the tyranid advance, but we cannot deploy the fleet until we know exactly where the attack will come.

Astropaths are reporting ripples and eddies in the warp, consistent with those that presage the arrival of a fleet, but the distortions caused by the Shadow in the Warp are making it impossible to pinpoint. We would end up chasing ghosts.'

'The Krieg regiment will have its men and armoured units on the ground within the next three days,' said Stagler. 'We will begin augmenting the city's defences and I have devised a training regime that will ensure our readiness for when these aliens arrive. These aliens will not soon forget the Death Korp.'

Uriel said, 'I shall assign Sergeant Learchus and a squad of Ultramarines to you to aid your training program. He is the finest instructor sergeant Agiselus has ever produced and I am sure will be of great help to you.'

'Thank you, Captain Ventris,' acknowledged Stagler. 'I welcome your aid.'

Rabelaq spoke next. 'My soldiers will be deployed by the end of the day. We have far less armour to land than Colonel Stagler's regiment and by morning I will have units moving throughout the continent to escort people back to the safety of the city. As the soldiers of the Logres regiment are raised from an ice world, this climate will present no difficulties for them, and we may also be able to teach you all a thing or two about cold weather injuries as well. To be honest, our main duties to this point have been protecting krill farmers from raiding Tarellian dog soldiers. It will do them good to have a taste of proper soldiering.'

Fabricator Montante said, 'My PDF regiments have been drilling ever since we received warning of the tyranids. As head of the PDF, I've ordered increased training over the last two months and called up all the citizen militia units to participate too. The vast majority of them have been on training exercises recently and are looking top notch, if I do say so myself. We've also begun stockpiling medical supplies, ammunition, fuel and food and drink in the caverns below the city.'

Kryptman looked surprised at this new side of the Fabricator Marshal and nodded.

'Excellent. That was to be my next point of concern.'

'Oh, don't worry about that, Inquisitor Kryptman. If there's one thing I know, its organisational logistics. I may not be a soldier, but I can organise your supplies better than anyone and make sure that every soldier has a full pack of ammunition and three hot meals a day.'

Kryptman chuckled. 'And therein lies half the battle.'

'Indeed,' beamed Montante, pleased to have something he could contribute.

The next two hours were spent in meticulous planning of the coming campaign. Everything from fleet operations to the precise deployment of men and machines throughout the city was discussed, debated and eventually decided upon. The situation was grim, but as the council of war drew to a close, there was a feeling of cautious optimism.

The lord inquisitor summed up that optimism, saying, 'Tyranids are creatures from our darkest nightmares. But remember this: they can bleed and they can die...'

Uriel poured himself a goblet of wine as the door at the far end of the chamber opened and a PDF vox-officer entered. He hurriedly made his way towards Montante, handing the Fabricator Marshal a data-slate before withdrawing.

Montante scanned its contents swiftly, his smile growing the more of the message he read. He handed the slate to Kryptman and said, 'I do believe we have them.'

Kryptman read the slate as Montante continued. 'Surveyors on listening station Trajen at the system's edge picked up an unknown contact in the Barbarus Cluster and directed fighter squadrons from the *Kharloss Vincennes* to intercept it. It seems they engaged and destroyed a tyranid scout vessel. Their astropath also reports an approaching disturbance in the immaterium. Gentlemen, I believe we now know where the enemy is coming from.'

TYREN MALLICK PUSHED forward the safety catch of his autogun and opened the breech. He lifted a clip of bullets from the pocket of his flak jacket, ensuring that the rounds were clean, and placed them in the weapon's charger guide. He pushed down on the clip until the top round was under the magazine lip then closed the breech and snapped off the safety. He lifted the rifle to his shoulder and sighted along the barrel at the three rocks he'd set up across the slope of the mountain. He breathed deeply, letting it out slowly and squeezed the trigger, expertly blasting one of the rocks from its perch.

He lowered the rifle and watched as his son, Kyle, copied his movements exactly. The crack of his shot echoed from the dark mountains, and another rock toppled from its perch. He could see several people in the township below jump at the noise before returning to erecting barricades at the town's entrance.

'Alright, son, nice work,' he said. 'Now do it again. You got to be able to do it real quick when these alien bastards come. When you can load that rifle with your eyes shut, we'll go in for supper.'

Kyle beamed at his father's praise, unloaded the rifle and began again. Tyren watched his son as he swiftly reloaded the rifle and repeated the actions they had been practising for the last two days. Though only eleven, Kyle was a natural and had the weapon loaded and ready to fire in less than six seconds. The final rock vanished in a puff of smoke as Kyle shot it dead centre.

Father and son spent another half hour practising with the rifle before a hard rain began falling and they quickly made their way down the waterlogged path that led to the small mining community of Hadley's Hope. They climbed over the slippery ore barrels erected before the town's main road and made their way towards their home, taking shelter from the rain under the wide eaves of the buildings lining the road.

Tyren could see that the far end of the road was barricaded as well, timber sawhorses looped with razorwire stacked alongside ore barrels filled with rocks and sand. It wasn't much, but it was the best they could do.

Sitting alongside the town's schoolhouse, the largest building in the settlement, Tyren Mallick's home was a sturdily constructed adobe structure, built by his own hands. He'd had twenty-five good years in this house, raised three children and worked hard in the mines that made Barbarus Prime worth inhabiting. He had been as faithful an Imperial servant as he could be, attending Preacher Cascu's sermons every week down in Pelotas Ridge and also spending a month of every year helping those less fortunate than himself.

Twenty-five good years, and he was damned if some faceless adept on Tarsis Ultra was going to tell him to leave his home because there were some alien raiders approaching. Well, the people of Hadley's Hope had come together in times of crisis before now and this would be no different. Already the entrance to their mine had been sealed, the town was barricaded, and its populace ready to defend their hearth and homes.

Heavy grey clouds gathered overhead and further down the road that led to the valley below, Tyren saw the powerful tower-lights of several other communities flicker on as night drew in. Even from here he could see that the other towns had made defensive preparations similar to those of Hadley's Hope. The shared sense of solidarity in the face of adversity was humbling, and Tyren once again gave thanks to the Emperor that he had been blessed with such fine friends and neighbours.

He and Kyle reached the heavy timber door to the house and removed their mud-caked boots before entering. Merria kept a clean house and both knew better than to dirty the place up before supper.

Warmth and the aroma of a home cooked meal enveloped him as he led Kyle inside. His wife and two daughters busied themselves with steaming plates and dishes, setting the table for supper as he hung the rifles beside the door, checking that both were properly unloaded first.

'You boys have fun up there?' asked Merria without turning from the hot stove.

'We sure did,' said Tyren, tousling his son's hair. 'Kyle here's a natural. Never missed once, did you, son?'

'Nope, not once, da,' confirmed Kyle.

His mother tutted as she turned and saw the bedraggled state of her son and husband. She cleaned her hands on her apron and shooed them towards the bedrooms.

'Both of you get out of those wet clothes before you catch your death. I'll not have you dripping all over my floor. Go on now, hurry up. Supper'll be on the table in five minutes.'

Both father and son knew it was pointless to argue and put aside their hunger while they dried off and changed into fresh clothing. They returned to the table as Merria began dishing supper, Tyren taking his customary place at the head of the table.

When everybody's plate was full, Tyren clasped his hands on the table, closed his eyes and bowed his head as he recited the Emperor's grace.

'Holy Father who watches over us all, we give thanks for this meal before us. Grant us the wisdom of your servants and the strength to prevail against the evil of sinners and aliens. This we ask in your name.'

His family echoed his amen and began tucking into their food. Hissing gas lamps hung from the roof beams provided a warm light as the family ate, the harsh glare from the arc lights outside blocked by the sheet metal Tyren had bolted over the windows.

He smiled at his wife and took a bite of his dinner.

Let these damned raiders come, whoever they were.

They would find Tyren Mallick and the people of Hadley's Hope ready for them.

SWEAT GATHERED ON Third Technician Osric Neru's brow and he wished the astropath would just shut up and give them all some peace. Her moans had been unnerving at first, but now they were just annoying, filling listening post Trajen's cramped control room with her never-ending drone. Osric's fingers beat a nervous tattoo on the console before him, as he stared in frustration at its display. The readings couldn't be right, they just couldn't. He rubbed a hand across his unshaven jaw and, even though he knew it was pointless, checked the figures once again.

The numbers scrolled across the slate once more, defiantly remaining the same as before.

He wiped the sweat from his tonsured skull and updated the parchment list beside him as his superiors on Tarsis Ultra had instructed him. Osric felt very alone and very frightened, dearly wishing he was back on Chordelis, serving in one of that world's many forge temples. If these numbers were correct, then there was an enemy fleet of unheard of magnitude approaching this system.

Vessels of the Imperial Navy were en route from Tarsis Ultra, but Osric knew they would not reach Trajen before this new fleet on his console did, and the thought terrified him. He caught the eye of the adept at the next console and tried to smile reassuringly, but failed to convince him.

He glanced over his shoulder at the senior magos and, despite his master's many augmentations, Osric could tell he was also extremely worried by what was drawing near.

Repeated requests to Admiral de Corte for permission to abandon the listening post had been denied and they could only wait and hope that the approaching fleet would pass them by.

The astropath sat in a reclined couch seat next to the magos, her teeth clenched, her skin drawn and pale. She twitched and muttered, her face alive with tics and nervous flutters. Her groans filled the control room, unnerving the six man staff of the listening post further still.

Suddenly she sat bolt upright, screaming at the top of her lungs.

Everyone jumped as the girl lurched from her chair, pulling at her green robes and tearing at her face with her fingernails. She fell to her knees, shrieking piteously, digging and clawing at her skin. Blood streamed down her face as she ripped open the stitching sealing her ravaged eye sockets and plunged her fingers inside, as though trying to pluck the brain from her skull.

'They are coming!' she wailed. 'They're scratching my mind, scratching, screaming, roaring – so many voices. They're coming for us – flesh and blood, body and soul!'

Osric put his hands over his ears to shut out her screams as she staggered to her feet and reached out towards him with bloody fingers, pleading for him to stop the pain.

But he could do nothing as she pitched forward and fell to the floor.

Blood pooled around her head and her cries were silenced.

URIEL JOINED LORD Admiral Tiberius and Philotas, his deck officer, as they examined the system map displayed on the stone-rimmed plotting table in the transept of the command bridge of the *Vae Victus*. A bewildering amount of information filled the embedded slate, displaying a topographical representation of the Tarsis Ultra system. Curling lines of system defence ship patrol circuits, orbits of planets and local celestial phenomena were picked out, as well as the major shipping lanes. Jump points at the system's edge were marked in yellow and each planet glowed with a soft green light. Numbers scrolled across the side of the slate, though Uriel had no idea what they indicated.

'Show me,' ordered Tiberius.

Philotas adjusted the runes on the plotting table and the background information faded from the display, leaving only the planetary details illuminated.

'At the furthest extent of the Tarsis Ultra system lies the planet of Barbarus Prime,' said Philotas, as curling High Gothic script in a gold edged box flashed next to the planet.

'A mining world,' noted Uriel. 'Precious metals and gem mines mostly, though there are a few vauable minerals used in the production of the metals that make up starship hulls.'

'Population?' asked Tiberius.

Philotas checked the information box and said. 'Quite low, the last census puts it at a little over nine thousand souls, mostly scattered throughout the uplands of the eastern continental mountain ranges.'

'What is being done about getting those people off there?' asked the lord admiral.

'A warning has been issued to the local adept, and there is a bulk freighter en route from Chordelis, though it will be touch and go whether it can reach Barbarus Prime before the first tyranid organisms.'

'Damn,' swore Tiberius. 'The more worlds that fall to the tyranids, the stronger and more numerous they become.'

'Further in towards the core worlds are two uninhabited planets. The first, Parosa, has an atmosphere largely composed of a benzene-hydrogen compound. Highly toxic and though the Adeptus Mechanicus have attempted to terraform its atmosphere several times, they have thus far been unsuccessful. The second is called Yulan. It's a geologically unstable rock, wracked by volcanic storms, though it does boast several gargantuan hydrogen-plasma mining stations in permanent geo-stationary orbit.'

Philotas zoomed in on the system map as they drew closer to the core worlds.

'Next we have Chordelis, a small, but populous world, mostly given over to industrial manufacture. Population in the region of sixteen million, with a PDF strength of fifty thousand soldiers. Evacuation protocols are in effect, though I would advise giving Chordelis a wide berth. There are a great many ships arriving and departing and there have been several accidents already.

'After Chordelis, there are two agri-worlds, Calumet and Calydon, both with a largely caretaker population. These worlds are being evacuated as we speak. Then we have Tarsis Ultra itself, with a population in excess of sixty million.'

'How long before we are in a position to intercept the hive fleet?' asked Uriel.

Philotas adjusted the runes at the side of the plotting table once more and a series of lines snaked across the surface of the slate. The line began at the group of icons representing the *Vae Victus* and the ships of the Imperial fleet and quickly extended through the system to Barbarus Prime.

More numbers flashed across the slate. Philotas used a steel ruler and calipers to plot time and distance over the system map.

'At current speed, it will be seven days before we can achieve orbit around Barbarus Prime,' said Philotas. 'The tyranids will get there first.'

OSRIC NERU WATCHED the approaching cloud of objects in the viewing bay with genuine, bowel-loosening terror, prayers of protection he had not given voice to since he was a child spilling from his lips. He gripped onto his console as the alien cloud enveloped them and another explosive impact rocked the listening station. For the last twenty minutes, spore-like objects had drifted from the advancing fleet, floating aimlessly through space until they neared the listening post, whereupon they pulsated rhythmically and homed unerringly on their position.

Some exploded like mines, others burst like wet sacks of liquid, spraying corrosive acids across the structure of the station. Already there were hull breaches all over the station where acids and viruses had eaten through the hull.

The size of the approaching fleet was simply too vast to comprehend. Thousands of drifting objects surrounded the alien vessels, dead lumps that the station's pitifully inadequate turrets had managed to blast apart before running out of ammunition.

Osric checked the firing log of the various turrets, calculating how many rounds had been expended. Over twenty thousand shells had been fired into the approaching cloud though the losses they had inflicted were insignificant against a force of such scale. They were now effectively defenceless.

Osric dropped to his knees and prayed as more of the alien spores drew near.

'Neru!' barked the senior magos. 'Return to your post.'

Osric stood as yet more explosions rocked the station and a fresh clutch of warning lights flashed into life on the console.

'We're going to die!' cried Osric. 'What does it matter if I'm at my post?'

'It matters because that is what we are here for,' said the magos with a calm he did not feel. 'Yes, we will die, but we will die doing our duty to the Omnissiah and the Emperor. No man can ask for more.'

Osric nodded, bowing his head and returning to his seat as the groan of buckling metal echoed from outside the control room. Another hull breach warning bell rang and the terrified crew of the listening station heard the grinding noise of pressure doors slowly sealing off the affected area.

Then they heard the scratching of alien claws at the door to the control room.

TYREN MALLICK SHUT out the pain of his torn shoulder and painfully reloaded his rifle, the trembling of his fingers making it that much more difficult. A blood-soaked bandage wrapped his shoulder and chest where fragments of an exploding spore had ripped into his flesh. Merria had pulled out the sizzling pieces of bony shrapnel from his shoulder, but the wound had refused to heal, weeping a constant gruel of infected blood.

'Why's the sky gone a funny colour, da?' asked Kyle, his voice trembling in fear as he looked through the molten remains of the sheet metal over the windows. The normally slate grey sky boiled a loathsome, bruised purple and unnatural lightning speared through the violet sky, lighting the mountains in a lurid, unfamiliar light. A rain of dark objects fell to the plains below, amid the burning rain that ate away at the metal roofs of Hadley's Hope and had forced its people to abandon the barricades and take refuge in the schoolhouse, the only structure large enough to contain everyone.

The men of Hadley's Hope carried a mix of weapons, from ancient rifles that would be lucky not to misfire and take their wielder's hand off, to freshly oiled lasguns earned in service of the local defence forces. Twenty-three crying children huddled in the centre of the schoolhouse, their mothers and teachers doing their best to calm them with songs and prayers.

'I don't know why, son,' admitted Tyren, finally pushing the bullets home in his rifle. He rose from the table and joined his son at the window. Alien spores like grotesquely swollen and veined balloons had been falling from the sky since daybreak, and though most of them had been carried into the high peaks of the mountains by updrafts from the plains below, more were drifting back down as night fell and the air cooled.

At first, the people of Hadley's Hope had watched them with fearful curiosity, until a pulsating spore with a frill of trumpet-like cones and trailing fronds had drifted into the settlement. Pastor Upden had confidently walked up to the mysterious object and shot it at point blank range, expecting it to simply deflate. Tyren had watched in horror as the vile globule exploded, showering the pastor with a thick, viscous fluid and his screams echoed from the farthest corners of the settlement. Tyren had run to help Upden, but it was too late, his skin was already blistering and sloughing from his bones as the alien acids ate his flesh away. He screamed piteously until his throat melted and his lifeless body dissolved into a stinking slime.

Since then they had taken great care to shoot down any spores before they reached the settlement.

'You stay alert, Kyle, and holler if you see anything,' Tyren said, staring through the dripping, corroded holes in the metal. The lights from the townships below were gone, and he had been unable to reach anyone in Pelotas Ridge for several hours now.

The lights here were failing too, as the acid rain burned through the cables that didn't run underground, and Tyren knew that soon the entire community would be in darkness. He tried to ignore the sobbing of the children and the trembling voices of the women as he saw movement on the road below. The ground undulated as though it was alive and the rain glistened from the carapaces of thousands of... *things* as they ran towards the small settlement.

He knelt and fished a battered but serviceable pair of magnoculars from his pack and trained them on the road. The unnatural darkness made it hard to see much of anything, but his breath caught in his throat as he saw a sea of creatures, all fangs and talons, swarming uphill.

'Emperor save us,' he whispered, dropping the magnoculars. 'Everyone with a gun get to someplace they can shoot from,' he shouted.

He grabbed a pale-faced man next to him and said, 'Radek, take ten men upstairs and shoot from the balcony, the canopy will give you shelter from the rain.'

Radek nodded and ran off to obey Tyren's command.

Tyren looked over to his wife and daughters, giving them a wave of reassurance before finding a loophole in the wall to fire his rifle from.

Kyle shouldered his rifle and stood beside his father, a nervous smile creasing his face.

'I'm proud of you, son,' said Tyren and Kyle nodded.

Tyren peered into the gloom, seeing the rippling swarm of creatures leaping and bounding across the barricades at the end of the road.

'Here they come!' he yelled. 'Open fire!'

Children screamed as the schoolhouse was suddenly filled with noise. Gunsmoke fogged the air and the crack of weapon fire in such a confined space was deafening. Tyren saw several creatures fall, hearing more shots from upstairs.

Over the crack of gunfire, he heard a whistling scream, similar to that of incoming artillery fire, and flinched as something heavy smashed into the roof of the building. He heard timber splinter and screams from upstairs, but knew he could do nothing to help the men stationed there. The ground trembled as more objects fell from the sky and struck with incredible force.

He shot again and again into the mass of beasts, their swollen skulls and armoured carapaces deflecting all but the most accurate shots. They swarmed into the town, spreading out and closing on the schoolhouse.

A thunderous impact outside threw Tyren to the floor and blew out the windows facing the street. A section of wall collapsed and the sheet metal was blasted from the walls. Hot, reeking air blew in.

Through the hole, Tyren could see that the generator building was on fire, and there was a huge object, like a lumpen boulder, rocking in the wide crater its impact had caused.

Smaller creatures leapt towards the hole in the wall and Tyren rolled to his feet, firing wildly into the breach. Flames from across the street silhouetted the creatures and, together with another three men, they were able to kill all the monsters attempting to force their way inside. The roof of the generator building collapsed, sending sparks soaring into the darkness, a shriek of something in pain echoing from beneath the rubble.

'Get something to block this!' he yelled, firing into the mass of creatures until his rifle was empty. He fumbled for another clip as three women dragged over a heavy table and some desks, overturning them before the gap in the wall.

Gunfire and the sound of screaming children filled Tyren's senses as he reloaded his rifle. He heard impacts on the few remaining windows covered by the sheet metal and saw another give way as a horrific alien creature forced its way inside.

It leapt into the room, rain steaming from its glossy, armoured carapace. Hunched over and six-limbed, its bestial face hissed in alien hunger.

Tyren shot at it, but missed, blasting a chunk of plaster from the wall beside it. The beast ignored him, pouncing on the defenders at the northern wall. He screamed as he saw Kyle turn to face the monster and raise his rifle. But the creature was inhumanly fast and its scything claws slashed out, disembowelling his son before he could fire.

'No! No! No!' Tyren screamed, firing again. His bullet caught the creature at the base of its neck and exploded its head in a spray of dark ichor. He dropped his rifle and ran towards his son, but it was too late, his boy was already dead.

He cried out in anguish, cradling his son's body. Through a mist of tears he saw the ruins of the generator building heave upwards, as something vast hauled itself from the wreckage.

He fumbled for his rifle, as more cries filled the schoolhouse. A huge shape lumbered across the street and slammed into the side of the schoolhouse, smashing down the wall and tearing a portion of the ceiling with it. The thing's body was on fire and it shrieked in fury and pain as it battered its way inside.

Tyren felt his knees sag as a monster from his worst imaginings took a thunderous step into the schoolhouse. Larger than a mining bulldozer, it reared above him on powerful, hooved legs, two pairs of thick arms ending in long, razor-sharp talons raised above its head. Its tapered jaw was filled with hundreds of drooling fangs and its dark eyes reflected the fires that consumed it.

The horrifying creature shrieked deafeningly, lashing out with its claws and hacking men in two with every blow. It stepped further into the schoolhouse, its weight smashing the floorboards and its deadly claws killing everything within reach.

Tyren screamed and fired his rifle at the monster, its chitinous carapace absorbing every shot without effect. Another of the smaller beasts clambered through the window beside Tyren. He shot it in the head and pushed home another clip.

The giant beast continued screaming as it demolished the schoolhouse, beams crashing down as its armoured head smashed through the ceiling. The upper storey collapsed, men falling to the ground floor, only to be crushed beneath its tread. Children wept in terror. The beast's piercing shriek grew in volume, until a seething ball of greenish light vomited from its jaws, immolating the screaming women and children.

Tyren screamed in horror and ran at the alien creature, knowing it would kill him, but unwilling to live knowing his family was dead. He fired his rifle until it was empty then used it as a bludgeon, smashing it to splinters against the monster's armoured legs.

The monster struck Tyren with its powerful claws, tearing off his arm and smashing him through the wall. He splashed onto the ground outside the schoolhouse, numb with pain and loss.

The acid rain burned his skin and he could feel nothing below his neck.

Hissing aliens gathered around him, stabbing him again and again with long claws like swords. Tyren felt nothing. His life ended in a blur of razor claws and fangs.

FIVE

A DYING WORLD filled the observation bay. Like monstrous, suckling parasites, the creatures of the hive fleet gathered around Barbarus Prime in a blurred, indistinct halo. Flickering lightning flashed through the atmosphere, and though the effect from space was striking, almost beautiful, Uriel knew that it signified the world was in its death throes, ravaged by storms of titanic proportions strong enough to topple mountains and drown entire continents.

The surface of Barbarus Prime heaved as its mantle cracked, split apart by gargantuan feeder tentacles that burrowed deep into its body, devouring anything capable of being broken down into its constituent organic components.

There could be nothing left alive on Barbarus Prime; soon all the world's genetic material would be absorbed by the tyranids and used as fuel for the ever-hungry reproductive chambers of the hive ships. Even now, the biological matter that had been the population of the planet would be churning within the belly of these beasts. The thought sickened Uriel and the hate he had felt on the fields of Ichar IV returned, bright and hot.

'Emperor, watch over thee,' whispered Uriel, swearing that the souls of this world would be avenged. He stood with Lord Admiral Tiberius on the bridge of the *Vae Victus*, powerless to help the world below, but ready to do anything he could to prevent any more Imperial servants losing their lives to the Great Devourer.

Tiberius strode to his command pulpit and mounted the steps that took him to his elevated commander's position. Unconsciously, he scratched at the spiderweb of scars that crisscrossed the side of his face, scars he had received fighting the tyranids at the Battle of Macragge, over two hundred and fifty years ago when he had been one of many deck officers to serve on this proud ship before rising to become its captain.

He pressed his thumb to the pict-slate on the polished mahogany lectern in front of him and the tactical plot swam into focus before him, displaying the doomed world and the Imperial fleet that had come to fight its destroyers. Alongside the *Vae Victus* was the *Mortis Probati*, the Mortifactors' ship, and to either side of them was arranged the might of an Imperial battlefleet.

They could not save the people of Barbarus Prime, but the battle to avenge them would be fought in the shadow of their dying world.

'They will be coming soon,' he said.

'How can you tell?' asked Uriel.

'See,' said Tiberius, pointing to where a gigantic creature rose ponderously from the feeding below. 'They are responding to our presence.'

Longer than the biggest battleship Uriel had ever seen, the monster's hide was gnarled and ancient, pitted with asteroid impacts and hardened by millennia travelling through the void. Its underside rippled with waving, frond-like tentacles and great, sucking orifices in its surface drooled a thick, viscous fluid as it rose to meet them. At what Uriel supposed was its rear, long feeders ending in barbed claws trailed behind it, pulsating with a grotesque motion. Nothing so huge should be capable of animation, thought Uriel, or should be allowed to manifest such a horrid mockery of life.

A host of vanguard organisms drifted up before the monster: giant, manta-like creatures with vast, cavern mouths filled with teeth as large as a Thunderhawk and razor-edged wings; spinning creatures that defied any classification of form, all rippling armour plates, blades, talons and trailing tentacles. Dozens of these beasts swarmed around the larger ship, like loyal servants protecting a queen. As they rose towards the Imperial vessels Uriel was reminded of carrion beasts that hunted in packs, picking off the weakest members of a herd that, once brought down, would be guarded with tenacious ferocity while the pack leaders fed off the carcass.

'What are their tactics? How will they attack?'

'I do not know, Uriel. They will test us first, probe us for weakness and learn what they can before committing their main force. We are fortunate to have caught them feeding. We won't have to face their full strength.'

Uriel watched the multitude of organisms advancing on the *Vae Victus* and gave thanks for that small mercy. For if this was but a fraction of the strength of the tyranids, then their full might was something to be truly dreaded.

LORD INQUISITOR KRYPTMAN watched the same scene from the bridge of the *Argus*, the flagship of Admiral Bregant de Corte and this battlefleet. He watched the enormous creature detach from feeding and rise to challenge them. He had fought the tyranids for almost the entire span of his life and he could remember no emotion save hatred towards them. As he watched the planet below die, he was gratified to note that his hatred burned no less strongly than before.

The approaching hive ship was not the biggest he had ever seen, that honour belonged to the beast at the head of the hive fleet that had engulfed the world of Graia, but it was still a giant, perhaps three kilometres in length.

'Loathsome things,' observed Admiral de Corte.

'Aye,' agreed Kryptman, 'but lethal. They are armed with fearsome symbiote weaponry, sprays of acid, bio-plasma and hordes of warrior organisms that can be ejaculated from the orifices in its stony hide.'

'Our weapons are blessed by the Emperor and we will prevail,' de Corte assured him.

Kryptman nodded and pointed to the mist of spores surrounding the beast. 'Look here, admiral. That veil of spores is so thick it will protect the creature from all but the most determined of attackers.'

'Lord inquisitor,' said Admiral de Corte, his voice betraying the tension the entire bridge crew were feeling. 'I request your permission to commence the attack.'

'Yes…' nodded Kryptman, staring in macabre fascination at the wide tactics table depicting the converging fleets. 'Commence the attack.'

Blank faced logisticians connected directly to the ship's surveyor systems ringed the wide table – gridded with spatial co-ordinates – using long, flat-headed poles to move scale representations of the various ships of the fleet.

The Admiral nodded curtly and spun on his heel, marching towards his commander's lectern. Bregant de Corte was a tall, wiry man, with gaunt, pinched features and a thin, pencil moustache. His admiral's uniform hung from his emaciated frame and, upon meeting him for the first time, many found it hard to believe that this was the man who had destroyed the Ork raiders of Charadax, who had ended the piracy of Khaarx Bloodaxe and whose masterful strategy had halted the K'Nib from invading the Sulacus Rim.

He stood behind the lectern, pouring himself a glass of amasec from the crystal decanter that always sat there and taking a deep breath. He took a moment to look around his bridge, allowing seconds to pass before issuing his orders. It was important that he not appear intimidated by the alien fleet approaching and his calm demeanour would be a guide for the rest of his crew to follow.

He drained the glass of amasec and said, 'My compliments to you all, and I wish you honour in this glorious battle.'

Jaemar, the ship's commissar, nodded in approval at the admiral's words.

A naval rating, traditionally the youngest man on the ship, approached the admiral. Sweat glistened on his brow as he asked, 'Is the word given, admiral?'

Admiral de Corte replaced the glass on the lectern and said, 'The word is given. Issue all ships with the order to attack. *Gloriam Imperator.*'

THE TWO FLEETS drew closer, though the ranges between them could still be measured in tens of thousands of kilometres. The ships of the Imperial fleet spread out as the attack order filtered through to the various captains and the admiral's plan

began to unfold. There appeared to be no strategy evident in
the tyranids' approach, the bio-creatures rising to meet their
enemy in a homogenous mass.

The Space Marine strike cruisers, together with the rapid
strike cruisers of Arx Praetora squadron, advanced before the
armoured behemoths of the battleship *Argus* and the Overlord battlecruiser, *Sword of Retribution*.

A trio of Sword frigates flew in a picket line before the fleet,
supported by two Dauntless light cruisers, the *Yermetov* and
the *Luxor*. Their fearsome lance arrays were sure to be decisive
in the coming engagement and de Corte was taking no
chances with their safety.

To either flank of the fleet, two squadrons of Cobra destroyers, Cypria and Hydra, surged ahead of the main fleet, their
cavernous torpedo bays loaded with sanctified weapons and
their pilots eager to unleash them upon the foe.

The massive hive ship at the centre of the tyranid swarm
shuddered as though in the grips of a powerful seizure and
expelled millions of spores, trailing glistening birth streamers
as they sped away from its toughened hide.

The majestically swooping manta creatures moved as
though swimming in a deep ocean, their wide, chitinous
wings rippling with the motion of the solar wind. The bladed
creatures that flocked around their birth queen swarmed forwards in a wave of seething claws, overcome with the
instinctual urge to destroy those who threatened the hive.

The Battle of Barbarus had begun.

'ORDER THE SWORD frigates to push forwards,' said Admiral de
Corte. 'Those beasts at the head of the fleet are increasing
speed. I don't want them in my battle line.'

'Aye, sir,' replied Jex Viert, his senior flag lieutenant, convey-
ing the order to the signals officer.

De Corte studied the observation bay, trying to guess how
the tyranids would react to their movements. So far, he did
not rate the tactical acumen of the enemy, if such a thing
existed in the tyranid fleet, and he allowed himself a tight
smile. He watched as the logisticians began moving the Sword
frigates forward with their poles.

'These ships that approach us, Lord Kryptman, what can
you tell me about them?'

The inquisitor walked stiffly along the nave of the command bridge to stand before the apse of the observation bay. He leaned closer, as though studying the creatures more closely and shook his head slowly.

'They are drone creatures, nothing more, though they are extremely resilient. I call them kraken and the will of the hive mind controls them. Do not allow them to close with you, they are filled with all manner of deadly warrior creatures.'

'I understand. Mister Viert, issue orders that no captain is to allow any alien organisms to approach to within five thousand kilometres of his ship.'

'Five thousand kilometres. Aye, sir.'

Satisfied his order would be obeyed with alacrity, de Corte returned his gaze to the observation bay. One of the larger creatures was detaching itself from the main body of the tyranid fleet, using short flaps of its wide wings to power itself forwards in sporadic spurts of motion.

'Hydra squadron to take up blocking position on the right flank. Order the *Sword of Retribution* to follow the frigates in. *Yermetov* and *Luxor* to escort her.'

'Aye, sir,' said Viert, punching in the admiral's orders. 'Might I also suggest that the strike cruisers of the Space Marines advance with the Cobras of Cypria squadron? If these alien vessels are indeed as resilient as Lord Kryptman suggests, then their heavy bombardment cannons will be of great use.'

'Your suggestion has merit, Mister Viert. Make it so, and confirm readiness of lance decks and gun crews.'

The admiral watched the dance of ships on the plotting table, seeing the plan of the battle unfold as the captains of his fleet obeyed his orders.

'All weapon decks report readiness, sir. Senior gunner Mabon reports he has a firing solution for the nova cannon.'

'Understood, inform him that he may fire when ready,' said de Corte.

He saw that the Cobras of Hydra squadron would soon be in a position to fire as well, and the Swords had rapidly closed on the first wave of the ships Kryptman called kraken.

The gap between the two fleets was closing fast and he knew it would not be long before aliens would be dying.

* * *

DEEP IN THE bowels of the *Argus*, the fifty-metre wide door of
the nova cannon's breech groaned shut as thousands of sweating naval ratings dragged the massive weapon's recoil
compensators into position. Hot steam and noise filled the
long chamber, its cavernous structure fogged with the furnace
heat of lifting mechanisms that hauled the enormous projectiles from the armoured magazines below.

The chamber ran almost the entire length of the ship and
stank of grease, sweat and blood. A booming hymnal echoed
from ancient brass speakers set into grilled alcoves in the
wall accompanied by the droning chant of thousands of
men.

Senior gunner Mabon watched from his gantry above the
firing chamber as a series of bells chimed and a row of lights
lit up along a battered iron panel before him. He couldn't
hear the bells, his long service as a gunner in the Imperial
Navy having deafened him decades ago.

The shell was loaded and he muttered the gunner's prayer
to the warhead as he squinted through a bronze optical
attachment that lifted on groaning hinges from the panel. He
clamped his augmetic monocle to the optical, lining up the
thin crosshairs on the red triangle that represented his target.
The target was closing on them so he didn't have to make any
adjustments for crosswise motion. It was a simple shot, one
he could have easily made, even in the earliest days following
his press-ganging on Carpathia.

Satisfied that the shell would be on target, he lifted his head
and ran his gaze across the chamber, checking that his gunnery crew gangs were clear of the greased rails that ran the
length of the chamber and that each had their green flag
raised to indicate that all the blast dampers had been closed.
He reached up and took hold of the firing chain that hung
above his station.

He grunted in satisfaction and pulled hard on the chain,
shouting, 'Spirits of war and fire, I invoke thee with the wrath
of the Machine God. Go forth and purify!'

Steam hissed from juddering pipes and a high-pitched
screech filled the weapon chamber as the gravometric
impellers built up power in the breech.

Mabon rushed to the edge of the gantry and gripped the
iron railings. Seeing a weapon of such power discharge was a

potent symbol of the might of the Imperial Navy and he never tired of the sight.

The screeching rose to an incredible volume, though Mabon was oblivious to it, until the nova cannon fired, and the enormous pressure wave slammed through the chamber. The weapon's firing sent the three-hundred metre barrel hurtling back with the ferocious recoil. The air blazed with sparks and burning steam as the grease coating the rails vaporised in the heat of the recoil, the stench of scorched metal and propellant filling the chamber with choking fumes.

Mabon roared in triumph, gagging on the stinking clouds of gas that boiled around him.

Juddering vibrations attempted to topple him from the gantry, but he had long since grown used to them and easily kept his balance.

The smoke started to clear and his gunnery overseers began whipping their gangs into dragging the massive weapon back into its firing position once more. The armoured bays in the floor groaned open and the looped chains descended to be attached to a fresh shell.

Mabon had drilled his gunnery teams without mercy and he prided himself that he could have the nova cannon ready to fire again within thirty minutes. This time would be no different.

THE SHELL FROM the *Argus* streaked like a blur of light through space, exploding like a miniature sun in the heart of the tyranid ships. More potent than a dozen plasma bombs, the shell detonated only a few kilometres from one of the manta-like creatures, instantly incinerating it in a roiling cloud of fire, which also scattered a nearby flotilla of smaller creatures. One creature fell away from its pack, glutinous fluids leaking from its ruptured belly. It thrashed as it died, eventually becoming still as it haemorrhaged fatally.

The swarm scattered from the blast, though a host of small organisms, each no larger than a drop pod, converged on the shrinking cloud of organic debris, exploding with terrific violence as they neared the centre of the blast.

A group of creatures surged forward, as though galvanised into action by the blast, and closed on the approaching Sword frigates. Behind the frigates came *Sword of Retribution*, the

Cobras of Cypria squadron and the strike cruisers of the Ultramarines and the Mortifactors.

First blood had gone to the Imperial fleet, but the battle had
only just begun.

URIEL GRIPPED THE hilt of his power sword, listening to the
sounds of the *Vae Victus* as her hull groaned and creaked as
she manoeuvred in the battle line. The lights in the corridor
were dimmed as he and his squad waited in one of the strike
cruiser's reaction points. When going into battle, the Space
Marines aboard a ship of war were stationed throughout the
corridors of the ship in places where enemy forces were likely
to try and board.

His helmet's vox-bead was tuned to the ship's bridge and he
could hear the excited chatter of the various captains travelling between their ships. He listened to the cheers as it became
apparent that the fleet's flagship had just scored a direct hit on
an enemy vessel with her first shot. Such an auspicious beginning boded well for the coming engagement, though Uriel
could not rid himself of feelings of apprehension.

He did not like the arbitrary nature of space combat, where
a warrior's fate was in the hands of others, no matter how skil-
ful or competent they might be. Uriel knew he would rather
face a thousand enemies on the field of battle than wait in the
sweating darkness of a starship, not knowing whether death
would reach out its long, grave-dirt encrusted fingers and
sweep its terrible scythe around to claim his soul. He shuddered at the thought.

Pasanius saw him shiver and said, 'Captain?'

Uriel shook his head. 'It's nothing, I just had a strange sensation of déjà vu.'

'Are you getting another one of your "feelings"?' asked Pasanius.

'No, do not worry, old friend. I just do not like the idea of
waiting here for a foe who may not come. Part of me wishes I
had stayed with Learchus on Tarsis Ultra.'

'Now I know you're insane,' joked Pasanius. Though the
rivalry Uriel and Learchus had endured on Macragge during
their training had long since been forgotten, they would never
be true friends. Where Uriel had learned the virtue of personal
initiative from his mentor, Captain Idaeus, Learchus seemed

incapable of making that leap. He was an Ultramarine and that was to be expected, but Uriel knew that there were times when such rigid stricture was not always the answer.

Such thoughts disturbed Uriel. He knew it was but a short step from there to beginning down the path of the Mortifactors. Was that how their descent had started? Small breaches of the codex's teachings that over the centuries became greater and greater until there was nothing left of the blessed primarch's work? Astador had claimed that their Chapter venerated the primarch, but could you hold him highest above all else and yet not follow his words?

Had Idaeus been the first step towards the end of everything the Ultramarines held dear? Could he have been wrong in his teachings, and was Uriel on the path that lead to ultimate damnation? Already he had gone against the teachings laid down in the codex, most recently on Pavonis.

In the dim light of the *Vae Victus*, Uriel felt the stirrings of doubt for the first time in his life.

ABOARD THE BRIDGE of the Sword class frigate *Mariatus*, Captain Payne watched the tyranid bio-ships closing on his vessel with a mixture of anticipation and dread. It stunned him that creatures so huge could be alive, though he assumed that, in the way of the larger beasts on his homeworld, they would be as stupid as they were massive.

A clutch of drifting objects floated before the bladed ships, pulsing ahead of the alien vessel as it continued closing the distance between them.

The captain folded his arms and nodded to where his gunnery officer stood by the weapons station.

'You have a firing solution?' he asked.

'Aye, sir, the lead enemy vessel will be in range in just under a minute.'

'Very good. Order all ships to begin firing as soon as the enemy ships are in range.'

Payne marched back towards his command chair, perched atop a raised dais at the centre of the bridge. He followed the progress of the other ships in his squadron, *Von Becken* and *Heroic Endeavour*, on the pict-slate before him, satisfied that they were holding proper station – allowing their leader to take the first shot. A shiver of premonition went down his

spine as he watched the creatures before his ship turn ponderously to face him and he felt he could see their dead,
expressionless eyes staring deep into his soul. Such a notion
was plainly ridiculous; these beasts would have been blinded
by spatial debris were they to rely on sight alone. But still the
notion persisted and he bunched his fists to halt the sudden
tremors that seized him.

'All guns firing now,' reported the gunnery officer calmly as
the ship juddered with the recoil of its powerful guns. The
vibrations running along the worn teak flooring did not do
justice to the violence of his guns' firing. Right now, hundreds
of massive projectiles and powerful lasblasts would be
hurtling through space to unleash a torrent of explosive death
amongst these vile aliens.

He watched a flurry of detonations explode around the
nearest bio-ship, gradually drawing in as his gunners bracketed it. Some even managed to score direct hits, their shells
blasting one of the creature's giant, bladed limbs from its
body. Vast streams of fluid pumped from the bio-ship's
innards as the remainder of his squadron opened fire and the
flash of distant explosions momentarily obscured the tyranid
ships. When the viewing bay cleared, he saw that one had
been completely blown apart and another was drifting list-
lessly in space. He surged from his chair and punched the air
in triumph.

'Damn me, but that was some fine shooting. My compliments to the gun deck.'

'Aye, sir,' replied the gunnery officer, proudly.

He watched the viewing bay, seeing the remaining enemy
ships shuddering, as though gripped by some form of
spasm.

'What in the Emperor's name is that?' he wondered aloud.

Before he realised what he was seeing, bolts of gelatinous
liquid spurted from the front section of the bio-ships.

'All ships, hard to starboard!' he yelled, suddenly understanding what was happening.

The bridge of the *Mariatus* heeled sideway as emergency
power was routed to the engines, but a ship of war does not
react quickly, even if her captain does. With terrifying speed
the bolts hurtled towards his ships, streaking through space in
a tightly focussed stream. Payne gripped the armrests of his

chair as his ship fought against her forward momentum to turn away from the incoming fire.

Even as the bolts slid to the side of the viewing bay, he saw that it would not be enough. The *Mariatus* would escape significant harm, but there was no way either of her sister ships could possibly evade in time.

THREE CORROSIVE ACID bolts struck *Heroic Endeavour* on the lower section of her engine compartment. In panic, her Adeptus Mechanicus engineers shut the engines down, venting her combustion chambers as they realised the acid was eating away at the plasma cells that powered the engines. Their quick thinking undoubtedly saved the ship and, to their immense relief, emergency procedures were able to halt the damage before the acids could breach the volatile fuel stores. Four hundred and thirty-seven men lost their lives in the attack, but her sister ship, *Von Becken*, was not so fortunate.

The full force of the tyranid weapons struck *Von Becken* broadside on, just behind her swept prow. The sheer force of impact smashed the bolts through the first layered sections of armoured panels, before the bio-acids ate through the remainder and the full force of the tyranid weapons engulfed the mid-level decks of the ship.

Hundreds died in the first moments of impact, smashed to pulp or sucked into space as explosive decompression blew out adjacent sections of the hull. The acids filled compartments with burning fluids that dissolved flesh and metal in a heartbeat, the fumes as lethal as any nerve agent devised by the Adeptus Mechanicus. Blast doors rumbled closed, sealing off the area of the impact, but the corrosive fluid liquefied the doors and spilled onwards, dissolving decks and pouring down onto the screaming men below.

The *Von Becken's* hull, already weakened by the acids and under stress from the violent manoeuvring screeched in protest, finally buckling as the venerable ship split in two.

TORPEDOES LAUNCHED FROM the Cobras of Hydra squadron streaked through space on blazing tail plumes, arcing for the nearest of the giant manta-like creatures. A cloud of spores drifted before the ship, and as the torpedoes closed the gap, a swarm of them surged forwards to intercept the missiles. Explosions rippled through the cloud of spores as the torpedoes smashed through them, some detonating prematurely, some broken apart by the acidic explosions of the spores.

Not all the torpedoes could be stopped and a handful slammed into the body of the mantis creature, the primary warheads vaporising a chunk of its hide, before the tail sections exploded, thrusting the powerful centre section of the weapons deep inside the creature to detonate.

The monster's belly heaved as the torpedoes exploded one after the other and it listed drunkenly as its lifeblood poured from its gaping wounds. But as grievously wounded as it was, the creature was by no means finished, and it could still fight back. A swelling of intercostal motion pulsed along the top of the creature and a flurry of jagged spines rippled from its flanks, thousands hurtling towards its attackers like enormous javelins. At such range, the odds of hitting a relatively fast moving target such as a destroyer were huge, but if you factored in the sheer number and density of the spine cloud the odds changed dramatically.

Two Cobras exploded as hundred metre spines hammered through their armour, smashing through the armaplas and ceramite hulls with horrifying ease. The lead vessel's bridge was destroyed upon first impact, penetrated from prow to stern by a dozen spines, while the second was reduced to a blazing hulk as three giant spines penetrated her engine core and started dozens of uncontrollable conflagrations.

The last vessel, shielded from instant annihilation by her sister ships, was nevertheless struck several glancing blows and suffered horrendous damage as several torpedoes being readied for launch exploded in her launch bays. Her crews fought to bring the damage under control, but her captain was forced to disengage from the battle. His ship's primary weapon systems were damaged beyond immediate repair and there was nothing more he or his ship could do to alter the outcome of the battle.

THE HIVE SHIP moved ponderously forward, explosions bursting around it as the incoming fire from the Imperial ships came within range. Hundreds of spores vaporised in the hail of blossoming explosions, but there were always more

pumped into space from the ship's churning reproductive vats
to replace them.

The Dauntless cruisers *Luxor* and *Yermetov* passed the listing
remains of the frigates *Von Becken* and *Heroic Endeavour*, their
lance arrays spearing towards the hive ship. Turning as a single entity, a number of smaller bio-ships sped forward,
hurling themselves into the path of the burning lance beams.
Three exploded, torn apart by high-powered energy weapons
and another was cut in two along its length. A salvo of torpedoes launched from the Cobras of Cypria squadron slammed
into the hive ship, passing through an expanding cloud of fire
and spores and detonated against the craft's stony carapace.

Ichor spilled from the wound, but almost as soon as the fire
of the torpedoes' explosion had faded, the tear in the creature's hide began reknitting as fresh tissue formed across the
beast's flank.

Suddenly a fleshy fold in the bio-ship's underside eased
open and scores of finned creatures shot from its belly, trailing sinewy streams of amniotic birth fluids. A handful were
blasted to atoms by fire from the *Sword of Retribution* as it powered forward and the *Argus* angled her course around the
coreward flank of the hive ship, manoeuvring into a position
to bring her broadside lances to bear. But none of the fleshy
creatures launched from the hive ship were bound for either of
the battleships of the fleet. They converged upon the Space
Marine strike cruisers that escorted them.

ADMIRAL DE CORTE watched the hive ship slip to the left of the
viewing bay and counted down the minutes until his portside
lances could fire. So far the battle was proceeding much as he
had planned, though the durability of these alien craft had
surprised him, despite the inquisitor's warning. There had
been losses, but precise figures and exact information was
slow to reach him.

'Mister Viert, status report,' he demanded impatiently.

'The Swords are out of action, Lord Admiral, and Von
Becken has been completely destroyed. The *Heroic Endeavour's*
engines have been shut down though her enginseers are
attempting to relight them. Hydra squadron has lost two
ships and initial reports suggest that neither will fight again
without spending years in dock.'

De Corte bunched his jaw as the scale of their losses became apparent. 'I fear that we may have underestimated the cunning of these aliens,' he whispered.

'You would not be the first, admiral,' observed Kryptman.

'Did the tyranids lure us into this attack?' demanded de Corte. 'I have four ships out of action already and we have barely scratched the surface of the hive ship.'

'Fighting the tyranids, you must be prepared to accept losses, lord admiral.'

'Losses? Have you any idea how many men have died already?'

'A great many, I know. But many more will die if we fail here. We must press the attack and destroy that hive ship.'

Before de Corte could answer, Jex Viert intervened. 'Admiral! We are at optimum lance range!'

De Corte gave Kryptman a last, disgusted look before hurrying towards the tactical plot at his bridge's centre. He saw that the *Sword of Retribution* had punched a hole in the hive ship's forward screen of bio-ships with its lances and a well-placed volley of torpedoes. It raked the hive ship with its broadside guns, but only a fraction were impacting on the massive creature. A flurry of smaller craft were closing with the battlecruiser and the strike cruisers, but de Corte was confident that their close-in defences could handle them.

'Order the lance decks to fire on the craft around the gap in the tyranid line, we need space for a clear shot at that monster!'

'Aye, sir!' said Viert, punching in the admiral's orders. He placed a hand over the vox-bead in his ear and looked up, saying, 'Sir! Captain Payne on the *Mariatus* requests permission to close with the enemy. He claims to be in a position for a strafing run.'

De Corte could see that the *Mariatus* would not survive running so close to the hive ship without support. The *Argus* was almost behind the hive ship and the admiral felt the deck vibrate with the continued firing of his ship's guns.

'Tell him no, Mister Viert. We will need every ship in the coming days and I'll not allow any needless heroics. Order Payne to withdraw and come about to support the *Yermetov!*'

'Aye, sir.'

* * *

THE SMALLER FLESHY organisms fired from the belly of the hive ship sped like bullets towards the Imperial fleet, streaking past the majestic form of the *Sword of Retribution* and arcing towards the strike cruiser of the Space Marines. Supporting fire from the nearby battlecruiser's gun turrets obliterated the majority of the approaching organisms, and the combined guns of the Space Marine vessels and Arx Praetora squadron helped further thin their numbers. But still they kept coming.

On the bridge of the *Vae Victus*, Admiral Tiberius sweated as he watched the swarm of approaching craft. Thus far their close-in guns were holding them at bay, but it would not take much for the balance to swing against them.

'Sir!' shouted Philotas in dismay. 'The *Mortis Probati* is disengaging!'

Tiberius saw with mounting horror that Philotas was correct: the Mortifactors' strike cruiser's engines were flaring brightly as she pushed forward, her course angled upwards towards the hive ship. Her defensive guns had stopped firing and she was leaving the *Vae Victus* in her wake.

'What the hell are they doing?' demanded Tiberius, even as he saw the answer. A gap had been torn in the defences of the massive hive ship, its protective screen of drone ships stripped away by the relentless fire of the *Sword of Retribution* and her escorting Dauntless cruisers.

'They are going for the hive ship!' said Philotas.

'Can they make it before the tyranids re-establish their cover?' asked Tiberius.

Philotas consulted the plotting table, hurriedly scribbling distances and trajectories on a tablet beside him. He silently mouthed his calculations, shaking his head in exasperation.

'I think they might, lord admiral, but they will be cut off almost as soon as they breach the alien's defences.'

Tiberius slammed his fist into the lectern, cracking the glass of the slate. 'Damn them, what in the nine hells do they think they are doing? The codex clearly states that this kind of manoeuvre should only be attempted with a three to one superiority of fire.'

'I do not think Captain Gaiseric is familiar with that part of the codex, sir. And we have more pressing concerns now!' said Philotas pointing at the viewing bay.

Without the supporting fire from the *Mortis Probati's* turrets, perhaps half a dozen of the fleshy bullets fired from the hive ship had penetrated their defences and were, at best, seconds from contact.

'Emperor save us, no!' hissed Tiberius as he felt the impact of the tyranid organisms on his beloved ship.

URIEL RACED TOWARDS where the stony-surfaced object had smashed through the hull, filling the width of the corridor. Emergency bells and a hellish red glow bathed everything the colour of blood.

'Fan out!' he shouted. 'Make sure none of them get past you!' he shouted, directing his warriors to other damaged portions of the ship.

He kicked over a smouldering lump of chitin, approaching the cracked object that sat like a giant, toothed egg in the rubble of the corridor. Yellow slime dripped from its broken edges and hot steam billowed all around it. A piece of the object dropped to the deck, revealing an inner skin of a translucent, veined membrane.

'Pasanius, get up here. I need your flamer!' shouted Uriel as a ripple of motion shuddered through the membrane. He raised his bolt pistol and fired a succession of shots into the object, tearing the membrane and drawing an alien screech of pain from within.

A long claw ripped through the membrane and a grotesque creature bounded from the object. Its hide glistened wetly, dripping fluids from its bony exoskeleton, its mucus-wreathed head filled with needle-like fangs. Two pairs of arms, each ending in vicious barbed claws, clicked together as it landed lightly on the mesh deck. It hissed at Uriel, its black eyes nictating as it adjusted to its new surroundings. A trio of identical creatures followed it from the steaming chrysalis. Uriel could see many more behind them and unloaded his pistol into the mass of creatures as Pasanius finally arrived at his side.

Two of the creatures exploded as the mass-reactive shells detonated within their bodies, spattering yet more as they poured from the organism. A liquid wash of fire filled the corridor as Pasanius bathed the corridor in flame, simultaneously begging the ancient ship's forgiveness.

A burning creature bounded from the roaring flames, its teeth bared in its death fury. Uriel thrust his sword into its belly as it leapt, blasting its head from its shoulders with a single shot from his pistol. Elsewhere he could hear shots and screams of aliens as his men fought the horrific boarders.

Even as the flames died, a host of fresh creatures boiled from the object and Uriel wondered how closely packed these beasts must have been to fit within it. He swept out his sword, hacking two down with a single blow and sidestepping a third as it leapt for his head, bringing its hind legs up to rake his body with its claws.

It struck a stanchion, landing badly and Uriel stamped down on its neck, reaching for a reload for his pistol with trained economy of motion. Pasanius grappled with a pair of clawed beasts that tore at his armour with frenzied slashes of their talons. But Terminator armour had been designed with just this kind of close quarter battle in mind and they could not defeat it. Pasanius smashed their heads together, breaking their skulls open with a sickening, wet crack.

He dropped the twitching corpses, his flamer lying useless beside him, its fuel tank ruptured and leaking volatile fumes. Yet more creatures hurdled the bodies of their fallen siblings, desperate to reach their enemies. Uriel and Pasanius fought back-to-back as the alien tide threatened to overwhelm them, forced to fall back from the tide of clawed killers. They could not hold here, there were simply too many. Had they been reinforced from another boarding spore?

Uriel grunted as a razor edged claw slashed through the armour on his thigh, tearing into the muscle and ripping down to his knee. He toppled backwards, the alien's claw tearing from his flesh in a wash of bright blood. Uriel kicked out, breaking its neck and pulled himself backwards. The reek of promethium in the corridor was intense and as Pasanius helped him to his feet, he snatched a grenade from his belt.

'Run!' he shouted, pushing Pasanius down the corridor and hurling the grenade back the way they had come.

Pasanius gripped his captain's arm and pulled him to the deck as the grenade detonated, filling the corridor with lethal, scything fragments and igniting the choking promethium fumes. Roiling flames exploded with a whoosh of roaring air and the entire corridor was engulfed in a fiery explosion that billowed along its length, incinerating everything in its path. Uriel felt the flames wash over him, watching the external temperature reading on his visor rocket skywards. But neither his nor Pasanius's armour failed them and as the lethal flame wall burnt out, they found themselves in a blackened, corpse-choked passageway, littered with charred alien limbs and burning pools of promethium.

The two Space Marines struggled to their feet as the sounds of battle continued to rage throughout their ship.

There was more death yet to be done.

ADMIRAL DE CORTE watched the charging *Mortis Probati* close with the hive ship with a mixture of anger and admiration. The Mortifactors had broken his battle line, but by the Emperor they were courageous! The strike cruiser's bombardment cannon pounded the hive ship at, in spatial terms, point blank range, tearing great gouges in its hide.

The long feeder tentacles at the hive ship's rear lashed forward, swiping ponderously at the ship, but its captain swung his ship out of harm's way at the last possible second.

A host of bio-ships swung in behind the strike cruiser, blocking any escape as another cluster spun around and moved to attack. Bio acids and spurts of plasma struck the ship and flames erupted from her hull.

Inquisitor Kryptman watched the uneven battle with fierce pride, his knuckles white on the pommel of his cane. He spun to face de Corte. 'We must help them. Bring us about.'

'I cannot,' said de Corte. 'We are too far beyond them. It will be impossible to turn in time. We are manoeuvring to a position behind the hive ship as planned.'

'Do it!' snapped Kryptman, hammering his cane on the deck. 'Do it now!'

Kryptman spun to face the black uniformed Jaemar, the ship's commissar. 'You! Make him turn this Emperor forsaken ship around and support these brave warriors.'

Jaemar unholstered his pistol, cowed by Kryptman's reputation.

'The admiral is correct, lord inquisitor, commissar,' said de Corte's flag lieutenant, Jex Viert, moving to stand between Jaemar and his admiral. He placed his hand on the hilt of his sword, the threat clear. 'The image you are seeing is from our port surveyors. Even were the order given now, we will not be able to turn quickly enough to matter. In this respect, the Mortifactors are on their own.'

But Jex Viert was wrong.

CAPTAIN PAYNE, ABOARD the wounded *Mariatus*, shouted, 'For the Emperor!' as he gripped the arms of his command chair. The hive ship loomed large in the viewing bay and he knew that even if he survived this battle, he would be summoned before a court martial for disobeying a direct order. But with two of his ships put out of action by this monstrosity, he would have risked much more to avenge their gallant crews.

The *Mariatus* shuddered as blazing gouts of plasma fired from the hive ship drooled over her hull. Her guns hammered the alien monster, blowing chunks of its armoured carapace spinning into space and leaving a trail of seeping wounds along its mountainous body.

Ahead, he saw the graceful form of the Mortifactors' ship locked together with a thrashing beast with claws as big as a Battle Titan that raked its side and tore great swathes of its armour away. More bio-ships surrounded her, ready to sweep down and attack. Despite this, the massive cannon mounted on its prow continued to fire on the hive ship and though the heroism of the Space Marines was truly magnificent, there could only be one outcome.

Well, not if Payne and the *Mariatus* had anything to say about it.

URIEL RACED TO the bridge, hearing the desperate vox-traffic travelling between the ships of the fleet, dismayed at the sheer carnage unleashed. His armour was blackened and his leg flared painfully as he ran. The tyranid creatures were all dead and the damaged areas of the ship were finally secured.

He couldn't believe what the Mortifactors had done. Breaking the battle line and charging forward to engage the hive ship at close quarters was about as far from the teachings of the primarch as it was possible to get.

He mounted the steps to the bridge three at a time, sheathing his bloodied sword and sprinting through the arched entrance to the command bridge. Lord Admiral Tiberius turned as he entered, his face set in a mask of controlled fury.

'Uriel, thank the Emperor,' said the master of the *Vae Victus*.

'The boarders are repelled,' reported Uriel, staring in horror at the viewing bay as the Mortifactors' ship was slowly engulfed by the tyranid craft. Its bombardment cannon continued to fire, even as it was slowly being taken apart.

'What have they done?' he whispered.

Tiberius shook his head, words failing the ancient admiral. Then the battered shape of a Sword class frigate hove into view, trailing blazing plumes of venting plasma and golden streamers of sparks and freezing oxygen.

'Guilliman's blood, look!' shouted Philotas, as the prow of the *Mariatus* swung around and ploughed straight into the heart of the creature attacking the *Mortis Probati*.

The hull of the Imperial vessel buckled as it struck the hardened carapace of the tyranid creature, but its forward momentum could not be denied and it cracked through the flesh of the beast, spewing its bodily fluids all across the hull of the Space Marine vessel. It thrashed in its death agonies, releasing the strike cruiser and tumbled away with the *Mariatus* embedded deep within its body.

As valiant as the sacrifice of the *Mariatus* had been, there were tyranid ships aplenty to finish off the *Mortis Probati*, but before any could react to its unexpected survival, she unleashed a final shot from her bombardment cannon that struck a knotted growth tucked away at the rear of the hive ship. Bright liquid spurted from the wound like an enormous geyser and a visible shudder ran the length of the hive ship as the main synapse link to its attendant bio-ships was severed.

KRYPTMAN SAW THE great wound spew the hive ship's lifeblood into space and the listless drifting of the drone ships that surrounded it. His eyes flickered from bio-ship to bio-ship as he saw them pause in their relentless attack.

'Their connection to the hive mind is severed!' yelled Kryptman, spinning to face de Corte so quickly he almost fell. 'We must attack before it is restored! Immediately!'

Admiral Bregant de Corte nodded to Lieutenant Viert, who still stood between him and Jaemar. 'Mr Viert, order all ships forward. Let's close and finish this beast.'

* * *

WHILE THE TYRANID ships drifted in confusion, the captains of the *Sword of Retribution*, the *Luxor*, the *Yermetov* and the *Argus* all closed as quickly as possible, their gun decks loading and firing as fast as their crew chiefs could whip their gun gangs. The *Vae Victus* and Arx Praetora squadron swooped in and tore the underside of the tyranid vessel apart in a flurry of well-aimed fire. Fusillade after fusillade of explosive shells and lasblasts hammered the tyranid ship, pulverising vast sections of its carapace and spraying jets of ichor in all directions.

Feeder tentacles vainly attempted to swat away the attacking craft, but their swipes were drunken and uncoordinated. The smaller organisms protecting the hive ship threw off their lethargy, returning to their basic, instinctual desires, but by then it was too late. The Imperial ships were in textbook positions to deliver the deathblow to nearly every one of the drone ships. As though on range practice at Bakka, the *Sword of Retribution* bracketed one tyranid ship after another, annihilating them with powerful broadsides.

The battered *Mortis Probati* limped towards the listing hive ship and, in respect to her crew's reckless heroism, every other ship in the fleet hung back, allowing Captain Gaiseric to take the killing shot.

Fluid and fleshy entrails drifted from the mortally wounded beast, its alien lifeblood pumping into space from ruptured arteries and ruined organs. Those tentacles that had not been blasted off twitched spasmodically, and through a great rent in its upper carapace a vast, pulsing organ could be seen, labouring to keep the beast alive.

A single shell from the strike cruiser's bombardment cannon punched through the tough, fleshy outer layer of the hive ship's heart and detonated within its massive ventricle chambers. The explosion blasted the organ to shredded tissue and with a final, juddering spasm, the hive ship died.

ADMIRAL DE CORTE breathed a sigh of relief and his bridge crew cheered as they watched the death of the hive ship, its massive heart utterly destroyed by the Mortifactors. De Corte knew he should be furious with Captain Gaiseric for breaking the battle line, but could not deny the fact that his actions had been key to the tyranids' defeat. They went against everything taught at the naval academies, but de Corte knew that the

truly great captains were the ones who could sometimes break
all the teachings and still emerge victorious.

He didn't yet know if Captain Gaiseric fell into that category,
or whether he had just been hugely lucky. Publicly, he would
espouse the former, but privately, he suspected the latter. Had
it not been for the valiant, but ultimately wasteful sacrifice of
Captain Payne's ship, then the corpses of the Mortifactors
would even now be joining the listing body of the hive ship.
Watching the massive vessel haemorrhaging into the darkness,
he mouthed a short prayer to the battle spirits that invested his
ship, thanking them for their faithful service in this fight.

'Make a note, Mr Viert,' said de Corte. 'Commission a new
victory seal to be added to our glorious ship's honour banner.'

'Aye sir, and perhaps a service of thanks?'

'Yes, a service of thanks to be held in the ship's chapels at
vespers for all crew. Thank you, Mr Viert.'

The admiral linked his hands behind his back and returned
to his command lectern as Inquisitor Kryptman shuffled
along the nave to join him.

'A great victory,' said the admiral, loud enough to be heard
by his entire bridge crew.

Kryptman nodded. 'A victory, yes. It remains to be seen
whether it is a great one.'

The admiral leaned in close to Kryptman and whispered,
'You and I both know that this engagement has cost us dearly,
but it will avail us nothing if we allow our crews to know how
costly. I would appreciate your support in this matter.'

Kryptman looked ready to snap back at de Corte, but nodded curtly. 'You are correct, Admiral de Corte. Morale is crucial
at this point.'

De Corte accepted Kryptman's acquiescence gracefully and
began issuing the orders that would see his fleet disengage from
Barbarus Prime and fall back to the orbital docks of Chordelis.

For the viewing bay was filled with a multitude of tyranid
creatures rising from their feeding; a collection of hive ships
and drones that dwarfed the group they had just destroyed.
The Battle of Barbarus had been won, but in the face of such
a vast fleet, it would be folly to fight again without first
regrouping and rearming.

This had been a great victory, but it was just the tip of the
iceberg. The real battles were yet to come.

SIX

LEARCHUS GAZED UP at the sloping wall that stretched to either side of him for nearly five kilometres towards the valley's flanks. Despite his disappointment in the manner in which this world upheld the ideals of Ultramar, he was pleased at the strength of its construction. Worthy of Macragge itself, he thought. Ten metres high and sheathed in smooth stone, the wall glittered like white marble in the low sun. A small revetment protected its golden gate and an icy moat drained below the level of the road into a sluggish river that wound its way to the plain below.

A foaming waterfall, pouring from the centre of the wall, roared down a copper channel embedded in its centre, fed the moat and filled the surrounding air with a chill mist of icy water. The morning was bitingly cold and his breath feathered before him, though his power armour isolated him from the worst of the frosty air.

Beside him stood a shivering officer of the Tarsis Ultra Citizens' Defence Legion, his blue, fur-collared coat and white peaked cap immaculately clean. In addition to his dress uniform, he wore a grey scarf around his lower jaw and thick

mittens, thrust deep in his coat's baggy pockets. His name was
Major Aries Satria and he commanded the armed forces of
this city in the name of the Fabricator Marshal. His iron
breastplate was polished to a silver sheen and the dress sword
buckled to his gleaming leather belt shone like gold.

'When winter comes, does this moat freeze?' asked
Learchus.

'This far out, yes,' nodded Major Satria, 'but as you get further into the city, the heat gets trapped by the valley sides and
keeps them from turning to ice.'

'How far in do they freeze?' pressed Learchus.

'The moats at the first and second walls always freeze, and
sometimes the third, but it really depends of the severity of
the winter.'

Learchus nodded, setting off for the gate in the wall. 'What
is the forecast for this coming winter?'

'The meteorologists say it will be a tough one,' said Satria,
hurrying to keep up with Learchus, 'but then they always say
that, don't they?'

The winters on Macragge had taught Learchus how tough
a winter could be on soldiers, and he knew that the war
could not have come at a worse time for this world. The cold
weather had caused them problems already, with men
reporting frostbite and other cold-related injuries. Corpsmen from the Logres regiment were instructing the men of
the Krieg and local defence forces how to cope with such
severe conditions, but it would take time for such practices
to be adopted.

The two men crossed the moat on a crowded steel bridge.
Its arching spars were limned with hoar frost and drifting floes
of ice were already forming in the water below. Learchus had
ordered the bridge to be rigged with explosives so that it could
be destroyed upon the first attacks, though he could see that
it would not be long before the moat was a solid sheet of thick
ice, as easily traversable as this bridge. Nevertheless, standard
practice was to destroy all approaches that the enemy could
make use of and thus he had ordered it prepared for destruction.

But while the bridge still stood, many of the citizens of Erebus were making good use of it. Its metal deck vibrated with
the passage of scores of vehicles, which rumbled past Learchus

and Satria in the direction of the main spaceport below. All manner of vehicles, from gleaming limousines to battered agri-transports, streamed through the wall's main gate, each crammed with people carrying as many of their possessions as they could fit inside.

They stepped from the bridge onto a rutted road caked in grit that led to one of the wall's few postern gates. Tightly packed trucks filled with frightened people passed them and the sudden roar of a nearby starship engine made conversation impossible for a few seconds. Both Learchus and Satria turned, watching a cargo vessel rise from the port facilities and climb into the pale sky on smoky trails. It was the eighth vessel to leave Tarsis Ultra this morning and, judging by the crowds pressing around the walls of the spaceport, would only be one of many.

'It is unseemly that your people do not stay to fight,' said Learchus, turning back to watch the labouring men below. 'Where is their spirit? Their world is threatened and they flee before the enemy.' He shook his head in disappointment. 'No citizen of Ultramar would desert their homeworld. I believed the news of the great victory at Barbarus Prime would have put some steel in these people's spines, but it only seems to have weakened them.'

'People are frightened,' shrugged Satria. 'And I can't say I blame them. If even half of what I've heard about these aliens is true, then I can understand their desire to get away.'

'Given the chance, would you flee?' asked Learchus.

'No,' admitted Satria with a smile, 'but I swore an oath to defend this world and I don't break my word.'

'That is good to know, Major Satria. The warrior spirit of Ultramar is in you.'

Satria beamed with pride at the compliment as they eased past a madly revving supply truck. Laden with two-dozen frightened citizens of Erebus, its back wheels had sunk into the churned soil of the road and, behind it, angry horns blared continuously, as though their owners believed sheer volume of noise alone could shift the immobilised truck. Fountains of mud and chunks of grit from its spinning back wheels sprayed the limousine behind the truck, cracking its windscreen and leaving streaks of bare metal where they ripped across its pristine bodywork.

The driver of the truck continued gunning the engine, oblivious to the damage he was causing, gasoline rainbows forming in the clouds of filthy blue oilsmoke jetting from the truck's exhaust. The limousine's passenger, a tall man with a slicked widow's peak and a prominent hooked nose, climbed from the back of the vehicle and began screaming at the truck driver, delivering choice insults regarding his parents' promiscuity and bodily hygiene.

Learchus stepped forward to berate the man for his uncivil behaviour and coarse language, but Major Satria quickly shook his head saying, 'Best let me handle this one, Sergeant Learchus, I know this fellow. A gentle touch required, I think.'

'Very well,' said Learchus reluctantly.

Major Satria banged on the cab of the truck and made a chopping motion across his throat to the driver. Immediately, its engine shut down and the noise of the protesting motor faded to a throaty rumble as Satria made his way towards the limousine.

'Come now, Mr van Gelder,' said Satria, nimbly hopping across the mud of the road to address the limousine's passenger. 'There's no need for such language.'

The tall man drew himself up to his full height and tucked his thumbs into the pockets of his long frock coat. A caustic sneer spread across his features as Satria approached.

'Did you see what that imbecile has done?' he snapped.

'I did indeed, Mr van Gelder, and if you'll just bear with us, we'll get you on your way as soon as we can find some planks to put under the back wheels of this truck and get it out of the mud.'

'I want that wretched driver's name so that I can be properly compensated upon my return to Tarsis Ultra.'

'I assure you that I shall attend to the matter, sir,' soothed Satria. 'Now, if you'll just return to the lovely heated interior of your limousine, we'll soon have you out of the city.'

Before van Gelder could reply, a groan of metal sounded from behind the major. Satria turned to see Sergeant Learchus effortlessly lifting the back end of the fully laden truck from the sucking mud and push it forwards to more solid ground. The sergeant dropped the truck to the road and almost immediately it sped off to the spaceport.

Satria had heard of the great strength of Space Marines, but had thought that most were overblown exaggerations. Now he knew better.

The sergeant's face was thunderous as he marched back along the road towards van Gelder.

He pointed at the crowd that had gathered and the line of vehicles extending from the gate, shouting, 'Enough! This stops now. There will be no more departures from Tarsis Ultra. Get back in your vehicles, turn them around and get back within the city walls where you belong!'

Satria grimaced at Learchus's lack of tact and even van Gelder was momentarily taken aback. But he was not a man to be cowed easily.

'Do you know who I am?' he blustered.

'No,' said Learchus, dismissively. 'Nor do I care. Now turn this vehicle around before I do it myself.'

Having seen the Space Marine's strength demonstrated upon the truck, van Gelder was under no illusions concerning Learchus's ability to do such a thing, and reluctantly climbed into the back of his limousine.

'The Fabricator Marshal shall hear of this,' said van Gelder as a parting shot.

'I will make it my business to see that he does,' promised Satria.

Van Gelder's eyes narrowed, unsure if the major was mocking him, and slammed the door in his face. The limousine's gears ground as its driver attempted to turn it on the narrow road.

'I think we might have upset him,' smiled Satria.

'Good,' replied Learchus.

MELTED SNOW STREAKED across the fogged glass of the land train's window, running in long, wobbling lines. Lieutenant Quinn briefly wondered how fast they were actually travelling; it was hard to tell when everything he could see beyond the glass was a uniform white. He gripped the handrail as the land train swept around a bend in the track and leaned over to wipe a gloved hand across the glass, smiling at the young family seated across from him.

'No need to worry,' he said. 'It won't be long before we're in Erebus. Just one more stop to pick up the people at Prandium.'

The man nodded, his wife looking fearfully at the white-steel of the lasgun he held across his knees. It was a look he had seen many times on this journey, the terror that armed conflict had come to their once-peaceful world, but he couldn't bring himself to feel sorry for them. After all, was it not the duty of every Imperial citizen to stand against the enemies of Mankind?

He and his platoon had emptied six farming collectives of their populace and packed them on this long land train in order to bring them to the safety of Erebus. Dozens of other platoons were performing the same job all across the continent and with any luck they would be able to complete their mission without incident. Over sixty carriages snaked back from the labouring engine car and they were already nearing capacity, each carriage crammed with fearful people.

Already Lieutenant Quinn could envision the scenes of outrage when he would have to order these people to discard their belongings to make room for the people of Prandium.

Sergeant Klein, his adjutant, made his way along the carriage's central aisle with difficulty, pushing past protesting citizens, his thick jacket and combat webbing catching almost everyone he passed. Klein held his rifle raised, the sling wrapped around his arm and said, 'Sir, we're just about to pull into Prandium.'

'Excellent. Nearly done, eh, sergeant?'

'Yes, sir.'

'Order the men to stand to. I'll take First squad, you take Second.'

Klein nodded and made his way back through the carriage as Quinn felt the train's deceleration. He rose from his seat and eased his way through the crowds packing the train towards the main doors where a knot of his soldiers from the Logres regiment waited to disembark. He sketched a quick salute and wiped his hand across the glass of the doors, seeing the silver steel of the platform approaching. Something struck him as odd, but it took him a second or two to realise what it was.

The platform was empty.

Whereas some communities had been reluctant to abandon their homes, most had been only too eager to be escorted back to the safety of Erebus, their departure points thronged with anxious people, packed and ready to leave.

But not here.

Quinn sighed as he realised they were probably going to have to convince more stubborn farmers to abandon their lands and come with them. He should be used to it, he supposed. Each time the Tarellians attacked one of the sea farms on Oceanus, they would run into bull-headed krill farmers who'd be damned if they'd abandon the holdings their family had farmed for generations. In Quinn's experience, those types always ended up dead sooner rather than later.

The train slid to a graceful halt and the doors smoothly opened. Freezing air sucked the warmth from the carriage, to the groans and complaints of its passengers. Quinn stepped onto the frosted platform, feeling ice crunch under his boot.

That was unusual. He would have expected the station's servitors to have kept the platform free from ice. The windows of the station building were opaque with frost and long icicles drooped from the eaves of the main station house. The hanging sign that creaked in the low wind clearly declared that this was Prandium.

He could see Sergeant Klein's squad further down the platform and waved his adjutant over.

'This is peculiar,' he said.

'I agree,' said Klein. 'No one's been here for a while.'

'Another train hasn't passed this way before us, has it?'

Klein pulled out the small orders pad he kept in his thick winter coat's breast pocket and shook his head. 'No, not according to my information, sir.'

'I don't like it,' stated Quinn.

'What do you want us to do?'

'Move into the town,' ordered Quinn. 'And stay sharp. Something doesn't feel right here.'

Klein saluted and made his way carefully along the platform to rejoin his squad.

'Right,' said Quinn, 'let's move out.'

Using small, careful steps, he crossed the slippery platform and flicked off the safety on his lasgun as he reached the top of the steps below a sign that indicated the exit. The stone steps were slick with ice and more icicles hung from the underside of the banister. Slowly, and with great care, Quinn and his squad made their way down the stairs, emerging into the farming collective of Prandium.

Its snow-filled streets were eerily quiet, only the low moan of the wind and the crunching footsteps of his platoon disturbing the silence. Not even the lonely call of a bird sounded. The buildings were sturdy-looking, prefabricated structures, similar to those on a thousand other worlds, fashioned from local materials and built with the sweat and toil of their inhabitants. A generatorium building stood abandoned beside them and a trio of vast grain silos towered above the community at the far end of the street.

There was a tension in the air; even Quinn could feel it. Prandium reeked of abandonment. There had been nobody here for a long time and the sense of neglect was painfully evident.

'Let's go,' he said and led his squad into the settlement, crunching through the knee-deep snow. The streets felt narrow and threatening. Through a gap in the buildings, he could see Klein's squad advancing on a parallel course to their own.

A door banged in the wind and everyone jumped, lasguns swinging to face the direction the sound had come from. Quinn's feeling that there was something wrong here rose from a suspicion to a certainty. Even if these people had left on an earlier transport that he didn't know about, any farmer worth his salt would have found the time to make sure his property was closed up for the winter.

Two large harvesters stood rusting at the end of the street in the shadow of the huge grain silos and Quinn motioned his squad to follow him towards them. Even though the icy air dampened any odours he might have smelled, he could still taste the reek of rotted grain. As they circled around the harvesters, he saw something that made him pull up short and raise his fist.

At the base of the nearest grain silo, a three-metre tear had been ripped in the skin of the tower, the metal peeled back and buckled. A sloping pile of frozen grain spread from the tear.

He advanced cautiously towards the torn hole, a sudden chill enveloping him as he moved into the long shadow cast by the tower. Quinn drew his chainsword, his thumb hovering above the activation rune. He stepped onto the gritty surface of the grain, flicking on the illuminator slung beneath

the barrel of his lasgun, and took a deep breath as he stared
into the darkness within the silo. A thick stench, disguised by
the cold air, filled his nostrils as he cautiously stepped into the
silo, playing the spear of light from his illuminator around its
interior. The light could only show the merest fragment of
what lay within, but even that was too much.

He numbly waved his vox-operator forward.

'Get Sergeant Klein over here,' he whispered, his voice trembling, 'and tell him to hurry…'

SERGEANT LEARCHUS, MAJOR Satria and Colonel Stagler of the
Krieg regiment stood atop the frosted rampart of the first wall
of Erebus city, watching the soldiers of its defence force training on the esplanade between this wall and the second. Men
sweated and grunted below, the sound of their training
eclipsed by the ringing of hammers and clang of shovels on
the frozen ground as other gangs of soldiers dug trench lines
before the walls.

Learchus watched the men below with a mixture of disappointment and resignation.

'You are not impressed, I take it,' said Satria.

Learchus shook his head. 'No, most of these men would not
survive a week at Agiselus.'

'That's one of the training barracks on Macragge, is it not?'
asked Stagler.

'Yes, it sits at the foot of the Mountains of Hera where
Roboute Guilliman himself trained. It is where myself and
Captain Ventris trained also.'

Soldiers worked in small sparring groups, practising bayonet drills and close combat techniques with one another,
making a poor show of the skills they would need to keep
them alive in the coming battles.

Upon his first inspection of the troops, Learchus had
watched each platoon fire off accurate volleys of disciplined
lasfire, blasting close groupings of holes in target silhouettes.
He had marched to the first platoon and grabbed a lasgun
from a nervous trooper, before returning to a surprised looking Major Satria.

'You are teaching them to shoot?'

'Well, yes. I thought that might be important in a soldier,'
Satria had replied.

'Not against tyranids,' said Learchus. 'Have you ever seen a tyranid swarm?'

'You know I haven't.'

'Well I have, and they come at you in a tide of creatures so thick a blind man could score a hit ten times out of ten. Any man who can hold a gun can hit a tyranid. But no matter how many you kill with your guns, there will always be more, and it is our job to teach the men how to fight the ones that reach our lines.'

Since then, the organisation of a coherent training program had fallen to Learchus and in the week since he had ordered the gates of Erebus closed, he had fought bureaucratic intransigence and years of ingrained dogma to implement a workable regime.

At dawn the men would rise, practise field stripping their weapons and perform exercises designed to enhance their stamina and aerobic strength. Corpsmen from the Logres regiment had been instrumental in instructing the soldiers in good practices while exercising in cold weather, as each activity had to be rigorously controlled, lest a soldier develop a layer of sweat beneath his winter clothes that would later condense, degrading its insulating properties dramatically.

'These men must learn faster,' said Learchus. 'They will all die in the first attack at this rate.'

'You expect the impossible from them, sergeant,' said Satria. 'At this rate they will hate us more than the tyranids.'

'Good. We must first strip them of all sense of self. We must strip away every notion of who they think they are and rebuild them into the soldiers they need to be to survive. I do not care that they hate me, only that they learn. And learn quickly.'

'That won't be easy,' said Satria.

'Irrelevant,' said Stagler. 'The weakest men will always be the first to fall anyway. When the chaff has been removed, the true warriors will remain.'

'Chaff?' said Satria. 'These are my soldiers and I'll not have them spoken of like that.'

'Your soldiers leave a lot to be desired, Major Satria,' pointed out Stagler, his hands clasped behind his back. His patrician features were pinched by the cold, and his stern gaze swept the training ground in disapproval. Learchus agreed with Stagler and though he knew that Satria's men were trying, effort had to be combined with results to mean anything.

He watched a group of soldiers practising thrusting and parrying with bayonets, their movements encumbered by thick winter clothing. Originally the soldiers had been training without their webbing and winter gear, but Learchus had swiftly put a stop to that. Where was the use in training in ideal conditions when the fighting was never going to be that way?

Learchus firmly believed in the philosophy of Agiselus: train hard, fight easy. Every training exercise undertaken by its cadets was fought against insurmountable odds, so that when the real fight came, it was never as hard.

Even after a week's training, Learchus saw that the soldiers were still too slow. Tyranid creatures were inhumanly quick, their razored limbs like a blur as they speared towards your heart, and he knew that the butcher's bill among these soldiers would be high indeed.

Without a word of explanation he turned on his heel and made his way down the gritted steps that led from the ramparts to the esplanade below. Satria and Stagler hurriedly followed him as he stepped onto its slick cobbles.

He strode into the middle of the training ground and stood with his hands planted squarely on his hips. Activity around him gradually diminished until the soldiers began to slowly gather around the Space Marine at their centre.

'You have strayed from the ideals of Ultramar that the blessed primarch left you as his legacy,' began Learchus. 'You have been seduced by the frippery and comfort that comes from lives of indulgence and peace. I am here to tell you that that time is over. Comfort is an illusion, a chimera bred from familiar things and ways.'

Learchus marched around the circumference of the circle of soldiers, punctuating his words by slapping his gauntleted fist into his palm.

'Comfort narrows the mind, weakens the flesh and robs your warrior spirit of fire and determination. Well, no more.'

He marched to stand in the centre of the circle and said, 'Comfort is neither welcome nor tolerated here. Get used to it.'

* * *

THE SKIN OF the soldier's foot was waxy-looking, a white, grey-ish yellow colour, and several ruptured blisters leaked a clear fluid onto the crisp white sheets of the bed. Joaniel Ledoyen shook her head at this soldier's foolishness, jabbing a sharp needle into the cold flesh on the sole of his foot. The man didn't react, though she couldn't tell whether that was a result of the frostbite or the half-bottle of amasec he'd downed to blot out the pain.

Probably a mix of both, she thought, discarding the needle into a sharps box and scrawling a note on the man's chart that hung from the end of his bed.

'Is it bad?' slurred the soldier.

'It's not good,' said Joaniel frankly. 'But if you're lucky we may be able to save your foot. Didn't you receive instruction on how to prevent these kinds of injuries?'

'Aye, but I don't read so good, sister. Never had no call for it on Krieg.'

'No?'

'Nah, soon as you're old enough you're sent to join the regiment. Colonel Stagler don't approve of educated men, says it was educated men that got Krieg bombed to shit in the first place. The colonel says that all a man needs to do is fight and die. That's the Krieg way.'

'Well, with any luck, I'll have you fighting again soon, but hopefully you can avoid the dying part,' said Joaniel.

The soldier shrugged. 'As the Emperor wills.'

'Yes,' nodded Joaniel sadly as she moved away. 'As the Emperor wills.'

So far today, she had treated perhaps fifty cases of mild hypothermia and a dozen cases of frostbite, ranging from mild blanching of the skin to this poor unfortunate, who, despite her optimistic words, would probably lose his foot.

Joaniel snapped off her rubber gloves and disposed of them as she made her way painfully back to the nurses' station at the end of the long row of beds. She favoured her right leg, pressing her palm against her hip and watching as corpsmen from the Logres regiment circulated in the long, vaulted chamber. They used thermal bandages to gradually restore heat to frostbitten limbs of the injured men in a controlled manner. Thankfully, the beds in the District Quintus Medicae facility were still largely empty – the building was designed to cope with over a thousand patients – though she knew that the steadily increasing trickle of soldiers being brought to her wards would soon become a raging torrent once the war began. Remian IV had taught her that.

She rubbed her temples and yawned, pulling out the cord that bound her ponytail and ran a hand through her long blonde hair. Tall and statuesque, Joaniel Ledoyen was a handsome woman of forty standard years, with smoky blue eyes and full features that spoke of great dignity and compassion. She wore a long, flowing white robe, bearing the crest of the Order of the Eternal Candle, one of the Orders Hospitaller of the Convent Sanctorum of the Adepta Sororitas, pulled in at the waist by a crimson sash.

Unlike the battle sisters of the Orders Militant, the sisters of the Orders Hospitaller provided medical care and support for the fighting men and women of the Imperial Guard, as well as setting up missions for the needy and impoverished of the Imperium.

Many wounded soldiers had the sisters of the Orders Hospitaller to thank for their survival and it was a source of great comfort to those on the front line to know that such aid awaited them should they be injured.

One of her junior nurses, Ardelia Ferria, looked up and smiled as she saw Joaniel approaching. Ardelia was young and pretty, fresh from her training as a novice and had only recently completed her vows on Ophelia VII. She liked her and though the youngster had yet to witness the true horrors of war, Joaniel felt Ardelia would make a fine nurse.

'All done for the night?' asked Ardelia.

'Yes, thank the Emperor. Most of these men will live to fight another day.'

'They are lucky to have you to look after them, Sister Ledoyen.'

'We all play our part, Sister Ferria,' said Joaniel modestly. 'Have the fresh supplies arrived from the upper valley yet?'

'No, not yet, though the city commissariat assures me that they will be here soon,' said Ardelia, with more than a trace of scepticism.

Joaniel nodded, sharing Ardelia's misgivings and well used to the vagaries of the city's commissariat, but knew that the supplies would be desperately needed in the coming days. She would need to contact the commissariat in the morning and demand to know what had become of them.

'I can look after the wards for the rest of the night,' said Ardelia. 'You should retire for the evening, Sister Ledoyen. You look tired.'

Joaniel tried not to be too hurt at Ardelia's remark, but supposed she did. The weight of responsibility and too many bad memories had aged her prematurely and though she still met her order's physical fitness requirements and could field strip a bolter in less than forty seconds, she knew that a life of moving from war to war had made her features melancholy.

The war on Remian IV had been the worst she had ever seen: screaming men begging for a merciful death rather than endure such pain. The stench of blood, voided bowels, antiseptic fluids and the acrid reek of war had stayed with her long after the war there had been won.

She remembered the months of counselling she had given the soldiers after the battle, bringing many of them back from the horror of their experiences on Remian. In response to her soothing words and gentle manner, the soldiers had dubbed her the Angel of Remian and that name had followed her since then. She had saved hundreds, if not thousands, of lives on Remian, but in the end, there had been no one there to soothe the horrors in her own head.

In her dreams she would find herself back there, weeping as she clamped a spraying artery, fighting to save a faceless soldier's life as he screamed and clawed at her with broken fingers. Severed limbs and the choking tang of burned human meat still filled her senses and every night she would wake with a pleading scream on the edge of her lips.

Joaniel thought of returning to her bare cell above the wards, but the prospect of such emptiness was too much for her to deal with right now.

'I shall offer a prayer to the Emperor before I retire. Call me if you need anything,' she told Ardelia, before bowing and making her way through the thick wooden doors that led from the main ward into the stone flagged vestibule.

She walked stiffly towards a low arch, stepping down into a short, candlelit passageway with a black door at its end. A carving of a hooded figure with golden wings filled the door and Joaniel pushed it open and entered the medicae's chapel.

The chapel was a simple affair, barely large enough to hold two-dozen worshippers. Three lines of hard, wooden pews ran in orderly lines from the alabaster statue at the end of the nave and scores of candles filled the air with a warm, smoky glow. Above the statue, a semi-circular window of stained glass threw a pool of coloured light across the polished wooden floor.

Joaniel bowed and made her way towards the two stone benches flanking the statue and knelt before it, bowing her head and clasping her hands together in prayer. Silently she whispered words of devotion and obedience, ignoring the dull ache that grew in her knees as the cold seeped into her bones from the bare floor. Tears filled her eyes as she prayed, the sights and sounds of Remian coming back so vividly that she could taste the smoke and smell the blood.

She finished her prayers and painfully pushed herself to her feet, the metal pins in her right thigh aching in the cold. The field hospital on Remian had taken a direct hit from an enemy artillery shell and she alone had been pulled from the wreckage, the bones of her leg shattered into fragments. The soldiers whose lives she had saved had rounded up the finest surgeons and her surgery had been performed beneath the flickering light of an artillery barrage. She had lived, but the thousands of her patients in the building had not, and the guilt of her survival gnawed at her soul like a cancer.

She rubbed the feeling back into her legs and bowed again to the Emperor's statue before turning to make her way back to her cold cell above.

'As the Emperor wills,' she said.

THE VOLCANIC WORLD of Yulan was beautiful from space, its flickering atmosphere riven with streaks of scarlet lightning and the swirls of ruby clouds painting streamers of bright colours across its northern hemisphere. A cluster of ships hung in orbit, buffeted by the planet's seismic discharges and flares of ignited gasses from the cracked surface.

Their captains fought to hold their vessels steady, their shields at full amplitude to protect them from a host of hazardous materials being ejected from the world below. Though even the smallest vessel was almost a kilometre long, they were all dwarfed by the three behemoths that

hung in geo-stationary orbit above Yulan. Hundreds of pilot
ships and powerful tugs from the docks above the nearby
planet of Chordelis fought the miasma of turbulence in the
planet's lower atmosphere to manoeuvre themselves into
position at the vast docking lugs at the front of the enormous creations.

Each behemoth was a hydrogen-plasma mining station that
drank deeply of the planet's violent atmosphere and refined it
into valuable fuels used by the tanks of the Imperial Guard,
the ships of the Navy and virtually every machine tended by
the Adeptus Mechanicus. They were largely automated, as the
handling of such volatile fuels was, to say the least, highly
dangerous.

For several hours, and at the cost of scores of servitor
drones, the first of the huge refinery ships was slowly dragged
from orbit, its vast bulk moving at a crawl into the darkness
of space.

Despite the danger of working in such a hostile environ-
ment, the work to moor the tug ships to the second refinery
was achieved in little under three hours and it moved to join
the first on the journey to Chordelis. The Adeptus Mechanicus
magos overseeing the mission to Yulan was pleased with the
speed with which the operation was proceeding, but knew
that time was running out to recover the third refinery.

Already the tyranid fleet had reached Parosa and was heading this way.

Time was of the essence and a further six, frustrating hours
passed as the tug crews tried again and again to attach themselves to the last refinery in the turbulent lower atmosphere.
The tug captains moved in again, their frustration and orders
for haste perhaps making them more reckless than was
healthy.

But haste and a billion-tonne refinery packed with lethally
combustible fuels are two things that do not sit well together.

The captain of the tug vessel *Truda* moved his vessel gingerly into position on the forward docking spar of the last
refinery, eschewing the normal safety procedures regarding
proximity protocols. As the *Truda* moved into final position,
her captain was so intent on the docking lugs ahead that he
failed to notice the *Cylla* coming around a sucking, gas intake
tower.

At the last second, both captains realised their danger and attempted to avoid the inevitable collision, the *Truda* veering right and barrelling into the intake tower. She smashed herself to destruction against its structure, buckling the hot metal of the tower and crashing through the thin plates before exploding as her fuel cells ruptured.

The *Truda* could not have struck the refinery in a worse place; designed to capture the hot gasses from the planet below, the intake tower sucked a huge breath of the tug's explosion, carrying the burning plasma of its engines to the very heart of the refinery's combustion chambers, where it ignited an uncontrolled chain reaction.

Emergency procedures initiated, but blast doors not shut since the refinery's construction thousands of years ago jammed and shutdown measures failed as ancient circuits failed to close, their wiring long having since degraded to the point of uselessness.

Within minutes of the crash, the internal chambers of the refinery began exploding sequentially, with each blast blowing apart more storage chambers and multiplying the force of the blast exponentially.

From high orbit, it appeared as though the giant refinery was convulsing and before any warning could be given to the ships still clustered nearby, it exploded in a flaring corona that eclipsed the brightness of the system's star.

Everything within a thousand kilometres of the blast was instantly vaporised and the shockwave ruptured the surface of the planet below, sending plumes of fiery gasses into space.

The blast wave faded, leaving nothing of the refinery or the hundreds of men that made up the Adeptus Mechanicus detachment tasked with its retrieval, save an expanding cloud of burning plasma gas.

Oblivious to the disaster in their wake, the flotilla of tugs continued onwards to Chordelis with the two surviving refineries lifted from geo-stationary orbit around Yulan in tow.

Why the Ultramarines' admiral had tasked them with this dangerous duty, they did not know, but theirs was not to question, simply to obey.

* * *

THE SIX TRUCKS sat silently in the dimly lit vehicle hangar; moonlight streaming in through the high windows providing the only illumination. A dozen soldiers grunted as they loaded crates onto the back of the trucks, overseen by a supply sergeant of the Erebus Commissariat, who, despite the fact that the temperature was below zero, sweated beneath the fur-lined hood of his winter coat.

He smoked a limp bac-stick and stamped his feet to ward off the cold as the last crate was loaded onto the truck, each one marked with a scorched burn where a Departmento Munitorum shipping number and regimental crest had been stamped. The tailgates of each truck were slammed shut and secured with chained locking-pins and as his soldiers filed passed him, he pressed a wad of promissory notes into each one's hand.

'Don't do anything dumb with this,' he warned.

As the last of the soldiers left the garage, he stubbed out his bac-stick and circled the trucks, checking that all the tailgates were secured. As he rattled the last one, a group of figures emerged from the shadows at the far end of the garage.

'You all done?' asked the figure at the front.

The supply sergeant jumped, his hand reaching for the pistol below his coat.

'I wouldn't do that if I was you,' growled a hulking figure behind the first and the sergeant raised his hands.

'Snowdog,' he breathed in relief, lowering his hands as the group came into the light. He flipped another bac-stick into his mouth.

'You expecting someone else, Tudeca?' asked Snowdog, his shotgun resting on his shoulder. The leader of the Night-crawlers wore a thick woollen coat to ward off the winter's chill and his bleached hair shone as silver as that of the girl beside him. Behind Snowdog stood the psychotic thug he called Jonny Stomp and a trio of painfully thin youths decorated with colourful, if badly drawn, tattoos across their faces. At a gesture from Snowdog, they jogged towards the cabs of three of the trucks, a redheaded girl in a tight catsuit climbing into the nearest one.

'No,' said Sergeant Tudeca. 'It's just you startled me. I wasn't expecting you so soon.'

'What can I say; I like to surprise people,' said Snowdog, nodding to Jonny Stomp. The brutish giant climbed onto the back of each of the trucks in turn, counting the number of crates in the back of each one. Sergeant Tudeca stepped nervously from foot to foot, surprised Jonny Stomp could count past his fingers, as Snowdog and Silver watched him carefully.

'It's all there?' asked Snowdog.

'Yeah, it's all there. Medical supplies and ration packs, just like you wanted. Didn't I tell you I could get them for you?'

'Yeah, you really came through for us,' agreed Snowdog, putting an arm around Tudeca's shoulders and lifting the pack of bac-sticks from his breast pocket.

Snowdog waited for a second, raising an eyebrow until Tudeca took the hint and lit the bac-stick for him, the flame wavering in his shaking hands. Snowdog reached up to steady the sergeant's hand.

'You okay, Tudeca?' said Snowdog with false concern. 'You look all jittery, man. Something on your mind?'

'It's going to cost more,' blurted Tudeca. 'I had to give my lads twice what they normally get for this. The commissariat provosts are coming down hard on anyone they catch stealing, and if they arrest me, it's a bullet in the head for sure.'

'Tudeca, Tudeca,' soothed Snowdog. 'Don't look at this as stealing; look at it as redistributing it to the people who really need it. Look, all this stuff was going to the medicae buildings for the regiments from off world. I'll make sure it gets to the people of Erebus... at a nominal charge.'

Tudeca laughed, a hoarse bray, and said, 'Nominal charge! You'll be selling this for four times its worth.'

'Hey man, it's a seller's market out there. If I can make a little money out of this war, then who's to say that's a bad thing?'

'Don't forget, you're hip-deep in this too,' pointed out Silver, her long hair glittering in the moonlight.

'Yeah, I know,' said Tudeca sourly, as Jonny Stomp dropped from the back of the last truck.

'It's all there, near as I can tell,' he said.

'Well, what the hell does that mean?' said Snowdog. 'It either is or it isn't.'

'I mean it looks right to me,' growled Jonny.

'Good enough, I guess,' said Snowdog with a shrug as Silver and Jonny Stomp each got behind the wheel of a truck. He vaulted into the cab of the truck next to him and slammed the

door behind him. He rolled down the side window and
leaned out, looking over his shoulder at Sergeant Tudeca as
the engines of trucks roared into life. He pulled out a wad of
bills, a chunk of the score from the Flesh Bar – minus what
he'd paid for a stolen shipment of guns from another crooked
supply sergeant the night before – and flicked it through the
air towards Tudeca.

The sergeant caught the money with a lopsided grin of
avarice.

'I can get more of this stuff in a little while,' he shouted, his
greed overcoming his natural cowardice. 'I just got to wait
until the heat dies down a little.'

Headlights speared from their mountings and the first truck
moved off into the night.

'Sounds good to me,' said Snowdog as he gunned the
engine of his truck.

'After all,' said Tudeca. 'Business is business.'

'Yeah,' agreed Snowdog. 'Business as usual.'

SEVEN

THE ORBITAL DOCKS of Chordelis were a scene of controlled anarchy, as every technician, shipwright and able-bodied man available was pressed into service repairing the terrible damage done by the tyranids to the vessels of the Imperial Navy following the Battle of Barbarus. A perimeter of local gunboats formed a picket line around the naval vessels, isolating them from the swarm of ships that rose from the surface of Chordelis in an uncontrolled tide.

Under the supervision of the Mortifactors' Techmarines, thick sheets of steel were welded onto the damaged sections of the *Mortis Probati* and fresh shells loaded into her magazines. The crews of the *Heroic Endeavour* and the sole surviving vessel of Hydra squadron swarmed around their hulls, jury-rigging repairs that would allow them to go into battle once more. No one was under any illusions that these repairs were anything more than temporary – each ship would need many months in dock to return to full service.

The *Vae Victus* had escaped comparatively unscathed. Her hull had been breached in four places, but none of the tyranid boarding organisms had penetrated further than the outer

decks and repairs would be a relatively simple matter. Not
that this was any consolation to Admiral Tiberius, who had
vowed that he would not forget the insult done to his ship by
the Mortifactors' impetuosity. The bulk of the work on her
hull had already been completed and beyond the picket line
of gunboats, Arx Praetora squadron and the Dauntless cruisers *Yermetov* and *Luxor* awaited to escort her on another
mission.

Since the warning of the tyranids' impending arrival had
reached Chordelis, the planet had been steadily emptying and
hundreds of vessels clogged the shipping lanes around the
world. Wealthy citizens with their own vessels were the first to
depart, closely followed by those able to book passage off-
world. Those with enough money fled deeper into the galactic
core while those unable to finance such a journey travelled on
commercial ships crammed with refugees that shuttled back
and forth between Chordelis and Tarsis Ultra. Greedy captains, scenting opportunity for profit, raised their prices
accordingly until even the wealthy fled as paupers.

But though millions escaped, millions more remained.
Panicked crowds flocked to every major spaceport, trying to
get to safety. Desperate to escape, men offered eternal service
and women offered themselves. Some were successful, more
were not, and fear spread like an epidemic through the people of Chordelis.

At Berliaas, desperate crowds demonstrated outside the governor's palace, demanding action be taken to evacuate the
populace. Tempers flared and thousands of angry citizens
stormed the palace only to find the planetary governor had
already fled Chordelis and that his missives for calm had been
broadcast from off-world.

In Dremander, the crew of a rogue trader's vessel opened
fire on people trying to commandeer their vessel, killing more
than seventy before being overrun and torn to pieces by the
angry mob.

Two days after this incident, more than eleven thousand
people died at Jaretaq, the planet's largest port, as terrified
crowds broke through the lines of Arbites guarding the
entrance and demanded passage on the fleet of departing
vessels thronging her landing platforms. As the luxury vessel *Cherrona* lifted from the planet's surface, angry crowds

prevented the ground crews from releasing her mooring cables. Her starboard engine was torn free of its mountings as her captain brought her about for departure. The engine dropped and blew apart like a bomb among the milling crowds and the ponderous vessel began sliding back towards the ground, the attraction of gravity too much for its remaining engine to fight. Fully laden with refugees and thousands of tonnes of fuel, the *Cherrona* swayed drunkenly in the air, striking the nearby control tower before slamming into the landing platforms of the spaceport.

The *Cherrona* exploded with the power of an orbital bombardment, hurling blazing sheets of fire and lethal fragments in all directions, scything through thousands of people and touching off scores of secondary explosions. The devastation ripped through the spaceport until almost nothing was left standing. The blazing pyres of this terrible disaster could be seen as far away as the planetary capital of Kaimes.

All across Chordelis, the same scenes played out as its terrified population fought to escape their doomed world.

THE COMMAND BRIDGE of the *Vae Victus* was tense and subdued as Admiral Tiberius kept his ship a respectable distance from the mighty structure that slid through space before them and filled the viewing bay. They had all heard of the disaster at Yulan and the loss of the third refinery, and Tiberius was determined that nothing similar would happen to this one.

'How close are we, Philotas?' whispered Tiberius, as though the volume of his voice would alert the tyranids to their presence, though the aliens must surely be aware of them by now. Garbled reports from Arx Praetora squadron and the Dauntless cruisers, some thirty thousand kilometres ahead of them, had spoken of the alien fleet moving in a solid mass of creatures, several hive ships scattered throughout the swarm. They were probably too far apart to catch more than one or two, but even one was a victory.

'Hard to say, admiral,' replied Philotas. 'Surveyor returns are being scattered by the refinery vessel, but I'd say no more than fifty thousand kilometres.'

'We're cutting this very close,' observed Uriel, staring at the plotting table. 'The first engagements at Barbarus were not much closer than this.'

'I know, Uriel, I know. But we only have one chance at this. Chordelis is depending on us. We cannot fail.'

Uriel nodded, determined that Chordelis would not suffer the horrible fate of Barbarus Prime. By now there was nothing left of that world but a dead hunk of rock, its people, wildlife and very ecosystem devoured by these monstrous aliens. Chordelis also faced obliteration, but in this case the threat did not come from the aliens, but from the very people supposed to be defending it.

The thought of Kryptman's cold, steel logic sent a shiver down Uriel's spine and he was reminded of the last time he had defied the will of an inquisitor. On this very ship, Inquisitor Ario Barzano had proposed the destruction of Pavonis to prevent a madman from obtaining a weapon capable of unmaking the stars themselves. Uriel had managed to persuade Barzano to give them one last chance to act and, by the grace of the Emperor, they had been successful, and Pavonis had been spared the horror of the ultimate sanction of viral bombing.

Once again he had been forced to stand against those he would have counted as his allies in defence of the ordinary men and women of the Imperium. It astounded him that Kryptman could be so unfeeling with the lives of millions of people, consigning an entire planet to death simply to prevent the enemy from taking it.

Only two days ago in the captain's chambers on the command deck of the *Argus*, Kryptman had told them of his decision to let Chordelis die.

'We have no choice,' the inquisitor had said. 'Fighters from the *Kharloss Vincennes* have harried the vanguard of the alien fleet from Barbarus, past Parosa and Yulan. The tyranids will be here within three or four days at the latest. There is simply no more time to get anyone else off Chordelis. If we stay any longer we will doom what little assets we have, and for what? We could fight, and we would gain perhaps a day's respite for the defenders on Tarsis Ultra. And once we are defeated, the tyranids will devour Chordelis as they did Barbarus Prime, swelling their numbers with an entire planet's biosphere.'

Kryptman shook his head. 'No, far better Chordelis dies by our own hand than that of the Great Devourer. Believe me, Exterminatus is a better, quicker death than the tyranids will offer.'

A stunned silence had greeted Kryptman's pronouncement. Admiral Bregant de Corte blanched and took a sip of amasec before taking a deep breath and casting his flinty gaze around the table. His assembled captains looked shocked, but took their lead from the admiral and said nothing. Captain Gaiseric and Astador nodded slowly.

Admiral Tiberius cleared his throat and leaned forwards, resting his elbows on the smooth table and steepling his fingers before him.

'There must be another way,' he said slowly, and Uriel was struck by yet another sense of déjà vu, remembering when Inquisitor Barzano had come to a similar decision.

'Admiral Tiberius is correct,' he said. 'What is the point of us being summoned to this system to defend it when our first reaction to these aliens' advance is to destroy everything in their path? You would have us stand victorious over a dead system.'

'You do not see the larger picture, Captain Ventris,' said Kryptman, emphasising the insignificance of his rank next to his own. 'We are at war with forces too terrible to comprehend, and one must sometimes sacrifice the smaller battles to be victorious in the larger war.'

'Listen to yourself,' snapped Uriel. 'You talk of sacrificing smaller battles. Do you not realise that you are talking about one of the Emperor's worlds, still populated by millions of His subjects, His soldiers? I think that it is you who forgets the "larger war".'

'No, Captain Ventris,' said Kryptman with finality. 'I do not.'

Uriel stood and slammed his fist on the table, splintering the wood. 'Every time these aliens invade the Emperor's realm we fall back. People like you claim we cannot fight them and we hear this so often we start to believe it. Well that stops now. I say we draw a line here and talk no more. This time, I say we stand and fight.'

'Captain Ventris, you forget your place,' said Chaplain Astador. 'We are here to fight the tyranids and if the learned inquisitor believes that this is the best course, who are you to question him?'

'I am a loyal servant of the Emperor and proud son of Roboute Guilliman. As I once thought you to be, and the fact that you even ask me that question shows me how wrong I was.'

Astador's face filled with thunder and the muscles along his jaw bunched in rage at Uriel's insult.

'While we are united in a common cause, I shall call you brother, but when this foe is defeated, there will be a reckoning between us,' promised Astador.

'I welcome it,' said Uriel, returning to his seat. 'You disgust me.'

'Gentlemen,' said Admiral de Corte. 'This is hardly the time for such discussions. The fate of an Imperial world lies before us and it ill becomes us to fight among ourselves like orks.'

'Thank you, Admiral de Corte,' said Kryptman. 'We waste valuable time in these discussions. The decision has already been made.'

'Lord inquisitor,' said Tiberius. 'I may have an alternative solution that you might consider. As we passed the orbital refineries of Yulan, I recalled my Ravensburg.'

Kryptman's eyes narrowed, his interest piqued by Tiberius's reference to the saviour of the Gothic sector, Lord Admiral Cornelius Ravensburg.

'Go on…'

And Tiberius went on to tell the story of the destruction of the *Unforgivable* and the actions of Commodore Kurtz during the defence of Delos IV. A buzz of excitement filled the room as Tiberius explained the actions he had set in motion upon passing Yulan and the potential it had.

Even now, days later, Uriel could not believe the ease with which Kryptman had decided the fate of millions. To the inquisitor these were just numbers, but to Uriel they were living, breathing people – subjects of the God-Emperor and deserving of protection. He shook himself from his reverie, focussing on the present as the sacristy bell began ringing and Tiberius descended from his command pulpit to stand beside the plotting table.

'All stop,' he ordered. 'Come to new heading zero-six-five.'

'All stop, aye,' confirmed Philotas. 'Altering heading now.'

Uriel and Tiberius shared a nervous look as the image before them slid to the left. As their engines decreased power, only the momentum of the ship kept them moving forwards. Slowly, but surely, the vast hydrogen-plasma refinery shrank in the viewing bay and a palpable sense of relief spread throughout the bridge as the distance between the *Vae Victus* and the perilous colossus increased.

As the refinery diminished, the hazy outline of an indistinct halo grew around its edges. At first, Uriel thought this was the corona of distant stars around the vast refinery, but as it drifted further away, he could see that it was actually the outer edges of the tyranid fleet's vanguard.

'Guilliman's oath,' breathed Uriel as the scale of the alien fleet became apparent. Truly they had engaged but a fraction around Barbarus Prime. The viewing bay was filled with specks of reflected light that could only be tyranid organisms and their sheer number defied counting. There seemed to be no end to the alien swarm and Uriel felt a stirring of unreasoning dread settle in his belly at the vastness of the tyranid fleet.

Even the tyranid forces he had fought on Ichar IV could not compare to the size of this fleet and, for the briefest second, he wondered if Kryptman might not have been right. Could they ever prevail against such a huge horde?

'Courage and honour,' said Tiberius, seeing the effect the size of the tyranid fleet was having on his crew. 'They are many, but we have seen they can die and we know they can be defeated. And more than this, we have faith in the Emperor. Trust in Him and the primarch and we will prevail.'

'Arx Praetora squadron is coming into view,' said Philotas. 'Some damage to all ships, but nothing serious.'

'Good. And the Dauntless cruisers?'

'*Yermetov* holding position on our portside, *Luxor* is moving forward to cover our rapid strike cruisers.'

'And the tyranids?'

'Following close behind.'

THE CREATURES INQUISITOR Kryptman had referred to as kraken drifted towards the gargantuan shape of the hydrogen-plasma refinery behind a protective screen of spores. As the spores drew near, they sped off on spurts of hot gasses towards the refinery, exploding and spraying its structure with chitinous shrapnel. But it was too vast to be more than scratched by such pinpricks.

Detecting that the spores were having little effect, a number of kraken sped forwards, spraying the colossal vessel with foaming bio-plasma and lashing its upper pylons with razor-edged tentacles. They tore huge chunks of armaplas and steel from its structure, but as vicious as their attacks were, they could do little to damage it.

More kraken surged past the refinery, speeding towards the vessels that escorted it, particularly the smaller darts of Arx Praetora squadron. Unbearably bright lances of powerful energy weapons stabbed from the prow weapons of the *Luxor*, slicing through a pair of kraken and the others scattered, abandoning their chase of the rapid strike cruisers in favour of this new, bigger prey. The *Luxor* heeled sideways as her engines fought to reverse her course and her bow swung smoothly around. More lance shots from the *Yermetov* raked the tyranid organisms as the *Luxor* made her turn until none remained close enough to threaten her.

The cruisers powered away from the creatures attacking the refinery ship as swarms of tyranids flocked towards the massive vessel. They latched on wherever they could and bit, dissolved or exploded as their genetic purpose determined. Within minutes the entire vessel was obscured by a teeming mass of frenzied creatures, each desperate to destroy this threat to their hive.

But such was the solidity of the refinery's construction that none of the creatures could penetrate its hull and soon it had drifted deep within the mass of the swarm, and a single hive ship, itself more massive than the refinery altered its course to attack. City-sized gouts of acidic sprays lashed the side of the refinery, organic matter running molten alongside inorganic as the hive ship lashed the refinery.

Giant feeder tentacles looped outwards from the hive ship's gnarled carapace and latched onto the massive vessel, effortlessly dragging it towards a cavernous orifice in its body ringed with thousands of grinding teeth.

URIEL AND TIBERUS marched to the end of the command nave and watched the massive hive ship begin to devour the vast refinery, now scarcely visible, its surface buried under a heaving mass of tyranid organisms. Tiberus paused to savour the moment before his next action.

Uriel watched the tyranid organisms attacking the refinery and felt his lip curl in a sneer of contempt. Aliens were going to die and the thought pleased him. In his mind's eye he could see the black spectre of death floating above the tyranid fleet and felt a surge of heady anticipation at the thought of the vast scale of destruction about to be unleashed. He felt the power that comes of knowing that another being lives only because you have chosen not to kill it yet, and the sensation surged like an electric charge around his body.

His fists clenched. He could feel hot anger flooding his system and the desire to strike out at these aliens, his head filling with visions of bloody fields littered with tyranid beasts.

Uriel tasted blood and realised he had bitten his own tongue, the sharp metallic taste bringing him back to the present with a jolt.

Uriel's hearts were beating a wild tattoo on his ribs and sweat beaded on his brow. He took a breath, feeling the purity of the incense-scented air run like a cleansing breath through him.

'Are you alright, Uriel?' asked Tiberius, noticing the captain's discomfort.

'Yes,' managed Uriel. 'I am.'

Tiberius nodded and returned his attention to the viewing bay.

'You have a firing solution?' he asked without turning.

'Yes, lord admiral,' said Philotas, unable to conceal the excitement in his voice.

A respectful silence enveloped the bridge as Tiberius turned and marched back to his command pulpit, leaving Uriel to stand at the viewing bay. He mounted the steps and took his place at the head of the bridge.

He placed both hands either side of the lectern and simply said, 'Fire.'

THE VAE VICTUS shuddered as her prow bombardment cannon unleashed a building-sized projectile from its flash-protected barrel. Travelling at phenomenal speed, it closed the distance between the *Vae Victus* and its target in less than a minute.

The target point had been carefully selected: the weakest point of the refinery's armour, where an explosion would cause the most damage to the internal plasma tanks. Packed with millions of tonnes of highly volatile hydrogen-plasma compound, the refinery vessel was now a gargantuan flying bomb. The shell from the bombardment cannon struck it amidships, punching through metres of thick reinforcement, a delayed fuse ensuring that it did not detonate until it was deep within the heart of its target.

The shell exploded within the largest of the plasma tanks, instantly igniting the unstable compound and setting in motion a chain reaction like the one that had destroyed the third refinery in orbit around Yulan.

As though sensing the danger, the hive ship released its grip on the refinery, but by then it was already too late. Millions of tonnes of flammable chemicals ignited and exploded like the birth of a new star. Every creature attacking the refinery was incinerated, the fireball expanding in a lethal wave front and engulfing countless other swarm creatures. Kraken, drones and spores were all burned to death in the initial fireball and thousands more suffered fatal concussive injuries from the massive blast front that followed the detonation.

The hive ship had spent millennia traversing the void between galaxies and its hide was as thick as any starship's armour, but even it was helpless in the face of so much ferocious energy. Its entire body vanished in the initial fireball, its remains blasted to atoms by the shockwave that followed in the wake of the fiery explosion.

In a fraction of a second, a creature that had taken centuries of years to grow and evolve into its current form was obliterated and wiped from the galaxy as though it had never existed.

FOR THE NINTH day in a row, the defenders of Tarsis Ultra collapsed in weary resignation. Learchus watched them, a fierce pride burning in his chest as he saw the last man drop to his haunches and remove his pack. He himself had not even broken a sweat, but his physique was such that he could have run for days before requiring any rest. He smiled as he wandered through the exhausted soldiers, aware of their angry stares and muttered curses.

The men of each regiment were performing well and a shared sense of comradeship had flourished in them all. That it had come about through a shared hatred of him did not concern him, he knew it was a passing thing. While the enemy was still distant, soldiers needed a common target for their hate and their aggression. Learchus vividly remembered Chaplain Clausel at Agiselus and how much he had hated him during his training. Clausel was now a trusted friend and mentor and had brought great spiritual solace to the men of Fourth company in the dark times of its long, proud history.

Major Satria staggered towards Learchus, his face red and streaked with sweat.

'Damn, but you're working us hard,' he gasped.

'The tyranids will work you harder,' said Learchus.

'True,' nodded Satria, bending over and resting his palms on his knees and sucking down great draughts of cool air. The major had lost weight and, since the training had begun, had shed the silver breastplate and peaked cap his rank entitled him to. His shoulder-length black hair was slicked with sweat and there was more of a swagger in his step now.

Orderlies and volunteers from the citizenry of Erebus began circulating among the panting soldiers, distributing hot food and potable water from sloshing drums. Dehydration among the soldiers had become a serious problem, with many simply eating unmelted snow, which could contain disease and dangerously lower the body's temperature.

Learchus had also put a stop to the men's rations of amasec, caffeine and bac-stics. All these vices made soldiers susceptible to dehydration and though it had almost caused a riot when first announced, Learchus knew that his decision was paying off as the number of reported dehydration injuries had dropped significantly.

Cases of foot-rot had been widespread in the early days of training, with the thick, rubberised boots of many of the soldiers trapping the moisture of their sweat and causing necrotic fungal growths to fester. Soldiers from the Logres regiment had allowed the design of their standard issue footwear to be copied by the factories of Erebus and within days, each company of soldiers was issued with dozens of pairs of socks, anti-fungal powder and brand new boots that allowed the pores of their feet to breathe.

Learchus had been impressed by the efficiency of Sebastien Montante, the Fabricator Marshal of Erebus. He had judged him an empty headed fool when they had first met. Though he was no soldier, the man's talents for organisational logistics was second to none and virtually every request Learchus had made for supplies or equipment had been met within hours.

Montante was proving to be a valuable ally, but the same could not be said for every member of the Council of Industry who helped govern Erebus. Only three days ago, Learchus had sat with the nine members of the council in the Chamber of the Mosaic, outlining his plans for the defence of the inner reaches of the valley. He remembered the shame of losing his temper at their foolishness. The foolishness of one member in particular.

Simon van Gelder.

The man Learchus had prevented from leaving the city carried the weight of his humiliation around his neck and was determined to return the favour.

'We simply cannot allow Sergeant Learchus to demolish the buildings between the walls,' said van Gelder, sipping his wine. 'Why, when the aliens are driven off, we will be penniless paupers, lords over a ruined city with nothing but its wreckage to call our own.'

'If you do not destroy them, you will have no city at all,' explained Learchus.

'The many years of peace we have enjoyed have made us complacent,' put in Montante, gesturing at the walls around them. 'Look at the mosaic here. It is clear from this that we should not have been so reckless in our building programs. The original city plans, designed by Roboute Guilliman himself, show us that there should be no structures in these areas.'

'Pah,' snapped van Gelder, with a wave of his hand. 'A faded mosaic, thousands of years old, is no basis for forcing us into economic ruin, Sebastien. What will we do when our brave defenders defeat the tyranids? How can we produce goods with no manufactories?'

'Simon, we can rebuild,' said Montante. 'But we must be alive to do so. Please listen to Sergeant Learchus.'

'Many of the buildings you own have been constructed too close to the walls, Mr van Gelder. If we are forced to pull back from a wall or the tyranids capture one, then we will be providing them with valuable cover under which to approach.'

'You speak of the regions around District Quintus? These regions are over thirty kilometres from the valley mouth. Do you mean to tell me that you expect these damnable aliens to breach our fair city that far? That you don't have the ability to stop them before that? Forgive me, but I had thought the

Ultramarines to be warriors of great strength and courage. It would seem I was misinformed.'

Learchus surged to his feet and grabbed van Gelder by the front of his robes, hauling him across the table and snarling in his face. Wine spilled over the table and a goblet shattered on the stone floor.

'You dare insult our honour?' spat Learchus. 'You would do well to consider your next words, van Gelder, for if you utter such an insult again, I will kill you.'

The council sat stunned as Learchus fought to control his rage, unwilling to intervene on their fellow council member's behalf for fear that the Space Marine's anger would be turned on them. The only sounds were van Gelder's panicked breath and the drip of wine to the floor. Sebastien Montante rose slowly from the bench and put a hand on Learchus's forearm.

'Sergeant Learchus,' he said softly. 'I am sure that Mr van Gelder meant no offence, did you Simon?'

Van Gelder hurriedly shook his head.

'There, you see?' continued Montante. 'They were words spoken in haste, in the heat of the moment. Please, Learchus, if you would be so kind, would you return Mr van Gelder to his seat?'

Learchus let out a hissing breath and released his grip on van Gelder, who collapsed back onto the bench opposite with a plaintive moan. His face was ashen, though it took only seconds for his anger to return to the surface. Montante saw it coming and headed him off.

'Simon, before you say anything, I believe we have come as far as we can today and should adjourn until tomorrow morning. Agreed?'

A hurried nod of heads signalled the council's assent and after a tense pause, van Gelder had also nodded, making his way from the chamber of the mosaic without another word.

At the following day's meeting, van Gelder had been conspicuous by his absence and a missive sent to his home in the high valley inviting him to the meeting was returned unopened. A vote was taken in the matter of the demolition of his properties, the council unanimously supporting Learchus's plan.

The memory of his loss of temper shamed Learchus and he had spent every night since that moment in penitent prayer.

'How goes the work in the lower valley?' asked Learchus as Satria gratefully took a mug of water from a robed orderly, gulping it down like sweet wine.

'We've almost finished preparing the ground between the first two walls, but it's slow going. The ground's frozen solid and takes an age to break apart, even with earth moving machines.'

'We need to have the trenches completed within the next two weeks. The tyranids will be upon us by then.'

'They will be, don't worry. The men are working as hard as they can, I assure you.'

'Good. They are a credit to you, Major Satria.'

'Thank you, though you may want to tell *them* that.'

'I intend to. When they hate me more than their worst nightmare.'

'Believe me, I think they hate you more than that already,' said Satria. 'The fact that you so easily outperform them in training infuriates them. I think they feel you are showing off.'

'They are correct; I am showing off by training with them,' said Learchus. 'I want them to know that I am superior to them, for when it comes time for me to build them up, they must feel that my praise truly means something. I will make them feel like they are heroes, I will make them believe they are the greatest warriors in the galaxy.'

'You're a sneaky one, aren't you?' said Satria eventually.

'I have my moments,' smiled Learchus.

THE SMALL FLOTILLA of Imperial ships made best speed towards Chordelis, the rapid strike cruisers of Arx Praetora leading the way with the *Vae Victus*, *Yermetov* and *Luxor* following closely behind. The mood aboard the ships was cautiously optimistic. If another hive ship could be destroyed in a similar manner, might not the orbital defences combined with the fleet and system defence ships hold the tyranid fleet at bay, perhaps even prevent the aliens from putting a single clawed foot upon the soil of Tarsis Ultra?

On the bridge of the *Vae Victus*, Admiral Tiberius sipped from a goblet of water, discussing the tactical possibilities that lay before them with Uriel.

'We might yet make these damned aliens regret they came this way, Uriel,' he said.

'I think we might,' agreed the captain of the Fourth company. 'The defences around Tarsis Ultra are strong, and the last refinery should even now be rigged with lethal explosives.'

'If we can destroy another hive ship, then the overmind might decide to avoid Chordelis.'

'And that will be a victory in more ways than one,' said Uriel darkly.

'Be careful, Uriel,' warned Tiberius. 'Kryptman is not a man to cross, the power of the Inquisition is his to command. Were it not for him, Macragge might well have fallen to hive fleet Behemoth.'

'Did you ever meet him during the war?'

'Aye,' nodded Tiberius. 'He was young back then, full of the fires of an inquisitor who had found his true vocation.'

'Did he ever advocate the destruction of Macragge?'

Tiberius laughed. 'No, Uriel, he did not. I do not think that even Inquisitor Kryptman, as he was back then, would have dared voice such a thought. Lord Calgar would never have allowed it.'

'Do you think Lord Calgar would have allowed Chordelis to be destroyed?'

Tiberius rubbed a hand across his skull, considering the question before replying.

'I do not know, Uriel. Our Chapter Master is a man of great wisdom and compassion, but he is also a strategist of sound logic and I think that perhaps you and I are too fond of the idea of saving everyone we can. Lord Inquisitor Kryptman was correct when he said that sometimes you need to lose the occasional battle to win the war.'

'I cannot accept that,' said Uriel. 'The destruction of the Emperor's loyal subjects cannot be right.'

'We cannot always do what is right, Uriel. There is often a great gulf in the difference between the way things are and the way we believe they should be. Sometimes we must learn to accept the things we cannot change.'

'No, lord admiral, I believe we must endeavour to change the things we cannot accept. It is by striving against that which is perceived as wrong that makes a great warrior. The primarch himself said that when a warrior makes peace with his fear and stands against it, he becomes a true hero. For if you do not fear a thing, where is the courage in standing against it?'

'You are an idealist, Uriel, and the galaxy can be a cruel place for people like you,' said Tiberius. 'But still I wish there were more who thought as you do. You are a great warrior, able to bring swift death to your enemies, but you have never lost sight of why you fight: the survival of the human race.'

Uriel bowed his head to the venerable admiral, pleased to have been complimented. He gripped the hilt of his sword as Philotas approached bearing a data-slate, his angular features sombre.

Tiberius took the slate and quickly scanned its contents, his mouth dropping open in horror and disbelief.

'Open the viewing bay, now!' he barked. 'Maximum magnification.'

The brass shutters concertinaed back smoothly from the bay at the front of the bridge as Tiberius descended to the table, calling up the tactical plots of the surrounding area. He muttered to himself and Uriel could see from the pulsing vein in the admiral's temple that his fury had built to an incandescent level. He had never seen Tiberius so angry before.

'Admiral, what is it?' he asked.

Tiberius handed Uriel the data-slate as the shutters of the viewing bay finally folded back. He read the words at the same time as what they said was displayed on the viewing bay.

Even at maximum magnification, the planet before them barely filled the viewing bay, reflected light from the distant sun rippling across its heaving, fiery surface. Firestorms were raging across the dead planet as flammable gasses released from oceans of decaying organic matter enveloped it, scouring the surface to bare, lifeless rock.

The tyranids themselves could do no more thorough a job.

'Sweet heavens, no…' breathed Uriel, the data-slate dropping from his fingers. 'How?'

'The Mortifactors,' said Tiberius sadly. 'Kryptman lied to us. He had no intention of making a stand here.'

Uriel said nothing as the world of Chordelis burned.

PHASE III – ATTACK

EIGHT

THE QUARTERS OF Captain Uriel Ventris were spartan and clean, as befitted the leader of the Fourth company of the Ultramarines. A simple cot bed with a single linen sheet sat in one corner of the cell below the Ventris family shield. Next to the bed stood a thin-legged table upon which sat a clay jug filled with wine and a pair of silver goblets. Various recording crystals sat in neat piles next to the jug and at the foot of the bed lay an open, gunmetal grey footlocker containing simple blue robes and exercise garments.

Uriel poured himself a generous measure of wine from the jug and sat on the edge of his bed, swirling the crimson liquid around the goblet. He tipped his head back and drained the glass in one long swallow. The strong flavour made him grimace as the sight of the burning world in the viewing bay returned to him. He wondered how many people had been on Chordelis when the virus bombs hit. How many hundreds of thousands had Kryptman sacrificed in the name of the larger war?

The thought saddened him and he poured another glass, raising it in a toast to the dead of Chordelis. He downed the

drink and poured yet another, suddenly desiring the oblivion
that only alcohol could provide.

He had been able to stop Inquisitor Barzano from destroying Pavonis, but he had not saved Chordelis and the weight of
that failure was now a dark stain upon his soul. Had the people even known what was happening when the first bombs
had exploded in the atmosphere?

The life-eater virus was quick to act and utterly lethal in its
effects. Perhaps some had an inkling of what was being done
to their world, but most would probably have succumbed
without realising the magnitude of the betrayal visited upon
them. The atmosphere would be saturated with mutagenic
toxins that attacked the biological glue that held organic matter together, breaking it down with horrifying rapidity. Within
hours there would be nothing left alive and the virus would
be forced to turn on itself in an unthinking act of viral self-
cannibalism. The planet's surface would be covered by a thick
layer of decayed sludge, wreathed in vast clouds of toxic waste
matter. All it would take was a single shot from orbit to ignite
the fumes and firestorms of apocalyptic magnitude would
sweep the entire surface of the planet bare.

Uriel had seen the horror of Exterminatus and had even
been part of an expedition to administer the ultimate sanction
once before, on a Chaos tainted planet whose population had
become base savages practising human sacrifice to their dark
gods. Under certain circumstances, such destruction was
appropriate, even necessary, but this act of murder sat badly
with Uriel and he could not find it in himself to forgive what
Kryptman and the Mortifactors had done.

His mind was filled with contradictions and doubt as he
pondered the ramifications of what had happened at
Chordelis. In following the plan of Admiral Tiberius, they had
exercised initiative and reacted to the developing situation
with an original idea. They had not referred to the Codex
Astartes and, much as he hated to admit it, the Mortifactors
were closer to the correct procedure as laid down in that holy
tome. What then did that tell him?

A knock came at his door and Uriel said, 'Enter.'

The door slid open and Pasanius stood in the doorway, his
bulk filling the frame. He wore his devotional robes; his
armour – like Uriel's – being repaired in the company forge

three decks below. The silver of his bionic arm reflected the flickering candlelight from the passageway outside.

'I have a problem, captain,' began Pasanius, 'I've got a jug of wine and if there's one thing I know, it's that it's not good to drink on your own. Care to help me finish it?'

Uriel managed a wan smile and waved Pasanius inside. There was nowhere to sit, so Pasanius sat on the floor, resting his back against the wall. Uriel handed him two goblets, and he filled them with wine. Pasanius handed one back to Uriel and raised the other to his nose. He closed his eyes and smelled the heady aroma of wild berries and blackcurrants laced with a subtle hint of aged oak.

'This is the good stuff,' said Pasanius. 'Bottled on Tarentus in the year seven hundred and eighty-three, which, I'm reliably informed, was a good year for the vineyards on the southern slopes of the Hill of the Red Blossoms.'

Uriel sipped the wine, nodding appreciatively and the pair lapsed into a companionable silence, each lost in his own thoughts.

Eventually, Pasanius said, 'So do you want to tell me what's bothering you, or do I need to wait until you're drunk?'

'I have not been drunk since Agiselus, you remember?' said Uriel.

Pasanius laughed. 'Aye, Chaplain Clausel shut us out on the mountains and left us there for three days.'

'Emperor save me, but he was a hard bastard back then.'

'He still is, it's just he's on our side now.'

'Clausel would assign you a month of fasting if he heard you say that.'

'Maybe, but I know you won't tell him.'

'True,' agreed Uriel, taking another drink. The wine would not get either of them remotely drunk thanks to the preomnor, an implanted pre-digestive stomach that analysed and neutralised virtually any toxins, including alcohol. Nevertheless the two friends still enjoyed the taste of a fine wine.

'I have been having doubts, Pasanius,' said Uriel finally.

'About what?'

'A lot of things,' said Uriel. 'I was thinking about Captain Idaeus and everything he taught me about thinking beyond the scope of the codex. At the time I could not make the leap of initiative to believe what he said, but the more we fought together, the more I could see what he said put into practice.'

'Aye, he was a wild one, was Idaeus,' agreed Pasanius. 'But clever too. He knew when to bend the rules and when not to.'

'That's the problem, Pasanius. I don't know if I can do what he did... if I can understand when to follow the codex and when to think laterally.'

'You're doing fine, captain. The men of the company trust you and would follow you into the very fires of hell. Isn't that enough?'

'No, Pasanius, not by a long way. I thought Captain Idaeus was right, but now I see the Mortifactors and I wonder where his line of thinking will lead. If we follow his beliefs to their logical conclusion, will we end up like them?'

'No, of course not. Chaplain Astador said it himself: he and his Chapter are a product of their homeworld. He told me all about Posul and, if you ask me, it sounds like a vision of hell. Permanently shrouded in darkness, with each tribe fighting to kill one another so they can prove that they're the most brutal and be chosen to become Space Marines of the Mortifactors. A culture like that breeds a contempt for life and we should have seen it the moment they sided with Kryptman.'

'But we didn't.'

'No,' shrugged Pasanius. 'Hindsight is a wonderful thing.'

'I know, but look at what happened to Chordelis. We broke with the Codex Astartes to send that refinery into the swarm, the Mortifactors followed an inquisitor's direction and an Imperial world died. But I know we did the right thing, morally, in trying to save Chordelis, despite the logic of Kryptman's argument.'

Uriel slammed his goblet down on the table, spilling wine across his data crystals and bedsheet. 'I feel like a blind man who cannot feel the path before him.'

'Well, nobody ever said that the Emperor's service was supposed to be easy,' said Pasanius, pouring another two goblets of wine.

LORD INQUISITOR KRYPTMAN watched the *Vae Victus* dock with the northern pier of the star fort through its central basilica's main viewing bay, feeling a surge of unfamiliar excitement pound through his veins. He stood with his hands laced behind his back, wearing the formal robes of an inquisitor of the Ordo Xenos. Captain Ventris would know by now that he had lied to him about giving Chordelis a chance to live, but there was no use now in pointless recriminations. The tyranids had to be defeated by any means necessary.

Admiral Tiberius would understand that, but Ventris was the protégé of Captain Idaeus, a captain he had seen on Macragge following the defeat of hive fleet Behemoth. He would need to be wary of Ventris's puritannical anger.

Fortunately, he had sufficient force to ensure that Ventris would be kept in line.

The blue and white curve of Tarsis Ultra shone at the bottom of the viewing bay, dozens of system ships and defence monitors hanging in orbit around the planet. There was a formidable force arrayed here and the Ultramarines' demonstration of how effective a weapon the refineries could be as floating bombs had not gone unnoticed. The last refinery hung in high orbit, a fleet of servitor-manned tugs ready to drag her into the heart of the tyranid fleet and unleash fiery destruction.

The inquisitor limped to his desk and sat behind its sweeping nalwood expanse. It had been commissioned hundreds of years ago for his mentor from a world whose name he could not now remember, and was a work of impressive craftsmanship. It never failed to intimidate those who came before him – not that he expected a Space Marine to be intimidated by a mere desk – but it gave him a sense of place whenever he sat behind it.

He knew that the Ultramarines would even now be on their way to his chambers.

Kryptman touched the vox-bead at his collar and said, 'Captain Bannon, could you and Chaplain Astador come in here.'

URIEL MARCHED PAST frightened-looking naval ratings and techs as he, Tiberius and Pasanius made their way towards the basilica of the star fort. The orbital space station was a massive construction, impossibly ancient and, together with the others in the linked chain, powerful enough to defeat a battleship together with any attendant escorts, and even through his anger, Uriel could see that they would be potent weapons in the fight against the tyranids.

As they had drawn closer to the star fort, he had seen the vast shape of the last refinery anchored thousands of kilometres away from the nearest vessel, remotely piloted ships packing its structure with even more explosives. Proof positive that Kryptman had never intended to save Chordelis.

The trio passed through the northern quadrant of the star fort, entering the central basilica where Inquisitor Kryptman awaited. A black uniformed armsman directed them to the chambers the inquisitor had requisitioned and as they approached the door, Admiral Tiberius took hold of Uriel's arm and said, 'Remember, Uriel. Kryptman is not a man to cross, so be mindful of what you say.'

'I will,' promised Uriel and rapped his gauntlet on the door, pushing inside without waiting for an answer. Tiberius nodded briskly to Pasanius, who swiftly followed his captain inside.

Uriel pulled up short as he saw Kryptman seated behind an ugly desk of a dark wood, two Space Marines flanking him. He recognised Astador and took the other for one of the Mortifactors until he saw the silver inquisitorial symbol on his left shoulder guard. The yellow of the Imperial Fists Chapter on his other shoulder was a stark contrast to the midnight black of his armour, his skin deeply tanned and his hair a close-cropped blond.

'Ah, Captain Ventris,' said Kryptman. 'Allow me to introduce Captain Bannon of the Deathwatch.'

'Deathwatch...' breathed Uriel. The Chamber Militant of the Ordo Xenos, the elite alien fighters in which he himself had once served for a decade. Kryptman had said that he had requested a Deathwatch kill team, but Uriel had not expected them to arrive in time for the coming conflict.

Formidable killers of xeno creatures, each member of the Deathwatch was chosen from the finest warriors of his Chapter to serve for a time with the Ordo Xenos to combat the threat of aliens throughout the galaxy. There were none better qualified to join this fight than the Deathwatch, and seeing the stylised skull symbol on Bannon's shoulder guard immediately filled Uriel with fresh hope.

He marched towards the gaudy desk and leaned forwards, resting his fists on its surface. He locked eyes with the inquisitor and said, 'You lied to us.'

'You allowed yourself be lied to, Uriel,' said Kryptman. 'Did you really think I was a man who changes his mind on a whim?'

'No, but I thought you were a man of your word. Everything I have learned of you has led me to believe that you were a man of honour.'

'Then you are naïve indeed,' said Kryptman. 'I am a man who gets the job done.'

'Even if that means murdering innocent people?'

'If it proves necessary, then yes.'

'I do not know who I hate more just now. You do not see the tyranids killing one another to achieve victory.'

'Not yet,' answered Kryptman with a sly smile.

'You would do well to watch your tone, Captain Ventris,' said Astador, circling the desk to stand face to face with Uriel. 'Your Chapter owes this man its very existence.'

'Get away from me, Astador,' warned Uriel.

'You will mind your place, Captain Ventris,' said Astador. 'We all have a part to play in this war. You must accept yours as I accept mine.'

Uriel felt his anger towards Astador flare and before he knew what he was doing, he hammered a thunderous right cross against the Chaplain's jaw. Astador spun backwards, crashing into the wall, but before Uriel could capitalise on the surprise of his attack, he felt a powerful grip encircle his neck and a burning heat prickle the skin beneath his jawline.

'If you so much as move, I will plunge this power knife up through your soft palate and into your brain,' said Captain Bannon. Astador surged to his feet, a killing light in his eyes, and in them, Uriel could see the feral tribal warrior he had been on Posul.

But before he could move, Pasanius was there, his massive hand wrapped around the Mortifactor's neck. He held the struggling Chaplain in a grip of steel.

'Don't,' he said.

'All of you, stop this madness now!' bellowed Tiberius, stepping into the centre of the room. He stared at Bannon and said, 'Take that knife away from my captain's throat,' before turning to Pasanius.

'Sergeant, let go of Chaplain Astador and step away from him.'

Pasanius looked round at Uriel, who nodded, the movement almost imperceptible due to the glowing amber blade at his neck, and released the Mortifactor. Astador's eyes blazed fury, but he made no aggressive moves and Pasanius stepped back, radiating threat and the promise of fresh violence should the Chaplain attempt anything further.

Bannon withdrew the knife from Uriel's neck and said, 'I know of you, Captain Ventris, and I have a great respect for what you have done in the past, but we must be united in this common cause. It ill becomes us to fight amongst ourselves when there is a terrible foe who seeks to destroy us all.'

Uriel nodded and unconsciously rubbed his neck where the burning edge of Bannon's power knife had singed his skin.

'Captain Bannon speaks true,' said Tiberius. 'We are all servants of the divine God-Emperor and must comport ourselves accordingly. We are not animals or blasphemers who have cast off the codes of moral behaviour. There is to be no more violence between us.'

The tension in the room slowly ebbed away and Bannon offered his hand to Uriel.

Uriel took a deep, calming breath before taking Bannon's hand, feeling the killing rage drain from his body, leaving him vulnerable and ashamed. Deep inside he felt the touch of an ancient being within him and heard its diabolical laughter echoing within his soul.

'Come,' said Kryptman, when he sensed his audience had calmed. 'We have much to discuss. While we have been fighting the tyranid fleet, Magos Locard has been busy in the biologis research labs on Tarsis Ultra and his findings are most illuminating...'

BLINDING CLOUDS OF hot steam filled the train platform as another land train pulled into its designated berth and Pren Fallows, the platform overseer, cursed as his snow goggles fogged with condensation. He pulled off the goggles and wiped the inner face clear with the sleeve of his overalls. There was precious little snow here anyway, the heat generated by the land trains and the hundreds of milling people soon turned the snow and ice to a shin deep mucky slush.

Trains had been arriving daily for the past month, each laden with frightened farming communities from the outlying regions and, as the largest city on Tarsis Ultra, Erebus had been receiving the majority of these refugees. As if the city wasn't crowded enough already. Pren shrugged, pushing his way through the crowds and making his way to the control booth that overlooked the platform.

Seventeen train berths and fifty track lines radiated from the docking bays. He and his staff of seventy men had pulled double shifts for the last two months, ensuring that each train had deposited its human cargo and then departed on time to pick up yet more. It was thankless, dirty work and there was precious little reward to be had, but it was the life the Emperor had chosen for him and though he knew it would do no good to complain, Pren Fallows was not the kind of man to let that stop him.

Powerful arc lights mounted on steel towers bathed the platforms in a ghostly white light, and despite the heat, his breath fogged before him. Yellow coated provosts from the city Commissariat directed people from the docking station, taking names on clipboards and directing them to the Ministorum camps further up the valley.

It was a scene of organised chaos, but this train had been the last of the day and there were no more scheduled until noon the following day, which would allow Pren and his crew to enjoy a well-earned break.

As the provosts escorted the last of the refugees from the station, a blessed calm descended. Pren stopped and smiled, enjoying the dead quiet of a winter's night and an empty station.

He climbed the rusted iron ladder to the control booth, stamping the slush from his boots before pushing open the door.

'Close the damn door!' shouted Halan Urquart, his deputy controller, who sat before a bank of controls, his feet up on the table, drinking a cup of hot caffeine. 'You're letting all the damn heat out.'

'Sometimes I wonder if you understand who's in charge here, Halan,' replied Pren, unfastening the wax-lubricated zipper on his winter coat and hanging it on a hook on the back of the door.

'Yeah, I wonder that sometimes too.'

'Anything to report?' asked Pren, brushing the ice from his beard.

'Nah, it's been real quiet. The provosts seem to have finally got the hang of moving people out of here without bothering us.'

'About bloody time,' commented Pren, pouring himself a mug of caffeine. It was lukewarm, but beggars couldn't be choosers. He pulled up a seat next to the window, watching as another flurry of snow began to fall, coating the platforms in a fresh blanket of pristine white.

Pren lifted the station logs from the basket tray beside Halan and began flicking through his deputy's scrawled handwriting. He sipped his caffeine, noting that the turnaround times for the land trains was as quick as it had been even before the war. He'd need to remember and say a few encouraging words to his staff come the morning.

He flipped over to another page, glancing up as a shiver passed down his spine. He put down his mug and stared out the misting window, squinting through the fogged glass at the twin pinpricks of light that were approaching the station.

'What the hell…' he muttered.

'What's up, chief?' asked Halan.

'Look,' said Pren, pointing in the direction of the mysterious lights.

'What the hell…' said Halan.

'I know,' said Pren. 'I thought we were all done for today.'

'We are, I don't know what that is.'

The men watched as the two points of light drew closer through the night's darkness, their sense of apprehension growing with their brightness. As the lights got closer, they came within the glow cast by the tower lights. Halan and Pren both breathed a sigh of relief as they saw the sleek shape of a land train glide smoothly into the station, its sides and roof coated in a thick layer of frost.

The train slowed and came to a complete halt at the end of the furthest platform, its doors jerkily sliding open. Pren and Halan waited for the inevitable crowds to emerge, but nobody disembarked from the train. It simply sat, silent and unmoving on the far end of the platform, steam venting from the grilles around its engines and the track.

Both men shared an uneasy glance.

'I guess we should go down and have a look,' suggested
Pren.

'I just knew you were going to say that,' said Halan, pulling
on his winter coat and gloves.

Pren grabbed a portable illuminator and donned his
winter gear, following his deputy outside into the biting
cold. He clambered down the frosted ladder and trudged
alongside Halan through the fresh snow towards the
unmoving land train. As they drew nearer, they could see
the windows of the train were dark and opaque with frost,
even those of the driver's cab, and their sense of unease
grew stronger.

The darkness and silence of the docking station, normally a
relief after the hectic bustle of a day's work now pressed in
around them and Pren wished some of the provosts were still
left in the station. At least they were armed.

He gripped Halan's arm and the man nearly jumped out of
his skin.

'Guilliman's oath!' swore Halan. 'Don't do that!'

'Look, you can see the train's number on the engine.'

'So?'

'Well we can tell which bloody train this is and why it's here
now, you idiot.'

'Oh, right,' said Halan, pulling out a data-slate from his coat
and scrolling through a list of numbers, eventually stopping
at the train's designation.

'Got it. This was due in last week.'

'Last week? And no one noticed it was missing?'

'I guess not, we've been pretty busy here you know.'

'True,' said Pren. 'Well, where's it come from?'

'According to this, it was under the supervision of a Lieutenant Quinn from the Logres regiment. They were picking up
refugees from across the north-eastern districts. Their last stop
was at Prandium and they should have been here six days ago.
I guess the train must've come in on auto.'

Halan tucked away the slate and the pair gingerly continued
towards the train, their steps cautious, hearts beating faster.
The train's doors stood open, but still no one got off. A light
flickered inside, briefly illuminating the train's interior and a
tinkle of broken glass made both men jump.

Steam gusted from the engine, melting the ice coating the train and cold water dripped from around the opened doors. Pren and Halan reached the doors and warily stepped into the darkness of the train.

Pren flicked on the illuminator and swept the beam around the interior of the carriage.

He heard Halan cry out in horror and fell to his knees as his mind attempted to cope with the butchery he saw all around him.

Bodies. Hundreds of gutted, flensed, dismembered and partially devoured bodies filled the carriage, like hunks of meat in a coldroom. Strung from the walls on resinous streamers of glistening mucus, their dead flesh hard and unyielding, their frozen eyes staring down in mute accusation at the station operators.

Stalactites of frozen blood reached down to the uneven floor and Pren felt a suffocating fear swell in his chest. He dropped the illuminator and it rolled down the carriage floor, casting lunatic shadows across the interior of the frozen charnel house, the spinning beam giving the rictus features of the corpses a hideous animation.

'Sweet Emperor–' wept Pren. 'What happened here?'

But the dead had no answers to give him, merely frozen eyes, emptied bellies, shorn limbs and gnawed flesh.

And further back along the train, a creature that had first come to Tarsis Ultra many months ago ghosted from its lair and vanished into the warm labyrinth of Erebus city.

THE COMBINED NAVAL might of the Imperial defenders of the Tarsis Ultra system hung in orbit around the world that gave it its name. A chain of linked space stations ringed the planet's equatorial belt, towed into position to face the approaching tyranids by a host of tugs and pilot boats. Dozens of defence monitors and system ships lumbered into their position in the battle line alongside Admiral de Corte's flagship *Argus*, the battlecruiser *Sword of Retribution*, and the Dauntless cruisers *Yermetov* and *Luxor*.

Gathered around the hulking form of the carrier *Kharloss Vincennes* were the Cobras of Cypria squadron, together with the one surviving vessel of Hydra squadron. The two strike cruisers of the Space Marines anchored in the shadow of the

Argus. Lord Inquisitor Kryptman and the Space Marines had already deployed to the surface of Tarsis Ultra, their presence there deemed more vital than aboard their vessels. As a result, the *Mortis Probati* and the *Vae Victus* would stand off from the main engagement and utilise their fearsome bombardment cannons, rather than entering into the thick of the battle. With only a limited number of thralls and servitors to defend them, there would be no possibility of them repelling boarders and such ancient craft were too valuable to be lost in such a manner.

The tyranid fleet first appeared as a sprinkling of light against the velvet backdrop of stars, its scale magnificent and terrible. Reflected starlight gleamed from city-sized chitinous armour plates and glittered on trailing tentacles that drooled thick, glutinous slime. Swarms of smaller creatures, their fronts crackling with twisting arcs of electrical discharge, surrounded the hive ships, surging ahead of the main fleet with a speed hitherto unseen among the organisms that made up the alien fleet.

Under the power of dozens of straining servitor-crewed tugs, the hydrogen-plasma refinery drifted forward to meet the tyranids. Its hull was packed with yet more explosives and volatile plasma cells, and the magnitude of the resultant explosion was sure to dwarf the detonation of the previous refineries.

ADMIRAL DE CORTE watched the tyranid creatures close on the refinery with a feral smile on his lips. Though tens of thousands of kilometres away, the refinery still dwarfed everything around it, and de Corte knew that the blast was certain to kill hundreds, if not thousands, of alien organisms. If they were lucky, perhaps another hive ship would be drawn to attack the refinery and yet another of the masters of this fleet could be destroyed.

Swarms of aliens surrounded the refinery, many passing close, but none yet attacking. De Corte resisted the temptation to order the *Argus's* nova cannon to fire until one of the larger beasts moved in to attack. His practiced eye watched the vanguard of the alien creatures smoothly part as they swept past the refinery, their movements as precise as the finest naval squadron's display manoeuvres.

'They're not attacking it,' said Jex Viert.

De Corte chewed his bottom lip, pondering whether to order the nova cannon to fire. So long as the refinery drifted before his fleet, he was reluctant to order a general advance and the damned aliens weren't taking the bait.

Something was wrong. The tyranids had reportedly swarmed all over the refinery the Ultramarines had sent towards them beyond Chordelis, so why weren't they doing the same now?

Four enormous creatures approached the massive construction, rippling orifices on their elongated prows filled with rotating blade-like fangs. They surged past the refinery, their long, trailing tentacles snagging on its superstructure. Whether their actions were accidental or deliberate, de Corte was unsure, but he did not like the synchronicity with which they had moved into position. Hordes of creatures with spined crests rippling upwards from their bodies like bizarre, reflective organic sails, emerged from the swarm, moving with a grotesque, peristaltic motion to take up position before the refinery.

'What in the name of the warp are they doing?' wondered de Corte aloud as another group of alien creatures, with crackling arcs of electricity spitting before them moved to surround the tentacled leviathans.

'Sir,' prompted Jex Viert, 'The kraken in the vanguard of the alien fleet are approaching engagement range.'

De Corte snapped his gaze to the plotting table and the automaton-like logisticians moving the markers representing the tyranid fleet forward towards his battle line. The refinery would have to wait. 'Mister Viert, order the monitors forward and issue clearance to engage to all ships. My compliments to each captain, and wish them all good hunting.'

'Aye, sir,' nodded his flag lieutenant.

LORD ADMIRAL TIBERIUS watched the same scenes from the bridge of the *Vae Victus*, his own confusion matching that of de Corte.

'This is damned peculiar,' he said, rubbing a hand across his jaw. 'Why doesn't de Corte shoot?'

'I believe he is waiting for one of the hive ships to attack the refinery,' said Philotas.

'Then he has underestimated the ability of these creatures to adapt to new battlefield situations.'

Tiberius did not know how right he was.

THE TENTACLED LEVIATHANS whose trailing appendages had caught on the refinery strained against its massive weight, their bodies little more than a colossal series of powerful, interlinked muscles. Though internal fibres ruptured within them, and each creature burned so much energy in halting the refinery's forward motion that they would soon be consumed in the process, they continued hauling on its gargantuan bulk.

The vast overmind cared nothing for the individual creatures that made up the majority of its mass and directed its monstrous will at the muscle beasts. Even in death, the muscle beasts would not be wasted, their organic mass would be reabsorbed by the hive fleet and used to produce fresh warrior creatures.

The hive ships lurked in the centre of the swarm, keeping a safe distance from the dangerous intruder in the midst of the fleet.

Slowly at first, but with greater speed as they overcame the refinery's inertia, the dying muscle beasts began dragging it behind them.

Fluids and muscle fibre was shed from their bodies as the single-minded purpose of the hive mind continued to destroy them.

And the refinery followed behind them, gaining more and more speed as it returned to the Imperial battle line.

ADMIRAL TIBERIUS SUDDENLY realised what was happening and shouted, 'Philotas, open a channel to Admiral de Corte. Now!'

'Admiral?'

'Hurry, Philotas!' shouted Tiberius, descending from his command pulpit and running to the communications station as Philotas held out the brass headset and hand-vox.

The vox officer nodded as the clipped tones of Admiral de Corte and hissing static crackled from the gold-rimmed speaker on the panel.

'Admiral Tiberius, make this quick, I have pressing concerns just now.'

'Destroy the refinery. Now. The tyranids are pulling it back towards our battle line.'

'What? Are you sure?'

'I'm sure, admiral. Check your auguries if you must, but do it quickly.'

'You must be mistaken, Tiberius. How could the tyranids possibly even have the capacity to understand our intentions?'

'They learn, admiral. I should have known that we could not pull the same trick twice with these beasts. Please, admiral, we don't have time for debate. Destroy it now!'

'I shall have my surveyor officers confirm what you say, but I am unwilling to destroy so potent a weapon on a whim. De Corte out.'

Tiberius handed the headset back to the Space Marine at the vox station and marched back to the plotting table. Quickly he scanned the positioning of the Imperial fleet and felt his skin crawl as he realised the scale of the disaster that could soon befall the Imperial fleet unless they took swift action. Philotas joined the admiral, furiously entering figures into his navigational slate.

'If we move now, we can intercept the refinery, lord admiral,' he said.

'Do it. All ahead full, divert all available power to the auto loaders for the prow cannon. I want to be able to hit that refinery with everything we've got. And contact Captain Gaiseric on the *Mortis Probati* and get him to join us, we'll need his ship too.'

'Aye, sir. All ahead full,' shouted Philotas, relaying the admiral's order.

Tiberius felt the deck shifting and prayed that they were in time.

'Well?' asked Admiral de Corte, impatiently.

'It would seem Admiral Tiberius is correct,' replied Jex Viert, his voice betraying his anxiety. 'The refinery does appears to be closing with us now.'

Hot fear dumped into Bregant de Corte's system as he realised the ramifications of this new information. He nodded to his flag lieutenant.

'Order the nova cannon to fire!' shouted Jex Viert. 'Signal all ships to open fire. Now, for the Emperor's sake, now!'

No, thought Admiral de Corte, not for the Emperor's, for ours.

COLOSSAL ENERGIES HURLED the explosive shell from the breech of the nova cannon on the prow of the *Argus* and sent it streaking on a blazing plume towards the tyranid fleet. Travelling at close to five thousand kilometres per second, the shell closed the gap between the foes in a little under twenty-five seconds. As it closed to within fifteen thousand kilometres, blazing arcs of blue lightning surged outwards from the rippling plates of the creatures that surrounded the muscle beasts dragging the refinery, enveloping the missile's shell. Instantly, the shell exploded in an expanding cloud of burning plasma, its shattered remnants spinning off into space.

The crackling, lightning spitters and the beasts with giant sail-like appendages took up station before the refinery as a flurry of shells and energy blasts slashed towards it. A thick morass of spores and tyranid creatures swarmed forward, exploding and spilling their lifeblood as they absorbed the mass of firepower directed at the refinery. Lance beams cut through spores and burned alien flesh before finally striking the reflective sails of the winged beasts that escorted the lightning spitters. The sails' honeycombed structure dissipated much of the lance beams' strength, rendering them harmless as they scored the structure of the refinery, but failed to penetrate its metal hide.

Starhawk bombers and Fury interceptors surged from the launch bays of the *Kharloss Vincennes*, attempting to punch a hole through the tyranid screen, but every gap they blasted was soon filled with even more alien beasts. Eventually, the commander of the furies, Captain Owen Morten, pulled his surviving craft back to the carrier to refuel and rearm. Just because a task was impossible was no reason to give up.

No matter how hard the Imperial Navy hit, they could not penetrate the screen of tyranid creatures protecting the refinery and without the drag of friction, its speed increased until it was hurtling towards the Imperial battle line.

* * *

'NOTHING IS GETTING through!' shouted Philotas.

'Keep firing,' ordered Tiberius, his voice strained.

'Aye, sir.'

Tiberius's jaw muscles bunched in anxiety as he watched the rippling series of explosions bursting before the *Vae Victus*. Her firepower, normally so fearsome in battle, was availing her nothing as every shell from her bombardment cannon was intercepted by a tyranid creature sent to its death by the alien imperative of the hive mind.

Hundreds of beasts were dying, but they were achieving what the hive mind desired.

Nothing could touch the refinery.

ADMIRAL DE CORTE gripped the arms of his command chair as the *Argus* canted to starboard. The massive vessel was slowly moving from the path of the oncoming refinery, but even without asking, he could tell they weren't going to make it. The fleet was scattering from its path as quickly as it could, but even at cruising speed a vessel as vast as a Victory class battleship took time to turn, and even longer from anchor.

Withering salvoes of massed gunnery from the defence monitors and system ships had prevented the approaching kraken from breaking their battle line, but nothing could halt the inexorable approach of the refinery.

'Estimated time to lethal range, Mr Viert?'

'Forty seconds, sir.'

'GET US CLEAR, Philotas,' ordered Tiberius. The closure speeds of the refinery and the *Vae Victus* was such that, in the time it would take to load and fire another shell from the bombardment cannon, the massive structure would be past them before the shell could arm itself.

Tiberius angled his stance as the prow of the strike cruiser rose and the refinery swiftly vanished from the viewing bay. The admiral could feel the deck shudder beneath him as its hull groaned under the pressure of such violent manoeuvring and the thump of fire from her broadsides and close-in guns as smaller tyranid organisms shearing from the refinery's protective swarm threatened to overwhelm her. Without her complement of Space Marine defenders, Tiberius knew that to allow the tyranids to board the *Victus* would seal its fate.

'Estimated time to lethal range, Philotas?'

'Twenty seconds, Lord admiral.'

SALVOES OF TORPEDOES exploded amongst the vanguard of the guardian swarm, killing alien organisms in their fiery blasts, but nothing could penetrate the thick mass of creatures forced to give up their existence in service of the hive mind. Less than sixty thousand kilometres separated the fleet from the refinery now.

And at its current speed, that meant about ten seconds.

'ALL HANDS, ABANDON ship!' bellowed Admiral de Corte as the proximity alarms of the *Argus* began blaring. The sacristy bell chimed again and again, warning – as though warning were needed – of the imminent collision of the refinery. He knew it was a wasted breath, none of the ship's lifeboats would be able to get clear of the blast radius of the refinery, but he had to try. Their doom filled the viewing bay, hurtling towards them with awful finality and, in the few seconds left to him, he stood and marched to the centre of the command nave.

He saluted his bridge crew and said, 'It has been an honour to serve with you all. The Emperor protects.'

AS THE REFINERY flew into the midst of the Imperial fleet, the lightning spitters that had protected the gargantuan construction turned, whipcord fast, and lashed their former charge with raw tongues of blue fire. Metal ran molten beneath the assault and, like bloated ticks, the lightning spitters bored their way within the softened plates of the structure.

Once inside, each creature pushed its magma-hot discharge before it like a drill bit, slashing through metre after metre of sheet metal to reach the storage chambers at its heart. The heat from their crackling arcs of energy rippled around them, melting their own armoured carapaces and scorching the flesh from their bones, but driven by the implacable will of the hive mind, each beast continued onwards until it reached its goal.

As the first beast punched through the armoured chemical tanks, the flaring, electric arcs flashed across the fuel chamber, instantaneously igniting the volatile hydrogen-plasma mix. Others penetrated fuel chambers across the length and breadth of the refinery and in a heartbeat, the colossal bomb of the refinery was ripped apart in a cataclysmic explosion.

HUNDREDS WERE BLINDED by the dazzling brightness of the explosion as it ripped across the heavens above Tarsis Ultra. The *Argus* vanished in the corona of the blast, its shields no protection against the violence of the detonation. Metres-thick sheets of adamantium were vaporised in an instant as the plasma fire engulfed the ancient vessel. Compartments vented into space, the oxygen igniting as the heat tore through the ship and its massive structure sagged as her keel melted in the incandescent heat. Thousands of men died instantly as their blood flashed to steam and the skin was scorched from their bones in the time it took to draw breath to scream.

The fires of the explosion expanded rapidly, quickly eclipsing the doomed *Argus* and smashing into the other vessels of the Imperial fleet. Six defence monitors and as many system ships vaporised as their magazines and fuel stores exploded. The Cobras of Cypria squadron broke apart as their store of torpedoes cooked off in the launch bays, though the ill-fated Cobra of Hydra squadron miraculously survived.

The launch bays of the *Kharloss Vincennes* blazed as fuel stores caught light, the blast doors melting shut and rendering them unable to recover previously launched squadrons of fighters and bombers. Well-practiced fire drills saved the ship and her captain's quick manoeuvring put her prow-first into the detonation and lessened the buffeting shockwave's effect.

The *Sword of Retribution*, the *Yermetov* and the *Luxor*, shielded from much of the blast's force, were spared the worst of the damage, though their corridors echoed to the sound of hull breach klaxons and yelling damage control gangs.

BLOOD-RED LIGHT bathed the control bridge of the *Vae Victus*, the sacristy bell ringing as though the ship herself was screaming. Sparks and jets of hydraulic fluid spurted from shattered control panels, but Tiberius knew they were lucky still to be in one piece.

The *Vae Victus* had been stern on to the explosion and its force had hurled her about like a leaf in a hurricane, but Admiral Tiberius's quick thinking had put her clear of the main destructive energies of the hell that had engulfed the majority of the Imperial fleet.

'Damage report!' bellowed Tiberius.

'We've got hull breaches on decks six, seven and nine,' reported Philotas. 'The engines are operating at fifty per cent efficiency and we've lost most of the turrets on our rear quarters'

'What of the rest of the fleet?' asked Tiberius, dreading the answer.

'I don't know sir. The surveyors are having trouble penetrating the electromagnetic radiation released by the blast.'

'Get me Admiral de Corte, we need to get control of this situation, now.'

'Aye, sir.'

Tiberius lurched across the buckled deck to stand beside the plotting table, trying to make sense of the confused hash of imagery displayed there. A red haze filled the bottom of the schematic, the slate unable to display enough symbols to represent the tyranid fleet. Scattered blue icons faded in and out of focus as the surveyors fought to lock down the positions of the Imperial vessels.

'Emperor save us,' whispered Tiberius as names of vessels began flickering up next to the blue icons. Precious few, he saw. He frowned, scanning the table for the icon representing the *Argus*. Tiberius looked up as Philotas said, 'The *Argus* is gone, sir.'

'Gone–' echoed Tiberius.

'She caught the full force of the blast. There's nothing left of her.'

The lord admiral fought down his shock at the destruction of so mighty a vessel as the *Argus* and the death of her crew.

'And the rest of the fleet?' he asked, quietly.

'It looks like the local ships took the worst of the blast, but we've lost the Cobras and the Argus. The *Sword of Retribution* is damaged, but under power, and the *Kharloss Vincennes* is still with us though her launch bays are out of action.'

Tiberius nodded curtly, assessing the scale of the catastrophe and knew that the campaign in space was over.

'Issue a general communication to all vessels. I am taking command of the fleet. Order all ships to disengage. Get clear of Tarsis Ultra and rendezvous at Calydon.'

'Admiral?'

'Do it!' snapped Tiberius. 'Fighting an unwinnable battle is of no value if by doing so we lose the war. Now do as I say.'

Philotas nodded and dispatched the admiral's orders as Tiberius gripped the edge of the plotting table. Nothing now could be gained by fighting the advancing tyranids in space and he would not be responsible for dooming every man of the Imperial fleet.

Whatever came next, the defenders on Tarsis Ultra would have to face it on their own.

NINE

A COLD WIND blew across the tops of the Cullin Mountains, howling across the rocky ground below and stripping any lingering warmth from the bright morning. The air was crisp, but the sun was bright and low, preventing the foaming waters of the mountain springs from freezing over. Splashes of emerald green forests dotted the lower slopes of the mountains and, here and there, herds of shaggy yrenbacks made their way back down slope to the warmer plains from their drinking grounds.

Suddenly, the motion of the herds halted, each animal raising its long, furry neck into the air, as though scenting a predator. The herds milled in confusion, drawing closer to one another, agitated at their inability to identify the threat they all felt. The animals brayed in confusion, ears flat against their skulls.

A scattershot darkness covered the flanks of the mountain as a host of shapes flashed across the sky. All across the mountains, puffs of snow and rock were thrown skyward by the tremendous impacts of falling objects. The herds scattered as more and more objects dropped from the sky, churning the surface of the mountains with their numbers.

The clouds above flashed with purple lightning as spores burst within them, dispersing a multitude of contaminants and viruses that instantly began working to alter the climatological balance of the planet's atmosphere. Heat built up rapidly, increasing the air pressure and causing actinic bolts of lightning to arc from cloud to cloud, dispersing them as a viscous, toxic rain.

In minutes, the newly risen sun was obscured by the sheer mass of spores falling from the heavens. Terrified yrenbacks ran backwards and forwards across the mountain sides, leaping through the deep snow in their blind panic. Churning motion erupted from the steaming spores that had landed in their midst, flashing claws and alien screeches as the creatures within them emerged and sought something to kill. Driven into a frenzied killing fury by the hive mind and bio-engineered, super-adrenal chemicals, the first wave of tyranid invaders hacked entire herds of the grazing animals to bloody ruin before collapsing and dying, spent by the fury of their assault and their inability to survive the freezing temperatures.

Thousands of tyranid organisms in the first wave perished as the numbing cold of Tarsis Ultra froze them within minutes of their arrival. After burning virtually all their bodily energies in their initial surge of violence, and without reserves of fat, none could survive more than a few minutes before perishing.

But none of this mattered, for as each creature died and the hive mind became aware of the local conditions on the prey planet, it simply adjusted the biological physiology of its warrior organisms, enabling them to produce more insulating tissue and energy reserves that would allow them to survive for longer periods.

AMID THE LOAMY earth of the lower forests, the thick, biological rain soaked into the tree canopy and saturated the earth with its bacteria-laden substance. Microbes containing the genetic blueprint of tyranid fauna spread rapidly through the ground, assessing and digesting the chemical content of the soil before turning that energy into horrifyingly fast growth spurts.

Multicoloured fronds ripped their way through the silver bark of the trees and twisting vines and creepers surged from

the moistened ground. Again, the cold of Tarsis Ultra dramatically shortened the plants' lifespan, but as each leaf and
creeper died, it vomited a host of fresh spores into the atmosphere and the cycle began again.

As each generation of plant went through its brief life cycle,
the chemical reactions fermenting in the ground began raising
the temperature of the surrounding air. Streamers of heated
air drifted from the ground, warming the burgeoning plant
life until the rate of growth was rising exponentially. Jagged
spore chimneys of thick, vegetable matter broke through the
hot earth and pushed skyward, their root structure burrowing
through the permafrost to the nutrient-rich soil below. Hot
steam and exhaust gasses from the biological conflagration
below belched from the chimneys, sending yet more spores
high into the atmosphere to be spread by the prevailing
winds. As the atmosphere heated even more, strong updrafts
of warm air rose, meeting the cold air descending from the
mountaintops to create freak weather patterns that spread the
contamination of the tyranid organisms even further.

The invasion of Tarsis Ultra had begun.

DESPITE THE INABILITY of the Imperial fleet to hold back the
tyranid invaders, Tarsis Ultra was not without defences of her
own. Ground-based batteries of defence lasers fired skyward
and hundreds of orbital torpedoes roared into the upper
atmosphere on blazing tail plumes.

The defence lasers slashed through the sky, but the rapidly
mutating content of the air had one more adaptive surprise
for the defenders of Tarsis Ultra.

One of the greatest problems for ground-based laser
weapons was the reduction in power they suffered over long
distances, called 'thermal blooming'. As a laser beam travels
through the air, small quantities of its energy are lost to the
surrounding atmosphere as heat, which causes disturbances
in the air and disrupts the optical path of the beam. Not only
does this impair accuracy, but it spreads the beam wider, thus
weakening the energy delivered to its target. For the colossal
energies produced by the defence lasers, this was not normally
a problem, but each beam was passing through dozens of
rapidly fluctuating temperature patches in the air, causing
them to impact with greatly reduced power.

Many of the smaller organisms suffered at the hands of the defence lasers, but the majority of the tyranid creatures had little to fear from them.

But torpedoes have no such barriers to performance and these weapons reaped a fearful tally amongst the gathering predators. Hundreds of torpedoes exploded amongst the bloated spore ships of the tyranid fleet, destroying some and fatally wounding others. Scores of alien creatures perished and fell through the atmosphere as bright, fleshy meteors, haemorrhaging their lifeblood like comets' tails.

The skies above Tarsis Ultra were what Imperial strategos referred to as 'target-heavy' and every torpedo found its mark in a tyranid creature. Within two hours, over five hundred confirmed kills had been reported by the silo commanders, along with desperate requests for additional ordnance to fire. Faced with so many targets, each silo exhausted its supply of weapons after another hour of firing.

Against any conventional invaders, the defences of Tarsis Ultra would have caused utter devastation and crippled any attempt to invade.

But the tyranids were far from conventional invaders.

FROM THE AIR, the hydro-skiff resembled a speeding silver bullet as it roared along the frozen surface of the hydroway. Its passenger compartments were laden with soldiers of the Logres regiment making their way back to Erebus, its speed approaching two hundred kilometres per hour as its giant, prop-driven engines hurled it along the frozen canal surface.

A mist of ice crystals billowed in its wake as the hydro-skis angled to take the skiff around a bend in the canal, rounding a series of low hills capped with a thatch of evergreen firs. Sparks flew as the offside ski grazed the mag-rails on the side of the canal, the pilot having taken the turn a little too fast for comfort. But concerns of safety were now outweighed by the need for speed. They had seen the heavens criss-crossed by bright streaks of lasfire, and the pale blue of the sky to the west was laced with cloudy pillars from firing torpedo silos. No one needed to tell the men of the Logres regiment what was happening, and that it was time to head for the safety of Erebus.

Unnatural twilight was falling as tyranid spores filled the
sky above, long shadows cast by chittering black clouds that
spun and swooped like flying oil slicks. Soldiers peered nervously through the steamed windows at the gathering
darkness, willing the skiff's pilot to coax his machine to yet
faster speeds.

A pair of the black clouds dropped through the air, looping
downwards to fly parallel to the skiff, a third descending in a
lazy spiral ahead of it. Officers watching through the roof
periscopes shouted at their men to stand to, chivvying them
to the windows and bellowing orders to fire at will.

Blasts of freezing air filled the skiff as windows were forced
open and barrels of lasguns pushed through. Lasbolts
snapped upwards, punching into the black flocks that pursued the skiff. Occasionally, a twisted shape would tumble to
the snow, but such precious victories were few, and despite the
terrific speed of the skiff, the flocks drew nearer still.

Cries of fear echoed along the length of the passenger compartments as the flocks began to overtake the skiff and the
soldiers had their first glimpse of the enemy. Grotesque, mem-
brane-winged creatures with leering, fang-filled maws and
clawed limbs surrounded them. Lasbolts tore amongst the
aliens, but for every one that was downed, a hundred more
remained. They swooped over and around the skiff, spitting
black gouts from weapon orifices that peppered its metal skin
like handfuls of thrown stones. Glass smashed and men
screamed as the aliens' fire struck them, their armour cracking
and dissolving under the impacts.

Medics ran to the wounded, peeling off bloody flak vests
and applying pressure to the ragged holes in the soldiers' bodies, then recoiled in horror as they saw clutches of writhing,
beetle-like creatures boring deep into the men's flesh.

Scrabbling claws tore at the skiff's roof, gouging long tears
in the thin metal. The skiff swayed from side to side, throwing
more sparks as the pilot fought to compensate for the additional weight and drag of the attackers. Soldiers fired through
the roof, killing the flying beasts in their dozens, but unable
to dislodge them all.

Muscular taloned arms reached in and dragged a screaming
soldier through a hole in the roof, his cries cut off as the rushing wind snatched away his breath. His comrades fought to

pull him back, but another volley of the flesh-eating creatures slew the would-be rescuers in a hail of fire.

The skiff screamed around another bend in the icy canal, only to be faced by yet another flock of the winged monsters, swirling in an impenetrable cloud and blocking the skiff's path with their bodies. The pilot reacted instinctively, slamming on the air brakes and wrenching the controls to one side. Barbed brakes deployed from the skis, throwing the skiff into an uncontrollable skid.

The rear end of the skiff fishtailed, the passenger compartment slewing around until it was travelling sideways. Wider than the canal, its back end caught the edge of the mag-rails and flipped it over onto its side. At such high speeds, the impact ripped the passenger compartment open and tore the coupling to the engine with it, sending it spinning into the air to crash down onto the ice a hundred metres further down the canal where it exploded in a searing orange fireball.

Flames billowed skywards as the wreckage skidded along the canal for another six hundred metres, the heat from the flames melting the ice as it slid. Amid the carnage of the crash, a few pitiful survivors crawled from the wreckage, battered, bloodied and dazed.

Even before they had a chance to freeze to death, the winged gargoyles were upon them, biting and clawing at their helpless prey until there was no one left alive.

The first victims of the land war of Tarsis Ultra had been claimed.

FROM THEIR PERCH high on the roof of their warehouse hideout, Snowdog and Silver watched the distant contrails of torpedoes as they climbed through the purple skies into the upper atmosphere.

The devotional holos, normally full of nameless preachers demanding prayers to the Emperor, had been displaying a non-stop procession of warnings against the dangers of contact with xeno species.

Snowdog didn't know what was happening with the war, but was pretty certain that there must have been a screw-up somewhere along the line, because you didn't start firing ground based weapons except to prevent an imminent invasion.

'This does not look good,' said Snowdog.

'Nope,' agreed Silver, 'It sure doesn't.'

LORD INQUISITOR KRYPTMAN stood in an armoured viewing bay atop the Governor's Palace, watching the same scenes with a similar feeling. With the news that the fleet had been forced to disengage, his hopes that this invasion could be stalled before it reached the surface of the planet had been shattered. He cast his gaze across the landscape one last time, knowing that even were they able to defeat the aliens, this world would never be the same again.

Orders had been issued to all officers on tactical doctrine and the proper conduct to be followed during conflict with the tyranids. Experience bought with uncounted lives was even now circulating amongst the soldiers of Tarsis Ultra and Kryptman hoped that the sacrifice of those who had died to gather that information would not have been in vain.

As he watched the beginning of the tyranid invasion, Magos Locard joined him in the bay, hands clasped before him and mechadendrites swaying gently above his head.

'So it begins again,' mused the inquisitor, watching the swirling, multi-coloured sky.

'Indeed,' said Locard. 'Were it not such a monstrous thing, it might be considered aesthetically pleasing. It is nature driven into paroxysms of creation.'

'Creation, yes, but there is nothing natural about this. It is creation designed to destroy and consume.'

'An interesting dichotomy, yes?' observed Locard.

'Yes, but one for another time perhaps. How goes your research?'

'It progresses. The facilities here are lacking in some regards, but they are sufficient for my needs. The samples taken from the xeno creatures recovered from the *Vae Victus* have helped immensely, but their genetic structure shows evidence of mutation. Evidently, the tyranids have entered another iteration of evolution since the consumption of Barbarus Prime.'

Kryptman turned to face the magos and nodded. 'I had suspected as much.'

'To achieve our goal, it seems clear we will need to somehow obtain a gene sample that is as close to the hive's original

structure as possible, one that has not been subjected to mutation at the behest of the overmind.'

'And how do you intend to obtain such a specimen?'

'Ah, well that I do not yet know,' admitted Locard.

'Find a way,' ordered Kryptman.

URIEL WATCHED LEARCHUS and Pasanius march along the front
lines of the city's defences and fought the urge to join them.
Little time had passed since he had been a veteran sergeant
himself, and the old desire to check on the men under his
command still came to the fore on the eve of battle. He had
greater concerns now, he reminded himself, as he checked the
data-slate to ensure that everything in his sector of responsibility was as it should be.

From above, the plain before the city walls resembled the
top of a racetrack with curved trenches linking the two sides
of the valley. Three entrenchments crossed it, progressively
narrowing as they neared the city walls, but Uriel knew that
these were nothing more than temporary defences. The first
wave of tyranids would come at them from the air, pinning
them down while the bulk of the tyranid army approached on
foot. Sebastien Montante had assured him that the valley
sides were well defended with enough guns to make any aerial attack unfeasible. Uriel had his doubts, knowing that the
sheer scale of a tyranid invasion was beyond the comprehension of most people who had never seen one.

Seven thousand men occupied the first trench, six thousand the second and another two thousand the third. The
remainder of the soldiers waited within the walls of Erebus
itself, held in reserve until needed. Rumbling before the wall,
its armoured flanks bristling with guns and its crenallated
battlements swarming with soldiers, was the Capitol Imperialis of Colonel Octavius Rabelaq. Emblazoned with the
heraldry of the Logres regiment, the massive rhomboid-
shaped command vehicle rose nearly fifty metres from the
ground. From here, Rabelaq could direct his soldiers and
maintain command and control over the battle. Its tracks
were wider than a road and four Leman Russ battle tanks
could fit within the barrel of its main gun. It was a fearsome
reminder of Imperial power and its might was plain for all to
see. Smaller tanks surrounded the Capitol Imperialis, like

ants around an elephant, passing through the gates in the wall towards the front line.

Those tanks that had already taken position idled in well-sited berms, with flared aprons of flattened snow behind them to allow them to reverse out and withdraw to the next line.

Soldiers in dirty overwhites huddled in their dugouts, clustered around plasma-wave generators, cooking their rations. The men clearly relished what might be their last hot meal for some time, and Uriel knew that little improved morale more than hot food and beverages. Here, Montante had excelled himself, handling the logistical nightmare of feeding and equipping tens of thousands of soldiers with the skill of a veteran quartermaster. He had organised vast kitchens to supply the soldiers defending his city with regular hot food and ensured that the commanders had a reliable supply train.

Everything had been organised with admirable efficiency and he could see the teachings of the Codex Astartes in the precise layout of the defences. Uriel was reminded of the schematics he had seen depicting the defences of the northern polar defence fortress on Macragge during the First Tyrannic War, though he hoped to avoid the outcome of that battle.

Satisfied that all was as it should be, he marched along the slush-covered duckboards of the trenches towards the front line. A thick, two-metre berm of snow had been built before the trench to absorb any incoming fire, since, rather than exploding away from projectiles like sand, snow would anneal under the impact and become a stronger, more effective barrier.

Buckets of water had been repeatedly poured down the slope of the snow barrier before the lip of the trench, making a glass-smooth surface that would hopefully prove extremely difficult for the aliens to scale.

'Any word on when we can expect to see them?' asked Pasanius, joining Uriel on the trench's firing step.

'Soon,' answered Uriel as Learchus marched over.

'You have done fine work, Learchus,' said Uriel, gripping his sergeant's hand in welcome.

Learchus nodded. 'The soldiers here are good men, brother-captain, they just needed reminding of the teachings of the Codex Astartes.'

'I'm sure you gave them a very pointed reminder,' noted Uriel.

'Where necessary,' admitted Learchus. 'I was no harsher than any other Agiselus drill sergeant.'

Both Pasanius and Uriel winced as they remembered the severity of their training on Macragge. Neither had any doubt that Learchus had put the soldiers here through hell in order to prepare them for the coming war. But if it made them better soldiers, then it was a price they should be thankful for.

'Where are the Mortifactors and the Deathwatch to be stationed?' asked Learchus.

Uriel pointed towards the southern reaches of the trenches, his brow furrowing at the memory of the confrontation with Astador and Kryptman in the orbiting space station. He had lost control and the shame of that lapse still burned inside him. He was a Space Marine in the service of the Emperor and was above such petty considerations as temper. But the death of so many innocents on Chordelis and the stain left within his soul by the Bringer of Darkness had overcome his normally unbreakable code of honour.

The thought of losing control and becoming little more than a killer without a conscience frightened him greatly. Briefly he thought of confessing to the growing darkness within him, but bit back the words, unsure of how to articulate his feelings. Such weaknesses were foreign to a Space Marine and he had not the humanity to reach out and express them.

The three Space Marines watched the boiling sky in the far distance with trepidation. None would ever forget the horrors they had witnessed on Ichar IV and the thought of facing such a foe again brought nothing but apprehension.

While they knew they could fight any foe and triumph, they were but a hundred warriors and, against such a numberless horde, there was only so much they could do.

The soldiers around them were numerous, though nowhere near as numerous as the tyranids. But where the defenders of Tarsis Ultra had the advantage over the alien horde was in their basic humanity, the courage that came from defending one's hearth and home.

The very thing Uriel and his sergeants lacked.

* * *

THE WESTERN MOUNTAINS writhed with motion. Thousands upon thousands of mycetic spores hammered the ground, each disgorging a mucus-covered creature that hissed and screeched in animal hunger. Swarms of beasts gathered in the shadow of the twisting, smoke-wreathed forests, the natural beauty of the ecology perverted into monstrous, alien flora that consumed the nutrients in the soil and spread a dark stain of necrotic growth across the landscape. Bubbling pools of acids and enzymes formed in sunken patches of ground, small devourer organisms plunging into the acid baths to give up the energy they had consumed to feed the voracious appetite of the alien fleet.

When enough creatures had gathered in a snapping, biting mass, the horde set off at some unseen signal, powerful hind limbs propelling the bounding swarm through the deep snow of the mountains and onto the plain below. Larger creatures stamped through the snow, their bestial jaws snapping and clawed hands sweeping aside the smaller aliens as they moved through the swarm. Tens of thousands of aliens charged down the mountains, directed to their prey by invisible cords of psychic hunger that connected them with thousands of flying gargoyles that swept ahead of the swarm and reeled them closer to their prey.

All across Tarsis Ultra, the beasts of the tyranid invasion closed on their targets.

GUARDSMAN PAVEL LEFORTO of the Erebus Defence Legion nervously licked his lips, then wished he hadn't as he felt the cold freeze the moisture within seconds. He desperately needed to empty his full bladder, but the latrine pits were three hundred metres behind his platoon's section of the forward trench. He cursed the need to drink so much water. At his age, his bladder wasn't the strongest in the world, and the need to drink five canteens of water every day to stave off dehydration – a very real danger in this cold climate – was a constant pain.

But the corpsmen of the Logres regiment were all humourless bastards when it came to cold weather injuries, and it was now a court martial offence to suffer from dehydration, frostbite or hypothermia.

The trench was not as cold as it had been in the weeks previous to this, though high on the periscope platform, a cold wind chilled him to the marrow despite the many-layered thermal overwhites he wore. The presence of so many soldiers raised the temperature by several degrees and the tanks had become a magnet for cold soldiers who basked in the heat radiating from their engine blocks. This section of trench alone was home to over three hundred soldiers, a mix of squads from the Logres and Krieg regiments. None of the off-world soldiers were that friendly, and treated the majority of the Defence Legion soldiers like weekend warriors, amateurs playing in the big boys' arena. This combined with fraying tempers caused by the miserable conditions, had made relations between the defenders of Tarsis Ultra strained to say the least. The initial excitement of leaving his regular post in the Erebus smelteries had long-since evaporated and he missed the predictable monotony of his work.

But more than that, he missed returning home to his wife and children at the end of the day and the cramped, yet homely hab-unit that they and three other families shared high on the north face of District Secundus. Sonya would be readying the evening meal about now and his two children, Hollia and little Solan, would be on their way back from the scholam. The ache of their absence was painful and Pavel looked forward to an end to this war when he could be reunited with them.

Banishing thoughts of home and family, he pressed his face to the rubberised eyecups of the bipod-mounted periscope magnoculars and pressed the button that flipped open the polarised lens covers. He shifted his balaclava under his helmet to get a good look through the magnoculars. The heat from his skin momentarily fogged the glass before the image resolved into clarity before him.

The bleak, unbroken whiteness of the landscape was empty as far as he could see, though he knew that the freezing temperatures reduced his depth perception and visual acuity. Still, he wasn't the only one watching this sector, so he wasn't too bothered that he couldn't see much. Seeing nothing was a good thing anyway, wasn't it?

'Anything?' asked his squad mate, Vadim Kotash, holding out a steaming tin mug filled with caffeine towards Pavel. At forty-five years old, Vadim was a year younger than Pavel and together, they were probably the oldest men in the platoon.

His friend's face was obscured by his balaclava and snow-goggles, a scarf wrapped around his mouth muffling his words.

'Nah,' said Pavel, snapping the covers back over the magnoculars. He took the mug and, pulling the scarf from his mouth, sipped his hot drink. 'Can't see anything worth a damn in this weather.'

'Aye, I hear that. Con tells me that Kellis got taken back to the medicae yesterday. Snow blindness got him. The young fool kept taking his goggles off.'

'The provosts will haul him over the coals for that.'

'I wouldn't mind being hauled over the coals, it might warm my old bones up,' chuckled Vadim.

'It would take the furnace back in the smeltery for that now,' said Pavel.

Vadim nodded as an officer in a long, mud-stained Krieg greatcoat and a thick, furred colback studded with a lieutenant's pips stalked down the trench. He carried his lasgun slung over his shoulder and he scowled in displeasure as he marched.

'Uh-oh, it's Konarski,' hissed Vadim, tapping Pavel's shoulder, but it was already too late.

'You!' snapped Konarski. 'Why the hell aren't you watching for the enemy?'

Pavel started at the sharp bark of Konarski's voice, spilling caffeine onto his overwhites.

'Uh, sorry, sir. I was just–'

'I don't give a damn what you were doing, you are supposed to be watching for the enemy. You might single-handedly condemn us all to death with your carelessness. I'll have you on report for this, you mark my words.'

Pavel groaned in frustration as Konarski fished out a battered, and obviously well-used, disciplinary infractions notebook and a worn-down nub of a pencil.

'Right then, soldier, name, rank and serial numb–'

Konarski never got a chance to finish his question as the alert sirens blared into life all along the front line. Wailing klaxons screamed a warning to the soldiers and the trenches erupted in panicked motion as troopers fumbled for their weapons and scrambled to the trench's firing step. Pavel dropped his mug and pressed his face to the trench periscope, the altercation with Konarski forgotten.

He snapped up the covers and gasped as he saw the swarming black shapes knifing through the air towards the trenches. The entire upper half of the viewer was filled with alien creatures and he could hear the rustling roar of thousands of beating wings as they drew nearer.

Realising he no longer needed the scope, Pavel dropped to the firing step and lifted his rifle to his shoulder. Engines belched smoke as Hydra flak tanks drove forward, sending frozen mud and snow flying as their tracks churned the ground. Ammunition trucks followed the tanks, each carrying three thousand shells in easy-to-load ammo panniers, since a Hydra could pump out up to a thousand rounds a minute.

Pavel watched the approaching cloud of flying aliens with a mixture of terror and anticipation. Never having journeyed far beyond the walls of Erebus, he was excited to have the chance to see real aliens from afar. But if even half of the information given in the platoon briefings on these creatures was true, then he knew that in all probability he wouldn't enjoy too close an encounter with a tyranid organism.

The noise of the sirens died, and the awful sound of the aliens' flapping wings echoed from the valley sides along with a brittle, high-pitched noise of millions of claws clicking together.

'Hold your fire until they get closer,' ordered a captain of the Logres regiment, calmly walking behind them with his sword drawn, the blade resting on his shoulder. 'Don't waste any of your shots, you'll need every one of them.'

Pavel caught Vadim's eye, seeing the fear behind his friend's nervous smile.

'Don't worry, Vadim,' said Pavel. 'Just keep a fresh power cell handy and you'll be fine.'

Vadim nodded shakily as the Hydras began firing and the noise of the quad-barrelled weapons as they began pumping shells into the approaching swarm was deafening. Hundreds of explosions burst among the flying creatures, painting the sky with dirty smears, and the distant screeches of dying creatures drifted through the cold air. Steam billowed from the air-cooled barrels and robed enginseers circled each tank, sprinkling their hulls with blessed water from their aspergillum as the guns sprayed the air with explosive shells.

Pavel watched the swarm above convulse as fire from the Hydras ripped through it, blasting apart hundreds of creatures with every passing second. The carnage wreaked among them was fearsome and hundreds of falling black objects drifted from the swarm. He wondered how they could possibly take so much punishment and still keep coming.

In perfect synchrony, a portion of the swarm dipped and flowed from the sky as another climbed, heading for the high peaks of the city. The lower swarm rapidly lost altitude to skim the ice and race towards the trenches like dark bullets.

The Hydras continued to spray the air with shells, the barrels depressing as the swarm heading for the trenches descended. The range was closing rapidly, the chittering screeches of the aliens clawing at the nerves of the thousands of men facing them.

Pavel watched the aliens through the scope of his lasgun, the blinking red crosshairs flashing to green as the aliens entered the weapon's lethal range.

'Fire! Fire at will!' bellowed an officer, and thousands of lasguns opened fire simultaneously. The black swarm jerked, hundreds upon hundreds of the beasts cartwheeling into the ice. Disciplined volleys pierced the swarm. Pavel fired without aiming. It simply wasn't necessary when the enemy came at you in such numbers.

The alien screeches rose to a howling gale and suddenly they were upon them.

Vadim ducked as a flying monster smashed into the lip of the trench, vestigial rear limbs scrabbling for purchase on the ice. Membranous wings flapped as its ribbed arms pointed towards him, a slime-dripping symbiotic weapon aimed at his heart.

Pavel shot the beast in the head and its thrashing carcass fell into the trench. A pair of hissing monsters swooped low, gobbets of black slime spattering the trench walls as Pavel pushed Vadim to the slush at the bottom of the trench. He rolled as the beasts came at him, oblivious to the screams and sounds of battle echoing from all along the trench line. He opened up on full-auto, filling the trench with bright lasbolts and cutting the creatures in two.

Vadim shot another beast as it clawed its way over the snow berm. He dragged Pavel to his feet. The air was thick with gargoyles, swooping and diving at the trenches, clawing and biting and firing their disgusting bio-weapons. Screams tore through the hissing of the monsters and the air reeked with the stench of blood and fear.

A clutch of the screeching beasts swooped down from the thinning swarm, bright spurts of bio-plasma melting snow and flesh with equal ease. Vadim screamed as he was lifted into the air by a gargoyle, his legs thrashing and his cries piteous as he was carried from the trench. Pavel jumped, grabbing hold of Vadim's legs, but his thick mittens couldn't get a grip and his friend was carried into the sky. Pavel fell back into the trench as another gargoyle swooped towards him. He dived to one side, desperately bringing up his lasgun to block its sweeping claws. Sparks flew as the alien's talons hacked through the barrel, ripping through his overwhites, but tearing free before cutting into his chest. He stumbled, falling to his rump on the firing step. He hurled his useless weapon aside, reaching for his war-knife as the beast spun in the air and came back for another pass.

Alien gore spattered him as the gargoyle exploded in midair, detonating from within as it was struck by a burst of fire from a Space Marine's bolter. He wiped dripping ichor from his goggles in time to see an Ultramarines captain and sergeant fight their way down the length of the trench, killing aliens and shrugging off their attacks as if they were on the parade ground.

'Thanks,' blurted Pavel, but the warriors had already moved on.

He dropped to his knees, retching as the reality of his near death flared and shock began to take hold. Sick dread filled him and hot fear dumped into his system as he realised how close he had come to leaving Sonya a widow.

He felt his limbs shake and rooted amongst the dead on the floor of the trench for a weapon, realising that action was his only hope of staving off the onset of this paralysing fear.

Pavel hurriedly loaded the lasgun, and surged to his feet. He clambered back to the firing step and fired into the mass of creatures boiling in the air above him. He fired and reloaded, losing count of how many power packs he slammed home, resorting to taking more from the pouches of the fallen when his own ran out. But even he could see that the swarm's numbers were diminishing.

Unable to land and fight, the gargoyles could never capture the trenches, and Pavel wondered what exactly the point of this attack was.

The answer was horrifyingly clear. The aliens were probing them... learning. This attack was nothing more than an exploration of their prey's capabilities, the merest hint of what was to come. This vanguard was a diversion only, and the beasts that died here in their thousands were expendable, fodder to be used in order to decide how best to defeat the creatures that defended this world.

The thought of such a cold, unfeeling logic chilled him to the core. If thousands might be sacrificed for the merest scrap of information, what more horrors might the aliens' leaders unleash?

The sounds of battle were beginning to diminish and here and there, Pavel could see the armoured forms of the Ultramarines and the Mortifactors despatching the last elements of the swarm, moving and firing their cumbersome weapons with an efficiency that came from decades of constant practice.

He steadied himself against the side of the trench as a crippling wash of sensations flooded him. Relief at his survival, an ache for his family and grief for Vadim – though he had no idea whether his friend was alive or dead.

He slumped to the trench's firing step as exhaustion filled his limbs with cold lead and his hands started to shake.

Pavel wept for his lost friend and the tears turned to ice on his cheeks.

SNOWDOG LET RIP with a huge burst of fire from the heavy stubber, the shells cutting a hissing gargoyle in two and sending it tumbling from the boarded-up window it had been attempting to batter its way through. Silver calmly double-tapped another as it tore at a hole in the ceiling and Tigerlily spun and wove her way through the aliens, tearing wings and plucking out eyes with her thin daggers.

Jonny Stomp and Trask fought back to back, blazing away with their purloined weapons at the bizarre-looking creatures that were trying to bust into their warehouse hideout. The guns' reports were deafening, and cries of panic and fear from those civilians who'd been lucky enough to reach the safety of the warehouse dopplered in and out of perception between the blasts of fire.

The doorway timbers finally splintered and half a dozen screeching monsters fought to get through the opening. Snowdog spun and braced himself, keeping his stance wide as he depressed the firing stud on the textured grip of the heavy stubber. A metre-long tongue of fire leapt from the perforated barrel and annihilated the aliens in a blood-and-smoke stained cloud. Even braced, the recoil staggered Snowdog, the stream of shells ripping upwards and blasting chunks of the plaster ceiling loose.

He swung the gun back down again, searching for fresh targets, but, for the moment, finding none. The panicked whimpers and muffled sobs from the two-dozen civilians at the back of the warehouse were already irritating him and he let out a deep, calming breath, running to the edge of the shattered window frame to risk a glance outside.

Since early evening, the roaring of defence guns had echoed from the valley sides and he'd watched the tops of the rock faces erupt in a furious storm of gunfire. At first he couldn't see what they were shooting at, but pretty soon a billowing cloud of creatures came into view. Trailing the monsters came a black rain, spores in their thousands, dropping towards the city at a terrific rate.

Explosions painted the sky, shells bursting amongst the dropping organisms and killing thousands of aliens. Snowdog had never seen such a magnificent display of the city's defences before, and the firepower they brought to bear on the spores was nothing short of incredible.

The scale of the tyranid invasion was of an order of magnitude greater than the city's architects had ever bargained for, and scattered pockets of the aerial bombardment were able to penetrate the umbrella of flak, mostly in the lower reaches of the city, far from where the extra guns studding the walls of the Imperial Palace of Sebastien Montante defeated the first wave.

Curious onlookers surrounded the spores that did manage to land, eager to see, first-hand, this threat to their world, most paying with their lives as the spores erupted with alien killers: slashing beasts and sickle-armed monsters with pitiless eyes and voracious appetites.

Snowdog had watched as a handful of spores had smashed through the thin, corrugated iron roofs of nearby dwellings, wincing at the impacts and knowing that the inhabitants were already dead. People scattered, shocked into action by the violence around them.

Nearly a hundred of the leaping, hissing beasts thronged the narrow streets before the warehouse building serving as their base. Screaming people, carrying children and pathetic bundles of personal possessions had fled before the aliens and, in a moment of weakness that he just knew he was going to regret, Snowdog had allowed them sanctuary in the warehouse.

Since then, he and his gang had been fighting for their lives as aliens fought tooth and nail to get inside. Jonny had held them at bay long enough for Snowdog to break out the weaponry they'd snagged from one of the many crooked supply sergeants at the busy port facilities, and with everyone carrying such powerful guns, they'd sent the aliens packing with their tails well and truly between their legs.

It pained Snowdog to use these guns, because the resale value would be a hell of a lot less now they'd been fired. Still, he figured, he had crates and crates of ration packs and medical supplies in storage and would bet the sun and the moon that there'd be a hell of a demand for them in the coming days.

He coughed as sudden quiet descended on the hab-unit, his lungs filled with acrid smoke from the heavy calibre weapons' fire. Trask and Jonny Stomp high-fived.

'You see that one I got between the eyes?' snarled Trask. 'Blew its Emperor-damned head clean off!'

'Aye. But what about the one I nailed with the grenade launcher? That was sweet,' said Jonny, miming firing his weapon again and again.

Snowdog left them to their bragging, shouldering the smoking heavy stubber and smiling at Silver, who nodded back and reloaded her pistols. Lex and Tigerlily slumped to the floor, sparking up a couple of obscura sticks and Snowdog let them, figuring the threat was over for now.

Silver sidled next to him and rubbed the back of his neck, leaning up to kiss his cheek. She smiled and nodded towards the crowd of terrified people at the back of the warehouse, her normally icy demeanour melting.

'That was a good thing you did, letting those people in,' she said.

'Yeah, ain't I the hero?' snapped Snowdog.

'No,' replied Silver, 'but I think maybe you're a sentimentalist.'

'Me? Don't bet on it, honey. I don't even know why I did it. If I'd had time to think about it, I'd have shut the door in their faces.'

'Really?'

'Really.'

Silver searched his eyes for any sign that he was joking, then removed her hand from his neck when she found none. He saw her aloof exterior reassert itself as her stare penetrated his apparent altruism to the white heat of his self-interest.

She turned away and said, 'I just bet you would have.'

Snowdog returned his gaze to the snow-covered city through the window. He didn't blame Silver for thinking the best of him; he could be charming when he wanted to be, but he knew that he was basically a guy whose selfishness was too deeply ingrained for him to change. He knew his faults and they weren't his defining characteristics, they were casual attributes – a monument to his desire to look out for number one.

He cursed softly to himself as he remembered how Silver had looked at him when she believed he had let the fleeing people into the warehouse through unselfish motives. There was no guile in that look and its naked honesty scared him with how it made him feel. Snowdog rested the stubber against the wall and pulled a pack of bac-sticks from his trouser pocket, lighting one as he considered what would happen next.

He'd have to feed these people, and keep them safe, a duty that went against every instinct in his body. He looked out for his nearest and dearest and that most certainly did not include civilians. Damn. He glanced over at Silver, feeling the chill of her eyes and cursed again.

He ran a hand through his bleached hair, hearing the sound of screams and gunfire as more aliens ran into resistance in

other parts of the city. He looked at the huddled people and
shook his head.

What had he been thinking? What *was* he thinking?

Stacked crates stretched all the way back into the darkness
of the warehouse; it was a veritable treasure trove of weapons,
medical supplies, food, clothing, blankets – all the things a
city in the grip of winter and invasion would desperately
need.

He switched his gaze from the crates to the huddled people
and as he saw the desperate longing in their eyes, he pictured
the contents of the crates.

Snowdog smiled, suddenly scenting opportunities multiplying.

TEN

URIEL AND LEARCHUS surveyed the wreckage of the trench lines with practiced eyes, realising that against another aerial assault they would probably hold, but against a combined assault of land and airborne creatures, they would not. Reconnaissance provided by the Fury pilots stranded on Tarsis Ultra after the *Kharloss Vincennes* had been unable to recover them had indicated that a chitinous tide of unimaginable proportions was barely sixty kilometres to the west.

A conservative estimate of their speed of advance put the tyranid horde less than hour away. Three aircraft had been lost to discover this information, brought down by roving packs of gargoyles lurking in the coloured clouds that billowed up from the mutant growths propagated by the alien spores.

'We will not hold this line, brother-captain,' said Learchus.

'I know, but it will be a bitter blow to morale to have to pull back so soon after the first attack.'

Stretcher bearers and field medics moved along the trenches, applying battlefield triage where they could and marking those who needed immediate removal to the medicae facilities with charcoal sticks. The soldiers of all the regiments had performed heroically, but Uriel knew that heroics alone were not enough to win this war.

Further along the trenches, Uriel could see Chaplain Astador of the Mortifactors, kneeling in prayer within a circle of his brother Space Marines. Smoke from an iron brazier set before Astador drifted skyward and even over the stench of today's battle, Uriel's enhanced senses could pick out the scent of boiling blood.

Learchus followed his captain's gaze, his lip curling in distaste as he too caught the scent of blood in the dark smoke.

'What devilment are they about now?' wondered Learchus.

'I do not know, sergeant, but I'll wager that you will not find its like within the pages of the Codex Astartes.'

Learchus grunted in agreement as Major Satria of the Erebus Defence Legion and Captain Bannon of the Deathwatch made their way towards the two Space Marines. Bannon moved with the leisurely stride of a born warrior; his armour was blood-stained, the yellow and black symbol of the Imperial Fists obscured with purple ichor. Satria's features were bloody and exhausted. A red-stained bandage bound his left arm and his helmet bore deep grooves, scarred by alien claws.

'Sergeant Learchus,' he said.

'Major Satria. Your men have fought bravely,' said Learchus.

'Thank you,' replied Satria. 'There's steel in these lads. We won't let you down.'

'Your fighting spirit is commendable, Major Satria, but I fear this is but a taster of what is to come,' said Uriel.

'You may be right, Captain Ventris, I've just received reports that seven other cities have been attacked already. And we can't raise many of the smaller settlements.'

'They are already dead,' said Bannon.

'You can't know that,' protested Satria.

'But I can, Major Satria,' answered Bannon. 'I have fought the tyranids before and we can expect more attacks very soon, launched with even more ferocity and cunning.'

'So what do we do?'

'We will fight,' stated Bannon, his tone brooking no argument. 'This is the largest settlement on Tarsis Ultra and the tyranids will see it as the most vital organ of their prey to strike. They will attack throughout Tarsis Ultra, of course, but their greatest effort will be directed at us.'

Uriel nodded, his blood flaming with the certainty and passion of Bannon's voice, feeling the killing rage and hatred of the tyranids boil upwards through his veins.

'Where are your men?' asked Learchus.

'I have stationed them at key points in the defence line,' answered Bannon. 'Each has the Litany of Hatred of the Xenos carved on his breastplate and will recite them to the soldiers around them as they fight. The Emperor's holy wrath will infuse every man with the courage to do his duty.'

'They will do so anyway,' promised Satria.

Uriel let the words of his companions drift over him as the scent of blood in his nostrils suddenly leapt in clarity, swelling to fill his perception until he could see and feel nothing beyond the desire to see it shed. He could feel the pace of his heart rates increase until he realised he was in danger of hyperventilating.

'Captain Ventris?' asked Bannon. 'Are you alright?'

With an effort of will, Uriel dragged his perceptions back to the present, feeling the real world suddenly snap back into focus and the overpowering stench of blood recede like a forgotten dream. He unclenched his fists and nodded.

'Yes, yes, I am fine,' he said slowly. 'I am simply eager to spill more alien blood.'

Uriel swore he could feel the amusement of a dark spirit lurking just behind his eyes.

IN ANOTHER SECTION of the trenches, Pasanius wiped black streaks of alien blood from his silvered bionic arm, a frown of consternation creasing his features. He picked up a handful of snow and smeared it over the gleaming metal, watching as it melted and washed yet more of the blood from his arm. Finally, he stooped and picked up a fallen scarf, wiping the surface of his arm clean.

The metal beneath was gleaming like new, its surface smooth and unblemished by so much as a scratch.

Pasanius caught his breath and closed his eyes.

He held his arm close to his body and prayed.

AGAIN THE WARNING klaxons blared and soldiers rushed to man the trenches. Distant swarms of gargoyles swooped in the sky as a swelling, rustling noise built from a whisper to a roar.

Uriel recognised it as the sound of millions of creatures frantically jostling together as they churned forwards in an
unstoppable mass, driven to kill and fight by the implacable
will of the hive mind.

A rippling black line appeared on the horizon, an undulating tide of claws, armoured carapaces and leaping monsters.
He flexed his fingers on the grip of his sword, his thumb hovering over the activation rune, willing the tyranids closer so
that he might slake this bloodlust in their ripped entrails.

The horizon seethed with motion, the entire width of the
valley filled with alien monsters intent on killing. Imperial
artillery pieces, placed nearer the city walls, boomed and
plumes of black smoke and explosions of ice fountained on
the ice plain. Defence turrets and hastily constructed pillboxes
opened fire, filling the air with deafening noise and lethal projectiles. Howling Lightning and Marauder aircraft streaked
over the trenches to strafe the forward elements of the tyranid
swarm or send high explosive bombs to crater the ice and
incinerate tyranid creatures in their hundreds. Imperial Guard
tanks lobbed shells on a high trajectory, their commanders
knowing they would find targets without the need to aim. The
vast cannon on the frontal cliff of Colonel Rabelaq's Capitol
Imperialis fired, its thunderous shot sounding like the crack of
doom. Sheets of ice and snow fell from the mountains as the
thunderous barrage of a well dug-in force unleashed the full
fury of its firepower against the enemy.

Thousands of tyranid organisms were killed, their carcasses
trampled in the furious rush of the surviving creatures to
reach their prey, but Uriel could see that the actual damage
inflicted was negligible. Thousands were dead, but a hundred
times that number remained.

Among the swarm, he could see larger, more threatening
looking beasts, their shape suggesting giant, living battering
rams. Creatures that felt no pain and whose nervous systems
were so rudimentary that it could take their bodies many minutes to realise that they were in fact dead. Crackling arcs of
blue energy sparked amongst the swarm and the screeching
wails of the aliens echoed from the valley sides, plucking at
the strained nerves of the soldiers.

He glanced at the nervous faces around him, seeing the regimental insignia of Krieg, Logres and Erebus Defence Legion

units. Every face was wrapped in snow goggles, scarves and helmets, but he could sense the fear in all of them.

'Place your trust in the Emperor,' shouted Uriel, 'He is both your shield and your weapon. Trust to His wisdom that there is purpose in everything, and you will prevail. Kill your enemies with His name on your lips and fight with the strength that He has given you. And if it is your fate to give your life in His name, rejoice that you have served His will.'

Uriel activated his power sword, coils of energy wreathing the blade in deadly energy.

'Let the aliens come,' he snarled. 'We will show them what it means to fight the soldiers of the Emperor.'

CHAPLAIN ASTADOR FELT the pulse of the world through the ceramite plates of his armour, sensing the planet's pain at this invasion in every strand of life that took its sustenance from its spirit. The scent of his own burning blood filled his senses and allowed his ghost-self to commune with those who had gone before him, who had worn the holy suit of armour in ages past, whose perceptions of the universe were uncluttered by the fetters of mortal flesh.

He could feel the flaring energies of the soldiers around him, fear radiating hot and urgent, but also courage and determination. It was a potent combination, but Astador could not yet tell whether it would be enough to stand before these creatures that gave neither thought nor obeisance to the spirits of the dead and all that they could know.

Though he could sense individual intelligences lurking within the swarm, he could feel a single keening voice that lanced through the swarm, a single driving imperative that gave them great strength of purpose, but no will of their own. It felt like cold steel, a glacial spike driven through his ghost-self. The sheer horror of this utterly alien consciousness threatened to overwhelm Astador, and the awesome scale of such domination of the self beggared belief.

There was no hunger, no anger, no courage, or ambition in that imperative, only a single-minded desire to consume.

There was strength in that, to be sure, but also great weakness.

But should that cold steel imperative be broken, what then could such slave creatures achieve with no will of their own?

Casting his ghost-self further into the chill of the ghastly tyranid psyche, Astador probed for ways to do just that.

CAPTAIN OWEN MORTEN hauled violently on the stick of his Fury interceptor, pulling a hard dive for the deck. Whiteness flashed past his canopy and he levelled his wings as he pulled out some forty metres above the ice. He feathered the engines, pulling around and craning his neck over his right shoulder. A trail of bright explosions bloomed in his wake, alien carcasses cartwheeling through the air and Morten's icy countenance hardened even further.

Hastily reconfigured to carry air-to-ground munitions following their landing on Tarsis Ultra, Captain Morten's squadron of Furies were taking the fight back to the tyranids. His last sight of the *Kharloss Vincennes* was of her launch bays in flames before the violence of the refinery's explosion had eclipsed her death throes. A blood price had to be paid for all their shipmates and the Angel squadrons were reaping it in the blood of these damned aliens.

Erin Harlen's Fury looped overhead, the bombs on his centre pylon pickling off in sequence to impact in a string of detonations that merged into one continuous roar.

Morten rolled his Fury, screaming back across the trenches below and checking that his two wingmen were still on station with him. High above, Lightning interceptors looped in lunatic acrobatics with packs of gargoyles, their pilots keeping the flying creatures busy while they delivered their explosive payloads. Even a cursory glance told him that the Lightnings would not be able to hold the flocks of aerial killers off their backs for much longer.

He thumbed the vox-link on his control column.

'We're going in again,' he said. 'Low altitude strafing run. Follow on my lead.'

'Captain,' warned Kiell Pelaur, his gunnery officer, 'we're all out of missiles. We don't have anything left to drop.'

'I know, lieutenant. Switching to guns.'

Morten pushed the nose of the aircraft towards the ground, the swarm rushing towards him through the canopy. The shuddering of the airframe increased and a red light flashed on the panel before him as the proximity alarms shrieked as the Fury's altitude dropped to a mere thirty metres. Flying at such height required the steadiest of hands on the stick, as the slightest error would smear the Fury across the ice.

But the commander of the Angel squadrons was amongst the best pilots the *Kharloss Vincennes* battlegroup could put in the air and his control was second only to that of Erin Harlen. The tyranids rushed towards them, plumes of ice crystals foaming in the wake of the screaming Furies.

Captain Morten pulled the trigger on his control column, sending lancing bolts of energy from the Fury's lascannon into the horde. Explosions of blood and ice tore through them as the powerful weapon fired again and again. Morten screamed as he fired, feeling the burning desire to kill every single one of these abominations in one fell swoop. He pictured a blooming red fireball, the destruction he could achieve by simply letting go of the Fury and allowing her a final, glorious death in the heat of battle.

Another red light began blinking as the last energy cell for the lascannon was ejected from the Fury's underside and the frequency of the proximity alarm rose to a shrill new height.

'Captain!' screamed Pelaur, 'Pull up! For the Emperor's sake pull up!'

Pelaur's shout snapped Morten from his visions of death and he took a deep breath, pulling back and hauling the Fury into a looping climb.

'Imperator, captain! That was some real close flying,' breathed Pelaur. 'That's the kind of thing I expect from Harlen.'

Captain Owen Morten didn't reply, picturing a giant valedictory explosion.

PAVEL LEFORTO FIRED into the mass of aliens, terrified beyond thought at the scale of what he was seeing. Giant monsters lumbered through the charging mass of beasts, their snapping talons bigger than the claws on the lifting rigs that hauled girders in the smeltery.

The alien advance had faltered about ten metres from the trenches, the smooth ice coating the snow berm defeating their attempts to close the final gap. But already the smaller beasts were chopping into the ice to pull themselves closer. They died in droves, but following creatures used the corpses to push even closer. The advance had stalled, but it had granted the Imperial forces only the briefest of respites.

The noise of battle was tremendous: roaring guns, explosions, screaming and the inhuman rasping of the tyranids. A huge mushroom cloud erupted in the centre of the aliens as the Capitol Imperialis fired again, throwing ice and alien bodies hundreds of metres into the air.

The platoon briefings told him to shoot at the larger tyranid creatures, the sergeants claiming that this would disrupt the smaller beasts. Quite how that would work was a mystery to him, but he had spent his entire adult life obeying orders and wasn't about to stop now.

He ejected a spent power cell and slotted home a fresh one with trembling hands. Raising the rifle to his shoulder, he sighted along the barrel at a towering monster with a flaring bone crest rising from the back of its skull. Powerful, clawed arms held a long gristly tube that dripped slime, and surrounding the monster were dome-skulled creatures with bony protuberances growing from their upper limbs. He aimed a shot at the largest creature's skull, his bolt ricocheting from the thick fringe of bone. A missile streaked from behind him towards the giant monster, exploding against the bony growths of one its chitinous protectors.

Realising there wasn't much he could do to scratch this monster, he switched targets as a hissing alien, having finally climbed the carpet of dead, planted its claws in the top of the snow berm. He shot it full in the face, blowing its head off and leaving its body anchored to the trench by its long talons.

Soldiers all around him fired frantically into the masses of aliens, knowing that to survive they had to prevent them from reaching their lines.

But Pavel could already see they wouldn't succeed.

URIEL SLASHED HIS sword through a hormagaunt's midsection and kicked another's head from its shoulders as it clawed its way over the snow berm. Beside him, Pasanius's flamer seared a clutch of aliens as they attempted to scale their dead. Snow and ice steamed in the heat and droplets of promethium melted small holes in the ice.

Uriel saw a brace of monsters drop into the trench further along the line and shouted to Pasanius, 'With me, sergeant!'

He dropped from the firing step and sprinted towards the breach in the lines, firing his bolt pistol as he ran. The explosive shells blasted apart a handful of the creatures and he burst amongst the rest like a thunderbolt, slashing left and right with furious strokes of his power sword. Aliens died by the score as the two Space Marines smashed their way through their hissing bodies.

Claws scraped at their armour, their speed blinding, but these warriors were the very best of the Emperor's soldiers and none of the aliens' blows could halt them. Uriel felt ancestral hatred of these beasts pound in his veins as he slew, attacking, always attacking, with no thought to his own defence.

A pack of hormagaunts landed atop him, driving him to his knees. Chitinous claws hammered his armour, one penetrating the joint of his breastplate and hip. Blood burst from the wound, clotting instantly as his enhanced bloodstream formed a protective layer over the tear in his flesh. He rolled, crushing several of the beasts beneath his weight and thrashed like a madman to dislodge the others. He slammed his elbow downwards, feeling bone break, and swung his arm in a wide circle, leaving severed alien limbs and opened bellies in the wake of his blade.

He clambered to his feet, spinning with his sword raised as he felt a powerful grip encircle his arm. He roared in hate, diverting his stroke at the last second as he saw Pasanius before him, hammering his sword into the packed snow of the trench wall.

Pasanius ducked past Uriel and poured a tongue of fire down the length of the trench from his flamer. Duckboards caught light and aliens screeched as the fire consumed them. More were pouring over the top of the berm and dropping into the trench.

The Space Marines turned and fought with all the skill and ferocity the Adeptus Astartes were famed for, shrugging off blows that would have killed a normal man twice over and fighting beyond the limits of courage and endurance.

Then the tide of smaller beasts parted and a giant beast with massive clawed arms stomped across the mass of dead aliens towards them. Three metres tall, the warrior organism was all rippling armour plates and glistening organs, layered beneath a bony exo-skeleton coated with an encrusted layer of fatty tissue. Its jaw opened, letting loose a terrifying screech as its scythe-taloned arms raised to strike. A drooling bio-weapon spat a phlegmy wad of slime.

Uriel dived aside, the sparkling slime blasting a huge chunk of ice from the wall behind him. He sprang to his feet as the monster smashed its way through the snow berm, standing at the lip of the trench. He fired his last remaining bolts at the huge creature, blowing off chunks of its chitinous armour, but failing to stop its murderous progress. Pasanius bathed the creature in fire, the insulating fat on its bones sizzling and filling the trench with a disgusting odour. Dozens of hormagaunts followed in its steps.

Uriel leapt to meet the monster, swinging his power sword at its thorax. A bladed limb swept down, blocking the blow as another slammed into his breastplate, cracking the ceramite and knocking him from his feet. He rolled with the blow and dove around the side of the beast, hacking his blade through its legs just above its giant hooves. The beast howled in pain, crashing to its knees and toppling forwards into the trench where it lay thrashing its clawed arms impotently.

Pasanius fought the hormagaunts back as yet more poured through the gap their larger sibling had battered.

'Captain!' bellowed Pasanius.

'I know!' shouted Uriel, leaping onto the bucking monster's back. The giant tyranid beast struggled to right itself, but Uriel reversed the grip of his sword and drove the blade downwards through its skull.

Instantly its motion ceased and Uriel roared as he ripped his blade free in an arc of black blood. He jumped from the monster's back as Pasanius cut his way through the suddenly dazed-looking hormagaunts. Uriel and his sergeant didn't give the disorientated creatures time to recover their wits, hacking them down without mercy.

Uriel killed them without pity, hating them for driving him to this frenzy of slaughter. His blade rose and fell, its surface coated with blood as he waded in alien gore. The battle around him receded until he could see nothing beyond the death that surrounded him, the blood and the sudden fear of creatures that had no will of their own, having had the blanket of connection stripped away from them.

Thunderous footfalls shook him from his reverie of blood. He saw Pasanius hurled through the air and the shadow of another gigantic monster rear up through the mist of ice and blood.

Larger than a dreadnought, the carnifex shrieked with a rasping of plates deep in its shark-like maw. Its carapace was battered and cracked, alien blood pouring from numerous wounds punched through its body. Rearing up, it blocked the sun and four massively clawed arms reached towards him.

Then its jaw opened wider still and an emerald green torrent of bio-plasmic fire vomited from inside it.

Uriel threw up his arms to ward off the energised plasma, but the force of the alien's discharge smashed him to the ground.

He fought to stand, the hissing green ichor coating his visor and rendering him blind. He lashed out with his sword, feeling it bite through alien flesh.

The ground shook as the carnifex towered over him and Uriel felt the heat of its breath on his face.

ASTADOR FELT HIS grip on his ghost-self slip as he neared the cold fire at the centre of the swarm's mind. A giant presence like the chill at the heart of a glacier bathed his soul in ice-water and he could feel its presence echo from the sides of the valley like a cavern-deep river. This was it, this was the control, this was the heart of the cold mind.

He could sense its awareness only as a fragment of something unimaginable vaster, and deep on the edges of its perception, he knew that it too was aware of him. Cold ripples of horror reached for him, but his ghost-self was already returning to his body.

Astador opened his eyes and smoothly rose to his feet.

The warriors who had loaned him their strength did likewise and he blinked as his normal sight restored itself. All around him battle raged, but he felt disconnected from it, his spirit resisting the imprecations of flesh and the limitations that imposed.

Mortifactors and members of the Deathwatch battled the tyranids all around them, fighting to keep the alien creatures from breaking his trance.

Captain Bannon marched towards him, his armour bloody.
'Well?' he asked. 'Do you know?'

'I know,' said Astador.

PAVEL HURLED HIS last grenade into the mass of creatures, ducking as the concussive force of the detonation dislodged a
section of the trench. He had passed beyond fear now, acting
simply on adrenaline and training. So many things had happened to him that he could not function were fear to take
hold. His body's own sense of self-preservation clamped
down on his fear and drove him ever onwards.

He shot, stabbed and hacked his way through the alien
creatures, scavenging whatever munitions and weaponry he
could find when his own ran out. He tripped, rolling over the
dissolving corpses of two soldiers wearing Krieg greatcoats,
slamming his face against the cold steel of their fallen
weapon. Hissing slime ate away their flesh and Pavel recoiled,
spitting blood as he pushed himself upright.

Jade light lit up the trench and he saw a hulking monster
with a vividly patterned carapace smash its way through the
trench barricades, green fire spewing from between toothed
mandibles. Dozens of hissing beasts gathered behind the
massive creature, ready to pour into the trench. An Ultramarines sergeant lay unconscious on the snow and the same
captain who had saved his life from the gargoyles sprawled in
a steaming pool of the creature's green fire.

Pavel acted without thinking and lifted the Krieg gunners'
weapon onto his shoulder, praying that they had loaded the
missile launcher before they'd died.

URIEL SCRAMBLED BACKWARDS, desperately wiping hissing bio-
plasma from his visor.

He looked up and saw death in the black eyes of the
carnifex. They were black, lidless and devoid of life, like a
doll's. He felt the wall of the trench at his back and knew there
was nowhere else to go.

His sword arm came up, but he knew it was too late.

Then a blistering streak flashed through his vision and
struck the carnifex square in the centre of its skull. A powerful
shockwave buffeted Uriel and he felt bony shrapnel spray
him. As the echoes of the explosion faded, he looked up

through the cloud of smoke at the massive organism and saw that its head had vanished, leaving nothing but a charred blood basin, oozing brain and skull fragments.

The carnifex swayed for a second until its body registered the fact that it was dead and its knees buckled. The massive creature collapsed and Uriel rolled aside as it fell, the impact throwing up blood-streaked bio-plasma and ice.

Further along the trench he caught sight of a soldier with the insignia of the Erebus Defence Legion stencilled on his helmet, a smoking missile launcher cradled on his shoulder.

He pushed himself to his feet as a tide of hormagaunts poured through the gap bludgeoned by the carnifex.

Raising his sword, he leapt to meet them.

PAVEL TOSSED ASIDE the smoking missile launcher and swiftly rolled over one of the Krieg gunners, searching for more weapons. He unholstered the man's laspistol and drew his sword from a wide scabbard. The blade was toothed and heavy, and Pavel recognised a chainsword, though he had never used such a weapon before.

He searched for an activation stud, finding it on the base of the pommel, and the sword roared into life, the toothed blade spinning like a chainsaw. He rose and sprinted to where the Ultramarines captain was desperately fending off a horde of beasts that were pouring into the trenches.

He swung the heavy chainsword, feeling the blade judder as it tore through alien bones and sprayed him with alien fluids. He fired into the mass of creatures, blasting another to death and ripping his sword free in the same instant.

Pavel fought without the skill of the Ultramarines captain, but his fear and the desire to protect his home empowered him with fury and courage.

Together he and the Space Marine captain fought the aliens like heroes of legend. His arm ached from swinging the sword and he switched to using it two-handed when the laspistol ran out of charge.

He hacked a screeching beast in half as another giant figure in blue armour joined him and the captain, a sergeant with a gleaming silver arm. He grinned as he killed another alien, picturing the stories he'd be able to tell Hollia and Solan when this was all over.

He tried to pull the chainsword free from the creature's chest, but the toothed blade was jammed in its bony exoskeleton. He desperately tugged again as another monster bounded over the trench barricade.

Its claws slashed for his head and he swayed aside.

But not quickly enough as a scything blade hammered into his helmet, tearing it from his head. A lower set of clawed limbs stabbed at him, tearing through his overwhites and hot pain shrieked along his nerve endings. Blood sprayed from the wound and he collapsed, feeling gore-melted snow slam into his face.

Pavel rolled, drawing his war-knife and, through a blur of red water and tears of pain, raised it in time to skewer the beast's throat as it leapt at him. It claws scrabbled at him as it died. Pavel wrenched the knife upwards, impaling its skull on the blade.

Releasing the knife, he weakly pushed himself to his feet, using the side of the trench for support. His vision swam and he felt his legs turn to water as a wave of sick dizziness swamped him. He numbly peeled the sodden fabric of his torn overwhites from his shoulder. Sticky blood oozed wetly from a deep gash and a glistening black claw was wedged in the cut. Strange, he thought dreamily.

His wound didn't seem to hurt. There was no pain.

He wondered why, but was saved from the answer by collapsing, face first, into the bloody snow.

He was unconscious before he hit the ground.

URIEL RAN THROUGH the twisting passages of the trench, racing towards where he could see a group of black armoured warriors mounting up in five Rhino armoured personnel carriers. Colonel Rabelaq was feeding in reserves from the second trench to stabilise the front and yet more troops were moving up from the third line. The defences were holding, but only just. If the tyranids kept up this ferocious assault, then it was only a matter of time until the front line was breached.

He vaulted mounds of the dead, hurrying past desperate combats to reach the southern salient, where the Rhinos growled as the drivers gunned the engines. He could see Captain Bannon of the Deathwatch and the bone-rimmed armour of Chaplain Astador as he made his way through his kneeling men, administering the Mortis Astartes blessing to each one.

Captain Bannon rose to his feet as he caught sight of Uriel approaching, and moved to intercept him.

'What are you doing?' demanded Uriel.

'What must be done to hold the line,' answered Bannon, blocking Uriel's route.

'You are taking the fight to the aliens, aren't you?'

'Yes. Chaplain Astador has located the beast he believes is controlling this element of the tyranid swarm.'

'What? How?'

'The spirits of his ancestors have guided him to it.'

'Are you serious?'

'Deadly serious,' stated Bannon. 'I trust his judgement on this implicitly.'

Uriel was stunned. To hear a brother Space Marine place such faith in ritual and superstition was beyond belief, but it was happening right here in front of him. He wondered what Idaeus would do.

Uriel nodded, his expression hardening. 'Very well then, I'm coming with you.'

Bannon's eyebrows arched. 'Really?'

'Aye. If we can end this now, then you'll need all the help you can get.'

Bannon searched Uriel's face for any sign of an ulterior motive, but finding none, slapped a palm on his shoulder guard and said, 'So be it. Find a transport and let's go.'

Uriel jogged towards the Rhinos and, realising there would be no room for him inside, clambered onto the roof of the nearest one. Its every panel was black, fastened with rivets stamped with tiny brass skulls and a grinning skull topped each exhaust, blue oilsmoke jetting from each jaw. The engine roared and Uriel gripped the edge of the roof as the rest of the Mortifactors and seven members of the Deathwatch climbed aboard the five transports.

The Rhino spun as the tracks fought for purchase on the slushy ground, before lurching forward as they finally bit. Thick timbers had been laid across the trench and the Rhino reared upwards as it hit the edge of the snow berm, slamming down hard onto the ice on the other side. Uriel's Rhino took the lead at the head of a wedge of transports, crushing those aliens not quick enough to get out of the way.

Alien screeches rose to new heights as they reacted to the interlopers in their midst, and a section of the swarm smoothly altered the direction of its charge to intercept the Rhinos. Scores of bounding, clawed monsters drew close and Uriel pulled himself along the roof as the front hatch opened and a warrior of the Mortifactors pulled himself up to man the pintle-mounted storm bolter. He snapped back the action and checked that it was equipped with a full load, before pulling the trigger and working the bucking weapon left and right, clearing a path for the Rhino to follow.

Uriel hung on for dear life as the Rhino swayed crazily through the aliens, gripping his sword in his other hand as the vehicles crushed a path towards a monstrous, humped creature lurking in the centre of the swarm. Its glistening, segmented body rippled with motion and, even from here, Uriel could feel a sickening sense of dread permeate his soul as the Rhino drew nearer.

A flash of gleaming claws brought him back to the present with a jolt as a hormagaunt leapt from the swarm towards him. He brought his sword up in the nick of time, hacking the creature in two with one sweep.

The Rhino's speed was dropping. Dozens of beasts clambered across the vehicle's hull as it sped closer to its objective,.alien bodies clogging the tracks and allowing others to climb over them to reach the prey on top.

Uriel stabbed and slashed with his sword, keeping the monsters from reaching the gunner who continued spraying bolts into the mass of creatures. Wind whipped by him as the Rhino ploughed onwards.

An explosion behind him rocked the vehicle with its force. He risked a glance over his shoulder, seeing the second Rhino burning fiercely, bright flames leaping from its ruptured hull. Blazing Space Marines stumbled from the wreck, still fighting as they burned. Hissing creatures surrounded them and soon the warriors were lost to sight as hundreds of clawing, biting creatures buried them beneath their bodies.

Uriel looked to see where the shot had come from, and saw a grotesque monster drifting above the ice, its long, sinuous tail whipping beneath its bulbous head. Withered limbs hung uselessly beneath its hissing maw and a crackling haze surrounded the rippling frill of skin beneath its armoured skull.

As though sensing his scrutiny, the monster hissed, slowly turning its unnatural gaze towards the speeding Rhino. Uriel leaned forwards and rapped his fist across the shoulder guard of the gunner.

'One o'clock!' he yelled, jabbing his sword towards the floating beast.

The gunner nodded, and the storm bolter roared, spitting a hurricane of mass-reactive bolts at the monster. Uriel saw a firefly blossom of purple light flare around the creature and cursed as he saw that the volley had left it unharmed. Almost immediately, a flaring corona of psychic energy built around the creature's head, and Uriel gripped the edge of the Rhino, realising what would come next.

A bolt of pure white light streaked from the creature's overlarge head, slamming into the front of the Rhino. Uriel was hurled from his perch by the impact. He sailed through the air, just barely grabbing onto the edge of the roof panel, his feet scrabbling for purchase on the running boards.

The Rhino slewed sideways, but its recently blessed armour held firm against the abomination's attack. Ichor-slick ice hurtled beneath Uriel's feet as he fought for grip.

A screeching creature leapt for him and he kicked out as yet more hormaguants closed in. He lashed out with his feet and sword, breaking bones and splitting skulls.

Finally gaining his balance, he sheathed his sword and swung himself back onto the roof as he felt the Rhino veer off to the side. Uriel knew that they would not be lucky enough to survive another blast from the warp creature and as he looked up, he realised that the Rhino's driver had reached the same conclusion.

The floating beast was directly before them, drifting backwards in an attempt to get clear, but there was no escape as the Rhino's spiked bull bar slammed into its withered body and dragged it beneath the armoured tracks of the transport. Uriel heard a satisfying crack as it was crushed beneath the weight of the vehicle, seeing the giant stain on the ice of its crushed carcass as the Rhino drove onwards.

Their charge had been broken up, but the four surviving Rhinos were now within striking distance of their prey. From his vantage point on the Rhino's roof, Uriel could see a swirling motion amongst the swarm as its leader alerted its minions to the danger. With a precision unseen except on the parade ground, whole swathes of the alien beasts altered direction, abandoning their attack on the trenches to come to the aid of their master.

Gunfire from the Rhinos hammered the disgusting beast, its antlered head retreating within its carapace as bolts exploded all around it. Crackling energies flared from its head and the sense of dread Uriel had felt earlier grew stronger still. His innate horror at this creature threatened to overwhelm him with its alien otherworldliness, until thoughts of the Bringer of Darkness surged, unbidden, into his mind, and the sheer evil of its existence made him laugh at the insignificance of this creature.

Guardian warrior organisms rushed to the alien's defence as the Rhinos skidded to a halt beside the lumbering beast and the Space Marines debarked with speed and precision. Uriel leapt feet first from the roof of his transport, hammering into the face of the closest monster. He felt fangs snap under his boots and rolled to his feet.

He stabbed his glowing sword through its bloody head and charged across the snow to face the next beast. Giant claws scythed towards him and he dived beneath them, aiming a gigantic, disembowelling sweep at the organism's belly. Black blood sprayed and its alien screech was cut short as Uriel hammered his blade through its neck.

More creatures closed in around him as he fought his way towards the giant master of the horde. Claws and razor-edged hooves bludgeoned him, but he cared not for the pain as a dark mist closed on his sight and he hacked about him, severing limbs and opening bellies in his frenzied charge.

He could hear a roar of animal hate and spun, searching for the source of such an atavistic howl, before realising that it was his own. Shocked at his loss of control, the battle snapped into a slow-moving ballet of utter clarity. He could see the Mortifactors forming a cordon around the seven members of the Deathwatch who jammed melta charges into the flesh of the thrashing, segmented body of the swarm leader.

And he could see the soulless, black eyes of the monster as it realised its doom was at hand. Even as he watched, its horned, beetle-like head surged from its carapace and hammered into his chest, digging deep and lifting him high into the air. A massive, toothed orifice opened beneath its horns and Uriel was powerless to prevent himself from sliding into its fanged maw. He gripped its bony horns with one hand and desperately tried to pull himself free.

The monster's eyes rolled back as a nictitating membrane blinked and the orifice closed on his body. He felt the fangs bite into his armour, and knew that the incredible strength of the beast would soon break open its toughened plates. Uriel spun his sword, holding it blade downwards.

He felt fangs pierce his flesh. Blood flowed.

He stabbed the blade into the beast's chitin-plated skull, roaring as he drove it into its brain as a dazzling brightness suddenly lit up the world.

Sudden, intense heat flared as the Deathwatch's melta bombs detonated, and he could feel the death-grip on his body relax. The snowy ground rushed up to meet him and he grunted as he slammed into the ice. A deathly silence fell across the valley and even Uriel could feel a keening sense of loss rip through the tyranid swarm.

Swiftly he cut himself free of the giant tyranid beast's maw and dragged his legs from the glutinous, sucking orifice. He felt a hand on his shoulder and pushed himself to his feet in time to see Bannon and the rest of the Space Marines backing away from the charred carcass of the monster towards the Rhinos.

'Come on,' snapped Bannon, his tone angry. 'It is dead. We must get away.'

'Aye,' gasped Uriel, staggering after the captain of the Deathwatch.

As he climbed inside the scorched and ichor-stained Rhino he felt nothing but shame as he pictured his frenzied, uncontrolled raging attack.

DARKNESS WAS SEVERAL hours old by the time the all clear sounded. With the death of the swarm leader, the tyranid attack had foundered, the alien creatures milling in panicked confusion as the controlling will was stripped from the majority of them. Furious counterattacks from the Space Marines and disciplined firing protocols soon despatched any remaining creatures that still appeared capable of independent action and as the temperature dropped to twenty below freezing, most of the tyranids froze to death where they stood.

Some survived by burrowing into the depths of the snow, where their increased reserves of fat allowed them to enter a form of short-lived hibernation, but these were few and far between. There were not, however, the resources to hunt them down as the subzero temperatures prohibited all but the most essential movements among the defenders.

Such a manoeuvre was even now being undertaken as the Imperial forces retreated to the second trench line. Realising that the first line would not hold against another attack, Colonels Stagler and Rabelaq had decided to pull back on the heels of what was being promoted as a great victory.

But with aerial reconnaissance promising yet more incoming swarms, at least triple the size of this vanguard, and each counting towering beasts that rivalled the size of Battle Titans among their number, there were no illusions among the high command that this victory was anything other than a stay of execution.

ELEVEN

A BLUE GLOW filled the command bridge of the Capitol Imperialis, throwing the faces of the command staff into stark relief. Hooded servitors sat immobile before their consoles, insulated bundles of cables snaking from the backs of their robes to sockets in the grilled floor. A lilting chant of imprecations to the machine god drifted from bronze speakers on the ceiling. Sputtering recyc-units tried to keep the atmosphere cool, but the temperature in the command bridge was still stifling.

Uriel did not like being in this armoured leviathan: it ill-suited the Space Marine way of war to be so static and the Codex Astartes frequently pointed out the need for mobility on the battlefield. But recently he had paid little more than lip service to the teachings of his primarch's holy tome. Learchus had made no secret of his disapproval of Uriel's helter-skelter journey on the roof of a Mortifactors' Rhino, claiming it was a foolish stunt more in keeping with the Sons of Russ than a proud Ultramarine, and Uriel was inclined to agree with him.

He shook his head clear of the memory and returned his attention to matters at hand.

The situation was not good.

A holo-map with a rippling green representation of the landscape surrounding Erebus filled the centre of the columned chamber, grainy static washing through the image every few seconds. Information received from various sources fed into the display, picking out Imperial units and positions of incoming swarms. Colonel Rabelaq stood at the end of the map, flanked by his aides and adjutants, while Uriel and Colonel Stagler stood on one side of the map with Chaplain Astador and Captain Bannon on the other.

'It appears that Hera's Gate and Parmenis have both fallen,' began Rabelaq. 'We've been unable to raise Imperial forces in either one of them, and the squadron of Lightnings we sent to obtain visual reports on Konoris and Inyiriam have failed to return. We must assume that the forces that destroyed them are now inbound on our position.'

'And what of the forces that are already moving towards us?' asked Stagler, still wearing his Krieg greatcoat and colback despite the heat.

Rabelaq didn't answer immediately, his consternation evident. 'Ah, well, that we're not sure of. It appears a great many of them have scattered or gone to ground, and we're assuming that they've burrowed into the snow for shelter, as animals are wont to do in winter, to await the arrival of the other swarms. A great many of our reconnaissance assets have already been lost and I felt it would be unwise to lose any more for what would in all likelihood not gain us much more information than we already know.'

Stunned silence greeted his pronouncement, before Bannon leaned over the map and said, 'It is a mistake, Colonel Rabelaq, to assume that these aliens will behave like animals, and if there is one thing I have learned about the tyranids, it is that you do not want to let them out of your sight, even for a second.'

'Yes, well, that's as maybe, Captain Bannon, but if you look at the map, you'll see that we have three distinct swarms of creatures closing on our position. Originally, the southern-most swarm would have reached us first, but it appears as though it has altered the speed of its advance so that all three will arrive together.'

'Clever,' mused Astador, 'very clever. They have learned that we can defeat one swarm, and gather to overrun in one massive charge.'

Uriel watched the icons on the holo-map crawl slowly across the flickering representation of the surface of Tarsis Ultra. Something nagged at the back of his mind, but he could not put his finger on what. He knew it was something simple, but of great import.

'And what is happening in space?' asked Captain Bannon. 'Have we been able to make contact with the fleet?'

Uriel said, 'The Shadow in the Warp is still making astropathic communication impossible, but we have been able to make brief contact with Lord Admiral Tiberius over the long-range vox-caster. Communications are still very fragmentary and we are having trouble maintaining the link through the electromagnetic interference generated by the hive fleet.'

'And what is his situation?' said Astador.

'The admiral has the fleet at anchor around the agri-world of Calydon, though he tells me that a great many vessels are heavily damaged.'

'Have the tyranids not tried to engage him?' asked Bannon.

'Not in any strength, no. It would appear that there are only two hive ships remaining in orbit, so the aliens do not have the capability to effectively control their forces here and despatch an expeditionary force to destroy the fleet.'

Bannon asked, 'Then is the fleet in any shape to offer us support?'

'Potentially,' said Uriel. 'Admiral Tiberius has suggested a plan of attack, but I need to confer with the Fabricator Marshal before expounding further on this. For the moment, no, we are on our own.'

Heads nodded around the map table as each commander digested Uriel's information.

'Then, in short, gentlemen, we have no other choice but to pull back behind the city walls,' said Rabelaq. 'The trenches simply can't hold against these numbers. The walls will prevent the smaller brood organisms from attacking and we have ample guns positioned there to pick off the larger beasts.'

'I agree with Colonel Rabelaq,' said Astador. 'We must accept that the city will suffer under the attack. Better to fight on our terms than theirs.'

Reluctantly, Colonel Stagler nodded, though Uriel could see it irked him to give ground, even when it would be suicide to stand and fight.

'The Krieg regiment will provide the rearguard for the retreat,' he said, almost spitting the words. Uriel looked at the map again and suddenly his nagging worry came to the fore of his mind.

'Were there not four swarms approaching us earlier?' he asked.

'Yes, Captain Ventris,' nodded Rabelaq, 'but we believe that the smaller northern swarm has simply merged with the one moving in from Parmenis. They were, after all, less than thirty kilometres apart.'

'Are you sure about that?' asked Uriel.

'Well, no, but where else could they be? The northern mountains are impenetrable, Fabricator Montante has assured me.'

'With all due respect to Fabricator Montante, he is not a soldier. Can we trust our security to the conclusions of a logistician?'

'He has local knowledge, Captain Ventris. Major Satria concurred also and having seen hololithic topography of the region in question, I am in agreement.'

Uriel could see the others around the room were alarmed at the prospect of a potentially missing swarm, but since there was no proof as to its existence, none had any answer as to what could be done about it.

'How long do we have before they reach us?' asked Bannon.

'Five, maybe six hours at most,' said Rabelaq.

'Then let's get to work,' said Stagler.

SNOW SWIRLED IN obscuring blizzards around the crumbling hab units of District Secundus, gathering in windblown drifts and deadening the sounds of the column of refugees that trudged through the knee deep white carpet that enveloped Erebus.

Displaced by the rain of organic bombs and those creatures whose cocoon spores were able to penetrate the flak umbrella protecting the city, nearly six hundred people trudged through the blizzard towards a nondescript collection of buildings constructed against the rocky sides of the southern slopes.

Armed men stood watch at the splintered timbers barring the entrance and a ragged tarpaulin flapped behind them.

Since the first days of the tyranid attack, word had spread of the hero Snowdog who had saved the people of the Secundus shanties from the tide of alien beasts that dropped from the skies. That his reputation as a murderer and thief were well known was secondary to the fact that people said he had food and medical supplies.

The winters of Tarsis Ultra were harsh and those without wealth or dwellings would soon perish without shelter.

And there was a brutal killer on the loose somewhere in Erebus.

Even amid the chaos of an alien invasion, its depredations could not go unnoticed: small, isolated groups of citizens found butchered like livestock, their bodies hacked to pieces and their flesh devoured. Fear whipped through the poorest quarters of the city, and those that could not escape to the high valley, where the soldiers of the Fabricator Marshal patrolled the streets and thoroughfares where the monied citizens of Erebus dwelled, were forced to band together for mutual protection.

As the fear of this mysterious butcher grew, so too did its violence, as though the very terror it spawned drove it to new heights of slaughter. Whole communities were murdered in their homes and only the ruthlessly patrolled area around the territory of the Nightcrawlers seemed to escape the killer's attention.

For people with no hope, Snowdog was their only hope.

Papa Gallo, the unofficial but acknowledged leader of the group, pulled back his hood and approached the two men guarding the door. The shorter of the pair racked his shotgun and jammed it in his face.

'We've come for shelter from the monsters,' explained Papa Gallo.

'Shelter's not cheap,' came the muffled reply.

Pappa Gallo laughed, turning to face the wretched people behind him. 'Look at us. What do you think we can offer you? We don't have anything left.'

'Oh, I don't know,' laughed the other man, eyeing the younger women. 'What do you say, Lomax? I bet we could come to some arrangement with these good people.'

'Shut up, Trask,' said the man who had spoken first. 'That's for Snowdog to decide.'

Pappa Gallo sighed. They might live through this winter, but if they did, they would emerge more desperate than before.

DEEP IN THE shadows of the ruined habs, crouched beneath a buckled sheet of corrugated iron, a creature watched the column of refugees through multi-faceted eyes, scenting the fear and despair as coloured washes through its various senses. Its flesh rippled a silvery grey as its chameleonic scales mirrored the surfaces around it and, with a stealth surprising for such a large creature, it slipped away from its shelter.

Its reserves of fatty tissue were low and it would need to kill again to replenish them, the freezing temperatures of Tarsis Ultra almost too much for even its fearsome adaptive qualities to cope with.

Since its virtual hibernation in the grain silos of Prandium, the beast, a species known by Imperial troops as a spook or mantis stalker, but more correctly as a lictor, smoothly loped across the snow to shadow the shambling people. It leapt onto the wall of a crumbling brick building, powerful intercostal muscles lashing fleshy barbs towards the top of the wall, which retracted to pull the beast rapidly up the sheer surface.

Long scythe-like claws unsheathed from chitinous hoods on its upper arms and dug into the wall as it smoothly swung its muscled bulk onto the roof.

Worm-like tendrils surrounding its jaw scented the air, and the beast set off again, following the column of refugees from on high.

Pheromone sacs situated along the ridge of its armoured spine atomised powerful attractants that would serve to lure more tyranid creatures to this place. Thus far it had roamed the city unmolested, careful to avoid the many dangers in such a heavily populated place.

But now the overmind, for whom it had travelled far ahead, was upon this place and it could afford to throw off its stealthy mantle and kill with all the ferocity it had been bred for.

The lictor stalked to the edge of the roof, squatting on its haunches as it watched a figure detach from the column and approach a building that stank of prey.

TRASK LET LOMAX do the talking as his eyes roamed over the women, though it was hard to spot the lookers thanks to the winter clothing most were wearing. He rested his shotgun on his shoulder and wondered again how the hell Snowdog had managed to pull one over on all these people. One moment of foolish altruism had spread the word throughout the city that he was running some kind of refuge from the cold and the aliens.

It made Trask want to laugh fit to burst at the thought of how wrong people could be. Those that had been allowed to stay were paying through the nose for everything they needed: shelter, food and even basic medical supplies. Some wanted narcotics, an escape from the terror, and that was available too. Also at a price. And if someone couldn't pay with hard currency or in valuables, then there were always other ways. A man with a comely wife or daughter could obtain things a single man could not, and amongst Snowdog's gang, there were plenty willing to accept that currency.

Snowdog had put a stop to that because it didn't bring any profit, which hadn't stopped Trask of course, he'd just had to become more circumspect.

In a group this size there was sure to be some money to be made and a few fillies to pluck. As he was contemplating the prospect of fresh conquests, a blur of motion caught his eye atop the smashed ruins of the old munitions factory. He raised a hand, squinting against the glare and through the flurries of snow.

What the hell was that?

He couldn't see anything now, but he was sure his eyes weren't playing tricks on him.

There! There it was again! Something dropped from the roof of the building, landing in a snowdrift with a piercing shriek. Whatever it was, it moved like quicksilver, charging into the mass of refugees before he could shout a warning. He brought his shotgun down and racked the slide as the screaming began.

Bright arcs of blood sprayed the snow and Trask caught sight of a neatly severed head fly across the street. Screams of terror echoed from the side of the valley as people scattered from the deadly killer in their midst. Trask saw a clear space form around a collection of gory rags that only superficially resembled human remains. A blurred creature pounced from the bloodbath onto the back of man carrying a swaddled infant.

The man went down in a tangle of limbs as a giant set of bony claws stabbed downwards, skewering him to the street. His death cry made Trask flinch in terror.

The thing moved fast, darting through its feast of victims and eviscerating anyone within reach of its claws.

Papa Gallo grabbed Trask's long coat and shouted, 'You've got a gun damn you, use it!'

The old man's hands shook him from his paralysis. Trask punched the old man away and stepped onto the road. He levelled his shotgun. Screaming people streamed past, too many to stop and he let them go, figuring Snowdog could sort out this mess later.

Lomax joined him. 'What the hell is it?' he yelled.

'Damned if I know,' replied Trask as more and more people buffeted him. A knot of people trying to escape down a side street were brutally hacked down by the murderous assailant and Trask levelled his shotgun as he saw the murderer clearly for the first time. Its hide was slathered in blood and gore and whatever chameleonic properties it might once have had were now rendered moot.

It stood on two legs, nearly three metres tall, its body powerfully muscled and ridged with bony armour plates. It was bigger than any of the beasts Trask had seen so far and its upper claws were gargantuan, hooking blades that clove people in two with each swipe. Beneath those monstrous claws, muscular arms ending in fierce, taloned fists lifted shrieking victims to its fang-filled jaws.

It spun quickly, its stock of victims exhausted, moving rapidly across the icy ground towards him and Lomax.

Suddenly he was struck by the absurdity of what he was doing. Why the hell was he risking his neck for these dumb people?

He turned tail and sprinted back for the warehouse as the beast charged.

Lomax spun and shouted, 'Where the hell–' as Trask ran, but was cut off as something shot from between the bony plates of the creature's chest and punched clean through his body. Lomax dropped his gun and stared in shocked disbelief at the barbs protruding from his chest before being yanked off his feet and stabbed to death by the monster's claws.

Trask ran like he'd never run before, tossing aside his gun, arms pumping. He took the steps to the warehouse two at a time, slipping on the ice on the top step and falling face first onto the concrete.

It saved his life. Gigantic blade talons smashed through the wall of the warehouse where his head would have been. He whimpered in fear, rolling aside as the talons came at him again, striking sparks from the ground as he desperately evaded the alien's attacks. He squeezed shut his eyes, feeling his bladder empty in naked terror.

A shotgun blast fired, deafeningly close, and he screamed. More gunshots sounded. A howling screech of pain echoed.

Something whipped by his face, a spatter of warm liquid splashed his face and neck. He curled into a ball and waited to die.

After long seconds, he plucked up the courage to open his eyes. The creature was gone, and relief washed over him. He wiped stinking slime from his face, looking up to see Snowdog and Silver staring down at him, disgust clear on their faces. Wisps of smoke curled from the barrel of Snowdog's shotgun and Silver had both her pistols drawn.

'Man, I don't know why the hell I keep you around,' snapped Snowdog, offering him a hand up. He smiled weakly at Silver, who didn't even deign to look at him, too busy taking in the horror of the massacre before them.

'Where's Lomax?' asked Snowdog.

Trask tried to answer but the words wouldn't come.

'I asked you a question, man,' said Snowdog.

'He's… he's gone,' managed Trask. 'That thing got him.'

'No thanks to you, I'll bet,' sneered Silver.

He tried to shoot her a venomous look, but it came off as merely petulant.

'Did you see what it was?' asked the albino-haired gang leader.

'No,' said Trask, shaking his head. 'I didn't, but it was big, man, real big. Bigger than anything we've seen. It was fast too, fast like on spur or something, you know?'

'It was fast all right,' shot back Silver, 'but not fast enough to catch you, eh, Trask?'

'Frag you, Silver,' said Trask, some of his cocksure attitude returning now that the monster was gone.

'Not this lifetime,' she said, spinning on her heel and heading back inside the warehouse.

'Get yourself cleaned up, Trask,' snapped Snowdog. 'We got work to do. These people ain't gonna get fleeced all by themselves, now are they?'

Snowdog turned and left him standing on the icy steps, the wetness in his crotch beginning to freeze.

Feeling his earlier fear turn to anger and resentment, Trask followed Snowdog inside, rubbing at a stinging patch of skin on his neck and face.

THE DOORS WERE emblazoned with the caduceus, a staff with two winged snakes entwined around it, and even before Uriel pushed them open he could hear screams and smell the stench of death and blood.

The walls of the District Quintus Medicae facility rang to the agonised cries of over a thousand wounded men, the reek of antiseptic sprays and camphorated oils unable to mask the bitter stench of infected flesh and weeping wounds. His breath misted before him, the temperature of the room close to freezing. Sisters of the Order Hospitaller scurried through the long, vaulted chamber, their flowing white robes stiffened with dried blood. The desperation and fear in this place was palpable and it tore at Uriel's heart to see so many brave men brought low by the vile aliens.

Shrieks of wounded men and sobs of those soon to go under the bone saw echoed. Three orderlies held down a screaming Krieg Guardsman, his legs nothing more than thrashing stumps, as they attempted to clamp the spray of blood from his femoral artery. Stretcher bearers passed Uriel, carrying a woman whose arm was severed just above the elbow and Uriel could see the wound had festered, no doubt frostbitten as she had lain awaiting rescue. The stump wept pus onto the rough blanket that covered her.

Droning priests chanted the *Finis Rerum* from high pulpits, but their words were inaudible over the screaming.

It seemed that the screaming would never stop. He watched one of the sisters pull a sheet over a dead man's face and nod to the orderlies. Uriel was no stranger to death, but this simple evocation of human suffering touched him in a way he could not explain.

The woman looked up from the corpse and saw him. She wiped a dirty sleeve across her eyes and limped around the bed towards him. Her blonde hair was pulled in a greasy ponytail and Uriel could see she had not slept in days. Her smoky blue eyes were dull and bloodshot, but she had strength in her, that much was obvious.

'Brother-captain,' she said. 'Sister Joaniel Ledoyen, senior nursing officer at your service, but we are sorely pressed, so whatever you need, please be quick.'

'Why is it so cold in here?' asked Uriel.

'Because one of those damned… things hit our generator before the first attack and the blasted tech-priests haven't been able to get us a new one,' snapped Joaniel. 'Now do you have any more stupid questions, or can I get on with trying to save some lives?'

'I am sorry, sister, I am weary from the battle and my manners escape me. I am Brother-Captain Uriel Ventris and I need to find a soldier I had brought here. His name is Pavel Leforto and he belongs to the Erebus Defence Legion. He saved my life and I wish to offer my thanks.'

Joaniel's expression softened and she pointed to a nurses' station in the centre of the chamber.

'There. My deputy, Ardelia, will try to find him for you, though you should be prepared for the fact that he may be dead.'

'As the Emperor wills,' said Uriel. The corner of the woman's mouth twitched at the familiar phrase and she nodded.

'Now, if you will excuse me, I have work to do,' she said and turned away.

Uriel watched Sister Joaniel Ledoyen limp towards the next bed and the next bloodstained soldier, then turned on his heel and marched to the nurses' station.

* * *

IT TOOK AN hour to locate Pavel Leforto. The bed Ardelia first indicated held only a pitiful wretch whose burned face was encased in gauze bandages, but was obviously not Pavel as his shoulder was uninjured. Eventually, Uriel located him on the second floor of the building, his upper shoulder and neck wrapped tightly in a plasflesh bandage. An intravenous drip bag was wedged under his arm – presumably to keep it from freezing – which in turn was draped outside the sheets to allow the liquid in the bag to flow.

His eyes were closed, but his breathing was deep and even. Even Uriel's limited knowledge of human physiology told him that Pavel Leforto would live, though he would have a vivid scar to remind him of his battle with the tyranids. Uriel remembered the last time he had seen Pavel's face, screaming and contorted in agony as Pasanius had rushed him back to the triage station. His features were at peace now, oblivious to the cries echoing from the floor below and the miasma of death that filled this place.

Clutched in the sleeping man's hand was a hololithic slate, and Uriel bent to lift it, seeing the image of a homely, but attractive woman with two beaming children clutched close to her. Uriel stared at the picture for several minutes, seeing the love these people had for this man through the grainy image. Pavel Leforto had a family to cleave to, a home to defend and a future to protect…

Things he could never have.

Replacing the picture, Uriel removed a purity seal from his armour and set it on Pavel's chest, before retreating from the bed, unwilling to disturb the wounded soldier's rest. He left the upper floor and made his way down to the medicae building's vestibule. Through a low arch to his left he saw a small passageway that led to an open doorway, from which a warm, softly glowing light spilled. He caught the soothing scent of incense over the stench of blood and stepped through the arch and into the medicae building's small chapel.

Simple and elegant, the chapel was spartanly furnished, the only concession to ostentation a semi-circular stained glass window depicting sisters of the Order Hospitaller ministering to the sick and providing alms to the needy. Uriel felt a peace and serenity he had not experienced in many months, as though a dark shadow that smothered the better angels of his nature could not violate this holy place.

He closed the door and walked to the end of the nave, bowing to the effigy of the Emperor and kneeling beneath His majestic gaze.

'Emperor of Mankind, in this time of war I seek the solace that only you can provide. Too often I feel hate poisoning my dreams. A darkness gathers in me and I fear for my soul in the coming days. Help me to overcome the taint that was placed within me and save me from becoming that which I have spent my entire life fighting in your name.'

Uriel took a shuddering breath and said, 'I am afraid that I may soon lose sight of what it is to serve you, that I am not worthy of your love.'

'No, Captain Ventris,' said a voice behind him. 'All who serve the Emperor are worthy of that.'

Uriel spun, rising to his feet. Sister Joaniel stood framed in the light from the window, the warm colours imparting a ruddy, healthy glow to her skin.

'Sister,' said Uriel. 'I did not notice you.'

'I know, I'm sorry for disturbing you. Would you like me to go?'

'No, no, of course not.'

'Then may I join you?'

'Yes, please do.'

Sister Joaniel nodded and limped to the end of the nave, genuflecting before the Emperor's statue and wincing as her hip joint cracked noisily. She sat on the front pew and said, 'I often come here when I have time. It is very peaceful.'

'It is,' agreed Uriel moving to join her on the pew, dwarfing the Adepta Sororitas nurse. The timber creaked under his bulk. 'I felt as though a great weight might unburden itself from me here.'

'You carry a burden?' asked Joaniel.

Uriel did not answer, his eyes cast down at the polished wooden floor. Eventually he said, 'You heard what I was saying when you came in.'

'True, but I do not know what you were referring to. Would you like to talk about it? I have counselled a great many warriors who carried emotional wounds as well as physical. Trust me, it can be very cathartic to give voice to thoughts that trouble you.'

'I do not know, sister... I am... not good at expressing such things.'

'Does it have something to do with the soldier you came to see?'

'No, more to do with a monstrous alien I fought on a distant world.'

'What kind of alien, a tyranid?'

Uriel shook his head. 'No. To this day I am not exactly sure what it was. All I know is that it was an ancient creature, old when the galaxy was young, that lived for slaughter and revelled in murder. An inquisitor I knew called it the Bringer of Darkness, and such a name was aptly given, for it could reach into a man's thoughts and drag his basest instincts to the fore.'

Uriel's hands began to shake as he relived the battle beneath the world on Pavonis. 'I saw men rend and tear themselves apart in an orgy of bloodletting and I felt my own urge to kill driven to new heights that sicken me to this very day. Visions of madness and death surrounded the creature and when its mind briefly touched mine, I saw everything, all the slaughter in the universe, and it bathed my soul in blood.'

'But you defeated it?'

'After a fashion. We drove it away and lived to tell the tale, though what became of it, I do not know.'

'You are haunted by the things it showed you,' stated Joaniel.

'Aye,' nodded Uriel, placing his head in his hands. 'I close my eyes and all I see is blood, death and mutilation. When I fight, I can barely hold back the killing rages born from the taint of the Bringer of Darkness.'

'I do not pretend to understand the nature of this monstrous being, but I feel you are tormenting yourself needlessly, Uriel. To have your mind touched, however briefly, by something of such power is bound to leave scars. To believe otherwise is folly.'

Joaniel reached out and took Uriel's hand. 'Every injury, whether physical or psychological, leaves behind its mark and sometimes they come tumbling out like daemons in the dark. Scars heal, Uriel, but only if you let them.'

'You do not think I am tainted?'

Joaniel smiled. 'No, I do not, Uriel. The power of this Bringer of Darkness must have been prodigious, but you defeated it. Yes, it showed you the depths to which man can sully himself with blood and death, but such barbarity is in all of us. You must accept that aspect of yourself and understand that part of the Bringer of Darkness will always be with you. With acceptance will come release. That you feel such pain tells me you are not tainted.'

Uriel nodded, already feeling the shadow within him recede at Joaniel's words. The two sat in companionable silence for many minutes until the vox bead in his ear crackled into life and the clipped tones of Learchus said, 'Brother-Captain, your presence is required at the main wall.'

He stood, acknowledging the message and bowed to the seated woman. 'My thanks for your understanding, Sister Joaniel,' said Uriel. 'But I must go now.'

Joaniel pushed herself from the pew and offered him her hand. Uriel shook it, his gauntlet swallowing her delicate hand utterly.

'I am always here, Uriel, should you feel the need to talk some more.'

'Thank you, I should like that,' said Uriel, bowing once more and marching quickly from the chapel.

MOVING THOUSANDS OF men and machines along with their attendant supplies, munitions and vehicles was potentially a nightmare, but with the well-drilled provosts of Erebus directing the soldiers of the Imperial Guard, there were precious few snarl-ups on the roads leading back to the city.

A thousand men of the Krieg regiment manned the second line of trenches as the Logres regiment and the Erebus Defence Legion pulled out. Those supplies that could not be brought back within the city walls were torched, bright pyres burning in the late afternoon sun. Supply trucks ferried troops back to barracks within Erebus at an admirable speed, and high in his Capitol Imperialis, Colonel Rabelaq was satisfied that the evacuation of the trenches was proceeding about as well as could be expected.

But random chance and misfortune have always played a part in any military operation and two things were to happen that would cost the Imperial defenders greatly.

On the high road to the northern gate, trucks laden with ordnance for the tanks bounced along a road which had become heavily rutted due to the immense volume of traffic passing along it and a supply truck loaded with this volatile payload dropped into a pothole, bouncing out with a teeth rattling jolt. Whether one or more shells had a faulty fuse mechanism or a careless soldier had accidentally removed one of the arming pins would never be known, but as the shells clattered around inside, the truck suddenly exploded in a devastating fireball. Secondary blasts ripped apart what little remained of the truck as the full complement of ordnance cooked off in the heat and detonated in a string of concussive booms that obliterated the road and everything within a hundred and fifty metres. Those vehicles spared the horror of the blast halted, backed up for half a kilometre and trapped on a narrow road with little room to turn around and head for another gate.

As the provosts attempted to sort out the logjam of vehicles, a swirling black cloud, fully a kilometre wide, appeared on the horizon far to the east, swooping and screeching low over the peaks of the high valley. Warning sirens blared and the city's guns opened fire. Fearing they were under attack, many of the Imperial units immediately adopted a defensive posture, slamming down the hatches of their tanks and readying their weapons to fire.

In many cases, this undoubtedly saved their lives.

From the ridges of the northern mountain slopes, hundreds of tyranid organisms poured down the treacherous, rocky slopes to fall upon the strung-out Imperial forces.

Soon, fierce battles were raging before the city walls as a tide of alien killers, having traversed the supposedly impassable mountains, fell upon the unsuspecting Guardsmen.

Alien and human blood flowed in rivers as the two forces clashed.

But there was worse to come.

'OH, SWEET EMPEROR, no…' moaned Colonel Rabelaq as the images on the holo-map suddenly leapt forwards. Fresh enemy icons appeared on the northern mountains and he realised that Captain Ventris had been right to doubt Fabricator Montante's word regarding their impassability. Fear settled in his belly and the blood drained from his face. The tyranids had fooled them all. The calculus-logi of the Capitol Imperialis had projected the speed of the advancing swarms and assumed that they were moving at optimum speed. Naively, he had fallen to thinking the same thing, but as he watched the icons of the three swarms closing rapidly with Erebus, he realised that he had fatally underestimated the cunning of these aliens.

He rushed towards the vox-station, and grabbed the carved nalwood handset from the console.

'All Krieg units, be advised that the tyranids will be on you imminently! I repeat, the tyranids will be attacking your position within minutes! Get out of there now!'

'WHAT THE HELL are you talking about?' snapped Lieutenant Konarski, grabbing the headphones from the vox-operator and jamming them to his ear. His eyes widened as he heard the panicked voice of Colonel Rabelaq screaming for them to evacuate the trenches.

He tossed back the handset and ran to the trench periscope, pressing his face to the viewing plate. Biting back a curse he swung the scope from left to right and felt a cold band of iron close around his chest as he saw a tide of alien monsters hurtling towards their position.

'Shit,' said Konarski and unslung his lasgun from his shoulder.

He ran along the trench, shouting at his men to stand to.

'Sir!' called his vox-operator. 'We're not evacuating?'

Casting his gaze along the line of the trench and seeing other Krieg officers pushing their men onto the trench's firing step, he said, 'No, son, we're not.'

'But Colonel Rabelaq's orders...'

'Damn Rabelaq!' snapped Konarski. 'We're the Death Korp of Krieg, son. Did you think that was just a pretty name? We never retreat. We fight and we die, that's the Krieg way.'

AS TERRIFYING AS the first attacks on the trenches had been, they were but a shadow of this assault. A massive, multi-limbed beast stamped forwards, smashing giant craters in the ice as it charged. Steaming jets of scalding acids sprayed from grotesque organic tubes slung beneath its massive jaws, dissolving snow, ice and flesh in smoking conflagrations.

Hundreds of spines fired with monstrous muscular contractions hammered the trenches, punching through metres of snow to skewer both men and tanks.

A boiling tide of creatures swarmed around the legs of the gargantuan beast. Chitin-clad organisms with bony prows and curled forelimbs hurled fleshy pods which burst in lethal sprays of razor-sharp bone and bio acids. Slow moving, each creature excreted another organic missile as it slithered across the ice.

Similarly bulky creatures, with fused, bony forelimbs that resembled long, organic cannons spat crackling chitin shells that hammered the retreating tanks with sprays of corrosive viruses and acids. Crackling electric energy leapt from the giant claws of thick, serpentine creatures that hurtled across the ice, their rasping armoured hides throwing up clouds of ice crystals in their wake.

But leading the charge, faster even than the multitude of ravening organisms that made up the bulk of the tyranid swarm, was a clutch of enormous creatures that smashed their way forwards on gigantic claws that dragged their bloated bodies across the ice with terrifying rapidity. Brood nests pulsed with a grotesque peristaltic motion between the bony plates of their hides and rippling muscle contractions hurled razor-edged spines towards the trenches.

A dark cloud of gargoyles massed above the attacking aliens, a massive black brood-mother moving amongst them, its monstrous wings flapping ponderously as it descended towards the men of Krieg.

LIEUTENANT KONARSKI RETCHED as he pushed the dissolving remains of his vox-operator from his legs to fall into a pool of smoking acids that melted its way through the trench's duckboards. He tried to stand, but the acrid stink of seared flesh doubled him in up with a fierce coughing fit. Blood and smoke filled the trench as tyranid missiles burst around their shattered defences. Here and there shots were returned, but it was a drop in the ocean compared to the fire they were receiving.

Finally overcoming his nausea, he shouted, 'For Krieg!' and fired over the lip of the trench. A dark shadow blotted out the light from the sun and Konarski looked up in time to see a gigantic monstrosity with wings tens of metres wide swooping low towards the trenches. Scores of smaller beasts clung to its belly and a swirling fire built between its jaws.

He risked a glance over his shoulder to see why no one was shooting the damn thing down. As he saw the nearest Hydra he realised why.

Its frontal section was a molten, twisted mass, thick armour plating liquefied by corrosive viruses and acids. Gory slime oozed from the vehicle's interior, the disintegrating flesh of its crew steaming in the cold air. But Konarski saw the Hydra's gun section was still intact.

He dropped his rifle and sprinted towards the quad-barrelled gun. He had to get it firing again. Huge, shrieking creatures with scything arms and horrific organic weapons poured over the trenches, tearing his men apart. Swarms of smaller creatures leapt and killed around them.

Desperate hand-to-hand combat raged as troopers vainly attempted to stem the alien tide. Giant, fleshy monstrosities disgorged hordes of clawed monsters that he recognised as genestealers. Everywhere, they were being overrun.

Konarski crouched low and held his gloved hand across his nose and mouth as the stench of melted human flesh assailed him. He scrambled across the stinking remains of the crew, sliding up into the gunner's compartment.

'Yes!' he shouted as he saw that the guns were still powered up and fully loaded. Gripping the firing handles, he slewed the four-barrelled turret around to face the giant flapping monster. Konarski punched the firing studs and a four-metre tongue of flame roared from the muzzles to strafe the sky with fiery explosions. The gun rocked with powerful recoil, pumping out hundreds of shells every few seconds. Konarski screamed as he fired, the horror of the last few days washing from his body in a storm of adrenaline.

Through the vision blocks he saw the flying beast torn apart as the close range blasts ripped through its bony armour plates to detonate within its vital organs. Screeching, it tumbled from the sky, rolling in a flurry of snow and alien blood to crush the broods it carried with its bulk. Explosions of coloured fumes erupted from its belly, noxious clouds of alien toxins blanketing the ground and green tendrils spilling into the trenches.

Working the gun left and right, he shredded every alien he could see, keeping the firing studs depressed long after the ammunition had run out.

COLONEL RABELAQ WATCHED through the viewing bay of the Capitol Imperialis and immediately saw that the Krieg rearguard was sure to be annihilated unless they were reinforced. Cries for help and desperate pleas for fire missions clogged the vox-circuits. The scale of the disaster staggered him.

The elements ambushed on the road to the city were holding, and in many places driving the tyranids back. Given time, Rabelaq guessed they could probably fight their way behind the walls. But time was the one thing they did not have.

The soldiers of Krieg could not hope to hold the tyranid advance long enough.

There was only one thing to do.

He marched to the centre of his command bridge and buttoned his frock coat, pulling the collar straight and brushing a piece of lint from his epaulettes.

'General advance, ready main gun,' he ordered.

'Sir?' queried his adjutant.

'You heard me, damn you! General advance, I'll not leave those brave lads to fight and die on their own. That's not the Logres way. Now do as I order!'

'Aye, aye, sir,' nodded the man, hurrying to obey.

Colonel Octavius Rabelaq came to attention as he felt the rumbling vibrations of the gigantic tracks and the Capitol Imperialis began its ponderous advance.

THE GROUND SHOOK, the charge of hundreds of alien monsters dislodging snow, ice and timber from the walls of the trenches. Konarski grabbed whatever men he could find through the stinking clouds of alien fumes, hauling them back towards the city wall. They had done as much as they could, and it was time to get his men to safety.

Huge vibrations rumbled through the ground, and briefly he wondered if they were in the grip of an earthquake. A screeching roar behind him echoed with alien hunger and he turned to raise his lasgun in a final show of defiance.

Suddenly the earth heaved and a thunderous string of explosions filled the world with noise. Bright light flared

behind him and the crack of displaced air threatened to
deafen him. He felt himself flying through the air as massive
tremors split the ground before him. He hit hard and rolled,
swallowing snow as stars burst before his eyes.

Flames leaped before him and he pushed himself dizzily to
his knees.

What the hell had just happened?

Then the smoke parted and he saw a towering cliff of steel
rising before him. Grinding forward on lumbering tracks that
crushed the earth, it split the very bedrock with its mass,
throwing up tank-sized chunks of ice and rock. The blessed
sight of the aquila was emblazoned on the soaring leviathan,
just below the gigantic, smoking barrel of the Behemoth cannon mounted on the Capitol Imperialis. Konarski laughed as
the mammoth war-machine rumbled past him, his cry of
exultation snatched away as its cannon fired again, the concussive force hurling him through the air once more.

The landing knocked the breath out of his body, but fuelled
by adrenalin, he quickly staggered to his feet and lurched off
in the direction of the city.

Colonel Rabelaq had bought them time and he wasn't
about to waste it.

COLONEL STAGLER KEPT the compress bandage tight against his
stomach, dizzy from blood loss, but unwilling to accept medical attention until he knew the fate of his men. Even from his
vantage point on a snow-capped gun tower atop the main
wall, billowing clouds of smoke and fumes obscured his view
of the trenches. He could get nothing from the vox-caster, simply screams and alien howls. His men were probably lost, but
they had died in the Krieg manner: fighting hard and dying
well.

The fool Rabelaq had surprised him, pushing his precious
mobile command post into the alien mass. He'd bought the
men fighting the ambushing aliens enough time to break free
of the noose and escape to the transient safety of the city.
Entire broods of aliens had circumvented the walls, dropping
from the high cliffs and into the depths of the city, but he
couldn't worry about them right now.

The Capitol Imperialis fired again and more snow tumbled
from the highest peaks of the mountains. Hundreds of aliens

swarmed up the flanks of the mighty vehicle, many more slamming their bulk into its tracks. Electrical discharges erupted around its hull and bright explosions surrounded it. Its close-in defences stripped away whole swathes of attacking aliens, but could not cope with the sheer volume of attackers.

Stagler snapped his fingers in the direction of his vox-operator.

'Get me Colonel Rabelaq,' he ordered as he saw a sight that would stay with him until his dying day.

'WHY ARE WE slowing, damn you?' demanded Colonel Rabelaq.

'Sir, the track units are jammed. We can't move,' came the reply.

The commander of the Logres regiment rushed to the surveyor station, where dozens of small pict-slates displayed images from the external viewers. Flickering scenes of carnage filled every one, thousands of tyranid brood creatures swarming around the Capitol Imperialis. Hundreds of short-range bolters fired a continuous stream of explosive shells into the alien horde, but could not stop them all.

He felt the recoil-dampened vibration of the main gun and even through the thick hull of his command vehicle, he could hear the shrieks of the deadly aliens as they fought to get at the humans inside his armoured behemoth.

Hundreds, perhaps thousands of aliens had thrown themselves into the mighty tracks of the Capitol Imperialis to prevent it from escaping, and the scale of such unthinking devotion terrified Rabelaq to the soles of his boots. Not even the ruthlessly driven Macharius or the charismatic Slaydo had inspired such obedience from their warriors.

A horrified intake of breath lifted him from his reverie and he looked up to see the gargantuan beast emerge from the billowing clouds of ice and poisonous clouds, crushing everything before it.

Multiple mandibles slavered around a cavern-sized sphincter mouth ringed with thousands of thick fangs. Dripping ichor spilled from the orifice in thick ropes of corrosive drool. Chitinous legs, reverse jointed like a spider's, dragged its bloated body across the ice, hundreds of scuttling organisms crawling across the thick bony plates of its upper armour.

'Great saints,' whispered Rabelaq. 'All power to the auto loaders! Fire the main gun, for the Emperor's sake. Now!'

'Sir! Colonel Stagler on the vox!'

'I don't have time for that fanatic now,' he snapped. 'Fire the main gun!'

Even through metres of adamantium deck and noise suppressors, he felt the thunderous recoil of the Behemoth cannon. The monster rocked under the impact and a huge cheer filled the command bridge. Huge chunks of excised flesh sailed through the air and parade-ground sized sheets of blood sprayed from a huge crater in the beast's flank.

It sagged to one side, its foreleg hanging by gory ribbons of torn muscle. Dark blood gouted from the wound, flooding the trenches below and melting the ice with its heat. A split opened along the sac of its belly, tearing wider as the screaming monster continued to drag itself towards the Capitol Imperialis. Thousands of leaping, snapping creatures and bloated egg sacs tumbled from the wound, only to be crushed beneath the massive beast's weight.

'Come on, come on,' hissed Rabelaq as he watched the indicator lights on the main panel charting the reloading process far below on the gun decks. He willed the gunnery overseer to whip his men harder and get the damn gun loaded. Forcing himself to look away from the panel, he watched in horror as the tyranid monster reared up again, the flesh already reknitting where their shells had struck it. Ichor no longer spilled from its belly and already new strands of muscle and tissue were slithering along the wounded leg to reconnect severed tendons and bone.

'Sir, hull breaches on decks two, three and five!'

'Sir, engine room reports intruders!'

'Colonel, close-in defences are out of ammunition!'

Rabelaq listened to more incoming reports, each more damning than the last, and knew that his career as a soldier in the Emperor's armies was finally over. This was one battle he would not walk away from and raise a toast to in the officers' mess in years to come.

Strangely, the thought did not discomfort him as much as he thought it might.

He felt a terrific impact rock the command bridge as the gigantic tyranid creature slammed into the side of the Capitol

Imperialis. He grabbed onto the brass rail that surrounded the holo-map table as the deck lurched sickeningly.

Servitors slid from their chairs, dangling on the cables that attached them to the deck, and his fellow officers screamed as they were thrown to the walls as the mighty leviathan was pushed over. He could see nothing through the viewing bay, simply a heaving mass of purulent flesh. Warning bells chimed and flames leapt from shattered consoles. Glass splinters flew as buckled metal fell onto the map table and steam spurted from ruptured pipes.

The deck continued to tilt and Rabelaq snatched the vox-handset from the side of the sparking map table.

'This is Colonel Octavius Rabelaq,' he said calmly. 'Colonel Stagler, if you can hear this, then you know what to do. Rabelaq out.'

The colonel dropped the handset, finally losing his grip on the map table as the Capitol Imperialis passed its centre of gravity and slammed into the ice. He sailed across the control room and smashed into the corner of a twisted console. He lay immobile in the exploding control bridge, blood and brain leaking from his ruptured cranium.

The only thing that consoled him as he slipped into uncon-sciousness was the fact that they would talk of his death for years to come in the regimental messes.

URIEL WATCHED THE enormous bulk of the bio-titan attacking the fallen Capitol Imperialis with a mixture of horror and sor-row. Colonel Rabelaq had been a good man and the soldiers of the Logres regiment would feel his loss keenly.

They had all heard Colonel Rabelaq's valedictory order and watched as Colonel Stagler passed the order to fire to the gun towers. Alien shrieks echoed from the valley sides as the bio-titan ripped open the toppled Capitol Imperialis with its gigantic claws, tearng open its thick armour as easily as a child might unwrap a gift.

Then the dusk was transformed into daylight as every heavy artillery piece on the walls opened fire on the fallen vehicle's engine section. Fiery explosions blasted from the shattered wreck, incinerating hundreds of the smaller crea-tures as they clawed their way inside the vehicle. Uriel knew that there may have been survivors within, but knew that this was a more merciful death than anything the tyranids would offer.

A huge mushroom cloud blossomed skyward as the combined weight of fire finally penetrated into the heart of the Capitol Imperialis and detonated the plasma reactor deep inside.

Streamers of unbearably bright light streaked from the wreck as the plasma chambers ignited and vaporised everything within half a kilometre. As the light faded, Uriel saw a deep crater, filled with hissing, molten flesh. The fatally wounded bio-titan floundered in a magma-hot soup of plasma, ice flashing to superheated steam and scalding its bones bare of flesh. Not even this monster's fearsome regenerative capabilities could save it and it screeched in agony, thrashing madly in its death throes.

Melting snow and ice poured into the crater, forming a lake of rapidly freezing water. Hissing clouds of steam billowed as the plasma boiled away much of the water, but within minutes there was nothing left to mark this titanic encounter save a frozen, ice-filled crater entombing the bodies of thousands of aliens and the mortal remains of Colonel Octavius Rabelaq.

'In Mortis est Gloriam,' whispered Uriel.

TWELVE

FOR THE NEXT four days the tyranids threw themselves at the walls of the city, each time losing thousands of their number, but their attacks never diminished in volume or ferocity. Ramps of dead aliens were piled so high at the base of the wall that their mass cracked the ice of the moat. Flamer units torched their remains as best they could, but the sheer volume of corpses could never be cleared in time before the next attack.

Each assault would begin with a barrage of crackling bio-shells fired from bloated creatures with pumping bony frills around their heads, whose fused forelimbs had evolved into vast, ribbed cannons. Huge chunks of the wall were blown away, but as it was built as a stepped structure into the slope of the ground, these did little more than blast the bedrock of the mountain. Following this, a rain of fleshy pods fired from the back of lumpen monsters with long, bony limbs would fall on the defenders.

Each missile would explode in the air, disgorging drifting clouds of poison that engulfed the front line and killed scores of soldiers and wounded hundreds more. As the medicae facilities filled with troopers blinded by corrosive fumes or coughing up their dissolving lungs, it became necessary for the first assaults to be met by the warriors of the Adeptus Astartes. They alone could hope to withstand the deadly toxins in the opening moments of the attack.

Following the bombardment, the plain before the city rapidly filled with hissing alien killers as they emerged from their snow caves, scooped out by sightless, burrowing creatures. Few tyranid species could survive at night without protection when the temperature plummeted to forty below zero, and the darkness was the only respite from the horror for the defenders of Erebus.

Electrical fires and gouts of poisonous flame, chittering devourer creatures and bony shrapnel bombs pounded the walls relentlessly and as casualties spiralled into the tens of thousands, the decision was made to abandon the first wall.

Barely anything remained of its parapet and the smaller creatures had entered another evolutionary iteration, spontaneously developing fleshy tendons equipped with jagged hooks that enabled them to scale the sheer surfaces of the walls. The many guns mounted on the sides of the valley were keeping the majority of the aerial creatures at bay, and after the ambush at the city wall, no one was dismissing the possibility of the tyranids attacking from avenues previously considered impossible.

Pockets of aliens had penetrated the city through drainage culverts, forgotten caves and even over the high peaks of the mountains, and, while they were wreaking havoc among the civilian population, not a single man from the front line could be spared to hunt them down.

For now, the people of Erebus would need to look to their own defence.

URIEL FELT THE cold against his skin as a burning sensation, but welcomed the pain as a sign he was still alive. His armour was dented, torn and gashed in innumerable places, stained with so much alien blood that its original colour was scarcely visible. The actuators in his left shoulder guard wheezed as he walked, the result of the none-too-tender ministrations of a gigantic tyranid warrior organism. Techmarine Harkus had done what he could to allow the auto-reactive shoulder guard to move freely, but without the proper blessed instruments, he had been forced to beg the armour's forgiveness and effect a temporary repair.

He had not slept since the destruction of Colonel Rabelaq's Capitol Imperialis, and while his catalepsean node had allowed him to continue to function, influencing the circadian rhythms of his brain and his response to sleep deprivation, he felt a marrow-deep tiredness saturate his body.

Looking at the thousands of men gathered around the lines of flaming braziers he felt his respect for them soar. If he was this tired, he could not imagine what the human soldiers must be feeling. Learchus, his armour similarly brutalised, looked well rested, his eyes bright and his stride sure as he marched beside his captain.

'Guilliman's oath, these men are weary,' said Uriel.

'Aye,' agreed Learchus. 'That they are, but they'll hold. I know they will.'

'You trained them well, brother-sergeant.'

'As well as the codex demands,' said Learchus, a hint of reproach in his tone.

Uriel ignored his sergeant's gentle rebuke as they emerged from the buildings of District Quatros and onto the ruined plain before the second wall.

Where once the area had been thronged with factories, production hangars and dwellings, there was now only iced rockcrete rectangles to indicate where they had once stood. Lines of burning oil drums packed with whatever flammable materials were to hand burned and kept the air just above freezing. Already scores of soldiers had perished in the cold nights, frozen to death where they lay, their comrades forced to pry their corpses from the ground as dawn broke.

The council of Erebus, initially supporting Learchus's decision to demolish the buildings so as to deny the tyranids cover between the walls had balked as the reality of the proposition had hit home. Simon van Gelder led the most vocal group of opposition and, in a move of surprising boldness, Sebastien Montante had dissolved the council of Erebus, giving command of his city to Colonel Stagler until such time as the tyranids were driven off.

It amazed Uriel to think that on the brink of annihilation, men could still squabble over such petty concerns as property

and wealth. This world might bear the name of the Ultramarines, but its leaders had long since forsaken the teachings
of the primarch.

But as he and Learchus marched towards the wall, he was
filled with love for the soldiers who stood defiant before the
tide of alien invaders. Here was the spirit of Ultramar best
exemplified. In the common man, who stood tall against the
horrors of the galaxy and was willing to die to protect what he
believed in.

The two Space Marines stopped by one of the blazing fires
on the edge of the wall, nodding in greeting to the soldiers
clustered around its fleeting warmth. Uriel cast his gaze out
over the ruined ground between the first two walls at the
masses of aliens gathered before him. The collective exhala-
tions of millions of creatures breathing in concert filled the
valley, sounding like a single slumbering monster.

It would likely not be that simple, but if Lord Admiral
Tiberius's plan succeeded then there was a chance that it
might be. He had conferred with Sebastien Montante following his dissolution of the council, finding him awkwardly
climbing into a suit of thermal overwhites and pulling on a
webbing belt of ammunition.

'What are you doing, Fabricator Montante?' Uriel had
asked.

'Well, now that the council has been dissolved, I think it's
about time I picked up a gun and started fighting, don't you?'

Uriel folded his arms and said, 'When was the last time you
fired a weapon, fabricator?'

'Ah, now let me think... probably during basic training,
when I did my regulation service in the Defence Legion.'

'And how many years ago was that?' pressed Uriel.

Montante had the decency to look abashed as he said,
'About thirty years ago, but I *need* to fight, don't you understand?'

'I do, Sebastien, have no fear of that. You are one of the
finest logisticians I have met, and your place is here. You have
kept the soldiers supplied with food and ammunition,
invested time, effort and money to ensure that all our military
needs are met. But you are not a soldier, Sebastien, and you
will die in the first minutes of an assault.'

'But–'

'No,' said Uriel firmly, but not unkindly, 'You can best serve your city in other ways.'

'Like how?'

'Well, you can start by telling me all about the orbital defences of Erebus: where they are, their status and how we get them firing again.'

Montante looked confused, 'But there's nothing left of them, Uriel. The torpedo silos expended their stocks of ordnance and the defence lasers fired until their power capacitors were dry.'

'Indulge me,' said Uriel.

And he had. Uriel and Montante spent the next two hours poring over maps, computing ranges, fuel to weight ratios, introducing all manner of variables into their discussions until they settled on the optimum course of action. Satisfied that the admiral's plan was indeed workable, Uriel had left, forcing Montante to swear an oath that he would not attempt to join the fighting men on the walls until the end came.

Then he had explained his idea to the other commanders. Initially sceptical, a cautious excitement gripped the senior officers as he outlined the results of his and Montante's labours, and they began to appreciate the scope of the plan.

Preparations were already underway and all they could do was hold until the battered remnants of the fleet were in position to strike. The operation was planned for the day after tomorrow and Uriel was anxious to begin. For too long they had retreated before the aliens. Now they had a chance to strike back.

Kryptman's pet Mechanicus had promised them a weapon to use against the tyranids, but had yet to deliver. Time was running out for Locard, and Uriel knew that the admiral's plan was the best shot they had at ending this war. It was a long shot, but as he looked down at the immensity of the tyranid swarm, he knew it was the only one they had.

He turned from the wall to see Learchus standing beside the brazier, his palms outstretched towards the flames. Uriel's brow furrowed in puzzlement, knowing Learchus was perfectly insulated from both the heat and cold within his power armour, before realising his sergeant was unconsciously copying the men around him. He smiled and listened to what Learchus was saying as he saw Chaplain Astador and Major

Satria approach from further along the length of the wall.
More men began drifting over from other fires as Learchus
raised his voice to carry further.

'You have fought with courage and honour,' said Learchus,
'giving your all for the fight and no man can do more than
that. Vile aliens assail us from all sides, yet amidst the death
and carnage not one amongst you is willing to take a backwards step. I am proud of you all.'

'You taught us well, Sergeant Learchus,' shouted Major
Satria.

'No, greatness was in all of you, I just knew where to look
for it. You are known as the Erebus Defence Legion, the protectors of your people. But you are more than this. The oath
of brotherhood sworn between your world and mine at the
dawn of the Imperium binds us together more surely than the
strongest chains of adamantium.'

Learchus raised his fist and shouted, 'You are warriors of
Ultramar, and I am proud to call you brothers.'

A huge cheer echoed from the sides of the valley.

SNOWDOG FISHED OUT the last pair of guns from a crate before
kicking it to splinters. Tigerlily and Lex collected the smashed
timbers in large plastic bags, for sale as firewood to the thousands of people that now filled the warehouse and its adjacent
buildings. He handed a freshly stamped lasgun with a pair of
power cells fixed to the stock with duct tape to Jonny Stomp.
The weapon looked absurdly tiny in Jonny's shovel-like hands
and Snowdog grinned.

'I'll try and find something better for you soon, big man,' he
promised.

'Good,' grunted Jonny. 'These pipsqueak guns just don't cut
it, Snowdog.'

'Hey, it's all we got.'

The ammo for Jonny's grenade launcher had long since run
out and he'd been unhappy with anything less destructive.
And they could certainly do with something more powerful:
the attacks on the warehouse had increased in ferocity and
number over the last few days, as though the aliens knew
there was a smorgasbord of prey just sitting here.

So far the guns they'd heisted from the Guard were doing
the job adequately, and Lex's bombs were proving to be as

effective against aliens as they were against the Arbites. But Snowdog knew that soon they'd need more.

He said, 'Hey, Trask, catch,' and tossed him a gleaming auto-gun with a bag of clips. Trask fumbled the catch, too busy scratching at an ugly red rash he'd developed on the side of his face and neck.

It made his dog-ugly features even more unpleasant to look at and he never stopped clawing at his flaking, mottled skin.

'Damn it, Trask, you gotta pay more attention,' said Snow-dog.

Trask made an obscene gesture and turned away, heading back into the noisy interior of the warehouse. Snowdog put Trask from his mind and made his way to where those men he'd deemed relatively trustworthy were guarding the remain-der of his purloined supplies.

Still plenty left and there were more people coming in every day. His stash was growing steadily as desperate people gave him all they had for what they needed. Analgesic spray? That'll cost you. Ration packs to feed your children? That'll cost you.

It was simple economics really, supply and demand.

They wanted his supplies, and he demanded their money.

When this was over, he was going to be rich, and then there'd be nothing he couldn't do. Take the Nightcrawlers legit or dump them and move on – he didn't know which yet, but with his pockets bulging with cash, there was no limit to the opportunities. Maybe even get off this planet and hit some virgin territory that was just waiting for a man with his talents to open it up.

Satisfied that all was as it should be, he slung his shotgun and made his way back into the warehouse. Crammed in tight, nearly three thousand people covered virtually every square metre of floor space. Smouldering braziers kept the worst of the night's biting chill away and stolen, high-calorie Imperial ration packs designed for winter operations were stretched to feed entire families. Ragged tarpaulins offered a little privacy to those who could scavenge them. Only the cold kept the stench of so many unwashed bodies from stinking the place up.

Tigerlily made her way through the crowded warehouse and, though he knew she was giving away firewood without taking anything in return, he let it go, figuring it was as well to keep her sweet. There was no one better with a knife and he'd seen her handiwork often enough to know that pissing her off wasn't a good idea. Soft sobbing and low voices filled the warehouse. Glares of hostility followed him everywhere, but he didn't care.

They might hate him, but they needed him. Without him, they were all as good as dead. It was that simple, and if he made a killing along the way, well that was just fine and dandy.

As he made his way to the front of the warehouse he heard a strangled cry from behind a tied-down tarp.

It was a common enough sound in here and Snowdog ignored it until he heard a familiar voice hiss, 'Shut your mouth, girl. Your man agreed to this, so shut your damn mouth and lie still.'

Immediately, Snowdog spun on his heel and racked his shotgun. He ripped aside the tarp, snarling in rage as he saw Trask holding down a weeping girl, her dress hitched up over her knees.

'Trask, damn you! I said no more of this!'

'Frag you, Snowdog,' snapped Trask, rising to his feet. 'They ain't got no money!'

'I said no,' repeated Snowdog. He stepped forwards and hammered his shotgun into Trask's face. The thick wooden stock broke his nose with a sharp crack. He followed up with a boot to the groin. Trask dropped, hands clutched to his crotch and blood spurting from his nose. Snowdog spun the shotgun and jammed the blue-steel barrel between Trask's legs.

'I even think you've done this again and I pull the trigger next time. You get me?'

Trask coughed a wad of blood and phlegm.

'I said, "do you get me?",' bellowed Snowdog.

'Yeah, yeah,' coughed Trask. 'I get you, you bastard.'

'Get out of my sight, Trask,' snapped Snowdog.

His face a bloody mask, Trask painfully picked himself up and lurched away, shouting at sniggering people to shut the hell up. Snowdog took a deep breath and held out his hand to the crying girl. She shook her head, tears cutting clear streaks down the dirt on her face.

'Whatever,' shrugged Snowdog, fishing out a couple of crumpled bills from his trousers. He tossed them to her and said, 'I might be many things, but I won't stoop that low. You understand?'

The girl nodded hurriedly, tucking the cash into her dress and scurrying away.

Snowdog watched her go as Silver came up behind him and slid her arms around his waist.

'He's gonna kill you if you don't kill him first,' she said.

'Not Trask,' said Snowdog, 'he ain't got the guts to come at me face to face.'

'I know, that's why you'd better watch your back.'

'I will,' promised Snowdog.

LORD INQUISITOR KRYPTMAN shivered, despite the thick robes he wore and the thermal generator burning brightly beside him. His breath misted in the air and the stench from the huge pile of corpses gathered on the esplanade behind the wall on the orders of Magos Locard was beginning to make him nauseous. He had studied, dissected and killed tyranids for over two centuries, but could never get used to their disgusting alien smell. The sooner this race was exterminated the better.

His personal retinue of Storm Troopers as well as two members of the Deathwatch led by Captain Bannon formed a cordon around them, hellguns and bolters pointed outwards into the night.

'Anything?' he shouted to Locard, who was waist-deep in tyranid viscera. His robes were filthy, his mechadendrites sifting through the organic waste and a genoprobe chiming softly in his hands.

'No, my lord. All the creatures I have examined so far are at least sixth generation iterations and therefore useless.'

'Damn,' swore Kryptman. 'Very well, burn them. Burn them all.'

CONCEALED BY THE night's darkness, the lictor slid through the darkness of the city, making its way towards where the pheromone signature of its alien kin was strongest.

Drawn towards the valley mouth, the lictor moved with stealth and speed, like a flickering shadow that darted from cover to cover, unseen and unheard, even by those it killed. On occasion it had encountered prey and killed them to bolster its energy reserves before moving onwards.

The lictor rounded the corner of a ruined building, feeling the scene before it wash through its sensory receptors in a heartbeat. It sensed heat, dead kin and a pheromone signature that surely indicated a leader beast of prey.

CAPTAIN BANNON'S EYES scanned from side to side as Inquisitor Kryptman and Locard performed their grisly autopsies on the tyranid corpses they had been ordered to gather. For what purpose, Bannon didn't know and didn't care, so long as it helped the defenders exterminate these xenos. He and his men had travelled the length and breadth of the city's armed forces, instructing every squad in the best methods of combating tyranids, pointing out weak spots in their natural armour, vulnerable organs and the correct hymnals to recite both prior to and following combat.

It was slow work, but it was paying off, as the daily casualty rosters, while still horrifying, were not as high as they might have been. Bannon understood that this could partly be accounted for by the weakest men having already fallen and the strongest remaining, but the men of Erebus had learned quickly and he knew that alien losses were much higher.

He had been impressed by the Ultramarines and the Mortifactors, though he found it hard to believe that both were descended from the same gene stock. His proud lineage came from the blessed Rogal Dorn and he briefly wondered how many of the successor Chapters of the Imperial Fists had deviated from their original teachings. Not many, he surmised, if the Black Templars were anything to go by.

'Captain Bannon,' said Inquisitor Kryptman.

'My lord?'

'There is nothing here of value. Burn it all.'

Bannon said, 'Aye,' and nodded to Brother Elwaine, originally of the Salamanders Chapter, who raised his flamer and sent a sheet of burning promethium over the mound of cadavers. His mouth twitched in a smile of satisfaction as he watched them immolate.

'Brother-captain,' snarled Henghast of the Space Wolves. 'Enemy near!'

Bannon knew better than to doubt the Space Wolf's senses, but before he could do more than face outwards, it was upon them.

One of the inquisitor's Storm Troopers was lifted from the ground, multiple barbs bursting from his back in a spray of blood and bone. Hellguns fired blindly into the dark, the soldiers having lost their night vision looking into the fire. Another soldier fell, his legs shorn from his body by a massive swipe of chitinous claws.

He saw it in the flickering glow of the flames. A lictor, its upper claws unsheathed and bloody. He raised his bolter, aiming for the junction of thorax and legs, and fired a hail of shells. The lictor spun away from his shots, speeding around the edge of the burning pyre of alien corpses.

Bannon ran around the fire, shouting, 'Henghast, go left! Elwaine, cover!'

Elwaine widened his stance, bracing his flamer as Henghast made his way around the other side. Kryptman had his pistol drawn and Locard twisted his head left and right, chattering excitedly to the inquisitor.

He scanned the ground before him, shutting out the screams of those wounded by the lictor. Damn, but it was quick. Where had it come from?

Bannon heard it a second before it attacked.

Powerful muscles hurled the lictor straight over the pyre, its claws aimed at his heart. He dropped, rolling and firing in one motion. Its claws ploughed the rockcrete, shearing through his shoulder guard and drawing blood. His shots went wild as a tongue of flame washed over the lictor.

But it was no longer there, vaulting from Elwaine's line of fire and smashing the Space Marine from his feet. Clawed hands ripped the flamer from his grip and tore his arms from his sockets in a flood of crimson. Elwaine dropped with a grunt of pain, still kicking at beast as it dismembered him.

Bannon fired again, this time drawing a screech of pain from the lictor as his bolts penetrated its chitinous hide. It spun, blindingly quick, and barbed tendons lashed out, skewering his bolter. The weapon exploded as the propellant in the ruptured shells ignited and Bannon fell back, his gauntlets melted in the blast.

Hellgun fire slashed at the lictor and over the screams Bannon head Kryptman's voice.

'Don't kill it! For the Emperor's sake, don't kill it!'

He rolled to his feet as the lictor came at him. drawing his combat knife and leaping to meet it.

As he leapt he realised that the lictor wasn't coming for him.

It was going for Inquisitor Kryptman.

Kryptman fired his pistol at point blank range, blasting clear a portion of the lictor's upper thigh. It stumbled, but its mantis-like upper claws swept down to eviscerate the inquisitor.

Then Henghast was there, his power sword sweeping down to intercept the blow. The former Space Wolf spun low and slashed his blade through the lictor's upper claws, drawing twin spurts of black blood. It roared in alien rage and once again its barbed hooks lashed out, entangling the Space Marine's sword arm. Its lower arms punched out, ripping through Henghast's armour and hurling him through the air. Blood pumped from its severed claws as Bannon fought to draw his own sword with his scorched hands. His power armour dispensed pain retardant drugs into his system.

The lictor spun away from the fire, its wounds driving it from the fight before he could reach it. He stumbled towards the inquisitor and Locard. Both were alive. Shaken, but alive.

'Get it, Bannon!' hissed Kryptman, 'but for the love of the Emperor, don't kill it. We need it alive!'

He stumbled after the monster as it sped towards the city walls, shouting into the vox, 'Uriel, Astador, anyone! I need help. I am in pursuit of a lictor heading north-westwards to the walls. Close on my position, and if you see it subdue it. I repeat, subdue it, do not kill it!'

URIEL, PASANIUS AND ten warriors from the Fourth company ran from the walls towards the source of Bannon's desperate call for aid. Leading his men in prayer, he had been amazed at the last portion of Bannon's message. A lictor on the loose and they were not to kill it?

'Spread out,' ordered Uriel.

'Why in the name of all that's holy can't we kill the damned thing?' said Pasanius.

'I don't know, but Bannon must have a good reason.'

'How are we supposed to see it, I thought these things were chameleons?'

'Just follow the screams,' said Uriel as he heard cries of pain a hundred metres or so to his left. His armour's auto-senses penetrated the darkness with ease and he saw the shimmering outline of the creature as it butchered its way through the picket line of squads protecting the army's rear.

'With me, now!' shouted Uriel and took off towards the lictor. He opened a channel to Bannon. 'I see it, it's in north sector delta!'

Whether the monster needed to kill or simply took pleasure in the act, Uriel didn't know, but it had stopped to slaughter the men stationed there. Uriel raised his gun, his finger tightening on the trigger before he remembered he was not to kill the creature. It spun away from him and leapt for the side of the rock face, its lashing hooks digging into the rock and hauling it rapidly upwards.

'It's getting away!' shouted Pasanius.

'Not if I can help it,' snarled Uriel, switching his bolter's shot selector to single shell. The lictor scaled the mountainside in jerky leaps, several of its fleshy grapnels hanging useless at its side.

Uriel said, 'Bolter-link,' and sighted carefully along the barrel of his weapon. Range vectors and an aiming reticule appeared on his visor, designating the point his shell would impact. He waited until the dot flashed red and pulled the trigger.

The weapon bucked in his hand and a portion of the rock face exploded as his shell blasted it apart. The lictor screeched in frustration as its flesh hooks were blown clear of the rocks and it tumbled hundreds of metres down the side of the mountain to slam into the ground with a sickening thud.

The lictor pushed itself groggily to its feet as Uriel and Pasanius leapt on it, pinning it to the ground with their weight. It thrashed weakly, tearing at their armour, but as more Ultramarines arrived, they eventually grappled the struggling monster to immobility.

Bannon skidded towards the battling Ultramarines with more of the Deathwatch behind him. Three of his men carried high-tensile cabling, capable of bearing the weight of a Land Raider.

'Bind it,' he ordered.

THIRTEEN

IN A CAVERNOUS hangar built into the rock face of the van
Gelder family's mountain estates, a veritable army of lifter-
servitors and indentured servants loaded a long, silver-grey
starship named *Magnificence* with scores of sealed crates. The
ship's sides were emblazoned with heraldic crests depicting
heroic van Gelders of history and her worth beyond measure.

Unwilling to entrust the loading of his entire estate to mere
workers, Simon van Gelder, former councillor of Erebus City,
watched impatiently from a high gantry as his harried overseers checked off each crate as it was wheeled up the ramp
into the *Magnificence's* capacious hold. The operation to load
her had been underway for several hours now, and Simon
knew that the abundance of his possessions would mean he
would be here for some time yet.

Well, no matter. All that concerned him was that the loading be done before this invasion progressed any further. He
was damned if he was going to stay and die with these fools
for the sake of some outmoded notion of honour. An oath
sworn with some long-dead – and probably mythical – figure
was no oath at all and certainly didn't bind him.

No, he was going to survive this war and if by some mis-
chance these fools were actually able to drive the aliens from
Tarsis Ultra, then he would return with his wealth intact, not
flattened in the name of military strategy. Those meek sheep
who blindly followed Montante's fawning over these Space
Marines were sure to be bankrupted by this war and even if
they survived, they would have no one to turn to for their continued economic life but him.

The thought of Montante begging him to return to the
council and pledge his financial support to prop up his inef-
fectual regime pleased him mightily and he wondered how
long it would be before he would be in a position to manoeuvre Montante from office. Not long, he was sure. The
industrial blocs were notoriously fickle and with the right
palms greased and pockets filled, it would be child's play to
ensure that his nomination was successful.

Simon pulled out a thick cigar from his long frock coat,
lighting it with a small gold lighter and puffing an expansive
series of smoke rings.

Scenting the smoke, a safety protocol servitor marched
stiffly towards him.

A red light flashed on its chest panel as it said, 'This area is
a protected zone and the ignition of combustible materials is
prohibited. Extinguish all flames and prepare for censure.'

Simon waved the servitor away, snapping, 'Go away. Autho-
risation code Gelder nine-alpha-prime.'

The servitor turned and marched away as Simon shook his
head and strolled along the gantry to an armoured blast door
that led onto a balcony overlooking the city. Another servitor
opened the door, wired into the rock of the wall, its arms augmented with powerful pistons that turned the heavy locking
wheel with ease.

The door ground open and cold air rushed in. Simon gathered his insulated coat about himself and walked into the
fading light of evening. This high on the valley sides, the wind
whipped by like a scalpel, cutting him to the marrow with its
icy blade. Far to the west he could hear the faint metallic ring
of battle, the cries of fighting men carried eastwards on the
wind that howled through Erebus. His contempt for what
these men of war had led them to knew no bounds and his
desire to live through this surged through him once more.

A chattering blast of gunfire sounded from further up the valley, close to Montante's palace. Simon watched as a flock of the flying aliens darted through the air above the source of the River Nevas. The servitor-manned guns on the valley sides tracked their movement, filling the air with explosive projectiles that burst in lethal clouds of shrapnel and shredded dozens of the beasts before they withdrew. They were clever these aliens, saw Simon. Testing each area of the valley for weak points to find a way in.

But Simon knew there were no weak points. His consortium, in conjunction with the Adeptus Mechanicus, had supplied and built the weapons as well as the servitors that controlled the guns and he knew that their coverage was nigh-on impenetrable.

Anything that flew above a certain altitude was interrogated by the machine spirits bound within each gun and should there be no response to that interrogation, the guns would open fire. Without clearance, flyers would be mercilessly engaged and destroyed the moment they entered the guns' coverage.

Simon smiled, his fingers playing over a plain metallic box in the pocket of his coat.

Unless you knew how to shut them down.

TECHS SWARMED AROUND the Ultramarines' Thunderhawk, stripping armoured panels from its hull and removing ammo hoppers from its frame under the watchful eye of Techmarine Harkus. His features were anxious and Uriel could hear frequent angry tirades passing between Harkus and the Adeptus Mechanicus cutters.

Sparks flew as extra weight was removed from the Thunderhawk with heavy cutting gear, thick plates of armour stripped and weapons removed to try and reduce the overall weight of the gunship from seventy-six tonnes to a mere forty.

A giant crane groaned as it lifted off the main battle cannon, tracked lifter-servitors unloading the shells through the front ramp. Adeptus Mechanicus tech-priests worked atop scaffolding built around the cockpit to remove the fore-mounted heavy bolters, while below them a procession of enginseers stripped out every unnecessary fitting. Teams of welders surrounded the stricken gunship, blue sparks flaring as they replaced its heaviest plates of armour with thin sheets of light-weight metal.

The sheets bent as augmented servitors lifted them into place to be welded and Uriel knew that they would be scant protection from even the most glancing of impacts.

'It breaks my heart to see such a noble vehicle so cruelly treated,' said Uriel. 'We must make our obeisance to its war-spirit that it might know we only do this out of the direst of circumstances.'

Beside him, Captain Bannon nodded in agreement. 'Aye, but your Techmarine will ensure that the correct supplications are made and prepare us with the proper prayers to offer.'

Crouched by the engine cowlings Harkus looked distraught at the drastic measures being taken to lighten his charge.

'I wonder who he is more terrified of just now?' wondered Bannon. 'The war-spirit of the Thunderhawk or his Master of Forges?'

'A little of both would be my guess,' chuckled Uriel, think-ing of the irascible Fennias Maxim back on Macragge who had balked at the idea of him forging his own blade when there were dozens of skilled artificers who could do a better job.

Harkus rose from the engine and jogged around his wounded gunship, his distress plain to see. He waved a hand at the Thunderhawk.

'These… these butchers are destroying my craft. Nine hun-dred years old, over two thousand campaigns and this is how we treat her. There will be words had when this is all over, mind. She can't take this kind of treatment.'

'How heavy is she?' asked Uriel.

'Too heavy,' snapped Harkus, 'she's still over fifty tonnes.'

'We need her at forty, Brother Harkus,' reminded Bannon.

'Don't you think I know that!' said Harkus in exasperation. 'But I'm a Techmarine, not a miracle-worker; I can't change the laws of aerodynamics. We can only take off so much before she'll become unflyable.'

'Find a way, brother,' said Uriel gently. 'Strip her down to her bare bones if you have to. Everything depends on you getting this honourable craft down to forty tonnes and still flyable.'

Harkus shook his head. 'I'll try, but I can't guarantee any-thing. I can feel her war-spirit's anger and it won't be easy to placate.'

'I know you'll do your best, Brother Harkus,' said Uriel as the furious Techmarine returned to yelling at the cutting crews as yet another armour plate clanged to the landing platform.

'Can he do it?' asked Bannon. 'Much depends on it.'

'He was an apprentice of Sevano Tomasin, one of our finest who died on Thracia. If anyone can achieve the impossible, it is Harkus.'

Bannon nodded. 'Even if we succeed, we may not make it back. You know this.'

'I know,' said Uriel slowly. 'But if we can end this, then it will be worth it.'

Bannon nodded, then paused before saying, 'You do not have to come on this mission, Uriel. We are the Deathwatch and this is what we are trained for.'

'I have served in the Deathwatch also, and if you go, I go. Besides, Harkus will want another Ultramarine there to make sure the Deathwatch treats his gunship with proper respect.'

SNOWDOG QUICKLY CHANGED power cells on his lasgun, his rate of reloading putting many veteran Guardsmen to shame. He fired over the barricade they'd built around the entrance to the warehouse, pitching another bladed killer backwards into the bloody snow. Jonny Stomp blazed away on full auto, and Silver blasted the aliens with carefully aimed shots from her twin pistols.

He'd drafted perhaps a hundred or so of the most able-bodied refugees and stuck guns in their hands, before bundling them outside to the barricades to fight. Some had complained that since they were paying him for protection, they shouldn't have to fight. Snowdog explained down the barrel of a gun that they didn't have an option.

Aliens poured from every street into the open ground before the warehouse, charging through the hail of fire that awaited them without fear or thought for their own lives. Before this had all gone nova he'd heard on some of the devotional vids that there were supposed to be large creatures that controlled the smaller ones, but thankfully they hadn't seen any of them yet. Perhaps they were all at the front line, which, judging by the noises coming from the west, was getting closer every day.

He wondered why no soldiers had come to their aid, but figured that they knew this was a Stank ghetto and that the city would be better off if the tyranids conveniently wiped out a few thousand Stankers. So it looked as though they'd have to do this on their own. So far, each attack had been sent packing by Snowdog and his gang, leaving more and more alien dead on the ground.

What he couldn't figure was why the hell were they so furiously attacking this place?

Trask fired his shotgun into the midst of the charging aliens, and even with one eye swollen shut by the rash that covered half his face, he still couldn't fail to hit something. A knot of aliens attacked that section of the barricade, and Snowdog opened up on full auto, cutting two in half and blowing another one's legs clean off.

Tigerlily, Rentzo and a dozen other members of the Nightcrawlers waited at the doors to the warehouse in reserve, fear etched on every face.

Another wave of screeching aliens poured into the square and now Snowdog knew he wasn't imagining things; the attacks on the warehouse *were* getting more frequent and more ferocious. It seemed as though every alien in the city was coming for him. What the hell was the matter with these aliens? Did they resent him making some money of the back of their invasion or something?

Silver crouched down to reload her pistols and raised her eyebrows. 'Some day, huh?' she said.

'Yeah, some day,' he agreed.

THE THUNDERHAWK WAS a dark shadow against the blackness of the night, the blue of its armoured hull visible only on the leading edges of its wings and tailfins, the rest having been stripped off to reduce its weight. Uriel and the members of the Deathwatch stood in a loose circle, their hands clasped in prayer. Each had made his peace with the Emperor and was prepared for the mission.

Uriel had cleaned and repaired his armour as best he could, but its fabric was still beaten and in need of months in the forge. Teams of struggling lifter-servitors carried the last of the Thunderhawk's cargo on board, the landing skids creaking under the strain.

As they finished loading the gunship, Harkus emerged from within and gave Uriel a nod of affirmation. Everything was

loaded and securely locked down. The Thunderhawk was
going to be doing some hard flying and the last thing they
needed was loose cargo spilling in the back. Looking at the
thin panels on the sides of the gunship, Uriel knew that the
cargo would go straight through it.

'We are ready,' said Bannon, slinging his weapon.

'Aye,' agreed Uriel, checking the action on his own weapon
and ensuring his sword was secure in its scabbard. The
remainder of the Deathwatch silently checked over their own
and each other's armaments with the silence of the elite soldiers they were. Satisfied, each man recited the first five verses
of the Catechism of the Xeno before turning and marching
aboard the gunship.

Uriel took a deep breath and looked around the soaring
peaks of the mountains. Distant specks spun in the starlit sky
far to the west. He shook his head as a sudden premonition
of doom passed through him and followed the Deathwatch
into the gunship's crew compartment.

There was barely room for the Space Marines to move
inside, with creaking pallets stacked to the roof and the gunship's other passengers taking up a great deal of room. There
were no armoured benches to sit on, their weight deemed
unnecessary, so he crouched with his back to the rumbling
fuselage.

The ramp whined closed, shutting out the starlight, and
Uriel's auto-senses took over.

A screaming whine built as the engines spooled up to verti-
cal take-off power and Uriel offered a quick prayer that
Harkus had not let them down and that Lord Admiral
Tiberius was near. He felt the Thunderhawk lurch as it lifted
easily into the air, and turn on its axis as Harkus set their
course. He was surprised at the ease with which the gunship
had lifted off before remembering that the problem was not
now its weight, but its range.

It was all a question of whether they could reach their
objective, carry out their mission and still have enough fuel to
get them back.

Uriel felt the acceleration of the gunship as the engines
built up to full power, pushing them eastwards across the
mountain tops. There was cloud cover higher up and while
nap-of-the-earth flying might keep them safe from being

spotted, it was hugely inefficient and burned up vast quantities of fuel.

As the gunship sped eastwards, Magos Gossin, the most senior of their Adeptus Mechanicus passengers, tapped him on the shoulder and pointed through the vision port.

'Even if we succeed here, will this world ever truly be ours again?'

Uriel twisted his head to look outside.

Purple clouds boiled in the distance and streamers of multi-coloured smog hugged the horizon, reaching into the upper atmosphere like a smeared painting.

Uriel wanted to lie, but felt he would choke on the words.

'No,' he said. 'No, it will not.'

The Thunderhawk streaked through the night sky.

THE VAE VICTUS was a far cry from the gleaming vessel that had set out from Macragge so many months ago. Her central nave was buckled and splintered, the polished timbers blackened and scorched. Many of her previously manned console stations sat empty, their systems damaged beyond repair without months of time in dock. Wisps of steam gusted from hastily sealed pipes and many of her weapons were unable to fire.

Her surveyors were functioning at minimum capacity, most of the external auguries having been incinerated in the fiery blast of the refinery's destruction. Much of her hull had been melted or stripped away in the explosion and her engines would only allow her captain to perform the most basic of manoeuvres.

And Tiberius knew that they had escaped relatively lightly.

They had lost the *Argus*, most of the local fleet and the *Kharloss Vincennes* would never launch fighters again. He had been forced to order all hands to abandon the Dauntless cruiser *Yermetov*, when it became apparent her warp drives had been damaged in the blast and would soon implode. Her crew had escaped to the *Sword of Retribution* and sent her into the warp on her last voyage.

The two remaining vessels of Arx Praetora squadron and the *Mortis Probati* of the Mortifactors limped alongside the *Vae Victus*. Captain Gaiseric and his crew were eager to exact a measure of revenge against the tyranids.

One Overlord battlecruiser, two battered Space Marine strike cruisers and a carrier that could not launch any strike craft was not much of a fleet to take on the full might of a hive fleet, but it was all they had.

Tiberius ran a hand over his scarred, hairless skull and chewed his bottom lip.

'Any word from Uriel?' he asked.

Philotas looked up from the cracked plotting table. Its slate was dark and his deck officer had rolled star charts spread across its surface.

He shook his head. 'No, lord admiral. The last message we were able to receive was over an hour and a half ago saying they were on schedule.'

'I don't like this, damn it. We could be sailing into a trap!'

'Indeed we could.'

'You're sure there's nothing from Uriel?'

'As sure as I can be. Most of our vox-casters were smashed in the explosion or had their internal workings fried by the electromagnetic pulse. We were lucky to make contact at all.'

'Then we're going to have to do this the old fashioned way,' said Tiberius.

Philotas nodded and returned to his charts as Tiberius stared in anticipation at the viewing bay. The world of Tarsis Ultra spun gently before him, tainted with several bruised areas of colour that were spreading across its surface. He could see distant specks of tyranid organisms and felt his hate grow. Like parasites, they suckled on this world, draining it of its life without thought for the billions of creatures that called it home. Even as he watched them, several of the vanguard drone creatures altered direction to face the incoming Imperial fleet.

'All ships, this is Tiberius. Battle stations. They're coming.'

He closed his eyes and muttered a prayer that Uriel was currently hurtling towards his objective.

Whether he was or he wasn't, there was nothing Tiberius could do about it.

All he could do was lead his ships into battle and fight.

SPOUTS OF MUD and water were thrown up as the Thunderhawk touched down on the upper slopes of the eastern mountains in a cloud of shrieking jetwash. Its skids slid

briefly on the slippery ground before finally finding purchase.
The front ramp slammed down into the mud and the five
members of the Deathwatch and Uriel surged from its interior.

Uriel jogged to a covering position and crouched low
behind a jagged black boulder, resting his bolter on it as he
surveyed the slopes below him for threats. A thick, viscous
rain fell and Uriel could tell that the temperature here was
many degrees higher than at Erebus. Already tyranid mutagenic viruses were working to raise the temperature of Tarsis
Ultra for ease of consumption.

The thick sheets of rain cut visibility dramatically and he
could see no more than three hundred metres through it.
Thunder rumbled, followed shortly by jagged bolts of lightning that speared the sky, throwing patchy illumination onto
the plains below. He cursed as he realised they would have little or no warning of any attack.

He signalled to one of the Deathwatch to take his place
and climbed the mud-slick slope to where Bannon co-ordi-
nated the unloading of the Thunderhawk's cargo. Another
whip of lightning seared the sky and Uriel saw what they had
come for, thrown into shadow by the bright atmospheric discharge.

From the outside it was nothing remarkable, simply an
oversized rockcrete bunker some thirty metres square, with an
armoured blast door leading within. A hemispherical dome
topped with eight long gun barrels squatted atop the bunker,
its bronze surface streaked with oxides.

Four lifter-servitors struggled under the weight of cargo pallets while Magos Gossin and his three drenched Adeptus
Mechanicus tech-priests hitched up their robes and hurriedly
made their way towards the bunker. Behind them, the servitors carried the precious cargo, fully charged capacitors to
power the defence lasers, into the bunker with the utmost
care.

Bannon strode downhill to meet Uriel, his black armour
glossy in the heavy rain.

'Anything?'

'No, but they could be right on top of us and we wouldn't
know,' replied Uriel, having to shout to be heard over the rain
and whine of the Thunderhawk's engines.

Another tense half an hour passed until eventually the last of the charged capacitors was unloaded from the belly of the Thunderhawk and taken inside the bunker. By now the Adeptus Mechanicus should be hooking them up to the main power grid. Silently Uriel prayed they would work fast.

He slid downhill through the thick mud to his earlier vantage point and squinted down into the murk. Movement rippled below him, but was it incoming tyranids or a trick of the light and rain?

Then a sheet of lightning flashed in conjunction with booming peals of thunder and the night was suddenly and vividly illuminated.

The slippery slopes of the mountain teemed with tyranid creatures, swarming uphill in their thousands. Leaping hormagaunts led the charge, but in his brief glimpse he saw a trio of lumbering, crab-clawed carnifex and a great winged beast with a long, barbed tail and a huge bony crest that stretched high above its bellowing jaws. Giant blades on its upper limbs cut the rain and a steaming bio-weapon oozed from its midsection.

He scrambled back uphill, fighting through the thick, sucking mud.

He opened a channel to the captain of the Deathwatch and Techmarine Harkus.

'Bannon, ready your men! Harkus, get the Thunderhawk off the ground,' he yelled.

Seconds later, the gunship's engines roared as it lifted off to assume a holding pattern until the Space Marines were ready for extraction.

Uriel looked back down the slopes of the mountain.

'And tell Gossin to work faster,' he said. 'They're here…'

'FIRE BOMBARDMENT CANNON!' shouted Tiberius as the two pincered kraken moved slowly across the viewing bay. Without many of their targeting auguries, gunnery was a far from exact science and only his and Philotas's experience gave them any chance of scoring hits on their foe.

The bridge shuddered as the ship's main gun fired and Tiberius winced as a fresh batch of red runes began flashing on the damage control panels.

'Hull breach reopened on deck six!'

'Come to new heading, zero-five-seven,' ordered Tiberius. 'Flank speed. We've got to get past their cordon.'

The entire bridge groaned as the battered ship forced itself into the turn, her buckled keel squealing in protest.

'Come on, hold on,' Tiberius whispered to the spirit of the *Vae Victus*.

Sprays of ichor burst before his ship as the bombardment cannon's shells impacted on the kraken's hide, detonating in a giant fleshy burst of gore. An angular prow slid into view as the *Mortis Probati* crossed the bow of the Ultramarines' ship. Her starboard guns hammered the listing remains of the kraken, blasting its thrashing body to expanding clouds of scorched flesh.

The second kraken ponderously moved to engage the Mortifactors' ship, its blade wings rippling as it changed course. Behind it, Tiberius could see the outline of one of the massive hive ships, limned in the glow of the planet's atmosphere.

'All ahead full,' shouted Tiberius. 'Twenty-degree down angle. Take us through the gap!'

Tiberius gripped the cracked timbers of his command pulpit as the *Vae Victus* shook violently and accelerated through the gap the strike cruisers had blasted.

Smaller drone creatures peeled off from their attack on the *Sword of Retribution*, swooping around to come for Tiberius's vessel.

'Lord admiral!'

'I see them, Philotas. Engage with port batteries.'

'We won't hit much without the targeting surveyors.'

'Fire anyway.'

'If they board us, we will be unable to repel them.'

'Damn them! Our only priority is the hive ships. Stay on target!'

THE *Sword of Retribution* pushed deeper into the swarming tyranid creatures, firing devastating broadsides from its many gun decks, filling the space around it with vast explosions. It had suffered the least of the Imperial fleet and its captain had volunteered to take the lead position in the attack.

Lethal strikes from the dorsal lances punched a hole in the tyranid fleet through which the smaller vessels of the fleet sailed. Alien vessels surged to close the gap, but the Space

Marine vessels were too fast, slipping past the vanguard organisms on a course for the hive ships.

The *Kharloss Vincennes* limped behind the *Sword of Retribution*, her ruptured hull and damaged engines causing her to fall behind the speeding Space Marine ships. As the tyranid creatures closed the gap in their forces, they also closed inexorably on the wounded carrier. Unable to launch fighters or bombers to defend herself, she was easy prey. Close-in turrets and broadside batteries kept the alien creatures at bay for a time, but as more and more closed with her, there was no doubting the outcome of the battle.

Snaking tentacles drifted forwards from a dozen cone-shaped drones, latching limpet-like to the hull of the battling carrier. Acidic secretions bound the creatures to the ship and their maws irised open, revealing caverns of giant teeth that burrowed into their prey at a horrifying rate.

Larger ships closed, then suddenly altered course to head back towards the planet, recalled by the hive mind to catch its attackers in a trap.

As the *Kharloss Vincennes* fought the losing battle for its life, the remainder of the Imperial fleet pushed on into the swarm.

THE NEAREST HIVE ship lay before the *Vae Victus*, its gargantuan shape filling the viewing bay before him. Attendant guardian creatures formed an impenetrable barrier between her and her escorting ships.

'All ships, fire all weapons!' shouted Tiberius. 'We have to break through.'

Massive projectiles hurtled through space, exploding in vivid blossoms of fire ahead, but none were reaching their target. Kraken and drones moved in an intricate ballet that would have been virtually impossible for the Imperial Navy to emulate, screening the hive ship from the incoming firepower. Tiberius saw a handful of shots penetrate the living shield, but precious few were causing any real damage.

Tiberius opened a vox-link to the captain of the *Sword of Retribution*.

'Captain, you must clear us a path! Use whatever means are necessary.'

He snapped off the link without waiting for an answer and said, 'Philotas, try and raise Uriel. Tell him that whatever he's doing, he'd better do it fast, because we won't last much longer here.'

RAIN HAMMERED THE mountainside and lightning provided stroboscopic illumination across the rocky slopes as the thousands-strong horde scrambled up towards the bunker. Rivers of foaming water flooded downhill, sweeping great swathes of the aliens with it.

For once, the tyranids' metamorphosis of a planet's surface was working against them, saw Uriel. The glutinous mud was as much of a hindrance to them as it was to the Space Marines. Bolter fire raked the slopes, blasting apart horma-gaunts and other nameless horrors in stuttering blazes of shells. Uriel hurled a pair of grenades, ducking back behind a rock as they detonated, sending up showers of mud and alien body parts.

Screeching carnifex struggled in the mud, their bulk causing them to sink knee deep. The winged monster flapped above the horde, buffeting winds keeping it from advancing for now.

The Deathwatch picked off aliens with single shots to their vulnerable organs, careful to conserve their ammunition. Bannon scrambled across the slopes to Uriel's position, his armour caked in clods of mud, the symbol of the Imperial Fists barely visible.

'They're circling around behind us. We need to get inside!'

Uriel looked up into the filthy downpour, seeing indistinct shapes bounding across the rocks towards the bunker. Bannon was right, given a few minutes, they would be surrounded.

'Let's get going then,' he said, rising from behind the rock.

Uriel felt the ground shift under his feet and leapt back-wards as a huge portion of mud suddenly detached from the slope, sliding downhill as the torrential downpour washed it from the side of the mountain. He landed on his back and rolled, grabbing onto the rock as he felt himself slipping. His bolter clattered behind the rock.

He heard Bannon cry out and saw the captain of the Death-watch desperately scrambling in the mud to keep from sliding into the mass of aliens below. Uriel braced himself on the rock and held out his hand towards Bannon. The two warriors gripped wrists and Uriel began pulling.

'Uriel!' shouted Bannon.

He looked up, seeing a monstrous beast with a fang-filled maw clawing its way up the slope. Its long, taloned fist clamped around Bannon's ankle and squeezed. The ceramite cracked under its awful strength and its black eyes locked with Uriel's. Bolter shells burst around the battle as the Death-watch bought time for Uriel to rescue their captain.

Uriel roared as he fought against the tyranid's strength, knowing that he could not defeat it. Bunching the muscles in his thighs, he braced his boots against the rock and gave a her-culean pull, reaching down to sweep up his bolt-gun with his free hand.

Feeling the tendons in his arm crack, he straightened his legs, the counterbalance of the tyranid warrior pulling him to a standing position. Gripping his bolter in one hand he aimed at the creature's head.

'Let go,' he said simply and emptied the magazine into its face, its brains mushrooming from the back of its skull as his bolts detonated within its cranium. Its grip spasmed and Uriel hauled Bannon to the rock, pulling him to his feet as another streak of lightning lit up the sky.

The two Space Marines slipped and stumbled their way towards the bunker through the torrents of water and mud. Twice, tyranid creatures came close to overtaking them, but each time the unerringly accurate bolter fire of the Death-watch kept the aliens at bay. Uriel heard static-filled words in his helmet vox, but could make little sense of them. He recog-nised the voice as that of Philotas, the deck officer of the *Vae Victus*, but whatever he was saying was unintelligible.

Eventually they reached the rockcrete apron surrounding the bunker and slammed into its reassuringly solid bulk. As more lightning burst overhead, tyranid creatures slid down-hill from the slopes above, skidding in the mud as they tried to find their footing. Silhouetted in the glare, Uriel saw the carnifex and the monstrous winged beast finally crest the plateau and lumber towards the bunker.

'Everybody inside, now!' yelled Bannon, firing at the carnifex as he limped backwards. Uriel stood beside him, loading and firing off another magazine to little effect. The monster's screeching roar echoed from the mountains as it charged through the rain. Uriel ducked inside the bunker, grabbing the giant locking wheel and shouting, 'Bannon! Get inside, now!'

The Deathwatch captain kept firing and Uriel was about to repeat his order, when Bannon turned and ran inside, dropping his bolter and helping Uriel with the door. Armoured and sheathed in double layers of adamantium, the door weighed over four tonnes, and was normally closed by means of hydraulic pistons, but Uriel and Bannon pulled it shut in seconds, desperation lending their limbs extra strength.

The door slammed closed and Uriel spun the locking wheel.

'That was too close,' breathed Uriel.

'Aye,' agreed Bannon, scooping up his weapon.

The steel of the door buckled inwards with a resounding clang. Thunderous impacts rocked it and dust fell from the ceiling. Glow-globes on the ceiling flickered with each impact.

'Come on,' said Bannon, 'This door will not hold them for long,' and marched along the bare rockcrete corridor. Casting wary glances at the booming door, Uriel followed him, eventually arriving in the humid fire-control chamber. Banks of ancient technology lined the edge of the octagonal room and an iron ladder led up to a brass rimmed hatch in the ceiling.

Magos Gossin sat before what was presumably the main firing panel with his head bowed in prayer, his tech-priests kneeling behind him and chanting in counterpoint to their master's words. Mud-caked Deathwatch Space Marines stood at attention as the droning mantra continued, with no sign of drawing to a close.

'Magos Gossin,' snapped Bannon. 'When can you fire these guns?'

Gossin turned in his seat, his displeasure at having been interrupted plain. 'The capacitors are linked to the main grid, but the necessary prayers to begin the firing sequence are lengthy and intricate. It would be preferable if you did not interrupt me as I perform them.'

Bannon marched towards Gossin as another impact slammed into the main door.

'Do you hear that?' he demanded. 'We have minutes at best before the tyranids are upon us. Fire these guns now or they will not fire at all. Do you understand me?'

A tortured metallic screech echoed through the bunker. Gossin stared fearfully along the corridor and nodded.

'Deathwatch, with me!' shouted Bannon, heading back towards the door.

THE VIEWING BAY of the *Vae Victus* lit up with the destruction of the *Kharloss Vincennes*, reflected light from the explosion flaring from the glossy carapaces of the tyranid bio-ships.

'Emperor watch over thee,' whispered Tiberius as another impact rocked his vessel. Deathly red light bathed the command bridge as more and more tyranid weapons scored hits. Their defensive capabilities had been degraded comprehensively by hundreds of drifting spores and there was nothing he could do to stop it.

The *Sword of Retribution* still fought, her captain performing brilliantly in evading the tyranid creatures and hammering the hive ship's escorts.

'He's fighting to reach the second hive ship,' said Philotas.

But Tiberius could see he wouldn't make it. Already organisms were swarming over her hull and suffocating her firepower.

They had come so close! The first hive ship was right in front of them. The *Vae Victus* and the *Mortis Probati* had stripped away a huge portion of its defences, diverting much of the defences previously protecting it from attack from the planet's surface.

But there was no attack from the planet and Tiberius felt his heart sink at the thought that they had failed.

'All ships, prepare to disengage,' he said.

THE DOOR BLEW inwards, ripped in two by a massive pair of claws. Rain and wind howled inside the bunker as a dozen hormagaunts fought to squeeze past the screaming carnifex that smashed its claws into the rockcrete around the door in an attempt to squeeze its massive bulk inside.

A volley of disciplined bolter fire brought down the first and second waves.

A giant crack split the ceiling, the carnifex bludgeoning its way forwards.

Screeching howls and deafening blasts of gunfire filled the narrow corridor.

Uriel aimed at the carnifex's head, its blunt features expressionless as it hammered its way inside. His shot put out its eye, blasting a chunk of skull clear. The beast flinched, but simply lowered its bony head and slammed harder on the bunker's structure.

Leaping hormagaunts filled the corridor, screeching with alien fury as the Space Marines slowly fell back before them. Glow-globes shattered and the ceiling split apart with a booming crack. Huge chunks of rock dropped into the corridor. Uriel hurled himself clear as tonnes of rock collapsed and billowing clouds of dust filled the air.

He dragged himself to his feet, scrabbling for his fallen bolter as a mud-covered warrior organism leapt atop the steel-laced rubble. Its fangs spread wide and a secondary set of jaws lashed out, biting deep into Uriel's helm. His visor shattered and he felt blood on his face as the jaws withdrew. He dropped to his knees against the wall, disengaging the vacuum sockets on his gorget and tearing the helmet loose.

The tyranid warrior pounced and a hail of bolter shells stitched across its thorax, exploding wetly within and spraying Uriel with its blood. Bannon hauled him to his feet as the tyranids clambered over the rubble and the Deathwatch hammered them with more shells.

Without the protection of his helmet's auto-senses, the noise was deafening. Gunfire and thunder combined with the lightning to form a cacophonous backdrop to the battle. Dimly Uriel heard Bannon calling the Thunderhawk down as they fell back towards the control chamber.

As the Space Marines withdrew, Uriel was suddenly aware of a bitter, metallic taste on the air as a powerful static charge built around him. His scalp tingled and even over the noise of battle he could hear a deep, bass thrumming build beneath him.

He looked up through the shattered ceiling in time to see an incandescent streak of light spear skywards, looking like the manifest wrath of the Emperor

ONCE AGAIN THE viewing bay lit up, and it took Tiberius a moment to realise why. Another streak of light slashed past the *Vae Victus* blasting clean through the body of the hive ship. Another shot fired, followed closely by another and he surged from his command pulpit and punched the air.

'Damn you, Uriel. I knew you could do it!' he yelled over the ringing of alarm bells.

With atmospheric conditions more or less stable in the region selected by Uriel and Sebastien Montante, the beams from the defence laser silo were unaffected by the thermal blooming that had so hamstrung the defences in the opening stages of the invasion.

In low orbit, and with its planetward defences engaged in protecting it from the Imperial fleet, the hive ship was horribly vulnerable and was now paying the price. Explosions of flesh rippled across the hive ship's body as blasts from the defence lasers destroyed it.

'All ships, belay my last order!' he shouted. 'Target everything you can at that hive ship! We've got it, by the Emperor, we've got it!'

URIEL CLIMBED THE ladder in the centre of the control chamber, hauling on the rusted opening lever and pulling aside the hatch. The static hum was even stronger here and a soft blue glow illuminated the dome above the control chamber. Then a dazzling light flared and Uriel blinked away blistering afterimages as the flash of the defence laser's fire filled the interior of the dome. The guns were firing automatically now and would continue to do so until the capacitors they had brought ran dry.

'All clear!' he yelled.

The sounds of bolter fire intensified as the tyranids, perhaps sensing their prey was escaping, intensified their attack.

Uriel hauled himself up into the dome, reaching back and pulling up the tech-priests as they scrambled up the ladder. Outside the dome he could hear the roar of the Thunderhawk's engines as it hovered overhead.

One by one, the Deathwatch climbed to the dome, until only Bannon remained. He fired a last burst from his bolter before dropping it and leaping for the ladder. He climbed fast as the tyranids flooded the chamber below. Uriel and another Space Marine pulled Bannon through the hatch and slammed it shut.

'Time to get out of here, wouldn't you say?' said Bannon breathlessly.

'Way past time,' agreed Uriel, as the guns fired again.

With Uriel leading the way, the exhausted group made their way onto the roof of the bunker. The wind and rain had diminished and the scale of the swarm surrounding the bunker now became apparent. Howling jetwash from the hovering Thunderhawk's engines threatened to hurl them from the roof. Hormagaunts frenziedly tried to climb to the roof of the bunker as the carnifexes battered its walls. They had seconds at best.

Thick, rappelling cables hung from the crew ramp of the gunship and Uriel quickly grabbed them, distributing a cable to each of the Deathwatch as he saw swarms of gargoyles hurtling through the air towards the gunship.

'Look,' he said, pointing.

'I see them,' nodded Bannon, grasping a cable.

The Deathwatch gathered up the tech-priests and Magos Gossin as Harkus activated the winch to pull them up. Uriel wondered how the fleet had fared as he swung through the air below the gunship and the ramp above drew nearer. The flocks of gargoyles were closing rapidly and he silently urged the winch to haul them faster.

Deciding that he couldn't wait any longer, Harkus spun the gunship, feathering the engines to gain altitude. Uriel didn't blame him. The ground slid below him, thousands of aliens hissing with malevolence towards the sky as their prey escaped.

Then the world turned upside down.

Something huge buffeted him, smashing into his back and spinning him crazily.

He heard a screech of rage and a grunt of pain. Flapping wings spun him around. His vision swum, but he could see the giant, winged monster thrashing in the cables below the Thunderhawk's open crew ramp.

Its wings spurted blood, slashed to ribbons by the cable as it mauled a black-armoured figure who fought it with equal ferocity. As the combatants fought spinning on the cable, Uriel caught a flash of the yellow Imperial Fists insignia.

Captain Bannon stabbed the creature with his power knife, plunging it again and again into its hard, bony carapace. In return the monster's claws tore at his armour, ripping ceramite plates free and gouging bloody chunks from his body.

Swarms of gargoyles swooped down, closing to attack.

The Thunderhawk swayed in the air, unable to make its escape.

Hands reached down to grip Uriel's armour and pull him aboard. He collapsed exhausted onto the armoured deck, breath coming in great heaving gulps as he rolled over to the edge of the ramp.

Below him, man and monster fought in a battle the likes of which Uriel had never seen. The gunship altered course, attempting to put as much distance between it and the hundreds of approaching gargoyles. But with its crew ramp open, it could not accelerate fast enough.

Uriel could see the realisation of this pass through the Deathwatch captain.

He saw what Bannon intended and shouted, 'No!'

But it was too late. Bannon reached up and slashed his power knife through the cable.

He and his monstrous opponent plummeted to the mountainside below, landing amid the swarming creatures.

Cursing the tyranids with all his heart, Uriel pulled himself up the Thunderhawk's fuselage and hammered the ramp's closing mechanism. Now able to achieve escape velocity, Harkus spun the gunship on its axis, punching the engines and kicking in the afterburners. Flocks of gargoyles snapped at the gunship's wings, but he was able to break clear and the aircraft banked around, heading back towards Erebus with hundreds of flying monsters in hot pursuit.

Uriel stared through the vision port.

Below him, Captain Bannon fought his last battle against thousands of screeching killers.

PHASE IV – SUBDUAL

FOURTEEN

THE THUNDERHAWK STREAKED through the lightening sky, vaporous contrails streaming from the trailing edges of its wings. The flight from the gargoyles had burned much of their precious fuel and Harkus was forced to climb to where the air was thinner and every kilometre of range could be squeezed from what little fuel the gunship's tanks still contained.

Should that not prove sufficient, then there was no way they would survive to reach Erebus.

The interior of the gunship was eerily empty, the five members of the Deathwatch, the tech-priests and Uriel all that filled its now spacious storage bays. Without the heavy capacitors, the Thunderhawk could fly much faster and had quickly outdistanced the pursuing gargoyles, concealing itself among the cloud layer.

The howl of the wind was deafening, but even over the tremendous noise, Uriel could hear the valedictions of the Deathwatch and though he too felt Captain Bannon's loss keenly, he respected their need to say their farewell privately.

Uriel closed his eyes and offered a short prayer for the departed captain of the Deathwatch.

It was the least he could do to honour his memory.

HEAVY BLAST DOORS slid smoothly aside, the freezing chill of an Erebus morning rushing in to fill the wide hangar as the *Magnificence* lifted from her moorings in a haze of screaming jets, heavy blast deflectors venting her exhaust fumes into the cold air.

The vessel ponderously nosed out of the hangar, its pilot proceeding with extra care since the owner of the starship was seated directly behind him and with the hold filled with such a vast array of wealth, she handled less deftly than usual. Hardwired into the controls of the ship, he was aware of every aspect of the *Magnificence*, but with a master as volatile as Simon van Gelder it never paid to take chances.

Simon watched the rocky interior of the hangar slide past through the viewing bay, to be replaced by the pristine white of the sky. He smiled as he saw his mountain estates below the ship, still guarded by his privately funded army. Though he expected Erebus to fall any day, there was no reason to leave his property unprotected. If he did return, he would require to reside in prestigious lodgings once again.

The ground slowly fell away as the pilot gained altitude. Simon could see tiny figures lower down the valley pointing at his ship and felt a smug glow of satisfaction as he pictured their dismay at his escape.

A buzzing warning sounded from the speakers, drawing his attention away from the rapidly diminishing landmarks of Erebus.

'The valley defence guns are interrogating us,' said the pilot, with a nervous edge to his voice.

Simon nodded, looking up through the viewing bay to see the massive defence guns rotating in their housings to acquire his ship. He smiled and removed a plain, metallic box from his long coat, unwinding an insulated cable from one end and plugging it into the pilot's console. He pressed a black button on its side and said, 'Broadcast this signal on all frequencies. It will shut down the protocols controlling the guns.'

'We shall be quite safe,' said Simon, deciding to retire to his sumptuous quarters in the upper levels of the ship.

'HANG ON TO something,' shouted Harkus as the Thunderhawk banked sharply around the highest peak to the east of Erebus. 'We have incoming hostiles!'

Uriel strode through the crew compartment to join the pilot in the cockpit. Ahead he could see the gouge in the mountains that was Erebus. Rising from mountain roosts, black flocks of gargoyles and other, more lethal, flying beasts clustered around the highest peaks.

They sped through the air towards the Thunderhawk and Uriel saw it would be a close run thing whether they reached the covering fire of the city's guns before they were caught.

'How are we for fuel?' he asked.

'The reserve tanks are virtually dry. We're flying on fumes and prayers now,' answered Harkus testily.

'Not enough to use the afterburners?'

'Barely even enough to land safely.'

Uriel nodded, watching as the valley of Erebus grew in the windshield. So too did the growing flock of flying monsters that raced to intercept them.

The Thunderhawk's speed increased as Harkus dipped the nose and the mountainside raced up to meet them. Snow-covered rocks flashed beneath them. What he wouldn't have given for some of the gunship's weapon systems right now.

Suddenly the ground dropped away and Harkus hauled back on the controls, deploying the air brakes and pulling the gunship into a screaming turn. Daylight speared inside as bio-weapons fire punched through the thin sheets of lightweight metal welded to its side. Uriel heard one of Gossin's tech-priests screaming as alien organisms ate away his flesh.

He gripped onto the empty co-pilot's chair as the gunship swayed violently in the air and a warning light flashed on the controls.

'We're under the cover of the guns, but they're not firing!' yelled Harkus.

Uriel let out the breath he'd been holding, watching as fly-ing aliens closed in around them. Dozens of impacts perforated the thin hull of the gunship. Fresh screaming echoed.

'Emperor's blood!' shouted the Techmarine, and Uriel looked up in time to see a silver behemoth with heraldic crests emblazoned along the length of its hull rising through the air directly in front of them.

SIMON HEARD HIS pilot's shout of alarm and turned, ready to rebuke him, but the words died in his throat as he saw the roaring Thunderhawk hurtling towards them and the thousands of black, winged monsters that pursued it.

His legs sagged and he dropped to his knees.

'No,' he moaned, 'not like this…'

THE THUNDERHAWK BROKE left and dived, Harkus pushing the weakened airframe beyond the limits of its endurance. The pressure tore the thin sides free and hurricane-force winds roared through its interior. Uriel saw the reflective silver hull of the vessel before them streak past, so close he could have reached out and touched it. The Deathwatch managed to grip onto the bars and struts of the frame, but the three tech-priests were swept screaming to their deaths.

Uriel slammed into a thick stanchion, grabbing onto it as he slid along the violently heaving deck. Over the howling air he heard Harkus swearing and invoking the name of the machine god in equal measures.

The deck lurched again and Uriel saw the ground terrifyingly close through the gaps in the Thunderhawk's flanks. It raced past then vanished from sight as Harkus brought them level again. Uriel pulled himself upright, still clutching the stanchion tightly.

The noise of rushing air diminished, Harkus easing back on the thrusters and bringing the gunship level.

'Imperator, that was close!' breathed Uriel.

'Brace yourselves!' yelled Harkus. 'We're coming into land and it's going to be a rough one!'

THOUSANDS OF GARGOYLES swarmed across the *Magnificence*, clogging air intakes and smashing into control surfaces. Larger creatures skidded across its hull, tearing and biting through her metal hide with acidic saliva and diamond-hard teeth.

Scores of creatures attached themselves to the underside of the hull, clawing and biting open access panels and climbing through the open undercarriage ports. Within seconds, tonnes of extra weight had been added and the already overburdened craft began to list drunkenly to starboard.

Simon's pilot pushed the engines out in an attempt to dislodge the creatures, but with so much of the craft overbalanced and clogged with alien flesh, one simply flamed out, causing the vessel to yaw uncontrollably.

The ship's windshield blew out. Screeching creatures swarmed in and Simon screamed as they tore the flesh from his bones.

A sweeping silver wing struck the rock face and sheared from the hull.

The *Magnificence* tumbled from the skies, gaining speed as she fell until she crashed in a spectacular fireball amid the buildings of District Secundus.

STREAKING BLACK SHAPES spun in the sky above Snowdog as he made his way through the ruins of the destroyed warehouse. Smoking rubble tumbled from the shattered walls and the baleful orange glow from the twisted piles of blazing wreckage more than resembled his vision of hell.

Weeping families hugged the crushed bodies of loved ones and dazed survivors wandered through the ruins, blinded and burned by the crash of the falling starship. A silvered wing pointed towards the sky and a burning section of its hull was embedded in the ground before the warehouse.

Broken crates from the ship's hold littered the ground, spilling smashed porcelain and gilt-edged finery to the snow. A framed portrait of an ancient nobleman lay smashed in the ruins, rolled rugs and tapestries burned in a pool of fuel and fluttering pages from a library's worth of books filled the air. Fabulously expensive clothing soaked in pools of melted snow, ruined beyond repair, and valuables of all description lay scattered throughout the fiery hell of District Secundus.

There was a small fortune just lying on the ground, and Snowdog helped himself to as much as he could fit into his backpack, all the while keeping an eye on the wheeling shapes above and cursing the damn pilot who'd brought his vessel down on top of them. The rear of the warehouse was gone, obliterated by the impact of the plummeting starship. Every one of the crates of supplies he'd heisted, scammed from crooked supply sergeants or killed for was gone, burned to ashes in the searing conflagration.

Tigerlily stood numbed at the scale of the destruction unleashed by the crash, while Lex and Trask scooped up handfuls of gems and stuffed them into their pockets. Jonny helped himself to a vast hunting rifle that poked from a smashed crate, the size of the shells now looped around the big man's body in crosswise bandoliers simply staggering.

'You could bring down an angry grox with that, Jonny!' shouted Snowdog.

Jonny laughed and raised the rifle, miming the rifle's colossal recoil.

The grin fell from Snowdog's face as he saw Silver lying under a pile of cracked stones, her face bloody and arms outstretched. He ran over to her and checked her pulse. It was thready, but strong. She groaned, and Snowdog saw a length of reinforcement bar impaling her side. Blood leaked from the wound and he gently eased her off the steel bar, grimacing as he saw fully fifteen centimetres had stabbed into her.

He removed his scarf and plugged the hole in her side, tying it around her body. It wasn't much, but it was the best he could do for now.

A hand gripped his upper arm and spun him around. He reached for his pistol, but relaxed as he found himself facing a weather-beaten old man.

'What you want, grandfather? Can't you see I'm busy?'

Papa Gallo slapped Snowdog hard in the face.

'You owe these people, Stanker. You took their money and possessions in exchange for safety.'

'What?' snapped Snowdog, pulling his arm free of the old man's grip. He pointed to the sky and said, 'Hey, I gave 'em a place to stay out of the cold and kept these damned things from killing them. I think I done my share. I got problems of my own now.'

Tigerlily moved up to stand behind him and nudged him in the ribs, but Snowdog ignored her, too intent on the confrontation with the old man and the wounded Silver.

'I don't think so,' said Papa Gallo, folding his arms.

'Tough,' retorted Snowdog, 'Anyway, all the stuff they gave me's gone up in smoke.'

'Not our problem. You owe us.'

Tigerlily nudged him again and this time he shot her an irritated glance. She nodded in the direction of the blazing warehouse. He followed her gaze and felt a hot thrill of fear slide around his body. Hundreds of soot-stained civilians, gathered silhouetted in the flames, many of them armed. Armed with weapons Snowdog himself had given them.

They were on edge and looked ready to use them.

Snowdog locked eyes with Papa Gallo and saw the fierce determination there.

He saw Jonny slide a shell for his rifle from the bandoliers and shook his head.

'Okay, man, you win,' said Snowdog, kneeling beside the unconscious Silver. 'What do you want? But be quick.'

'There's a lot of wounded here and you don't have the supplies to deal with them any more.'

'And?'

'And we need to get these people some help. I want you to lead them to the nearest medicae facility,' stated Papa Gallo.

'Shit, man, the nearest one still standing's in District Quintus,' protested Snowdog.

'Not my problem,' repeated Papa Gallo, and as Snowdog looked at the bleeding girl beside him and the many weapons facing him, he realised he had no choice.

'Okay then,' he shrugged, shucking his backpack onto his shoulders and gathering up Silver in his arms. 'Let's get gone. We don't wanna be hanging around with those things flying overhead.'

THE LICTOR THRASHED against its restraints, flesh hooks lashing out at the armoured glass that separated it from those who observed it. Bound to three upright dissection tables pushed together, its powerful muscles bunched as it attempted to break free, but the restraints rendered it immobile. Even so, it had killed two magos-biologis who had unwisely failed to observe full xeno-containment procedures and wounded a third who had subsequently been put to death for his lapse.

With the lictor's capture, Magos Locard's work had progressed with a new urgency following the failed attempt to destroy both hive ships between the defence lasers and the Imperial fleet. Things had gone from bad to worse when the

cowardly Simon van Gelder had attempted to flee Tarsis Ultra
and treacherously shut down the valley's defences.

The aerial exclusion zone had eventually been re-established,
but not before hundreds of gargoyles and their monstrous
brood-mothers had penetrated deep into the valley of Erebus.
It appeared that they were without the controlling influence of
the hive mind, as the majority of the creatures had reverted to
their basic, animalistic instincts, nesting in the caves of the valley sides and attacking small groups of civilians. Others had
rampaged through the densely-populated quarters of the city,
killing in an orgy of random violence for two days before being
hunted down by volunteer groups from the Erebus Defence
Legion.

The fighting at the District Quintus wall raged with undiminished ferocity, the tyranid swarm almost doubling in size
with the addition of yet more creatures as they were drawn to
Erebus by the single remaining hive ship. Time was running
out for the defenders of Tarsis Ultra and Magos Locard was
their last, best hope.

Deep in one of the Adeptus Mechanicus vivisectoria, Magos
Locard held forth to an assembled audience of Colonel Stagler, Major Satria, Lord Inquisitor Kryptman, Chaplain
Astador and Uriel. A blank-faced servitor with augmented
bionics grafted to its head and upper body stood in atten-
dance to the magos, carrying a silver pistol case. They watched
the lictor through the armoured glass with revulsion, its physiology repugnant, its mental processes beyond their
comprehension.

'As you can observe,' began Locard, 'the lictor organism,
even restrained by level three xeno-containment – unfortu-
nately the highest level available in these facilities – is still
45.43% lethal.'

'So why are you keeping the damned thing alive?'
demanded Stagler. 'Why not just kill it?'

'To defeat these aliens, we must first understand them,'
explained Kryptman. 'When fighting the ork, the hrud, the
galthites, the lacrymole we do so armed with knowledge of
their undoing. To fight one tyranid is not to know another.
Their adaptive nature is what makes them such superlative
predators. It is their greatest asset and, potentially in this case,
the one weakness we might exploit.'

'In what way?' asked Uriel.

'Tell me, Captain Ventris, have you heard the phrase "to turn an enemy's strength against him"?'

'Of course.'

'That is exactly what we intend,' said Kryptman with a sly smile. 'Magos Locard, if you please.'

Locard nodded and turned to the servitor, his mechadendrites unlocking the pistol case with precise turns of cog-toothed keys that slid from their tooled digits. He lifted a magnificently crafted silver pistol and a large calibre glassy bullet from the foam interior. With exaggerated care he slid the bullet into the breech and handed the weapon to the servitor as his mechadendrites relieved it of the case. At a nod from Kryptman, he spun the locking wheel that led into the lictor's cell and said, 'Proceed with instruction one.'

The servitor turned and pushed open the heavy door, marching to stand beside the dissection tables. Locard sealed the door as the lictor renewed its efforts to break free. The servitor approached and raised the pistol, pressing it against the fleshy portion of the lictor's midsection.

'What in the name of the Emperor is it doing?' asked Uriel.

'Observe,' said Locard, with more than a hint of pride in his voice. He pressed a thumb to the intercom and said, 'Perform instruction two.'

The servitor pulled the trigger, firing the glassy shell into the lictor. Ichor spilled from the wound, hissing on the vivisectoria's floor. Without pausing, the servitor placed the pistol carefully on the floor as Locard released the dissection table restraints.

In a blur of motion the lictor pounced, its severed upper claws smashing the servitor across the room. Its heavily augmented body cracked the glass, drawing cries of alarm from the observers.

Uriel and Astador unholstered their bolt pistols and aimed them through the glass.

'Wait!' cried Kryptman.

The lictor charged the servitor, its lower arms tearing into its grey flesh in a frenzy of violence. Blood sprayed the walls as the beast ripped its victim to shreds, tearing and gouging its body until there was nothing even remotely humanoid remaining. The beast reared up and hammered against the glass. Fresh cracks spread wider, rapidly spiderwebbing across its surface.

'Kill it! Kill it!' shouted Colonel Stagler.

Before Uriel and Astador could fire, the lictor doubled up, dropping to the floor of its cell. The beast let out a keening wail, its entire body convulsing as a frenzy of rippling motion undulated within its flesh.

'Ah yes, now it begins,' noted Locard. 'Resilient, but I expected that, what with its genome being relatively fixed.'

'What's happening to it?' said Uriel, staring in disgust at the convulsing monster.

The lictor fell onto its back, wracked by massive spasms, its body heaving into a giant inverted 'U'. Even through the glass, Uriel heard a loud crack as its spine snapped. The lictor's flesh split and monstrous growths erupted from within, its flesh writhing in uncontrolled evolution. Semi-formed limbs writhed from its viscera and other unnameable organs swelled from its mutating body.

The monster let out a final, tortured screech as an explosion of black blood vomited from its every orifice. Finally it was still.

Uriel was repulsed beyond belief. The lictor was undoubtedly dead, but what had killed it? Simple poison? Sudden hope flared in him as he realised that they might have a weapon with which to defeat the entire tyranid race.

'Excellent work, magos,' said Kryptman as the servitor's blood dripped from the cracked glass.

'Thank you, my lord.'

'What did you do to it?' said Astador.

Locard smiled. 'Using the lictor's genetic sequence, I was able to isolate the base strands of this splinter fleet's original mutation. With that "key", if you will, I was able generate a massive over-stimulation of its adaptive processes. In effect, I drove it into a frenzy of hyper-evolution that not even a tyranid's body could stand. A lictor's genetic structure is normally extremely stable, hence the infection took a little longer to take effect than I anticipated, but I think you'll agree that the results speak for themselves.'

'This is incredible,' breathed Uriel.

'Indeed it is, Captain Ventris,' agreed Locard, with no hint of false modesty.

'With this weapon we can finally defeat the entire tyranid race!'

'Ah, regrettably, that is not the case,' explained Locard. 'Each hive fleet's gene sequence is vastly different and it was only due to the capture of such an early generation of creature that we were able to isolate this hive fleet's genetics at all.'

'So we can only utilise this weapon on this fleet?' said Stagler.

'Regrettably so, and it may not prove effective against these aliens either. Many of the creatures on Tarsis Ultra have evolved to the sixth or seventh iteration and may have deviated too far from the base strand to be affected.'

'So it may not work at all?' asked Uriel.

'I believe it will, though of course I cannot be certain,' answered Locard.

'We should distribute this ammunition as soon as possible,' said Major Satria excitedly.

Uriel saw a look pass between Kryptman and Locard and suddenly the purpose of the demonstration became clear.

'It it not that simple, Major Satria,' he said.

'No?'

'No, it is not. Is it, lord inquisitor?'

Kryptman stared at Uriel for long seconds before nodding sombrely.

'Captain Ventris is correct. It would be pointless to manufacture ammunition with this gene-poison at this stage in the battle. No, this must be taken to the heart of the enemy where it will do the most damage.'

'And what does that mean?' asked Satria.

'It means,' said Uriel, 'that we are going to have to fight our way into the hive ship. It means we must infect the hive queen.'

IN THINE EVERLASTING Glory had always been one of Sister Joaniel's favourite prayers, speaking as it did of the joy and duty of service to the Emperor. She had dedicated her life to the preservation of life and the healing of those whose frail bodies and minds had come back broken from the horrors of war. On Remian she had lived when those in her care had died and she wept as she prayed, feeling the same guilt burn within her at she thought of the poor unfortunates who lay bleeding and dying throughout the medicae building.

As she had known would happen, the flood of casualties had risen to a raging torrent, with hundreds of men being brought in every day. No matter how hard she scrubbed, she could not get the stench and taint of blood from her hands. No matter how many soldiers they mended, there were always more being brought in by the stretcher-bearers.

And as the front line had drawn ever closer to District Quintus, she and her staff had worked under the noise of artillery and gunfire. The noise of war, screams, explosions and sobbing was always with her, and the sight of so many wounded men haunted her dreams.

Their faces blurred together so that she could no longer tell who lived and who died. So many times she had thought of just giving up, driven to tears by the sheer impossibility of their task. But each time, she recited her favourite prayer and the doubts and guilt were pushed back for a time.

She began the prayer for a fourth time and was midway through the second verse when she heard slamming doors and sounds of a commotion from the vestibule. Rising painfully to her feet, she limped from the chapel to see what all the fuss was about.

Climbing the steps to the vestibule, Joaniel saw a throng of injured people gathered before the doors to the wards. Uniformed orderlies were barring their way, arguing with a youngish man with bleached hair who carried a silver-haired girl whose midriff was a bloody mess.

'What in the name of all that's holy is going on here?' she said, her voice cutting through the babble of voices that filled the vestibule.

The man with the girl in his arms turned and ran his gaze up and down her. A woman with her flame-red hair shaved into stripes flanked him, her face lined with exhaustion.

'I got injured here, figured you could take care of her,' said the man.

'And who are you?' asked Joaniel.

'Me? I'm Snowdog, but that don't matter. I got saddled with bringing these people here and that's what I did. This girl's hurt bad, can you help her?'

One of the orderlies pushed his way towards her through the crowded vestibule, his annoyance plain. He waved a hand at the crowd, more of whom were gathered outside the medicae building, and said, 'They're not military personnel. We can't take them. We're too crowded as it is.'

'Hey, man, you gotta help,' said Snowdog. 'Where the hell else am I gonna go?'

'Not my problem,' snapped the orderly.

'I have heard of you,' said Joaniel. 'You are a killer and a dealer in guns and narcotics.'

'So?'

'So why should I help you, when there are thousands of men risking their lives every day against the tyranids?'

'Because that's what you do. You help people,' said Snowdog, as though it were the most obvious thing in the world.

Joaniel smiled at Snowdog's simple sentiment, ready to rebuke him for such naivety, before it hit her that, yes, that was what she did. It was that simple and she suddenly realised that she could not turn these people away. To do so would betray everything her order stood for. And that she would not do.

Joaniel nodded to Snowdog and pointed to a wide set of stairs that led to the upper levels of the medicae building.

'The top level is not as crowded as the others. I will send food and corpsmen to see to your wounded. We have few staff and even fewer resources thanks to our supplies being stolen, but I promise we will do what we can.'

'But they're not military personnel!' protested the orderly.

She turned to the orderly and snapped, 'I don't care. They will be given shelter and all the care we can spare. Is that understood?'

The orderly nodded, taking the wounded woman from Snowdog's arms and carrying her inside to the wards.

'Thank you, sister,' said Snowdog.

'Shut up,' said Joaniel. 'I'm not doing this for you, it's for them. Let me make myself quite clear. I despise you and all that you are, but as you say, there are wounded people here, so let's get them in out of the cold.'

GIGANTIC YELLOW BULLDOZERS finished clearing the worst of the rubble from the long boulevard that led to the front line, teams of pioneers of the Departmento Munitorum overseeing the final sweeps of the makeshift runways for debris. A stray rock or pothole could spell doom for any aircraft unlucky enough to hit it and this mission was too important for a single craft to be lost. Fuel trucks and missile gurneys crisscrossed the rockcrete apron, delivering final payloads to the multitude of aircraft whose engines filled the air with a threatening rumble. Everywhere there was a sense of urgency as pilots and ground crew prepared their airborne steeds for battle.

Captain Owen Morten, commander of the *Kharloss Vincennes'* Angel squadrons, made a final circuit of his Fury interceptor, checking the techs had removed the arming pins on his missiles and that the leading edges of his wings were free from ice. The greatest danger in flying in such cold conditions was not the additional weight of any ice, but the disruption of the airflow over the wing and subsequent reduction in lift. Satisfied that the aircraft was ready for launch, Morten zipped his flight suit up to his neck and patted the armoured fuselage of the Fury.

'We'll do this one for the *Vincennes*,' he whispered to himself.

'You say something?' asked Kiell Pelaur from the cockpit where he was finishing his ministrations to the Fury's attack logister.

'No,' said Morten, watching as the enginseers continued their inspection of the ice ramp that would hopefully allow them to take off without the length of runway they were used to. The plazas, squares and streets surrounding him were filled with a veritable armada of craft. Every cutter, skiff, fighter, bomber or recon craft that could be put in the air was right now being prepped for immediate launch.

Owen knew that most of them would never return, sacrificed to ensure the Space Marines got through to their objective. The thought did not trouble him. He had long since resigned himself to the fact that this would be his final flight. The skies above him were where he was meant to be and where he had always known he would die.

The thought that he would soon see all his dead shipmates was a great comfort to Owen Morten as he clambered up the crew ladder and vaulted into the cockpit.

* * *

THE BLACK THUNDERHAWK was devoid of insignia or ornamentation. Or so it appeared until closer inspection. Every square centimetre of its hull was inscribed with filigreed scriptwork, carved by hand with painstaking care. Catechisms and prayers of hatred for the xeno decorated the aircraft's body from prow to stern.

Chanting tech-priests circled the aircraft and blessed armourers inscribed words of ire onto the seeker heads of the wing-mounted missiles. Each heavy calibre shell loaded into the ammo hoppers of the autocannons was dipped in sanctified water before being slotted home with chants that would ensure detonation.

The five surviving members of the Deathwatch knelt in prayer before the gunship, entreating it to see them safely to their destination. Henghast led the prayers, his wounds still paining him, but recovered enough from his battle with the lictor to accompany his battle-brothers. Brother Elwaine of the Salamanders had also survived, and was even now undergoing augmetic surgery to replace his arms. Despite Elwaine's protests, Henghast had not permitted him to join the mission.

Five men against the might of a hive ship. It was of such things that the legends of the Deathwatch were made and thoughts of the battle to come filled Henghast's Fenrisian soul with fire. Should they survive, it would make for a fine saga for the Rune Priests to tell around the feast tables of the Fang.

Henghast clasped his hands to his chest and said, 'We mourn the loss of Captain Bannon, and revere his memory. He was a fine leader of men and a worthy brother in arms. I dearly wish he could be here to lead us into battle once more, but wishes are for the saga poets and we will bring honour to him by fighting this battle in his name.'

A long shadow fell over Henghast and his lip curled over his fangs as he smoothly rose to his feet, ready to rebuke whoever had interrupted his men's devotions.

But the words died in his throat as he saw the figure standing before him.

A Space Marine, his armour painted midnight black, with a single bright blue shoulder.

'Ready your warriors, Brother Henghast,' said Captain Uriel Ventris of the Deathwatch, 'we go into battle.'

FIFTEEN

URIEL FELT THE lurch of the Thunderhawk lifting off and rested his helmeted head against the rumbling side of the roaring aircraft. A soft blue light filled the crew compartment, and a beatific choir of angels drifted from humming recyc-units that circulated sacred incense inimical to the xeno. The Deathwatch sat along the opposite fuselage, their heads bowed as they readied themselves for the coming fight.

Brother Henghast, the Space Wolf, led their prayers, and Uriel was not surprised to hear pious imprecations that were the mark of a warrior preparing himself for death in battle. He allowed his gaze to wander over the brothers he would be sharing his final battle with, knowing that their service in the Deathwatch already meant that they were amongst the best and bravest warriors their Chapter could boast.

Brother Jagatun of the White Scars sat sharpening a long, curved tulwar, a horsehair totem dangling from its skulled pommel. Brother Damias, an Apothecary of the Raven Guard, taciturn and solitary, his power fist etched with bizarre scars that reminded Uriel of those inflicted by zealous priests who worked themselves into a self-mortifying frenzy of devotion. Beside him sat Brother Alvarax of the Howling Griffons and Brother Pelantar of the White Consuls. Both individually loaded the hellfire shells of their heavy bolters, the mutagenic acids contained in each silver-cased bolt deadly to xeno organisms.

Seated beside Uriel was the final member to make up their number. He alone of this band of warriors retained his Chapter's original colours and his presence was as much of as reassurance to Uriel as the Deathwatch itself.

Veteran sergeant Pasanius gripped the barrel of his heavy flamer tightly in his silvered bionic hand, silently awaiting the coming battle.

Uriel had tried to dissuade his oldest friend from coming, but Pasanius was having none of it, and since Brother Elwaine and his flamer were unable to fight, Henghast had been only too glad for Pasanius to accompany them. In the close confines of the tyranid hive ship, a flamer was sure to be a vital element of their attack.

Seeing that Pasanius was absolutely entrenched in his position, Uriel knew he would need to have his sergeant dragged away to prevent him from coming and had reluctantly, but inwardly gratefully, allowed him to come. Astador and Learchus were more than capable of holding the defenders together and his presence would not affect the fate of Erebus one way or another.

Astador had embraced him, promising his mortal remains a place of honour in the Gallery of Bone. Uriel had not liked the finality in the Chaplain's voice as he intoned the Emperor's blessing upon him.

Learchus had offered no such blessings, his fury at what he saw as his captain's desertion of his men incandescent. 'Your place is with your men, not leading the Deathwatch!' he had argued.

'No, Learchus, my place is wherever I can do the most good,' he had replied.

'Show me where it says that in the codex,' snapped Learchus.

'You know I cannot, sergeant. But this is just something I have to do.'

'Lord Calgar shall hear of this.'

'You must do what you feel is right, Learchus, as must I,' said Uriel before leaving his furious sergeant to ready the Ultramarines for the last battle.

Uriel was saddened by Learchus's inability to see beyond the letter of the codex, feeling sure that Roboute Guilliman would have approved of his decision to lead the Deathwatch into battle. He knew that there was great wisdom in the pages of the Codex Astartes, but knew also that it was wisdom to learn from, that such dogmatic adherence to what its pages contained was, as Astador had said, not wisdom, but repetition.

But there was a danger in this: that such thoughts would lead inevitably to the path the Mortifactors walked. Uriel had no wish to pursue that path, but knew now that there was a balance to be had in following the spirit of the codex, if not the letter. He smiled as he imagined the silent approval of Captain Idaeus and watched through the vision port as the view darkened from the violet sky of Tarsis Ultra to the blackness of space.

He looked around the crew compartment once more at his comrades. Seven magnificent warriors going into battle.

A battle that would decide the fate of a world.

LEARCHUS WATCHED THE Thunderhawk blast into the upper atmosphere, surrounded by hundreds of escorting aircraft as bright spots of light against the darkness. Dawn was already lightening the horizon with a diffuse amber light and he could see the first stirrings beneath the snow as the tyranids emerged from the ground.

The cracked remnants of the wall were sagging in many places, but there was little that could be done about it. Some work had been done to ready it for the coming assault, but the bulk of work undertaken throughout the night had been in preparing the runways for the aircraft to launch.

He gripped the hilt of his chainsword tightly, his anger at Uriel and Pasanius still bright and hot despite their departure. He and the remaining eighty members of the Fourth company stood at parade rest behind the northern segment of the District Quintus wall, ready to receive the attack of the tyranids. Chaplain Astador and the sixty-three warriors of the Mortifactors held the southern portion of the wall, and Learchus made a mental note to keep an eye on these reckless descendants of his Chapter.

Astador had already offered him the chance to partake in one of their barbaric blood rituals before the battle, but he had refused, marching away in disgust before doing something he might regret.

'Courage and honour!' he bellowed as the first bloated creatures moved sluggishly forward, tensioned, bony arms stretching back to launch their organic bombs.

THE TASTE OF blood still strong in his mouth, Chaplain Astador watched the unyielding figure of Learchus as he stood ramrod-straight with his warriors. He knew Learchus was a great warrior, but Astador knew he could never be anything beyond that.

His ghost-self had only recently returned to his body and his spirit still rebelled at its incarceration in the prison of flesh. Briefly Astador considered telling Learchus what the spirits of his ancestors had shown him, but shook his head and returned his gaze to the advancing tyranids.

What would be the point in telling him?

He would not be thankful for the knowledge that his captain was going to die.

A PUNISHING TWO-HOUR barrage of spores hammered the District Quintus wall, wreathing the ramparts in drifting clouds of toxic vapours. High winds channelled down the length of the valley dispersed much of the poisonous filth, but interspersed with the gaseous spores were those that sprayed acidic viruses upon detonation. Huge portions of the parapet dissolved into puddles of molten rock, sliding down the face of the wall like thick rivulets of wax.

A section of the southern rampart slid from the liquefying ground, sending a trio of Mortifactors tumbling to the base of the wall. They smashed through the thin ice of the moat, plunging beneath the icy waters only to rise minutes later as they swam to the surface.

Learchus watched the black-armoured Space Marines take up firing stances as the hordes of aliens surged forwards in one homogenous mass. Immediately, he could see this was no normal attack, but a concerted hammer-blow designed to smash through their defences. The smaller, leaping organisms streamed forwards, a chittering black tide that covered the ground. Gunfire hammered their numbers, but such casualties were insignificant next to the size of the overall attack.

The weight of so many creatures broke the ice of the moat with an almighty crack and thousands of organisms plunged into its subzero waters. They kept coming, the vast numbers of frozen bodies in the moat providing a means of crossing for those behind.

Giant clawed beasts with entire broods of hissing aliens encased in their armour plates charged, throwing up great chunks of ice as they powered forward. Scorpion beasts that Learchus had not seen before scuttled forward, streaming weapons formed from bony outgrowths in their midsections firing at the wall.

Lightning-sheathed beasts with vast, slashing claws slithered, snake-like, towards them, arcs of energy lashing the wall and blasting free tank-sized chunks of rockcrete.

Learchus opened a channel to Major Satria of the Erebus Defence Legion.

'Lead your men forwards now, Major. Pattern alpha one.'

'ARE YOU SURE you're ready for this, sir?' asked Major Satria as he jogged towards the wall.

'I'm sure, major. Now stop fussing,' chided Sebastien Montante as he breathlessly tried to keep up with the major and the five thousand Defence Legion troopers. His webbing was loose and he was sweating profusely in his overwhites.

His lasgun felt like it weighed as much as a lascannon, but he was glad of its reassuring feel. He felt powerful just carrying it and only hoped he remembered how to fire it when the time came to fight.

DEEP IN THE many caves that riddled the high peaks of the eastern valley a keening screech built to a deafening howl that echoed around the upper echelons of the city. Many of the gargoyles that had penetrated the aerial cover of Erebus thanks to Simon van Gelder's treachery had been hunted down and killed, but a great many had not. The majority of these had been simple warrior organisms bred to fly, but nine had been much more.

Secreted in the deepest caves, the gargoyle brood-mothers had obeyed the overmind's command to nest and produce more of its kin. Driven into a frenzy of reproduction, the brood mothers had since expired, but not before giving birth to thousands upon thousands of offspring.

As the assault began on the wall, an implacable imperative seized the nesting gargoyles who took to the air in their thousands, and a black tide of monsters screeched from their hiding places to attack.

'You GOT THEM, lieutenant?' asked Captain Morten, tensing his fingers on the Fury's control column.

'Yes,' snarled Keill Pelaur. 'The attack logister can't keep up with all the signals it's getting. The bio-ships are altering formation to face us, but they're slow. We'll be on them before they're properly aligned.'

Morten grinned beneath his oxygen mask.

The target information on Pelaur's slate was being echoed on his own display and the sheer numbers they were about to face were beyond anything in the squadron's history.

Fitting then, that this should be its last battle.

A rune on Morten's armaments panel flashed, indicating that he was within his missiles' optimum kill range.

He opened a channel to the aircraft he led.

'All craft open fire!'

He pulled the trigger on the control column twice in quick succession, shouting, 'For the *Vincennes*!' Scores of missiles leapt from beneath the wings of hundreds of aircraft, streaking upwards towards the tyranid fleet. They had to punch a hole through the screen for the Thunderhawk. All other concerns were secondary.

The gap was rapidly closing between the two forces and Morten knew it would get real ugly, real quick. Even as he watched, the enemy creatures smoothly moved into blocking positions, scores of smaller, faster creatures moving to intercept them.

'Stay sharp,' called Morten, 'the enemy is turning into us.'

The initial volley had cut a swathe through the outer screen of tyranid spores, but hundreds more remained, all closing on his aerial armada. A lesser man might have been cowed, but

Owen Morten was a born and bred Fury pilot who lived for combat.

He pulled into a shallow climb and armed his last missiles.

Almost as soon as he'd done so, he and his squadron were tangled up in a madly spinning dogfight with dozens of fleshy, spore creatures that spun and wove almost as fast as the Furies. Morten rolled hard left, catching sight of a speeding organism and followed it down.

'I'm too close for a missile shot!' he yelled, switching to guns as the creature tried to shake him.

Every move the creature made, the Fury was with it, spinning around like insects in a bizarre mating ritual. The beast flashed across his gunsight and he pulled the trigger.

'Got you, you bastard!' he roared as bright lasbolts ripped the tyranid beast in two.

'Captain! Break right!' screamed Pelaur as a spuming bolt of light speared past the Fury's canopy.

He pulled around and breathed deeply, amazed at how close their near miss had been. He eased back on the throttle and switched back to missiles.

A warbling tone in his ear told him the missile's war-spirit had found a target and he pulled the trigger again.

'Captain!' called Erin Harlen. 'You've got one right behind you!'

Morten hauled right and checked his rear, twisting his Fury in an attempt to shake the pursuing organism.

'I can't get rid of it!' swore Morten as the beast matched his wild manoeuvrings.

'It's firing!' shouted Pelaur.

'Breaking left!' answered Morten, rolling hard and kicking in the afterburner. He felt his flight suit expand and his heartbeat race.

A bolt of crackling energy spat below him and he spun the plane round in a screaming, tight turn, chopping the throttle and almost stalling the engine.

The creature tried to match his turn, but was too slow.

Morten rolled inverted and pulled in behind the pulsing organism, lining it up in his sights and firing.

Bolts from the lascannon shredded the creature and it exploded in a bloody spray.

Listening to the vox-chatter, he heard screams and imprecations from the rest of the aircraft. The tyranids were slaughtering them, but he couldn't think about that just now. Not while there was a battle still to be fought. But as he scanned the space before him, he could see they'd blown a gap. The Thunderhawk was streaking through it, the blue glare of its plasma engines bright against the darkness of the massive hive ship's stony carapace.

Then he saw a giant, winged creature with spitting, electrical mandibles powering after the Space Marine gunship. Arcs of crackling energies lashed the Thunderhawk again and again, and Morten could see it wouldn't survive much longer.

His flight suit was soaked with perspiration and he knew he was at the edge of exhaustion, but he pushed out the engines to follow the Thunderhawk.

URIEL FELT THE gunship lurch, and leaping streaks of blue energy sparked from the fuselage. The pilot threw them in a series of wild turns, but Thunderhawks had never been designed for dogfights and Uriel knew it was only a matter of time before whatever was pursuing them was able to destroy them. Weapons and ammo packs tumbled from the lockers above him.

He pushed clear of the restraint harness and rose to his feet, turning to retrieve the weapon Inquisitor Kryptman had given him. To lose it now would end their mission before it had begun. He staggered as another impact smashed into the gunship. Flames erupted from a shattered fuel line and warning klaxons screamed.

Yet another hammer-blow struck the rear quarter of the Thunderhawk and one of the vision ports blew out with a decompressive boom.

Rushing air howled from the gunship, and Uriel felt his rage growing. They could not fail. Not after coming so close.

But as further impacts rocked the Thunderhawk, he knew they could not survive another.

CAPTAIN OWEN MORTEN pushed the Fury as fast as it could go. His fighter streaked past the tyranid organism pummelling the Thunderhawk as he armed the last of his missiles.

A flickering blue glow illuminated the interior of the Fury as bolts of lightning lashed from the mandibles of the creature. Fully six times the size of the Fury, Morten knew that only a direct hit on its most vulnerable location would destroy it.

'Captain!' shouted Pelaur, 'ease back on the throttle or we won't have enough fuel to get back to the planet.'

'We're not going back,' said Morten calmly as he neatly slotted the Fury between the giant tyranid beast and the Thunderhawk.

'What the hell are you doing?' screamed Pelaur.

'What needs to be done,' answered Morten, cutting the engines and spinning the Fury on its axis until it had turned a full one hundred and eighty degrees.

The crackling maw of the tyranid beast filled his canopy. Giant arcs of lighting enveloped the Fury. Sparks and flames filled the cockpit.

Captain Morten pulled the trigger, sending his last missile straight down the monster's throat.

URIEL FELT A huge detonation behind the gunship, and awaited the inevitable destruction of the Thunderhawk. But the fatal blow never landed and the Thunderhawk levelled out, weaving through the hail of spores that gathered around the monstrous hive ship.

He made his way up the central aisle of the gunship towards the cockpit. All he could see ahead was the craggy cliff of the hive ship's hide. Inquisitor Kryptman had shown them the most likely locations of possible entry points, and he scanned the grey moonscape before him for one.

The aerial armada had got them through and now it was time to make good on that sacrifice.

'There!' he said, pointing to a rippling, fleshy orifice on the side of the gargantuan creature, organic waste venting through it into space by peristaltic motion of flesh. A ribbed sphincter muscle expanded as more waste was expelled and Uriel knew they had found what they had come for.

'Hurry! If what Inquisitor Kryptman says is true, it will close in seconds!'

The pilot deftly guided the gunship forward, increasing power to the engines as the fleshy orifice began to contract.

Only as they approached did Uriel realise how vast it was, fully sixty metres in diameter.

Before it could close completely, the Thunderhawk sped into the ribbed, fleshy tunnel beyond.

Truly they were in the belly of the beast, thought Uriel as the sphincter vent closed and the faint light of the stars was snuffed out.

LEARCHUS SWEPT HIS chainsword through the neck of yet another tyranid creature, his blade clogged with alien meat and gristle. His bolter had long since run out of shells and he fought two-handed with his blade.

Clotted blood caked his shoulder where a screeching monster twice the height of a man had gained the walls and torn through his armour. The wall was a charnel house of alien and human dead. Cracked pillars and columns clustered at the wall's edge were hung with gory spatters of blood and entrails that spilled over the icy ground, making it treacherous underfoot. Learchus fought for balance with every step he took.

Major Satria fought alongside him, stabbing with his bayonet and firing with his lasgun whenever he had the chance to reload. Beside him, Fabricator Montante fought with desperation and courage, if not skill. Learchus had already saved his life on numerous occasions and though it was foolish of Montante to be here, he was forced to admire his bravery.

'Warriors of Ultramar hold fast!' bellowed Learchus.

Drifting spores exploded amongst the battling warriors, but they refused to give way. He kicked out at a screeching hormagaunt as it scrabbled over the lip of the wall, sending its shattered skull spinning to the heaving mass of aliens below.

Over the deafening clash of battle at the wall, Learchus heard the roar of guns behind him and risked a glance over his shoulder to see who was shooting. The few remaining Hydra flak tanks were firing eastwards and his hearts skipped a beat as he saw the impenetrable black cloud of gargoyles sweeping down the length of the valley.

'Guilliman save us…' whispered Learchus as he took in the numbers of enemy now closing on their rear.

'Astador!' he yelled over the vox.

'I see them!' replied the Chaplain.

The Hydras punched holes in the swarm, but Learchus could see the sheer scale of the attack would defeat them.

SEBASTIEN MONTANTE FOUGHT with a strength and courage he never knew he possessed. His arms ached from the fighting, but he was filled with elation at finally having proven himself worthy of the mantle of leadership of this world. He ducked behind a fluted pillar as he reached for a fresh energy cell for his lasgun. A Space Marine fell beside him, a smoking crater blasted in his armour where his chest had been.

Sebastien hastily reloaded and spun around the pillar, opening up on a swarm of scuttling creatures with wide, webbed hands circling behind Learchus and Major Satria.

He felled three with a single burst of full auto and crippled a fourth as a giant shadow reared over him.

Sebastien spun and raised his rifle. A lashing, spined whip hacked his gun in two and spun him from his feet. He scrambled upright, using the pillar for support and fumbled for his sabre as the huge warrior organism towered above him. Its bony carapace was brightly patterned with crimson streaks and its hissing jaws seemed to leer at him as the writhing whips on the end of its upper limb lashed out again.

Sebastien screamed as the razor-edged tendril gouged his flesh, binding him to the pillar as it tightened. The monster's claws reached out towards him…

Then Learchus was there, hacking through the fleshy lash with his sword and spinning inside the monster's guard. Its claws closed around his body as he stabbed his blade through its hard, chitinous plates. It screamed and gouged great holes in Learchus's armour.

Sebastien struggled to free himself, but gave up as the talons embedded in the whip's length continued to bite deep into his flesh.

Learchus roared as he finally drove his sword through the beast's throat and Major Satria rushed over to help.

A black shadow passed overhead and Sebastien saw a teeming multitude of creatures descend on the defenders at the wall. The carnage was terrible as men were lifted up and clawed to death by this new foe. As the resistance at the wall began to disintegrate, Major Satria unsheathed his knife.

'Soon have you free, my lord,' he said, moving around the back of the pillar.

Sebastien nodded, in too much pain to reply.

Then he saw a massive set of ridged claws hammer into the rampart and a vast, gurgling beast haul its incredible bulk over the wall. A flock of creatures, red and black, with the same webbed fists as those he'd killed, scuttled from the folds of its flesh and raced towards them.

'Major...' he croaked, too quietly to be heard.

The beasts paused, raising their bizarre looking hands, as though they were waving at him and the ridiculousness of the thought almost made him want to laugh.

Their fists expanded, as though filling with air and suddenly dozens of sharp spines blasted from their hands and slashed towards him.

He screamed as he felt them penetrate his flesh. How many he didn't know, all he could feel was pain and fire racing around his body. He sagged against the barbed alien cord binding him to the pillar, his body pierced by dozens of long organic spines. His head sagged on his neck and he saw a spreading pool of blood expanding around his boots.

He heard someone shout his name, but everything was growing dim and he couldn't make out who.

Then everything went black and consciousness slipped away.

URIEL CLIMBED DOWN from the battered Thunderhawk and stepped onto the soft, spongy flesh of the hive ship's interior. Inquisitor Kryptman's weapon was stored in a holster at his hip. It didn't fit exactly, but was close enough not to matter.

A diffuse green light lit up the ribbed chamber they found themselves in, its vastness filled with pungent fumes and knee-deep organic effluent. The stench was indescribable and Uriel turned down his olfactory auto-senses before his disgust overwhelmed him.

He waved forward the rest of his warriors, Pasanius taking the lead with the blue flame of his flamer burning brightly in the rich atmosphere of the hive ship. Uriel felt motion around his boots and saw grotesque, beetle-like creatures scuttling across the ribbed walls of the chamber, feasting on the waste embedded there.

They were no threat and he ignored them as they pushed deeper into the chamber. A pulsing rumble thumped from the walls like a gigantic heartbeat, or a series of heartbeats. Kryptman had said that a hive ship was a massive agglomeration of creatures blended into one gestalt beast that formed the overmind.

'This place is cursed,' said Brother Pelantar, moving up to take a flanking position, his heavy bolter slung low and ready to fire. Alvarax took up the same position on the opposite flank.

'You might be right,' agreed Uriel, remembering the depths of Pavonis where he had fought the Bringer of Darkness and how evil echoes of past horrors could saturate a place with their power.

Brother Damias moved to the centre of the group, reading from a specially modified auspex Inquisitor Kryptman had furnished him with. Its blue light reflected from the base of his helm, its soft chiming loud in the warm chamber.

Hissing gusts of steam vented from slitted orifices and a tremor ran through the floor of the chamber as the walls rippled with motion. Uriel saw the scurrying organisms speed into fleshy caverns set in the depths of the wall and said, 'Come on, let us be about our business. I do not believe we should linger in this place.'

With Pasanius leading the way, the Deathwatch moved off into the depths of the hive ship.

SNOWDOG SPRINTED DOWN the stone stairs of the medicae building as the sound of alarm bells rang throughout the facility. Sisters of the Order Hospitaller hurried through the building, directing those wounded men who could walk towards the upper levels. Others carried stretchers or boxes of medical equipment.

He skidded to the bottom level, finding the vestibule thronged with nurses as they guided those without their sight through the armoured door at the base of the stairs. Snowdog could almost taste the panic in the air.

'What's going on?' he demanded.

No one answered him, too wrapped up in their own fear to reply. He pushed his way through the crowds towards the main wards, finding many more wounded men being chivvied to

their feet by tearful sisters. Straight away he could see that there
were far too many wounded for them to cope with.

As he realised this, he saw Sister Joaniel marching towards
him.

'You!' she yelled, 'come here!'

He made his way along the ward, dodging wounded men as
they limped towards the main doors.

'What's going on?' he asked again.

'We've received the evacuation order,' said Joaniel desperately. 'We need to get these men out to safety. The front line is
about to fall.'

'What? But it's less than half a kilometre from here!'

'I know, that's why we can't waste any time. I need your
help.'

'*My* help? What do you think I can do?'

Joaniel gripped Snowdog's arms and said, 'The medicae
facility is built against the rock face of the valley's southern
wall. There is an entrance to the caves on the upper levels that
lead further up the valley.'

'And?'

'And I want you to lead these people out of here to safety,'
explained Joaniel.

'What? I just got them here!'

'I don't care, just do it,' snapped Joaniel.

'Okay, okay,' said Snowdog. 'What about you? What are you
gonna be doing?'

'I'm going to be making sure that my patients get out of this
building alive.'

OOZING SLIME DRIPPED from the ceiling, hissing as droplets
pattered against the shoulder guards of the Deathwatch. The
fleshy passageways of the hive ship were a cornucopia of biological horrors, fleshy folds of muscle and gristle lining every
wall and suppurating pools of digestive juices filling every
footprint they left. Tiny slave organisms hurried along every
passageway, ignoring the Space Marines as they pushed
deeper into the body of the beast.

The omnipresent rumble drifted from every orifice and the
noise of biological processes was thick in the air.

Uriel could feel a nascent claustrophobia as the walls of the
ribbed passage contracted in time with the rumble, expanding

again as though they were in some great breathing organ. Steaming jets of liquid sprayed them as they passed from the passageway into a wide, necrotic chamber of crackling gristle and pulped meat.

Row upon row of ruptured egg sacs and niches with cancerous organic pipes hanging inert within them lined the walls of the chamber from floor to ceiling.

'What is this place?' asked Henghast.

'They slept here,' said Damias, sweeping his softly chiming auspex around. 'They slept away the years while they travelled to Tarsis Ultra from wherever they came from.'

Uriel saw Damias was right as he spotted a tyranid warrior organism in one of the niches, its flesh withered and dead. Its four arms hung limply at is side, its bony head slumped over its shoulder.

A sudden hissing motion rippled through the walls, a greenish glow building from the smoke that drifted at ankle height. At the far end of the chamber, a fleshy fold of bone lifted aside and a wash of stinking chemicals spilled into the chamber carrying a tide of screeching tyranid creatures.

'Captain!' yelled Pasanius as he bathed them in flames.

Alvarax and Pelantar braced themselves and sprayed the creatures with shells from their heavy bolters. Uriel fired into the mass of aliens as a host of the ventricle valve doors rippled open and yet more beasts poured into the chamber.

A giant beast bounded towards them, its armoured carapace low and armoured like a scorpion. It bounded towards Jagatun, who ducked and slashed its soft underbelly with his razor-edged tulwar. Looping organs spilled from the wound.

Henghast howled and slashed his power sword through its body, dragging Jagatun to his feet while firing his bolter with his free hand. Pasanius fell back, each step accompanied by a spray of liquid fire into knots of screeching aliens.

Uriel blazed away at the creatures as they poured from the walls to assail them. He didn't know how many beasts the hive ship had at its disposal, but he knew they could not afford to find out.

'Deathwatch, fall back!' he ordered.

Alvarax and Pelantar backed away, firing as they went and closing on Uriel.

'Brother Damias!' yelled Uriel. 'Which way?'

Damias was blood-streaked, his power fist coated in alien gore. He consulted the auspex and said, 'This way.'

He set off through an oval hole in the wall as Uriel called, 'Everyone through here!'

Henghast dived through the hole, followed by Jagatun. The roar of heavy bolters covered them before Pelantar ducked into the gap. Uriel pushed Pasanius through and shouted, 'Alvarax! Come on, we are leaving!'

Alvarax raked his fire over the attacking beasts, his aim sure. Dozens of aliens fell, blown apart by his sanctified shells.

Then the ground opened up beneath him and he was gone, sucked into the depths of the ship.

Uriel shouted, 'Alvarax!' and moved to go to his battle-brother's aid, but a strong hand gripped him and hauled him back.

'He's gone,' yelled Pasanius, 'Come on!'

Uriel nodded and pushed into the close confines of the new passageway, feeling his way by touch rather than sight. He heard an oozing sound behind him as muscular contractions pulled the passage way wider to allow more of their pursuers to chase them. Pasanius pushed him ahead and turned to fill the passageway with flames. Screeching howls followed them as aliens burned. The fleshy passage shuddered in sympathy with their pain and Uriel was suddenly reminded of something Kryptman had told him before they left Tarsis Ultra: 'As you penetrate deeper into the ship, its nervous system will become more sophisticated. It will feel pain the closer you get to its centre.'

He followed his warriors as the passageway sloped downwards, the soggy texture of the ground squelching as he ran. He heard gunfire and saw a glow from up ahead as the passage widened into a vein-ridged chamber with a pulsing, mushroom shaped organism at its centre.

A score of dead creatures littered the ground before the thing. 'What is that?' asked Henghast.

'Does it matter? They were guarding it so it must be important to them,' said Jagatun, slashing his tulwar through its stem. Plumes of spores erupted from the organisms severed stalk and enveloped Jagatun like a cloud of buzzing insects. He batted them away before doubling up as the surface of his armour began corroding before Uriel's eyes.

He heard the White Scar's screams over the vox as the spores devoured him from within, his filters and rebreathers no defence against such a deadly attack. The Deathwatch backed away from the clouds of corrosive spores, unable to help their stricken battle-brother. Pasanius fired his flamer, consuming them in a cleansing burst of promethium.

Chittering screeches from the sucking passageway they had just come from echoed towards them.

'This way,' said Uriel plunging into a ridged opening in the far wall, emerging into a long, curving passage, knee-deep in sloshing fluids. Fronds of cilia dangled from the roof and walls of the passage, waving as though in a gentle breeze. The sludgy liquid flowed away to the right and Uriel waited for Brother Damias to join them.

As the Deathwatch assembled, Damias led them to the left, splashing through the foetid ordure against the flow. Worm-like organisms swam through the sludge, latching onto their armour and attempting to feed.

The Space Marines plucked them from their armour in disgust. They were annoying but hardly dangerous. Uriel pushed onwards through the circular tunnel, the fronds above him brushing against his helmet.

He halted as he heard a strange sound over the constant rumble of the hive ship. It sounded like distant thunder, like standing at the end of the Valley of Laponis on Macragge and listening to the noise of the far-off Hera's Falls.

As he realised what it was he shouted, 'Hold on to something!'

He punched his fist through the tough walls of the veined passage and gripped a handful of the hive ship's substance as hundreds of tonnes of organic waste thundered along the passageway towards them.

SNOWDOG HUSTLED THE wounded men up the stairs to the upper levels of the medicae building, wondering how long they had before the tyranids got here. The damned alarm bells were still ringing and he smashed the butt of his gun against one until it shut up. Jonny was on the landing above him and Lex was busy wiring the main door of the building with the mother of all explosive devices. Tigerlily was keeping an eye on Silver who was now stable, but still unconscious. He had no idea where Trask was, but didn't much care one way or another. He still carried the backpack filled with valuables taken from the crashed starship, so it wasn't as though Trask was off stealing that.

He pushed his way down to the vestibule, seeing the skinny shape of Lex still working at the door.

'Lex, whatever you're doing, do it quicker, man,' he said.

'Hey, I'm going as fast as I can. You know, if you helped, I could get done quicker.'

'No way, man. Me and explosives? Forget about it.'

'Well thanks for offering anyway,' sneered Lex.

'No problem. Everyone off this floor?'

'Yeah, I think so. Everyone except that crazy sister.'

Snowdog pushed his way into the main ward area. The place was deserted except for Sister Joaniel, who stood behind the central nursing station with a plain wooden box before her.

Snowdog jogged towards the nursing station and slung his lasgun. 'Hey, sister, we don't have time to hang around here. Time we was gone.'

'Is everyone safe?' asked Joaniel, tears streaking her face.

'Yeah, more or less. They're all on their way upstairs if that's what you mean.'

'Good,' nodded Joaniel. 'I couldn't save them before.'

'What? Save who?'

'All of them. On Remian. They called me the Angel of Remian because I put them back together after the war had broken them, but in the end I couldn't save them. They all died.'

Joaniel held up the wooden box and said, 'They gave me this for all the good work I'd done. It's a medicus ministo-rum... I don't deserve it.'

'Okay,' said Snowdog in puzzlement, 'as fun as it is to trip down memory lane, Sister Joaniel, I think we need to get going.'

As if to underscore his words, a thudding boom impacted on the thick wooden doors of the medicae building. Even through the thick walls, Snowdog could hear the scrape of hordes of aliens swarming around the building.

Lex stuck his head in the door to the wards and shouted, 'Come on, let's get the hell out of this place.'

Snowdog turned to Joaniel. 'You heard the man, now come on.'

She gathered up the wooden box, but didn't move. Cursing himself for a fool, Snowdog grabbed her by the arm and pulled her along the ward.

'Why the hell do I let myself get into these situations?' he wondered aloud.

Together they emerged into the vestibule, the doors already splintering under repeated blows from something massive. They skidded across the stone flags of the floor, sprinting for the armoured door that led to the stairs. Jonny Stomp stood at the bottom, his massive hunting rifle slung over his shoulder.

'Come on!' he yelled.

With a crash of shattered timbers, the main doors were ripped from their frame and scores of snarling creatures poured in around a massive battering ram of a monster. Its claws were massive, sheathed in splintered wood and its jaws screeched with burning fires.

It took a thunderous step into the medicae building, the stone cracking under its weight, just as Lex's bomb went off.

Snowdog gathered Joaniel in his arms and threw himself flat as the detonation slammed them both into the wall. Fire and dust and stone filled the air as the blast took out the aliens as well as the columns supporting the roof and walls of the entrance. The giant beast staggered, but didn't fall, its armoured hide painted with the gory ruin of its smaller kin. It reeled at the edge of a crater gouged in the ground, blocks of stone tumbling from the walls around it.

Snowdog rolled onto his stomach, his body one giant mass of pain. Strangely, his back felt fine, but then he remembered his backpack of valuables and figured it must have protected him from the worst of the blast. He tried to push himself to his feet and cried out in pain, feeling at least one rib broken.

Joaniel pushed herself up against the stone wall, still clutching her medicus ministorum. Snowdog groaned beside her as the gigantic monster recovered its wits enough to take another stamping step towards them.

Jonny Stomp stepped down into the vestibule, his enormous hunting rifle wedged tightly against his shoulder.

The massive beast was almost upon him, the fire building between its gnashing mandibles.

Jonny sighted along the barrel and pulled the trigger.

And the beast's head vanished in an explosion of blood and bone.

Jonny was hurled through the stair door by the recoil and landed in a sprawling heap. He whooped with glee, thumbing another shell into the breech.

The monster crashed backwards into the crater blown by Lex's bomb as Joaniel pulled Snowdog to his feet. He cried out in pain as she pushed him into Jonny's arms.

'Go on!' she shouted. 'Get him out of here!'

'What you gonna do?' said Jonny.

'I'm right behind you,' said Joaniel, crouching by the medicus ministorum and flipping open its lid.

Jonny saw hundreds more of the smaller beasts gathering outside. 'Whatever you say,' he shrugged and half-carried, half-dragged Snowdog after him.

Joaniel lifted a gleaming bolter from within the box and slid home a magazine of shells.

She glanced upstairs, seeing Jonny and Snowdog rounding the first landing.

And closed the door, hearing the heavy clang of the lock as it slammed home.

Hissing monsters cautiously stalked into the medicae building, wary of more traps.

Joaniel cocked her bolter and smiled to herself. She hadn't been able to save those on Remian, but here and now she was going to do everything that was expected of a Sister Hospitaller of the Order of the Eternal Candle.

'Come on!' she screamed. 'Are you going to make me wait all day?'

She smiled beatifically as she opened fire, blasting the nearest creatures apart in controlled bursts. She fired and fired, killing dozens until finally the hammer slammed down on an empty chamber.

She dropped the weapon and spread her arms wide as the beasts leapt forward.

The Angel of Remian died with the last of her guilt washed away in blood.

LEARCHUS RAN THROUGH the ruins of District Quintus, the last remnants of the defenders of Erebus falling back in disarray alongside him. Swooping creatures dived from above, tearing at the routing soldiers and even the formidable strength of the Space Marines was sorely tested.

The Ultramarines and the Mortifactors fought side-by-side, buying time for the Krieg, Logres and Defence Legion troops to rally at the next wall. Learchus could see it was hopeless, but he had the soul of a warrior and fought on. The tyranids had closed every avenue of escape, as though they knew every possible route through the city or they could anticipate every move the Space Marines made.

He fired a bolter he had taken from a dead Marine, bringing down a host of winged monsters carrying off a Krieg soldier and hacked down a pair of hissing beasts that were devouring the corpse of a fallen Ultramarine.

He reached down and grabbed the armour of his dead comrade and began dragging him backwards. Chaplain Astador stumbled alongside him and lent his strength to the task, smashing an alien's skull with his crozius arcanum as he did so. The warriors of the Fourth company and the Mortifactors gathered around their leaders, forming a defensive perimeter around them. Learchus saw how pitifully few they were now.

Less than forty Space Marines still fought.

But fewer than this number had won against impossible odds before and Learchus knew that while there was still blood pumping round his body, he would never surrender.

Together the Space Marines dragged the corpse back towards a wide plaza from where a great many aircraft had launched earlier. It crossed his mind to wonder how close Captain Ventris had come to succeeding, but supposed it didn't matter much now.

'Wait,' said Astador.

'What?' snapped Learchus. 'We have to keep moving.'

'No,' said Astador, pointing to the base of the next wall. 'It is already too late.'

Learchus saw hundreds of tyranid beasts sweeping around their flanks, cutting off their escape. Giant creatures, three times the height of a Space Marine, and hordes of warrior beasts filled the area between them and the next wall.

Astador was right. It was too late for escape.

PHASE V – CONSUMPTION

SIXTEEN

THOUSANDS OF LITRES of stinking bio-fluids roared past the Space Marines with the force of a tidal wave, pummelling their armour and ripping them from the walls of the pipe. Uriel felt alien flesh tear under his gauntlet and cursed as he was swept along.

He spun crazily in the flow, slamming into the sides of the tunnel and his battle-brothers, losing his orientation as he tumbled along with the waste matter. All he could see was murky fluids and occasional glimpses of the tunnel walls. He tried to grip the sides of the tunnel, but the waving cilia had withdrawn into the meat of the walls.

Uriel flipped upright for a second, seeing an outthrust gauntlet. He grabbed onto it, an iron grip clamping around his wrist and halting his headlong tumble. Thundering fluids threatened to rip him from his saviour's grip, but he found his footing in a fold of flesh and hauled himself upright.

His head broke the surface and he saw the Deathwatch clustered on a bony ledge above the raging torrent of filth. Pasanius hauled him from the tunnel and he collapsed wearily onto the reassuringly firm surface.

'Thank you, my friend,' he gasped.

Pasanius nodded, too exhausted to reply. Uriel pushed himself to his knees, taking a closer look at their surroundings. They lay in an oval chamber that obviously fed into the fluid-filled tunnel. Damias, Henghast and Pelantar crouched beside a mesh of sinew that blocked their passage from this chamber and Uriel speculated that they were perhaps in some form of filter chamber. Noxious gusts of gas soughed from beyond the mesh of fibres and the rumble of multiple hearts was even stronger.

'How close are we, Brother Damias?' asked Uriel.

'I do not know, brother-captain,' replied Damias, his voice full of reproach. 'I was careless enough to lose my grip on the auspex as I was swept along. I shall perform whatever penance you deem suitable upon our completion of the mission.'

Uriel cursed quietly, but contented himself with the thought that so long as they headed in the direction of the hive ship's heartbeats, they couldn't go far wrong. It had been a long-held belief of Kryptman's that the reproductive chambers of the Norn Queen, the brood mother of the hive, would be close to the hearts, where the nutrients and vital fluid flow was purest.

'Do not worry, brother. The Emperor shall guide us,' said Uriel, drawing his power sword and hacking through the fibrous mesh that blocked the chamber's exit. Once he had managed to relight his flamer, Pasanius took point again, leading them along the glistening passageway. Mucus-like saliva dripped from the walls and more of the slithering, worm-like beasts burrowed in and out of the walls and floors.

'By the Emperor, this is worse than Pavonis, and I thought that was bad,' said Pasanius.

Uriel nodded in agreement. The darkness beneath the world had been terrible, but this grotesque mockery of the gift of life was almost too much to countenance. The blasphemy of the tyranids was beyond measure and he could not fathom how a race that gave nothing back to the universe, that lived only to consume, could be allowed to come into existence.

'What is Pavonis?' asked Henghast.

'A world on the eastern fringe, but that is a tale for another day,' said Uriel.

'I shall hold you to that promise, brother-captain. I will need a saga of your bravery to take back with me to the Fang.'

Uriel was struck by the undiminished optimism of the Deathwatch. Despite their losses and the scale of the task before them, not one had uttered a single sentiment that suggested that they did not believe utterly that they would prevail.

He slapped a palm on Henghast's shoulder guard and said, 'When we return to Tarsis Ultra I shall share the victory wine with you and tell you all about Pavonis.'

'Wine! Pah, wine is for women. We will drain a barrel of Fenrisian mead and you will wake with a hangover like continents colliding.'

'I look forward to it,' said Uriel as Pasanius raised his hand.

Uriel joined his sergeant at the head of their column, listening as the boom of multiple hearts and other, less obvious organs rumbled close by. A low-ceilinged chamber with a heaving sphincter muscle at its centre rasped with tendrils of ochre vapours gusting through it. Booming echoes rang from the fleshy walls.

'I believe we are close, brother-captain. The sounds converge on this place' said Pasanius.

'I think you're right, my friend, but where is it coming from?'

Brother Henghast entered the chamber and removed his helmet, coughing briefly before his enhanced resiratory system was able to adapt to the toxic atmosphere.

'What are you doing?' demanded Uriel. 'Put your helmet back on!'

Henghast cocked his head to one side and whispered, 'Auto-senses are all well and good, but my own are better.'

The Space Wolf sniffed the air, his features twitching as he filtered the smells and sounds of the hive ship with senses more sensitive than even Uriel's. The Ultramarine's senses had been enhanced by the Apothecaries of his Chapter, but were still no match for those of a Space Wolf.

'The heartbeats are strongest from this passage,' said Henghast, replacing his helmet and standing clear to allow Pasanius to proceed. Uriel said, 'Well done, Brother Henghast.'

As they proceeded along this new passage, wisps of smoke filled the air and the sound of monstrous hearts beating in counterpoint grew louder and louder. The glow of Pasanius's flamer silhouetted his sergeant and cast a flickering blue glow around the dripping walls of the passage.

They followed the twisting passage for several kilometres until a sickly green glow replaced that of the flamer. The passageway angled downwards, gradually widening until Uriel could see and hear the booming organs whose noise they had been following.

Larger than super-heavy tanks, the pair of thudding hearts pulsed with massive intra-muscular motion, pumping life-sustaining fluids around the hive ship. Uriel fought the urge to open fire. Kryptman had warned him that these organs would be protected by metres of tough, fibrous skin and that there were sure to be others that could take over.

Hissing organisms prowled the chamber beyond, but whether they were aware of them yet, he could not say.

Uriel and the Deathwatch crouched at the end of the smoky passageway, staring into the heart of the hive ship.

They had reached the reproductive chambers of the Norn Queen.

SNOWDOG GRIMACED IN pain as Jonny hauled him upstairs, hearing the booming impacts against the door below. His head hurt and his ribs felt like he'd gone ten rounds with a Space Marine. He glanced down the stairs.

'Where's Sister Joaniel?' he gasped.

'Dunno,' said Jonny without breaking his stride. 'I guess she's dead.'

'What?'

'Yeah,' confirmed Jonny, 'she shut the door behind us.'

'She shut the door?'

'Yeah.'

Snowdog mentally shrugged. It was a shame she was dead, but if she was crazy enough to try and take on the entire tyranid race, then that was no concern of his. Crashing thumps on the door below made him glad she'd shut the door. He wasn't sure he'd have trusted Jonny to remember to do it. The door was armoured, but with these monsters, you couldn't count on any barrier holding for too long.

'Where are the others?'

'Upstairs I guess. Why you got to ask so many questions?' said Jonny.

'Because that's how I find things out,' snapped Snowdog, regretting it instantly as the pain in his ribs flared bright and urgent.

They rounded another landing and Snowdog could have sworn that there hadn't been this many stairs before. As his senses began returning to normal, he heard a soft pattering, like a wind-chime in a strong breeze, and wondered what it was. He realised a second later and cried out in alarm.

'Jonny! Stop! Stop!' he yelled. 'Turn around!'

'Huh?' said Jonny, but complied.

Snowdog moaned in frustration as he saw a cascade of gold, silver and precious stones forming a glittering trail back down the stairs. He wriggled free from Jonny's grasp and painfully shucked the backpack from his shoulders as the crashes on the door below became even more frenzied.

The backpack had saved him from the worst of Lex's bomb sure enough, but it was in a hell of a mess for having done so. Everything he'd taken from the wreck was spilling through long, burnt tears in the canvas. There was barely anything left.

He began transferring the remainder into his pockets, hearing the scream of buckling metal from below. He heard a footfall on the stairs behind him, but ignored it as he continued to stuff precious stones into his pockets.

'Hey, Trask,' said Jonny.

Snowdog felt his blood chill and reached for his pistol, but it was too late.

He heard the rack of a shotgun slide and rolled to one side, yelling in pain as the splintered ends of his ribs ground together.

But the shot wasn't aimed at him. Jonny Stomp toppled to the stairs, a halo of blood splattered on the wall behind him.

Snowdog squinted through a haze of tears of pain and raised his pistol.

Trask kicked him in the face. He felt teeth break and spat blood.

'You and me got some unfinished business, Snowdog,' said Trask.

* * *

THE SIGHT OF the Norn Queen was something that Uriel would never forget for as long as he lived. The creature was massive, easily the size of a Battle Titan, its bulk filling the chamber with countless means of producing its monstrous offspring. A vast, mucus-ribbed tube hung from the walls, pulsing with disgusting motion and dripping great swathes of egg sacs to a slime filled pool where nurse organisms carried them away in great, scooped pincers.

Huge pools of protoplasmic ooze bubbled and burst with motion as screeching infant beasts were drooled from its surface along bony chutes to begin growing almost as soon as they hit the ground. Thousands of gelatinous incubation larvae hung from resinous mucus on the great arched ceiling, supported on huge ribs of bone, each thicker than the columns in the Temple of Correction on Macragge. Stinking fluids coated the floor and foetid steam gusted from millions of tiny orifices in the walls. Ropes of dripping intestine and nutrients pumped viscous fluids into the belly of the Norn Queen, its vast, bloated head fused with the ribbed ceiling of the chamber. Six-legged creatures that resembled fat spiders crawled all over its body, cleaning, feeding and ministering to their queen. Huge javelin-like spines protruded from her bony carapace, each dripping with hissing poisons.

The Norn Queen itself was as much a part of the bio-ship as an individual creature. Warrior organisms patrolled the chamber, snapping their glossy claws at any of the slave-beasts that approached too near the queen. Bigger than the largest tyranid warrior Uriel had ever seen, these warrior beasts were bred for once purpose and one purpose alone – to defend their queen to the death.

'How do we proceed?' asked Damias.

'With this,' said Uriel, unholstering the weapon Kryptman had given him. It was the silvered pistol with which the servitor had administered the gene-poison to the lictor, but with an added refinement. Fitted atop the barrel was a long, metallic tube, its blue-steel sheen subtly crystalline. At the end of the tube was an offset ring of nine small spines that slotted over the barrel of Kryptman's pistol. It was always distasteful to use the weapons of the xeno, but Inquisitor Kryptman had assured him that hrud fusil technology was simply a symbiosis of melta and plasma technology. A product of vile alien heresy to be sure, but one that, in this case, would prove useful in administering the gene-poison.

'What is it?' asked Pelantar.

He slid the gun back into its ill-fitting holster and said, 'It is the means by which we can end this. Just get me to the hive-queen.'

Uriel rose to his feet and said, 'But first we need to fight our way in, and we'll have to do it the old-fashioned way, with flesh, blood and steel.'

The Deathwatch followed their captain as he marched into the Norn Queen's chamber, Pasanius beside him, Henghast on his left and Damias on his right, Pelantar covering them with his heavy bolter.

Almost immediately, a warning screech sounded from one of the nurse organisms and the guardian warriors spun to face the intruders. A cacophonous wailing echoed throughout the chamber, a furious beat thrashing the walls as the tyranids rushed to defend their queen.

Pasanius bathed the first attackers in fire, the guardian creatures howling in anger at such destructive energies being unleashed in their queen's chambers. Pelantar fired a hail of mutagenic bolts into the mass of aliens, chanting the rites of firing as he slew.

Uriel ran forwards, the energised blade of his power sword cleaving through alien flesh and bone with ease. The smaller beasts fell like wheat before the scythe and though he felt the killing rage building behind his eyes, he made his peace with it, turning the taint of the Bringer of Darkness into a positive force.

Flames lit up the hellish glow of the chamber and crackling arcs of energy flared from Damias's power glove as he battered his way forward. Henghast howled in fury as he charged the alien creatures. Pelantar's heavy bolter ripped a path through them.

Uriel spun under a scything blow from a leaping beast that was more fanged maw than anything else, hacking it in two as he sensed the presence of something huge behind him. He threw himself forward, barely avoiding being sliced in two by a guardian organism.

The alien beast towered above him, larger than a carnifex, but more slender and quick. Its jaw was filled with dripping fangs and its upper pair of limbs ended in flashing talons that slashed for his head. Uriel rolled aside as they gouged the floor and slashed his sword at its legs.

The creature bounded over his blow, smashing its claws against his armour. Ceramite parted under the blow and blood washed down his side before the larraman cells halted the flow. Pain-suppressors pumped into his body and he staggered as the beast struck him again. He flew through the air, landing on the edge of a bubbling pool of stinking ichor. Whipping tentacles burst from the pool and wrapped around his midriff.

Uriel cried out and slashed his sword through them, rolling to the base of the pool.

The guardian organism bounded across to him, its hooves throwing up gouts of stinking fluids. Uriel rolled desperately, pushing himself to his knees and raising his sword to block just as the claws hammered down towards him.

Sparks flew and he grunted as he held the strength of the beast at bay.

He rolled beneath the claws, releasing his block and thrust his sword upwards into the creature's groin. It howled and collapsed to one knee, driving the blade deeper into its flesh.

Uriel ripped the weapon clear and hacked it through the monster's midsection. It thrashed as it died, insectile creatures swarming over its corpse to devour it as food for their queen. Uriel staggered towards his target as Pasanius joined him. His sword was bloody and the armour of his silvered arm was missing.

Brother Damias fought with skill and cunning, his power fist reaping a bloody tally in the furious battle. Henghast killed with all the ferocity he and his Chapter were famed for as Pelantar sprayed shells throughout the chamber, bursting egg sacs and perforating the gristly tube that snaked across the chamber walls.

Three warrior organisms blocked their path, each as deadly as the one Uriel had killed.

Damias and Henghast fought their way towards the two Ultramarines.

'The old fashioned way,' he breathed. 'Straight through them, eh? Pasanius, Henghast and I will hold them, you get to the queen!'

Uriel nodded and the four Space Marines raced towards the guardian beasts.

Pelantar saw what they intended and fired a carefully aimed blast towards the tyranids. Two reeled from the fusillade, their carapaces no match for the blessed ammunition of the Deathwatch.

But in doing so, he neglected his own defence for a fraction of a second.

And that was all his foes needed.

With a snap of claws, the heavy bolter was smashed apart and Pelantar was lifted from his feet in a massive set of powerful talons. He fought with every last bit of strength, punching bloody holes in the beast's carapace, but it was too late. With a bellowing roar, the beast ripped Pelantar in two, tossing the shorn halves away for the scavenger beasts to feed on.

Damias and Pasanius attacked while the beasts Pelantar had given his life to wound still staggered from his shells. One burned in the flames as Damias punched through the other's carapace with the lethal energies of his power fist. Henghast joined Pasanius in attacking the burning monster.

Uriel ran for the bloated belly of the Norn Queen, his sword raised to strike down the final beast between him and his goal. Its claws snapped shut and Uriel swept his sword through them. He leapt to meet the creature, ducking inside its guard as it flailed its razored claws at him, slashing its own flesh to ruin.

Uriel pulled himself up the creature's body, its bony exoskeleton providing ready-made handholds. The creature thrashed as it sought to dislodge him, hacking itself bloody as its claws tried to pluck him from its body. Secondary jaws punched down through his breastplate, biting a fist-sized chunk of flesh from his chest and tearing free a portion of his pectoral muscle.

Uriel roared in pain, but kept his grip on the beast's ribs. He pulled himself to the armoured plates of its shoulders and drove his sword into its neck. Black blood spurted and the beast screeched in agony as it died. The monster's death spasm wrenched the sword from his grip.

Before it collapsed, Uriel vaulted from its shoulders onto the glistening walls of the chamber, his fingers closing on the hardened flesh of the Norn Queen's hide. Hordes of the scavenger organisms closed on him as he climbed, biting and clawing him. They clambered all over him, even squeezing inside his armour, their weight alone threatening to prise him loose.

Despite the pain-suppressors, his chest was bathed in agony. He batted clear the scavengers long enough to draw Kryptman's pistol and press it against the belly of the Norn Queen.

Feeling his grip on the queen's flesh sliding free, he pulled the trigger.

He felt a blast of unimaginable heat as the hrud mechanism activated, lancing a column of fire, hotter that the heart of a star, through the thick flesh of the Norn Queen. A fraction of a second later the pistol bucked in his hand as the shell containing the gene-poison fired into its body.

He dropped the pistol and felt himself sailing through the air as he finally lost his grip on the queen's hide. Uriel twisted as he fell, splashing into the slimy floor of the chamber. He screamed in pain as noxious fluids spilled into the wound on his chest.

He rolled, crushing the scavengers beneath his weight and weakly tried to rise to his feet. He saw Damias destroy the creature he fought with repeated blows of his power fist. Pasanius was hauled from his feet by his blazing foe and lifted high above the ground. Henghast hacked at the beast's legs, but it refused to die.

The beast's claws crushed Pasanius's silvered arm, the metal buckling under the creature's incredible strength. Uriel reached for his sword, before realising it was still embedded in the tyranid warrior creature.

He looked up at the hissing shape of the Norn Queen's head and felt a terrible despair flood through him.

The gene-poison had had no effect on the monster.

They had failed.

TRASK LIFTED THE backpack, its contents spilling from the tears like glittering, precious rain. His ugly swollen features were twisted in hate and anger.

He kicked Snowdog in the ribs and again in the face.

'You stupid bastard,' he snarled. 'Did you really think I was gonna take all the crap you kept shovelling me? Two years I gave you and this is all I get?'

Snowdog looked up through a mist of tears and his own swelling features. Over Trask's ranting he could hear the door several floors below finally give in to the inevitable. He pressed his back to the wall in an attempt to push himself to his feet. Trask kicked out at him again, but Snowdog rolled aside and Trask's boot smashed into the stone of the wall.

He howled in pain, but recovered before Snowdog could do much more than slide over on his side beside the supine Jonny. The big man was still alive, saw Snowdog. Bleeding badly, but still alive.

Not for much longer if he couldn't deal with Trask.

Hideous screeching filled the stairs below, and he could imagine the aliens scrambling over one another as they leapt and bounded towards the upper levels. He fumbled around beneath Jonny's body, smiling to himself as he felt metal and wood in his grip.

He twisted his head to look at Trask.

And suddenly it all made sense. The swelling on Trask's face wept a purple pus and Snowdog knew that the lone creature that had attacked the column of refugees must have sprayed Trask with some kind of scent that drew these aliens to him like flies to shit.

He smiled at the aptness of the phrase.

'What the hell you smiling at?' said Trask, reaching for fresh shotgun shells.

'You, man. It's been you they've wanted all along.'

'Huh?' said Trask as Snowdog rolled to face him, Jonny's hunting rifle held out before him.

'You want him?' he yelled to the aliens below. 'Well, here he is!'

Snowdog fired the huge rifle, feeling the monstrous recoil crack yet another rib. The impact hurled Trask back down the stairs, a huge portion of his torso simply blasted away by the shell. He crashed down onto the landing below, his body a mangled mess. Tyranid beasts swarmed over the landing, but halted at Trask's body, hacking and slashing it to shreds.

While the scent of whatever was on Trask was keeping the aliens busy, Snowdog used the rifle as a crutch and painfully got himself to his feet. Briefly he considered trying to lift Jonny, but quickly dismissed the idea as insane.

He heard more footsteps above him and laughed in relief as Tigerlily and Lex sprinted downstairs.

'What the hell's going on?' yelled Tigerlily.

'Later,' said Snowdog as he fought through the pain and climbed the stairs. Between them, Tigerlily and Lex managed to lift Jonny and the battered foursome limped up the final set of stairs to the top level of the medicae building.

Snowdog had never been so glad to reach somewhere in all his life.

'Where's Silver?' he said.

'She's safe,' said Tigerlily, pulling him onwards. 'Come on, the entrance to the caves isn't far. Let's get the hell out of here.'

'Best idea I've heard all day,' said Snowdog.

LESS THAN TWENTY Space Marines remained. Heroism the likes of which Learchus had only read about in history had kept them alive for nearly forty minutes, but the end was drawing near. Horrified men of the Guard watched the Space Marines' last stand from the District Sextus wall, unable to help them. Learchus would not have wanted their help anyway.

This was a glorious battle, a fitting way for any servant of the Emperor to meet his end. He and Chaplain Astador fought back-to-back, killing aliens with ferocity and skill.

A mound of alien corpses surrounded the Space Marines, hundreds deep, and the shrinking ring of fighting warriors stood atop the mound, battling like heroes of legend.

Another warrior fell, dragged down by alien claws and Learchus felt the spirit of the martyr move within him. As he hacked down another hissing beast, he began to sing, a rousing hymnal from the dawn of the Imperium, a battle song to stir the hearts of all who heard it.

Astador joined him and soon every one of the Space Marines was raising their voices to the heavens in praise of the Emperor as the tyranids closed in for the kill.

PASANIUS KICKED THE guardian beast in the face, crushing its skull and pulverising its brain as Henghast finally drove his sword through its guts. Its claws spasmed and released him. He fell to the floor with a splash.

Uriel saw the golden hilt of his sword protruding from the corpse of the warrior organism. He struggled to his feet to reach it, wishing no more than to die on his feet with a weapon in his hand. He wrenched it from the dissolving flesh of the beast and limped to stand beside Pasanius and the gore-streaked Damias and Henghast.

The four Space Marines stood with their weapons facing outwards, ready to fight and die like men. Hissing creatures closed in on them, fangs bared and claws poised to strike.

A sudden, violent tremor shook the chamber and a tormented, animal wail built from behind Uriel. The smaller creatures dropped to their haunches in terror as the throat of the Norn Queen, silent for hundreds of years, gave voice to a screech of unimaginable pain.

Its body convulsed, tearing free of its egg sac and mucus-hardened limbs fused to the walls broke with the violence of the spasms. Huge tears in the queen's belly ripped open, mutant growths erupting from every one. The queen's flesh boiled and ripped as her evolutionary genome was thrown into anarchy and stimulated beyond all control by Magos Locard's gene-poison.

Every creature in the chamber took up the wailing screech of agony as evolutionary imperatives were passed through the gestalt consciousness which linked every creature in the hive ship and every creature connected to the overmind.

The chamber shook, the very structure of the ship screaming as every creature was driven into a frenzy of uncontrolled mutation.

Uriel watched as creatures convulsed so violently they snapped their own spines, frothing at the mouth with aberrant growths and genetic deviancy.

'It's working!' shouted Uriel as portions of the chamber erupted in white-hot fluids and acidic slime fell from the ceiling in enormous clumps.

'Aye, it worked,' agreed Pasanius, cradling his mangled arm, 'but let's get out of here before it claims us as well.'

The Space Marines fought their way through the rapidly disintegrating chamber of the Norn Queen, the aliens jerking spastically as they died.

Uriel felt a tremendous sense of vindication as they fled the chamber, knowing that he had made the right choice to lead this mission.

He never saw the javelin-like spine shoot from the carapace of the Norn Queen as it slashed through the collapsing cavern. The two-metre barb hammered through his back and exploded from his stomach in an explosion of ceramite and flesh.

The jagged missile passed clean through him, juddering in the necrotising floor.

He slumped forward, the pain beyond anything he had ever felt before.

'Uriel!' screamed Pasanius.

He looked down at the wound. Strange that there was no blood. A hard red scab formed around the exit wound, but there was no blood. A sluggish feeling permeated his body and a sharp pain blossomed in his left side, spreading throughout his body.

Pasanius lifted him from the ground.

'Damias, you're an Apothecary! Help him!'

Uriel felt his vision grey, his limbs becoming heavier and heavier.

He couldn't understand. He'd been hurt worse than this before and not felt like this. He saw his heart rate spiralling downwards in the corner of his visor.

'Bones of Corax,' swore Damias. 'It's phage-cell poisoning. It's sending his larraman cells into overdrive and his blood is clotting throughout his body!'

'Then do something about it!' bellowed Pasanius.

Uriel felt their words fading and tried to open his mouth, but his vision greyed and he felt his hearts stop pumping as they clogged with coagulated blood.

He closed his eyes and the pain went away.

LEARCHUS KILLED ANOTHER tyranid creature and started another verse before he realised that the attacks were not coming with the same fury as before.

In fact, they were not coming at all.

The alien beasts thrashed in violent fits, their screeching roars rising to new heights. He saw packs of creatures turn on one another, slashing each other's bodies to red ruin without cease. Thrashing monsters filled the plaza, howling in pain as the overmind died, their bodies unable to survive the psychic shockwave of its death.

Tyranid organisms scuttled and ran through the streets of District Quintus, howling in berserk fury and falling on one another in an orgy of senseless bloodletting.

The Space Marines forgotten, the tyranids tore themselves to pieces.

Before any of the larger creatures were able to regain control, the sixteen surviving Space Marines made their way towards the wall of District Sextus. Very few creatures opposed them and those that did attacked with no cohesion or purpose and were butchered without mercy.

THE INTERNECINE SLAUGHTER continued throughout the rest of the day, the defenders watching with elation as the alien menace that had threatened their world for so long tore itself to pieces.

As night drew in and the temperatures plummeted, whole swathes of organisms perished as they succumbed to the freezing temperatures, unable to seek shelter without the control of the hive mind to direct them.

Some creatures survived, larger creatures with a degree of autonomy from the hive mind, and soon they accumulated small packs of desperate beasts, taking refuge in the warmer parts of the ruined city.

Night finally closed on Tarsis Ultra as a speck of light descended from the heavens, a battered Space Marine gunship, its wings dipped in mourning.

EPILOGUE

PASANIUS SAT ALONE on the ruins of the District Quintus wall, staring out into the white expanse of the plain before the devastated city. Stripped of his armour, he wore a simple chiton of blue cloth and cradled his silver arm close to his chest. He watched as a transport flashed overhead; returning from another ruined city with more bad news no doubt.

It had been six days since their return from the dying hive ship and Pasanius had spent much of his time in prayer, offering his thanks for their victory and his sorrows for those who had fallen in battle. There were so many dead, so many prayers to say. The vast chamber of the mosaic held a candle for every soldier dead or missing, and the glowing light from the crystal dome was visible from the far end of the valley.

Among the honoured dead was Sebastien Montante, his spine-pierced body discovered on the ruins of the very wall Pasanius now sat upon. His body lay in state in the Imperial palace and the priests of this world were already calling for his beatification. Pasanius knew it probably wouldn't be long before Sebastien was made into a saint and he chuckled, thinking how amusing the Fabricator Marshal would have found that idea. Saint Sebastien, it had a nice ring to it.

Colonel Stagler's body had been found by his men atop a mound of tyranid creatures, his frozen corpse brutally hacked to pieces. His men did not mourn him. He had died in the Krieg way and that was enough. With both Stagler and Rabelaq dead, Major Aries Satria of the Erebus Defence Legion assumed control of the Imperial Guard forces until such time as a more senior Guard officer could be appointed.

And such a time would not be long in coming. With the destruction of the hive ship, the Shadow in the Warp had lifted from the Tarsis Ultra system and a flood of astropathic communiqués were received by those telepaths who had not been driven insane by the tyranids' infernal psychic noise.

Imperial Navy vessels were less than a week away, ponderous battlecruisers and vast transports bringing in fresh troops to bolster the weakened defences.

The Mortifactors had left Tarsis Ultra yesterday, Chaplain Astador offering to take the mortal remains of the fallen Ultramarines and inter them within the ossuaries of the Basilica Mortis. Learchus, who had taken command of the surviving warriors of the Fourth company, had politely, but firmly, declined.

Inquisitor Kryptman and the Deathwatch still prowled the ruins of the city, gathering alien carcasses for Magos Locard to study. The gene-poison might only have worked on this hive fleet, but there was still much to learn about the tyranid race.

Volunteer kill teams were being assembled to hunt down the surviving tyranid monsters that had gone to ground in the depths of the ruined city and caves of the high valleys. The shadow of destruction had been lifted from this world, but Pasanius knew that there would be trouble with the tyranids for many years to come if his experiences on Ichar IV had taught him anything.

The winds from the plain were cold and Pasanius extended the silver fingers of his right arm, the metal gleaming and pristine.

Already more than one tech-priest had commented on the skill of the artificer who had repaired his bionic arm following the battle on the hive ship.

Pasanius shivered, closing his eyes as he tucked his arm inside the fabric of his chiton.

He could tell them nothing, because there had been no artificer.

The arm had repaired itself.

THERE WAS PAIN. He supposed pain was good, it meant he was still alive.

Uriel opened his eyes, gummed with so long spent unconscious. He blinked away the residue and tried to push himself upright, but fell back, exhausted, unable to do much more than turn his head.

He lay on a sturdy bed in a stone chamber with a vaulted roof. It was warm and he felt a comfortable numbness that could only be the result of pain balms. He pulled back the sheet to look at his bandage-wrapped body. Scars crisscrossed his chest and he could feel the ache of recent surgery. Whatever had happened to him, it had been serious.

Uriel drifted in and out of consciousness for several hours until he was aware of a figure standing beside his bed, adjusting a drip feed attached to his arm.

He tried to speak, the words coming out as little more than a hoarse croak.

'You'll find it hard to speak for a while, Uriel,' said a voice he recognised as belonging to Apothecary Selenus. He managed to say, 'What happened?'

'You were poisoned by tyranid phage cells that attacked the larraman cells in your bloodstream. The poison caused your blood to clot on a bodily scale and your hearts failed, clogged with agglomerated blood. Clinically, you were dead, but the Deathwatch were able to get you back to the Thunderhawk in time for Brother Damias to administer a massive dose of anticoagulants and begin infusions of fresh blood. Pasanius almost killed himself providing you with enough blood to keep you alive long enough to get you here. You are lucky indeed to have such a friend as he.'

Uriel nodded, trying to take in the information, but drifted off into unconsciousness. When he awoke again it was to see a man in the uniform of the Erebus Defence Legion with his arm in a sling sitting beside him. He wore a Space Marine purity seal pinned to his breast.

'You're awake,' he said, standing and extending his hand.

'Yes,' managed Uriel. 'You're–'

'Pavel Leforto, yes. You saved my life in the trenches.'

Uriel smiled in recognition. 'You saved mine too as I remember.'

'Yes, well, I was lucky with the missile launcher. On any normal day, I'd probably have hit you,' said Pavel.

'Well, thank you anyway, Pavel.'

'You're welcome, Captain Ventris. Anyway, I just came to say thank you, but I have to report to my unit now. You know, plenty more work to be done,' said Pavel.

Pavel came to attention and saluted before turning and marching from the room.

Uriel watched him go, thinking back to the picture of his family Pavel had hel when he had lain injured.

When it came time for Pavel Leforto to die he would have the legacy of his wife's memories and his children's lives to proclaim that he existed, that he had enriched the Emperor's realms for a brief span with his labours.

What would Brother-Captain Uriel Ventris leave behind?

A lifetime dedicated to the service of the Emperor, to the service of Humanity, even though he was no longer part of it? He only dimly remembered his parents, they had been dead for almost a century now, their memory a distant shadow, eclipsed by decades of devotion to the Chapter and the Emperor. There was nothing left to remind him of his humanity, no family and few friends. Once he was gone it would be as though he had never existed.

Uriel had sacrificed his chance to experience such a life the instant he had become an Ultramarines novice.

And knowing this, would he have been so willing to become a Space Marine had he realised the enormity of what he was sacrificing to become one of the Emperor's elite?

Uriel smiled, his features softening as the answer was suddenly so clear that he was amazed he had even questioned it.

Yes. He would have. In giving up the chance for a normal life, he had gained something far greater. The chance to make a difference. The chance to stand defiant before the enemies of Mankind and hold back the tide of degenerate aliens, traitorous heretics and servants of Chaos that sought dominion over the Emperor's realm.

That was something to be proud of. His strength came from ancient technology that made him stronger, faster and more deadly than any warrior had ever been before. He had sacrificed his chance to be truly human and, yes, he stood apart from the mass of Humanity, but countless lives would have been lost but for his sacrifice.

That was a noble gift and he was thankful for what and who he was.

Uriel smiled to himself as he drifted into a dreamless sleep.

SNOWDOG WINCED AS he limped over to the bed where Silver lay asleep. His side hurt like a cast-iron bitch and the swelling on his face didn't seem to want to go down. He pulled the blanket up over Silver and brushed a strand of white hair from her face.

She stirred, opening her eyes and reaching up to touch his bruised face.

'Hey,' she said.

'Hey, yourself. How you feeling?'

She groaned as she pushed herself upright. 'Terrible. Next dumb question?'

Snowdog leaned down to kiss her, his cracked ribs flaring painfully.

She saw the pain in his eyes and chuckled.

'Some time, huh?'

'Yeah,' he agreed, 'some time.'

'So what's next for us, then?'

Snowdog didn't reply immediately, glancing over his shoulder into the front room of the abandoned hab-unit they'd commandeered as a temporary base. Lex and Tigerlily played dice and Jonny Stomp snored loudly on a bed of rolled-up coats.

He'd lost most of what he'd lifted from the wreck of the crashed ship and as he looked at the shotgun and lasgun lying on the floor he smiled.

'Looks like it's business as usual, honey,' he said. 'Business as usual.'

ABOUT THE AUTHOR

Hailing from Scotland, Graham McNeill narrowly
escaped a career in surveying to join Games Workshop's Warhammer 40,000 development team,
working on the Tau, Necrons, Chaos Space Marines
and Daemonhunters codexes. As well as two previous novels, he has also written a host of short
stories for Inferno! and is planning to severely
curtail his free time by writing even more while
fending off demands for a sequel to *Storm of Iron*.
Though as it happens, he's just had
a cunning plan...